THE
BOOKFAIR
MURDERS

THE
BOOKFAIR
MURDERS

ANNA
PORTER

McArthur & Company

Toronto

© 1997 by ANNA PORTER

Canadian Cataloguing in Publication Data

Porter, Anna
The bookfair murders

ISBN 1-55278-045-7
I. Title.

PS8581.07553B66 1999   C813'.54   C99-930478-X
PR9199.3.P67B66 1999

First published by Little, Brown and Company (Canada) Limited
This edition published in 1999 by McArthur & Company

Illustration by SHARIF TARABAY

Jacket Design by TANIA CRAAN

Interior Design and Page Composition by JOSEPH GISINI
OF ANDREW SMITH GRAPHICS, INC.

Author Photo by TONY HAUSER

Printed and bound in Canada by Transcontinental Printing

McArthur & Company
322 King Street West, Suite # 402
Toronto, ON, M5V 1J2

10 9 8 7 6 5 4 3 2 1

*This book is dedicated to
all my friends in publishing,
particularly the
Quasimodo survival group.*

ACKNOWLEDGEMENTS

My thanks to Geraldine Sherman, John Pearce, Catherine Porter, Susan Renouf, Bob Sessions, Bev Burns, Linda Camp and, as ever, Julian.

CHAPTER

ONE

ASIDE FROM THE MURDER, IT WAS A PREDICTABLE
Bertelsmann party. A gathering of the usual crowd. Most of them
had been coming to the Frankfurt Bookfair for fifteen years or
more. You didn't earn the right to Frankfurt until you had been
around for a few years and you hadn't really arrived in publishing
until you had a few Frankfurts under your belt.

Some of the older men were veterans of the last War, survivors
of long-forgotten battlefields. At the Bookfair were representatives
of all the countries that had been bent on annihilating one another.
A dozen years ago, a senior man from Knopf recognized his former
prison guard inside the well-pressed suit of a Heibon-sha executive,
stood staring at him for a moment or two, then threw his champagne into the startled Japanese face. Both were well over sixty and
neither chose to pursue the matter beyond the public insult. The
following year, Heibon-sha sent a new man, one who had sat out
the War on a troop ship.

Despite Bertelsmann's avid support for the Jerusalem Bookfair, there were those who never felt comfortable at the party,

THE BOOKFAIR MURDERS

scanning the faces of elderly Germans wondering where they had been during the War. For that matter, some felt uncomfortable coming to Germany at all, but, everyone agreed, the Frankfurt Bookfair isn't really Germany.

Each year there were a few new arrivals — tentative, attentive, eager, displaying their plastic-covered name tags. They watched in awe as famous names in the publishing world paraded by, well-known faces from the pages of the *Bookseller* and *Publishers Weekly*.

The older generation bore its endurance with pride.

"This is my sixteenth Bertelsmann party."

"My twentieth Frankfurt."

"J'étais ici avec Flammarion, lui-même."

"Lequel?"

"Grandpère."

"Ah."

The background music was sixties. Dr. Ruth was tugging at Sonny Mehta's elbow, trying to tell him about her newest theory of sexual dysfunction. Ever since his arrival at Knopf, the most prestigious post on the New York publishing scene, Sonny had acquired a mien of infinite boredom when having to deal with people or subjects that did not interest him. The technique had proved infallible with most of his colleagues but had made not a dent in the good doctor's tireless enthusiasm.

Ivana Trump was showing off her latest makeover and a new ghost for her next best-seller. Her editor had whispered, rather peevishly, that Ivana's success was becoming a mixed blessing; the lovely creature was beginning to imagine that she had actually written some of her own material.

The big-time German wives were subdued this year. Gerhardt's wore a backless red silk dress, sedate gold clip-on earrings, and her trademark six-inch heels. Friederich's showed one breast only, not both as last year, a brilliant job of cross-tying velvet. You caught only a glimpse of her nipple as you reached for her hand in the receiving

10

line. Werner's wife was suited and sober, much to everyone's disappointment. She could usually be counted on to berate the determinedly polite executives from Bertelsmann's various subsidiaries. She was particularly hard on the fellows from New York, because she was certain that, like all Americans, they were lazy and played too many sports.

It was the year that both Günter Grass and Margaret Atwood came. He brooded uneasily in a corner avoiding the local TV crews while assiduously working on his third gin. She walked through the room, smiling fixedly, her European agent and British publisher attempting to form a protective phalanx around her. Doubleday's battle-weary publicity director brought up the rear.

Every year the party was held at the Intercontinental's ballroom, and spilled out into the grand foyer. There were only two entrances, both sternly guarded by forbiddingly uniformed hotel staff and a soft-bellied, middle-aged member of Bertelsmann International, someone who would be sure to distinguish old friends who had forgotten to bring their invitations from enterprising crashers attempting to run the gauntlet of the liveried doormen. Even as it swelled to over four hundred people, the party had remained strictly by invitation. And those invitations were not easy to come by. Each was for one person only, and no amount of begging would allow in a "friend."

Eight banquet tables staggered under the array of food, more an ostentatious display of success, Bertelsmann's worldwide trademark, than a chef's labour of love. There were trays of lobster in pink caviar sauce, Australian prawns, a side of veal, pickled pork, beef brochette bordelaise, pickled palm hearts, a dressed roast pig, ice sculptures, strawberries dipped in chocolate, a baked Alaska, Cake Esmeraude, Austrian dobos, and vanilla tartes ... machismo in food. No expense was spared but no feeding comforts were provided. Given one glass of champagne, one heaped plate, a knife, a fork, and only two hands, no one could eat unaided. One year, a woman from a new, trendy publishing consulting group in New York brought a plastic gadget you could attach to the side of your plate to hold your glass while you ate. The gadget became the talk of the party. People came from as far away as the Korean corner to admire how it clung, vicelike, not spilling a drop of wine, while the woman stabbed at her salami with the fork. It was a refreshing respite from talking about books.

This was, after all, the Frankfurt Bookfair, the annual meat market for all the books in the world. You buy them here, and sell them, you check their pedigrees, their past performance, their breeding (which publisher's stable), their backing (how much was spent on the advance, how much on the promotion), even their handlers' track records. "She used to be Tom Wolfe's editor," someone might say. Or, "He discovered *Lemprière's Dictionary*." "She has a nose for this kind of book." "She touted Elizabeth George when no one would have thought ..." "He has connections in the movies."

You bid on them, watching the vendor's eyes for signs of weakness or greed. Some feign indifference. You walk away to circle back an hour later, checking for an opening. Some throw out lures of shimmering plot lines, big names for endorsements, whatever it takes for a handshake deal. Written contracts are rarely signed in Frankfurt but, despite the occasional disappointments, Bookfair participants still pay obeisance to such old-fashioned gestures of the past.

Frankfurt is part of being on a roll. It is a world unto itself, a time to preen, to show off for your peers. And Bertelsmann's is the party that separates the players from the incidentals, those who have arrived from those busily clawing their way there.

This year, as every year for the past twelve, not counting the one when she had inadvertently lost her job, Marsha Hillier was a guest at the Bertelsmann party.

She was a cheerful, damp, and slightly dishevelled guest. She had walked from the Frankfurter Hof because it was raining, as it always was during the Bookfair, and because there were no cabs, as there rarely were enough to go around with more than two hundred thousand Fair-goers converging on a city barely able to accommodate its own inhabitants and the assault of the unification with the East. She was relatively cheerful, because an hour ago she had made a ridiculously low offer for a bizarrely scandalous biography of Adenauer by some German student of Kitty Kelley's historic excesses and, to her astonishment, Suhrkamp's overworked rights director had accepted. Marsha was convinced that Rita Fessenbach had had too much to do to have read the manuscript herself. That's why she had seemed so glad to be able to remove English language rights for Adenauer from her long list of tasks to accomplish before Monday noon when they would each return to the relative safety of their offices. Marsha had been able to parlay her Brown University Level Two German into several exceptional deals in Frankfurt, but none was as surprising as this one.

She was pleased with herself. Circling the seafood table, she had just managed to spear the last piece of lobster ahead of a diminutive Dutch publisher's descending fork. He was bubbling away at her about the decline of American fiction.

"You are stifled by your consumer society. Therefore and consequently you are unable to deal in excellence," he said earnestly to his shrimps. "It is understandable, if inexcusable at the intellectual level." He spat out bits of shrimp that had lodged between his teeth as he pronounced "intellectual."

"Hm," Marsha said cupping her glass protectively with her forked hand. Her own solution to the Bertelsmann party's drink versus food dilemma was to forego plates altogether, using her fork to skewer what she could.

"The great losers are the next generation."

"Is," Marsha said spitefully.

"Is?" inquired the Dutchman, smothering his shrimp in mayonnaise.

"One generation," Bertil said from Marsha's elbow. He was a Norwegian publisher and a stickler for correct English.

"Not one, not one," the Dutchman shouted triumphantly. "Many. Perhaps all future generations of Americans will be deprived. And the rest of the world, so how you'd say, enraptured? Yes, indeed, enraptured to your fictions. All deprived. There is no excuse for publishing the garbage you all put out in the interest of money." He shook his head sadly.

"Ah yes," Bertil said, nodding in sympathy.

Marsha murmured something about Dick Francis and Per Wahlöö and wheeled around to join a group of former Maxwell employees who hadn't tired of telling crazy Maxwell stories even though the old fraud had been dead for many years. Mark Newnes's tales had even acquired a certain resonance as they ripened into fiction. She had first met Mark when he was Maxwell's flunky, the guy who arranged the great man's public relations. In crowds, he would hover at Maxwell's elbow, reminding him of people's names. In the final years, before his possible suicide, murder, or accidental death (there were numerous versions), Maxwell came to Frankfurt in his private jet and met with the lucky few he considered worthy of his time. Often he would appear to be conversing with heads of state on his portable telephone as he strolled down the aisles at the Book-fair. Once, Mark had sent out gold-embossed invitations for a dinner with Maxwell at the Savoy, black tie and decorations. Maxwell arrived, talking into his telephone, and left after a quarter of an hour. Mark was left to explain.

"He was amazingly light on his feet," Mark was saying. "For a man weighing three hundred pounds you wouldn't expect an Olympic record, but he set one that day. He leapt over his desk and came at me, like an enraged bull, his hands grabbing for my throat...." He stopped in mid-sentence when he noticed Marsha. "My dear Marsha, looking as lovely as ever." He flicked the near-white cowlick out of his face, kissed her on the cheek, Frankfurt-style, and gave her one of his sly boyish grins. Marsha couldn't be called a classic beauty, but her blue eyes, wispy blond hair, and trim figure often caught men's attention. "Congratulations on your big deal with Andrew Myles. Into the eight figures, I heard."

There were appreciative grunts all around.

"Margaret Drury Carter?" the Dutchman said. He had followed Marsha's lead and joined the group around Mark. "Or is that yesterday's news?"

"We're expecting her here tomorrow," Marsha said, modestly evading the question. Not that she wasn't proud of the Carter deal, there hadn't been many deals in recent years she had been as confident to make, but here, in Frankfurt, only the boorish showed off their as yet unproven acquisitions. It was, she thought, bad form.

"Be lovely to meet the old bat," Mark said looking around the room. "I thought of taking a run at the British rights myself, but Andrew, uncharacteristically, rolled the whole lot into one and landed it in your lap, didn't he?" Mark was referring to Andrew Myles's decision to sell world rights to A&M. Normally, Andrew would have sold each territory separately.

Mark had recently found a new job as Fleetwood's editorial director. Everyone who knew him drew a deep breath of relief. He had been out of work for almost a year, since Maxwell's ghost laid waste to most of his companies. Sending his résumé to all his old cronies had been humbling for Mark and an embarrassing experience for those who had to turn him away. He had lost weight as he had lost status. Now, he once again filled out his black worsted suit, his belly barely covered by the restraining blue vest. He was exuding success, poised, enthusiastic, making sure his voice would be heard above the din.

Marsha spotted Andrew Myles through the double doors. He was wearing one of his trademark vermilion bow ties tied too close to his chin as he was almost neckless. His hair was plastered down over his broad forehead. He was leaning forward, gazing at the floor between his feet, seemingly ignoring his companions. He was wedged into one of the wide-backed black leather armchairs in the foyer, near the champagne bar. He was surrounded by a group of animated talkers. From time to time, they glanced in his direction, to make sure he didn't feel excluded. Marsha figured the group's exaggerated animation would have been for Andrew's benefit. He was that kind of agent. A man others were always trying to impress.

To Bertil she said, "Andrew Myles would probably like to meet you," and she headed towards Myles.

"I doubt it very much," Bertil said, and let Marsha go on, Mark close behind her.

"Let's see how the all-powerful one is feeling tonight," Mark said.

The group around Andrew parted reluctantly to make room for them. She recognized the feral Jerry Haines from London, and Hideo Tanake from Tokyo. Hachette's Brigitte Dombert was laughing at something Jerry had said, her head thrown back exposing her long slender neck. Performing for Andrew, Marsha thought.

As if by instinct, Mark picked up quickly on the conversation. "I haven't had time to read it all, of course," he intoned, flicking the tuft of grey hair off his forehead, "but enough to see six figures flash before my eyes. Deep insight into the soul of the new machine." He smirked at Hideo as he added: "Made in Japan, as you might have expected." Mark might have changed his appearance a little since his new job, but he had lost neither the mannerisms nor the youthful bullying techniques of the brash upstart he had once been.

Hideo bowed his head. It was rumoured that Andrew had chosen him to represent his clients in Japan. The competition had been fierce. If true, Hideo would rise to a new level of prestige, rivalled only by Japan's most ubiquitous agent, Tom Mori, who proved his success by joining not one, but six, golf clubs and owning ten American cars.

They were talking about the Big Book of the Fair.

At Frankfurt there was always a big book: the book that everybody had to have seen, been offered, bid on, or turned down. It was the book everyone talked about. To establish that you were a person of importance, a person to be reckoned with, you had to have touched that manuscript while you were at Frankfurt. Sometimes it was relatively predictable, like a new le Carré, or a Gabriel García Márquez. During the Cold War it was frequently something Russian. Once it was Gorbachev's memoirs. Once it was Mandelshtam. A long time ago: Pasternak. Later: Solzhenitsyn. There had been surprises, like Margaret Trudeau's memoirs; the obscure literary work, *Perfume*; *The Power of One* from Australia; Marilyn Monroe's unpublished photographs; and *Scarlett*, the unimaginable best-seller. There was the year Caradoc King, the leading British agent, did not come to the Fair so as to fuel the rumours about the Big First Novel of one of his authors — an Herculean feat, but one that earned a young man over five million dollars while King played hard to get and made ever so sure of the prey in his London office.

Last year, Marsha had bought the *Vatican Secrets* from Myles's assistant. It was said to be the book of that year's Fair. She had stayed up all night to read the manuscript because she had been told she had until ten the next morning, or Myles would accept an offer "already on the table" from one of her competitors who was willing to buy without a read.

These things were not unusual at Frankfurt. How many people had really read *The Closing of the American Mind*? Or more than a few pages of *A Brief History of Time*?

Marsha hadn't yet heard of the Big Book of this year's Fair, though she had been offered a couple of pretenders. She felt reasonably sure that the contract she had signed with Myles in New York last month was as close as she was going to come to her firm's "big one" for this and many other Fairs. It was a complicated three-book deal for Margaret Drury Carter's next romantic thrillers. The twenty million dollar price tag would have made Barbara Cartland blush, but not her rival's rapacious agent. Myles had said Marsha had done the only sensible thing she could do: bought three at once.

"The smell of all that cash should keep the old broad awake nights typing," he'd told her. "I'll have something for you at Frankfurt."

Marsha had hoped he meant the sizable chunk of manuscript, the ten thousand words the contract had agreed would be delivered before the 15th of October. "You've certainly built in the incentive to be early," Myles had told her somewhat accusingly. Two million dollars was due on these few words. The final manuscript for the first book was not expected till the end of January. He had agreed to deliver, at the same time, a two-page outline for the second book. ("Let's call it an indication, not an outline," Myles had suggested just before he saw the contract for signing. "You can't expect a writer of Margaret's calibre to deliver an actual *outline*, now, can you?" "Not even for the two million more she'll get when she does it?" Marsha had asked. "Two pages will do, then," they had agreed.)

When she sat down on the soft black leather arm of his chair, Andrew Myles slumped forward slightly. ("What exactly do you mean, *slumped*?" the police would ask later.) He was leaning, or listing like a ship, over to the left, away from where Marsha had perched. It hadn't seemed strange to her then, because that's where his elbow was resting.

Jerry Haines said something to him. Marsha hadn't heard what it was except for the word "Carter."

Myles didn't react.

He was gazing fixedly at some midpoint in the sea of legs before him. That was not altogether unusual for Myles, who had been known to fall asleep at parties he found dull. But never at a Bertelsmann party. This was Andrew's kind of event. These were his kind of people. There were young comers eager to show their worth, and Andrew knew just how to offer them the opportunity; there were old-timers keen to display their vestiges of power, and Andrew could sniff their desperation. There were intrigues, secrets, hints of deals to be made. There was money in the air.

Andrew Myles never missed a Bertelsmann party.

"Andrew," Marsha said lightly, "I wonder if you have something for me."

As Andrew was dead, he didn't reply.

"You had mentioned you would bring it to the Fair, and, well ..." she wanted to appear casual; with Andrew you must never show eagerness. He knew how to take advantage of it. "It would be good for Margaret if we could discuss it tomorrow in person." Myles knew, as well as she did, that Margaret disliked written comments from her editors.

Margaret Drury Carter was to arrive for the lunch Marsha was hosting in her honour the next day. It would be the most important event for Marsha at the Fair, the chance to display the best-selling author to the many publishers who were bidding for the rights to the next three books. It was the event that would make a success of this Fair for Marsha. That's why she had made sure Margaret's appearance was written into her contract.

Myles continued to stare, tilting leeward, his head drawn deeply between his shoulders, his wineglass empty at his feet.

Marsha who, as a rule, didn't take rejection well, decided to ignore his silence and bent to retrieve his glass and hand it to a passing waiter. She assumed Andrew would like a refill. As she glanced up at him from knee-level, she noticed that his eyes, even allowing for the lateness of the hour, were extraordinarily glassy.

"Andrew?" she began, tentatively. "Are you all right?"

Naturally, he didn't respond.

"Andrew?" she tried again, a little louder. When he remained silent, she patted his hand — the one dangling at the end of the arm he was leaning on. It was damp, and limp. As Marsha tugged at it, for greater emphasis, Myles's arm dislodged itself from its wedged-in position, and his head slumped forward.

"Good God," Marsha said to the hovering waiter who had been ready to refill Myles's empty glass. "I think he's dead!"

The waiter jumped back a step — without losing the tray — and glared suspiciously at Myles. "Was ist los?" he demanded of Marsha.

"Maybe he just passed out," Marsha suggested uncertainly. She tried to detect a pulse on Myles's wrist. Then she placed a tentative finger along his throat to feel for one there. Myles's throat was as cold and damp as his hand had been. His chin rested on his chest. Neither appeared to be moving. His face, as Marsha had observed from underneath, was strangely yellow, as if he had been experimenting with a cheap overnight tanning lotion. His lips were bluish and slightly parted.

"Tot?" asked the waiter in some panic. "Ist er tot?" He shouted. There was a clatter of falling tray and broken glass.

Heads in the grand foyer turned. The small group around Myles stopped talking and stared. A young woman in evening dress produced a compact from her silver shoulder bag, opened it, and held the small round mirror under Myles's nose. She shook her head to indicate that it hadn't fogged up with Myles's breath. A man wearing a black suit and chic collarless white shirt pressed two fingers into the base of Myles's neck.

"Is there a pulse?" Marsha asked him.

"No."

Mark Newnes looked at Marsha accusingly. "Is he all right?" he asked. Hideo moved forward uncertainly but stopped when Dr. Schneider, definitely not a medical doctor, inserted himself between him and Myles. "Mon Dieu, qu'est-ce qu'il se passe?" Brigitte Dombert asked. She, too, was glaring at Marsha.

Dr. Schneider, who had failed to appear for a ten o'clock meeting with Marsha that morning, bent over Myles, while he held up his hand for the noise to die down. When it didn't, he called out in a high falsetto Marsha had not imagined he had harboured all these years: "Gibt's einen Doktor hier?" When no one responded, he tried it in English: "A doctor?"

Conversation stopped in the grand foyer as news of Myles's indisposition spread, and as word reached the ballroom a hush fell over the crowd. Then the murmur of voices rose again as people started to crowd in for a closer view of Myles's slumped self.

Hideo lifted Myles's chin and tried to lift his eyelid with thumb and forefinger. A young man wearing a light-blue tuxedo waved a glass of water before his blue lips. Dr. Schneider batted his hand away, spilling the water down Myles's pink shirt-front.

"Idiot," he said in his new falsetto.

Bertil appeared at Marsha's elbow and suggested it might have been the seafood. Mark Newnes launched into some tale about his having been almost poisoned by a cordon bleu chef in New York once. The crowd parted to let Gerhardt, head of the Bertelsmann book clubs, through. He gazed at Myles's pink and yellow figure and began to talk rapid German to Schneider, who nodded vigorously, then disappeared towards the stairway.

Brigitte Dombert ducked around Gerhardt's menacing form and shoved her ear into Myles's chest. When she emerged, she shook her head. "Rien," she said, and grabbed Marsha by the shoulder. "Je crois qu'il est mort," she sobbed. Brigitte had always been theatrical — an asset in a successful rights person — and here she had found a perfect opportunity for theatre. Marsha had thought she hated Myles.

Someone from Crown — or what was left of it after the recent takeover — ushered forth Dr. Ruth. She took one look at Myles and called for an ambulance. She tried to loosen his shirt collar with her finger while Gerhardt looked at her with an expression of utter disdain. She said no to Mark when he suggested they lay Myles down on the marble floor. "He must not be moved."

Marsha went to the bar and poured herself a generous helping of whisky. It would be a long night.

CHAPTER
TWO

"HE WAS ONLY THIRTY-SEVEN YEARS OLD," BERTIL told Marsha.

That was one of the things Marsha liked about Bertil. He was generous. He was also willing to believe what he was told, unless he had incontrovertible proof to the contrary. She had known Bertil for twenty years and in all that time he had not become cynical. Occasionally, his white-blond eyebrows rose in consternation, sometimes he professed to be surprised, but he never quite disbelieved what he was told. Some thought that's what made him the star fiction editor in Norway — his ability to go with the story, however unlikely it was. It also contributed to Bertil's boyish quality, something that Marsha still found irresistible.

"He's been thirty-seven for the past ten years," Marsha said softly.

"More as forty," the Dutch publisher, who had reattached himself to Marsha, asserted enthusiastically.

For some time after the party, everyone believed that Andrew Myles had been taken ill. A few thought that he had had a heart attack. Dr. Ruth smilingly opined that it was poison, and she had some idea what kind, but no one paid any attention because she had built her not inconsiderable reputation and personal fortune on sexual advice for the self-confessed incompetent, incapable, or wildly prurient who spent nights tuning in to her bizarre television shows and buying her not very interesting books.

Most remained in the lobby of the Intercontinental long after the party had been ended by the arrival of the ambulance to take Myles away.

Jerry Haines was propped up against the Lippizaner bar, just off the lobby of the Frankfurter Hof hotel, where late night Bookfair revellers had gathered for decades sharing tales and whisky. Haines was working on his second Ballantine's double, and an overlong Havana cigar. "I was telling him why we decided to stay out of the Carter auction," he said expansively.

Mysteriously, Jerry had surfaced after the disastrous eighties as managing director of the Fennell conglomerate, named after the investment banker who had found the cash for the venture. The firm included a range of once-independent imprints, each named after its former publisher, some of whom had stayed on in lowly editorial positions, reluctant to leave their names behind.

In his previous job, Jerry had become rounded, somewhat chunky, perhaps in adulation of his master, George Weidenfeld. The new Jerry was thin, muscular, ferret-like. Perhaps to emphasize the recently reshaped body, he had draped himself in a spacious, wide-shouldered jacket and loose, belted linen pants that lent him an air of foppish wealth. He had also acquired a golden brown tan, slicked-back hair (surely not Brylcreem?), a white wide-cuffed shirt, and an incongruous blue bow tie that he pulled at from time to time, betraying both the rubber that kept the tie in place and Jerry's discomfort with it.

"You all know we were the underbidders last time," he said to the group close to him, many of whom had been around Myles at the Bertelsmann party. "We have published twelve of her books, and all of them are still in print in our Lavender line. Paperbacks, of course. She is simply not a hardback author, I say." He winked at Marsha. "Precious few of them around these days. Fewer still to come. I believe," he pronounced, swivelling his ass on the stool, to make sure that as many as were in hearing range would catch his remarks, "that the days of the hardback are past. It will go the way of the dodo bird and the dinosaur. Mark my words."

"*Conspiracy of Roses*," Marsha demurred, "did reasonably well in hardcover."

"Perhaps," Jerry said, rubbing his lightly sprouting beard. Marsha thought he was attempting to emulate the Hollywood early-morning, day's-growth look. "As you well know, it is a different market over here. What we find a reasonably good performance, and what you do are not the same at all. At all," he repeated, shaking his head. "Sometimes a writer doesn't know what's good for her," he added.

"That would make her none too different from the rest of us," Bertil said. He had been nursing a large brandy and soda. He had hung his jacket on the back of his stool, its arms grazing the floor. Marsha loved Bertil's carelessness. She also loved his heroic gestures, like coming to her rescue with Jerry, but she resented it at the same time. Marsha knew how to fend off attackers of Jerry's calibre; she had been offered plenty of chances to perfect her skills during her years in publishing. She no longer thought of it as a challenge. It was both endearing and annoying that Bertil should think she needed protection.

"That's what I was telling Andrew," Jerry said defensively. "Just before he sat in that armchair. While he was still in our circle. I was explaining why we dropped out of the auction. It wasn't the money, you know. It was the conditions attached."

"Naturally," Marsha said. "Andrew, I assume, was so surprised by this he keeled over."

"Probably her age," Jerry told Bertil, ignoring Marsha. "Some of them get into their dotage and they start looking for some fitting monument to a lifetime of scribbling. A paperback doesn't seem adequate any longer. It's pure vanity, that's all it is, and you know it." Jerry's attitude to authors tended towards the amused condescending, the tones of a parent exasperated by a child's antics — the posture that had peaked in New York in the late eighties, where Jerry spent some of his formative years.

"Our bookclubs sold twenty thousand of the hardcovers." Bertil, the unrepentant knight in faded armour, had done it again.

"Only in Norway." Jerry raised his eyes heavenward.

"He was fine when he came in," Mark Newnes said. He had been half-listening, it seemed, though he appeared to have been deeply involved in Brigitte's décolletage. She was reaching for the olives bowl. "I was behind him in the queue. He said it would be a long time before he'd reopen his London office. He didn't like the defeatist atmosphere." Mark glanced at Marsha, a big toothy grin lit up his face.

Another one to the joust, Marsha thought. During the long, dry spell while Mark had been out of work, Marsha had made a point of inviting him to lunch. She had been visiting agents in London, and had called him, herself. She had even offered him a bed (decidedly not her own) in her apartment when he came to New York to extend his search for a job. Most of his other erstwhile colleagues, he had told her, treated him as if he had been afflicted with a particularly virulent strain of flu. As if being out of work was catching. Marsha knew what that felt like. She had been there. Her unexpected departure from Doubleday had even been announced in *Publishers Weekly*, with the usual euphemism (in case anyone had missed it on the industry grapevine), "Marsha Hillier has left to pursue other interests ..."

Marsha sighed. "We're going out with a first printing of fifty thousand copies this month, Jerry," she said, clipping her words to a fine New York edge, "in England. Why don't you wait for the results before you give me the benefit of one more lesson on the obvious differences between our worlds."

"Well, Andrew could see my point," Jerry said, pulling at his tie. "Nothing personal, my dear, you know that. When you pay through the nose for something, you do have to appear confident. And we're all sure you're going to do your best. Can't have the new owners think they must write off all that lovely lolly now, can we?" He smiled at the others, conspiratorially. Most of them would have heard how much A&M had paid, and, in the unlikely event that Andrew encountered someone of importance who didn't know, he would have made sure they found out.

"Deep pockets," Hideo said, with relish.

"For the right authors," Marsha rejoined. The stalwart Canadians who had acquired A&M had approved. They had arrived with a winning theory about publishing: you publish only best-sellers. Let the other people experiment with the small books that don't make the best-seller list. This way, they had told the hastily assembled and somewhat astonished staff, you save all your money for the winners. You can reward them with more money than the competition who are spending a bundle on losers.

"You were with him at the top of the stairs, weren't you, Frans?" Mark asked the Dutchman who had finally cornered the elusive barman and was attempting to hold his attention long enough to order a drink.

"That settles it, then," Bertil whispered to Marsha, "Myles died of boredom."

"I?" Frans squawked. "Perhaps for only a moment."

"Longer," Mark insisted. He had unbuttoned his silk vest and allowed his belly the freedom to rest on his Lagerfeld belt buckle.

"I was largely with Miss Hillier. We were discussing the decline of American literature, actually. I was telling her how far it has gone — this publishing of books with no meaning." He used the tiny serviette square from under his glass to wipe his forehead. "It is stifling the true creativity. I was thinking it's like a garden we have been chosen to tend. And the weeds are taking over the flowerbeds ..."

"No," Mark said.

"But yes," Frans insisted. "The flowers, the real flowers are becoming scarcer and scarcer ..."

"No, dammit," Mark interrupted decisively. "Not the bleeding flowers, or whatever you're rabbitting on about. I saw you and Andrew at the top of the stairs. He had just pushed past me and the entire Kodansha group, saying the Japanese didn't believe in queuing, either — you should see how they treat one another on the subways in Tokyo. Charming as ever, he was. Then I saw he had been running up to see *you*."

"Must have been one shitload of the good stuff to put Andrew on a trot," Jerry said.

"There they were, their arms around each other, as we dutifully filed by to pay our respects to the gentle hosts," Mark said.

"More and more," Jerry whistled appreciatively.

"We were not hugging each other," Frans protested.

"Okay, so he had his arm around your shoulder. Pretty affectionate for Andrew, all in all. Not a chap widely recognized for his loving relationships with publishers."

"We were talking about a book," Frans blustered. "If you must know." He hoisted himself off the elevated seat with some difficulty, placing one hand on the back of the tall stool, the other on the bar. He made a brave effort to appear dignified when he thumped onto his feet, but it didn't quite work. He half acknowledged his failure by smiling at Marsha and threw the others just a bit more information to reassert himself as the centre of attention. "We are to sign the contracts next week. The deal, as you would say, is done."

"Where?" Jerry asked.

"In Amsterdam, naturally," Frans protested, as if Jerry had accused him of not living in a major city.

Jerry whistled. "A big one, then," he said. "Not much for tourism, Andrew."

It was odd, Marsha thought, that some people had already started to talk about Andrew in the past tense, while others hadn't yet accepted that he was dead.

"Never came to Paris," Brigitte Dombert said as she turned her back on her companions from the other French houses. "We don't pay much money for his kind of book in France."

"Hm," said Hideo, "Perhaps for the Mitterrand memoirs ..."

"He lied if he said he had them," Brigitte said softly. She unlocked her ankles and lifted one shapely knee. Her tight black satin dress rode farther up her thighs.

Black lace panties, Marsha noted. She had expected silk.

"You know Myles," Brigitte told Bertil. "He had his little pretenses. 'I have ze book,' he would say, 'how much is it worth to you?' If he liked the number, he would go after the author." She arched a finely plucked eyebrow at Marsha. "The American way, no?"

"Myles's way, I would have thought," said Alex Levine on his way to the bar. "We're not all of a kind, but I expect you would know that. The French, one assumes, are fairly sophisticated." Alex spoke with a clipped New England voice that made him sound a little haughty, which he wasn't. A Boston agent, he was proud of being off the beaten track. His authors found him accessible and willing to listen to them. It was well known that he hated Andrew Myles.

Brigitte shrugged, dislodging one of the thin black straps holding up her dress. "Me, I did not see him very much," she said, as the dress slid to her left nipple. She affected not to notice, a difficult feat as everyone's attention was riveted to the spot. "And now, he's dead."

"A heart attack," Frans said faintly.

"That," Alex said, "presupposes that the man had a heart." He was too busy with the barman to notice Brigitte's undress.

Brigitte stretched languorously, affording a long glance of pink nipple, adjusted her strap, and turned back to her crowd.

"A very nice act, that," Marsha said to Bertil, who was coming out of a trance, his eyes lighting on Brigitte's slender back.

"It's Frankfurt, that's all," Bertil said huskily. "We all use whatever talents we have. It's what she's got. You're not jealous, are you?"

Marsha laughed. The last thing she had expected of herself tonight was to be jealous of Brigitte, but Bertil, with his customary clear-sightedness, was right. She and Brigitte had endured a long history, none of it particularly friendly. There had been times of mutual business, when Marsha bought some book Brigitte had been offering, but never any favours. Brigitte did not call on Marsha unless she was conducting an auction, and even then, only when Brigitte's expectations had reached the six-figure range. Marsha was never the one to hear ahead of the others, she was never the one with the floor. Brigitte was strictly a man's woman. She had no interest in creating friendships with other women. The one with the floor was always a guy. The only time A&M received special treatment was when Aaron took the bidding. That's Aaron of the long black lashes, the wonder boy who came from the small literary press with one surprise winner on his conscience, the one book no one would have picked for a best-seller, some whiny love story set in, of all places, Iowa, whose plot Marsha could barely remember, but the book that booksellers were recommending to their favourite customers that year. Somehow, the slim little thing (no more than two hundred pages, it was) sold over a million copies before the big houses woke up, and when they did, no one put it down to a fluke. Everyone thought it was the magic of the one editor at the press, and Aaron had twenty offers to choose from. As luck would have it, he picked A&M.

"She seemed rather cavalier about Andrew's untimely demise, don't you think?" Bertil asked thoughtfully.

"Not particularly. At least no more cavalier than everyone else is. Andrew wasn't the most popular of men," Marsha said.

"Perhaps not. But he was certainly on Brigitte's personal best-seller list, or didn't you know that?"

Marsha shook her head. She hadn't known that. "Brigitte Dombert and Andrew Myles?"

"A while ago. Andrew had just set up his Paris office. He called on all the big houses and offered them the top writers in America. For the right price, of course. Brigitte was still sharpening her skills then, hardly the beauty she's become." Bertil rested his eyes on her again. "But Andrew knew talent when he saw it. They were an item for a couple of months. Shared rooms at the Groucho Club during the London Bookfair. I know. I called her one morning around seven and Andrew answered the phone."

"Why?"

"Why did he pick up the phone? I suppose because it was on his side of the bed."

"No, why were you calling?"

"To invite her to dinner," Bertil said.

That was over two years ago. Since then, as Bertil acknowledged, Brigitte had sharpened her skills, and while Marsha had no claim to a proprietary interest in Bertil, she didn't want Brigitte to spend the night with him.

Earlier this evening she would not have thought of it, but now, she wanted to spend the night with Bertil herself. Theirs had become a traditional Bookfair relationship, cozy, undemanding, comforting. For many of the older crowd such relationships provided a home away from home, something to look forward to on the way to Frankfurt, a safe haven in a rapacious environment. They were no longer interested in the random couplings that the newcomers favoured. Had someone asked Marsha if she still loved Bertil, she would likely have said yes. She loved him with all-encompassing familiarity. She could not imagine a world without Bertil, never mind Frankfurt without Bertil. The sex was pleasant and reassuring year after year, but it was almost incidental.

The Lippizaner had grown noisier and hazier as the night wore on. The smell of perfumes and cigarettes had become over-whelming. The music blared Sting and the Rolling Stones, for the generation now going to seed. Jerry Haines relit what was left of his Monte Cristo cigar. In the remainder buyers' corner, near the entrance, someone ordered a magnum of champagne.

It was time, Marsha thought, to go to bed.

CHAPTER

THREE

Bertil didn't stay very long in Marsha's room. He had a seven o'clock appointment and Bertil hated to be late. He also never overstayed his welcome. Making love with Bertil was rather like pulling a comfortable duvet over her head, shutting out the noises and the cold of an uninviting city. He was warm, considerate, and reliable. He took neither himself nor the occasion seriously. When he left, he made sure the curtains were drawn so that the morning light would not wake Marsha, he checked that her alarm clock was set, he dressed in the dark, kissed her lightly on the cheek, and let himself out.

It was only after he was gone that Marsha allowed herself to think of Andrew Myles again.

Chiefly, what came to her mind was the way Andrew had slumped in his chair, head over one shoulder, his arm wedged into the corner to prop him up. The greyness of his skin. How damp his wrist had been when she touched it. Whatever it was that had made Andrew a person had already left when she came near him, she was sure of that. There had been no energy in him, no power.

As Marsha lay curled in her bed, she tried very hard to think kind thoughts of Andrew Myles, some memory that would fill her with the kind of sadness appropriate for a man's dying.

None occurred.

She had known Andrew Myles for about ten years, since he had burst onto the New York publishing scene. She had first heard about him from a friend at Bantam. Myles had called him to say that he was now representing Joe Heller, a South African author whose last two books had appeared to excellent reviews and (according to *Publishers Weekly*) surprisingly respectable sales for a foreign new-comer. Myles had inquired whether Bantam would match an offer he already had for two hundred thousand to get Heller's next book. After a day of deliberation, Bantam had declined.

What had irked Marsha's friend, in hindsight, was the cavalier way Myles went about offering a writer — take it or leave it — without the customary packages of material, waiting period, guide-lines for offers; none of the accoutrements New York agents had acquired over the years. Well, Marsha had thought at the time, at least he had made an impression.

He succeeded in making an even greater impression on Marsha a few days later when he arrived at her office, uninvited and unan-nounced. How he had learnt the ways of A&M was still a mystery to her, but he had simply blustered past the receptionist on the 25th floor, carrying a manuscript under his arm and appearing in Marsha's doorway. He was a short man, thirty-something, with a ruddy complexion, thinning brown hair, wide chest and shoulders, narrow hips, round-rimmed sunglasses, wide freckled nose, a square face. He had been wearing a white-collared blue-striped shirt, dark-brown checked woollen jacket, tan pants with soft edges, and light calf-skin boots.

"You will certainly want to see this," he had told her belliger-ently, thrusting the slim manuscript at her.

One of the disadvantages of working in a large company (there are others) is that you can never be entirely sure that the person in your doorway does not also work there. Dressed like that, he could have been any one of a hundred A&M employees, including the several messengers who carry stuff from one floor to another and slowly acquire the clothes they think are right for the editorial department. Still ... those boots.

Marsha had taken the package from him and set it on her desk on top of about a dozen other manuscripts, most larger than this one, and she had continued to talk on the phone. Some minutes later, she had glanced up to see what the noise was at her door. The square-faced man was still standing there, tapping the floor with the toe of his boot, displaying impatience. Andrew did not like to be kept waiting.

"That," he had pointed to the top of the pile, "is the requisite few pages of Heller's new manuscript." (He had learnt a few things since his call on Bantam.) "The floor is two hundred thousand. As you brought him to America first, we are willing to give you a chance to make one bid. You have until tomorrow. Let's say ..." glancing at his elaborate gold watch as if he was going to synchronize times, "till ten." He had smiled at Marsha, his pink cheeks dimpling. "By the way, my name is Andrew Myles."

He hadn't offered to shake her hand.

"Who," Marsha had said in her iciest tone, "the hell are you?"

"I just told you," Andrew had said, "I'm Andrew Myles and I represent Joe Heller."

There had been something comic about the little man's extraordinary self-assurance. Later, when Marsha came to know him better, she realized that none of it was bluster; Andrew really did believe that he was entitled to success and that all people he came in contact with were his inferiors. When he had decided to become a literary agent — and Marsha had never found out what he was before then — he had simply assumed he would start at the top, and that was what he had done. Along with blithe self-assurance, he had harboured the conviction that most everyone else in the business was befuddled by doing things the way they had always been done. He had believed that the sole justification for following the rules was to give others the comfort of their ways. Andrew had had no intention of offering comfort.

Even now that he was most certainly dead, it was difficult to think kindly of him. Marsha resolved she would try for a little respect.

She had barely fallen asleep when the phone rang. Four strident rings. Five. She opened an eye hesitantly. There was no light between the curtains Bertil had so thoughtfully drawn. The electric clock glowed 6 in the dark, a full hour before she had to get up. She reached for the phone, knocking over a glass of something sticky along the way. "What?" she sighed into the telephone.

"Mar-cia," came the whispered response.

The voice was familiar but for the moment she could not place it. That breathless two-syllable rendition of her name. Marsha thought of her mother, wanting to impress the others holidaying at the Vineyard. She had started to call her Mar-cia, in two syllables, perhaps to counteract her father's habit of calling her Marsh, or, Lee. He had insisted his daughter's middle name be Lee, after General Lee, of course. Marsha's mother had successfully fought off the prospect of Grant, even though he had won the war and General Lee had lost. With Lee, she could pretend it was a girl's name, and Marsha's father still had himself a general. During the summers her mother's triumphs included pinafores, starched white aprons, and a bent sun-bonnet while her father raged that she should not be dressed like a doll.

"Did Ah awake you?" the whispered voice continued.

"Hm ..." Marsha mumbled, trying to arrive at the present.

"So tewwibly sorry. Ah've just heard the dweadful news. Ah was westing when it happened. Late awwival from New York. The Concooood, you know. Poor, pooor deah Andrew. Was it his haaat?" Overly soft 'r's, elongated vowels, phrases strung together as breathlessly as if she had just completed a fast mile run. Yet each phrase carried the same emphasis, rather like her writing. Margaret Drury Carter. Alex Levine had told Marsha that Margaret had developed that endearing fake Southern drawl around the time she went on tour to promote *Magnolias in the Rain*.

"Possibly," Marsha said, trying to sit up in bed. "We didn't know for sure when we left the party."

"How ..." Margaret Drury Carter hesitated, before she pronounced the dreaded words, "did he die?" Her voice cracked on the word "die," but she carried on bravely. "You were theah, with him."

"I was there," Marsha said. "But I doubt if one could say I was *with him*. I think he was already ... unconscious when I saw him. Very sorry, Margaret," she added quickly, remembering that Margaret might have regarded him with some devotion, after all the money he had obtained for her over the past five years.

There was a long silence at the end of the line.

Then Margaret said, softly: "He is not in a hospital. They have all been called. That would mean he is dead. A tewwible, tewwible tragedy." The soft "r" tended towards a "w" sound. Alex held Vivien Leigh responsible for that one, the English actress who had struggled mightily with a Southern accent in *Gone with the Wind*. Margaret waited a beat, then asked, "Today, the plans will be cancelled, Ah'm shuah?"

Marsha searched for the right tone, and when none presented itself, she said rather too matter-of-factly, "I'm afraid not. It's too late to change the plans. Lunch at the Fünf Hussars, at twelve. You know it's your only chance to meet the foreign publishers." In deference to Margaret's sorrow, she added, "Andrew would have wanted you to be there."

"Callous, my deah, wouldn't you say?"

"We have no choice. Some of them are here only to meet you," which was a bit of a stretch. What she really meant was that for A&M to earn back some of the twenty million dollar advance they had guaranteed her, they had to produce the author at the Fair. The foreign publishers bidding for the privilege of publishing her had every right to expect to see her in person.

Margaret breathed a tearful farewell and released Marsha.

She smelled the sticky substance in the glass by the phone, identified it as brandy, Bertil's last drink from the mind-bogglingly expensive minibar, and sipped it. There was still half an hour left for sleep and she needed the rest. It would be a gruelling day and Marsha was beginning to feel the weight of the years she had been coming to Frankfurt. In the beginning she could survive, sometimes even sparkle on a couple of hours of sleep, now, five to six hours were not quite enough. She might have to give up her early morning jog if the nights kept stretching into the days.

She pulled the rock-hard pillow over her head, bunched the thin white cover over her shoulders and tried once more to go back to sleep. It was futile. She could still feel the cold moisture of Andrew Myles's skin.

She went to the bathroom and ran hot water over her fingers without turning on the light. She soaped and scrubbed her hands once more and returned to bed to stare at the black walls.

In Toronto it would be a few minutes past midnight. Marsha picked up the phone and asked the operator to ring Judith's number. Unlike Marsha, Judith was a habitual night owl. She answered on the second ring.

"Hello," she said tentatively.

"It's me," Marsha said. "Who were you expecting?" She knew her friend well enough that she didn't have to ask why she had picked up the phone so quickly. Marsha knew where every stick of time-worn furniture was in Judith's small house, and the phone hung on a hook by the kitchen door. Judith had put it there so that it would be about equal distance from the kitchen and the living room. Her money did not run to an extra extension.

"James," Judith said. "All this shit going on with Jimmy's

school, I figured he had to find out sooner or later. Plus I asked him for last month's allowance. He is eight weeks late and we have a mortgage to pay." Marsha and Judith had been friends for so long that their conversations barely had beginnings and ends; they were of a continuous flow, as if stopped in mid-thought the last time. "How's Germany?"

"Lousy. Andrew Myles died last night. At a party. I was there when it happened."

"Isn't that the agent nobody likes?"

"He was a prick," Marsha admitted, "but I wish I'd been somewhere else when he chose to go. I can't get it out of my mind."

"That's hardly surprising," Judith said. "It's not every day you witness somebody dying. What happened?"

"No one knows. Might have been a heart attack. He drank too much."

"Don't we all?" Judith asked rhetorically. "And now you can't sleep, right?" She didn't wait for an answer. "Why don't you go for a run in an hour. It'd make you feel better. It wouldn't do much for me, but you were always the exercise freak. What do you mean you were there when he died?"

"Sitting on the arm of his chair. Talking to him. And all the time he was dead." Marsha took a deep breath. "Tell me what you're up to. Any work coming in?"

"None. I thought *Saturday Night* magazine might come through on a story I've been following about some nutcase militia type, but they're reluctant to send me all the way to New Brunswick to find out if it's worthwhile. Might cost them three hundred dollars in airfare. Cheap sods. To hell with them — I've decided to go anyway. We're leaving tomorrow."

"Is Jimmy up for going with you?" Marsha knew that Jimmy had been Judith's biggest problem over that past few months.

This should have been Jimmy's Grade 12 year, but he had stopped turning up at school halfway through Grade 11. Judith hadn't found out till March because Jimmy had mastered the art of faking her signature. On his sixteenth birthday, when the class and teacher had sent a giant plant of uncertain pedigree and a get-well card, Judith realized he had signed himself out of school with mononucleosis several months ago. From time to time, it seemed she had been sending the teacher update notes to keep him informed of Jimmy's dire condition.

Battle lines had been drawn. Most of the arguments were exhausted within a week. Jimmy was a tough opponent because he didn't engage on the designated turf; he retreated conceding nothing. He simply insisted there was no sense in working for a piece of paper you earned by the simple effort of answering sub-standard questions in a prescribed fashion. Judith couldn't think of a way to force him back to school. The principal had suggested, none too gently, that the boy needed proper supervision. It was clear to all three of them that he was not going to see much of that at home — not with a single working mother. Though the principal hadn't quite said so, it was obvious he felt Jimmy was another victim of a broken home.

"I think it would be good for him to get away from here for a while. He's been keeping his end of the bargain, staying on the computer, working on projects, not hanging out with street kids downtown, but it would be easier if he were in another place. You know."

Marsha did know. Jimmy was her godchild and she knew him well enough to recognize what a struggle he'd have with temptation. At first, she had recommended boarding school for him, after all, both she and Judith had survived some four years at Bishop Strachan, a toney Toronto school for girls, but they both knew Judith couldn't afford the exorbitant fees at any of the private schools. There was no point asking James, Judith's ex, for the money, and Judith would not have accepted it from Marsha. She had never accepted any financial help from her, not even a short-term loan.

Marsha had always thought Judith was too proud to accept her money. Perhaps that was true. But her main reason had nothing to do with pride. Judith feared that her accepting Marsha's charity might change their relationship. It would make her dependent, and while it might not make any difference to how Marsha felt about her, it would change how she felt about Marsha.

She had been dependent once, on James, and she never wanted to feel that way again.

Jimmy had provided an easy way out of the private-school dilemma. Having borrowed an Upper Canada College uniform from one of his friends, he had paraded around the living room in a white button-down shirt, striped school tie, too-tight blazer, and too-short pants. He had tied up his scraggly blond hair at the back to give the impression of a short cut, and the only part of his old self he had kept was the earring. He had looked like a pathetic scarecrow. No one, they had agreed, should be subjected to appearing in public like this.

In the end, Marsha had advised Judith to ride out the storm, put on a reasonable front, and persuade Jimmy to return to school the next year. They had arrived at an uneasy truce. Jimmy would work on his computer courses at home and Judith would question him less about his spare time activities if he came home by midnight, took no drugs, and didn't drink to excess.

"You could always send him to New York for a while. He likes it there, knows no one and I'd enjoy his company," Marsha said. "It would be a pleasant change to have a guy to come home to in the evenings. We could take in a few shows. He used to like the theatre."

"Thanks. A nice thought. I'll mention it to him if this damned story does not pan out." Judith was a freelance writer and lived, as they all do, from one assignment to the next. "Is Bertil there?" she changed the subject.

"As ever."

"Still beautiful?"

41

Marsha laughed. "Yes. Gorgeous. A pity in some ways."

"Hm," Judith agreed. "Why don't you try and get a few minutes sleep before your run." She could tell that Marsha was feeling better.

"Good luck with James."

"Thanks."

This time, when the phone rang, there was a shaft of grey light between the curtains and she knew exactly where to find the receiver without knocking over the brandy glass.

"Fräulein Hillier?" asked the thin metallic voice.

"What now," Marsha demanded.

"Zis is the Frankfurt police department," the voice informed her. "Ve are investigating."

"Very good," Marsha said. Nice to know that the Frankfurt police was doing its job.

There was a moment's hesitation, but not long enough for Marsha to hang up. "Excuse," the voice resumed. "Perhaps it is too early?"

"Damned right it's too early."

"In Chermany, ve start very early. Sorry. Did not vish to disturb, but ve vere vorried you vould be gone to your business. Now ve must speak to you about Mr. Myles." He did not sound apologetic in the least.

"Now?" Marsha intoned. Her glowing alarm clock told her it was a few minutes past seven. "Now is not convenient," she added firmly.

Either he didn't notice, or he didn't care. "Ve vill be coming up in the elevator," he told her cheerfully.

"Bloody hell," Marsha said into the dead receiver. Myles was proving to be as aggressively rude in death as he had been in life.

She searched in vain for a bathrobe. At the astonishing rate of $450 a night the Marriott failed to provide one. Frankfurt hotels triple their rates during the Bookfair, though they don't improve their services. In the end, she opted for her soft track pants and a large t-shirt she had packed for her morning jog through the back streets. She ran her fingers through her limp morning hair. For as long as she could remember, it hadn't changed: blond wisps in uneven lengths that her mother had tried to puff up by blow-drying and back combing during her teens, but the wisps took no notice. She splashed cold water on her face and took a swig of Scope to quell the taste of stale brandy.

She hadn't turned on the bathroom light. She had never liked her features in the morning.

Although she was expecting them, the sharp knocks made her jump. She put the chain on the door before she opened it a crack. Marsha Hillier knew how to take care of herself. She peered through the narrow crack in the door at a tall man in a tan mackintosh, a brown felt hat, a square moustache in a pale face with an uncertain smile. He thrust his police identification card towards Marsha, or where he assumed her to be behind the door. It was a great get up for a police officer, one who must have watched a lot of American movies and was nostalgic for the 1950s.

"Inspektor Hübsch," he said. "Ve are investigating the death of Andrew Myles." He waited for her to open the door, and when she didn't, he proceeded seemingly undisturbed. "I have been given to understand that you vere wiz Mr. Myles last night."

"I wasn't *with* Andrew Myles," Marsha said defensively. "I happened to be close to him at one point in the evening, but he appeared to be already dead then."

Inspektor Hübsch flicked open a small leather-bound notebook and jotted. Then he looked up at the crack in the door and asked: "How do you know ven somebody is already dead, Miss Hillier?"

Marsha did not like the attempt to intimidate her with the cold look from behind Hübsch's unrimmed glasses, nor his expensive notebook, nor his apparent lack of concern about her not opening the door to let him in. "He was slumped in his chair," she said. "He wasn't moving, or talking, he was lifeless ..."

"Lifeless," Hübsch repeated slowly, writing.

Marsha waited.

Hübsch's face came closer to the crack in the door. He looked intently at what he could see of Marsha's. "I thought ve had agreed you did not know if he was actually lifeless. Is that so?" he asked.

"He seemed lifeless. As if he were asleep ..."

"Not lifeless then," Hübsch interrupted. "Vat exactly do you mean by slumped?" he asked pleasantly.

"He was leaning awkwardly. His shoulders were hunched forward."

"Slumped?" Hübsch repeated, writing into his little book. "And zis vas at vat time exactly?"

"One doesn't keep track of the time at parties," Marsha said.

"Ungefähr?" Hübsch asked.

"Let's see..."

"Approximately, I think you say," Hübsch said. "You speak some German?"

Marsha ignored the question; it was too early for pleasantries. "I arrived around nine-thirty. Perhaps it was an hour later."

"You did not speak wiz him, then?"

"How would I be conversing with him if he was already dead?" Marsha protested.

Inspektor Hübsch shrugged. "Zat, I do not know," he said. "Yet ozers have told me that you were speaking to him. How'z zat?"

"I didn't know he was dead right away," Marsha said.

"You said just now that he was dead already when you got there."

"I did not say he was dead when I got there, I said he was dead when I sat down next to him." She had not wanted to become defensive, but he was making it difficult.

"So," Hübsch said thoughtfully, "he vas not dead when you

arrived at his side but he was dead later in ze evening." He took a package of Marlboros from the breast pocket of his mackintosh, extracted a cigarette from the package by shaking it with one hand, and stuck the cigarette between his lips. He returned the package to his pocket, took a Bic lighter from the same place, and lit the cigarette.

In the United States, Marsha thought, he would at least have inquired if she minded. She did mind.

"What time vas it zat you approached Mr. Myles?" he asked.

"I just told you I have no idea. Perhaps around ten-thirty. Maybe sooner. I wasn't paying particular attention to the time, because I didn't know I'd be spending this ungodly hour answering questions about it."

Hübsch nodded and exhaled a cloud of cigarette smoke that should have set off the hotel's alarm system. "You vere in ze Lippizaner bar wiz your friends at midnight, so it could have been later. Yes?"

"Yes."

"Your friends," Hübsch looked up from his jottings, "zey vere the same people who vere wiz Myles vere zey not?"

"If you mean that some of the same people who were at the Intercontinental happened to be also in the Lippizaner after the party ended so abruptly, you are right. Some were the same."

"Zis vas not exactly what I meant, no." Hübsch flicked over a few pages in his book, and tilted his head to read. "What I meant is zere vere ze same people viz Mr. Myles who later met viz each ozer in the bar. No?"

"I really don't know what you mean. Some of us stopped for a drink, and yes, some of the same people were in both places. What of it?"

"Perchance you could give me all zeir names?"

"Perchance"? Where had that come from? He was beginning to sound like he had not only studied the clothing of 50s movie detectives, he was emulating their speech habits. "Okay," she said, "Jerry Haines, Mark Newnes, Hideo, Brigitte Dombert, Connor Sagfield."

"Mr. Sagfield is from Australia?"

"Yes. Several others I didn't know."

"Mr. Levine?"

"He was in the bar. I don't remember seeing him at the party."

"But he vas zere?"

"I suppose he must've been. He always goes to that party."

Hübsch nodded. He'd heard about the Bertelsmann party before. "He was a competitor of Mr. Myles. Yes?"

"You could say that," Marsha agreed. "Andrew Myles had a lot of competitors. There are more than two hundred literary agents in New York alone."

"Mr. Nystrom? He vas wiz you at ze party?"

"No. He didn't come with me when I was with Andrew Myles."

"Later in ze bar, only?"

"Yes."

"Ah," Hübsch said regretfully. "And Mr. van Maeght?"

"The Dutchman? Perhaps. I do not remember that he was around Andrew Myles. Certainly not when I first saw him."

"He vas viz you at the party," Hübsch stated emphatically.

"He was not with me." Marsha was finding it harder to fight her irritation with each question he asked. "We were at the same party. We did not go together. We did not leave together. I wasn't sure what his name was until I saw him at the Lippizaner, after the party. We did talk, but that was before I went over to speak to Andrew."

"But later, he was in ze bar, yes?"

"Yes. So what?"

He smiled and jotted in his book. "All zese people, zey were friends of Mr. Myles?"

"Not exactly friends." Myles didn't have any friends, Marsha thought. It was difficult to imagine anyone being friends with Myles. "Colleagues. We're all in the same business, that's all."

"Not friends, zen." Hübsch had reached the end of his cigarette, spat on his thumb and forefinger, squeezed them over the stub, then stuck it into his pocket. "Did you happen to notice what he was drinking?"

"He was not drinking when I got there because as I just told you he was dead. And his glass was empty."

"So what were you doing wiz it?" Hübsch asked quickly.

"I gave it to the waiter. I was trying to get him a refill." Marsha answered. What the hell was he getting at?

"For a dead man?"

"I didn't know he was dead then." Marsha hadn't noticed that her voice had risen to a shout until the door opposite hers opened, and a man in pyjamas yelled in French for them to be quiet, he was trying to sleep.

"When would it be convenient if I come back to see you, Miss Hillier?" Hübsch asked in a whisper.

Marsha suggested three o'clock at the Fair. It was not convenient, but there were no convenient times in Frankfurt. But she didn't feel she had any other option.

Hübsch folded his leather booklet and stuck it back into his coat pocket. "Thank you for your co-operation," he said, "and your hospitality. Your country, it is famous for it." He turned on his heel to walk away.

"Just a minute," Marsha called after him. She had slid the chain off the door and stuck her head out. "What was all this about, anyway?"

Hübsch didn't slow his progress towards the elevators.

"He wasn't murdered, was he?"

"Ah, yes, he was," Hübsch called over his shoulder.

CHAPTER
FOUR

T HE TALK OF THE FAIR WAS ANDREW MYLES. HE HIM-self could not have wished for more notoriety or more attention. Already at the turnstiles there were people asking one another about what had happened at the Bertelsmann party. Though it was drizzling again, Marsha walked to Halle 9 where all the American booths were. It wasn't exactly fresh air, but she couldn't complain after what she was used to in New York. She had been breathing that air all her life except for the odd interruption on Martha's Vineyard.

The four early risers at the A&M booth had all heard of the murder of Andrew Myles, and one of them had even heard that the killer had been caught with the murder weapon still on him. "They say it was a steel stiletto."

"Another agent?"

"No. A publisher."

Marsha's first appointment was A&M's Spanish agent, who wanted to know all the details of the two new Margaret Drury Carter novels. She was sure she could get a princely sum from any one of the seven major contenders for two new Carters, but it would be a lot easier if she could entice them with a plot or two.

Marsha wished she had demanded something as stirring from Andrew when she signed away the twenty million dollars, but Andrew offered no information except that the heavenly Carter was willing to agree to a deal, one manuscript almost finished, the second well on the way — and that another house was already offering in the high seven figures for only one. Andrew had shopped Carter around before coming to Marsha. With two books on the best-seller list at once, Carter could command almost any price she wanted, and Andrew was the guy to get it for her.

Before Andrew had found her four years ago, when Carter had been with Alex Levine, she had signed option agreements and honoured them. She and Alex would go and see the publisher in New York for the signing, and celebrate it with champagne that Alex brought along. It had been Alex's theory that it was useful for an author to have friends inside a publishing house about to bring out the author's new book.

Andrew's theory was summed up in the cash he demanded. "Any publisher will be committed to a book for which he paid a bucket of money," he had told Marsha. After Andrew took over representing Margaret Drury Carter, she did not bother to come to New York to meet her editor any more.

"They are in the tradition of *Conspiracy of Roses*," Marsha assured A&M's eager Spanish agent. It was safe to assume that they would be, most of her books were. "Strong woman character. Lost love. She gambles all once more ... and," Marsha was making it up as she went. These were much the same words she had used in the contract request she had sent upstairs, and it had been good enough for them. Carter's record of sales spoke more eloquently than any book brief. "You'll have to find out for yourself. Both are vintage Carters. Her fans will love them." She had decided not to mention the third Carter at the Fair. If her sense of Carter's European market was right, the first two books would solidify her base, the third would blow the charts. It would require careful orchestration of publicity and news support, but Fay was the woman to do it. She had drawn up plans the day the deal was signed.

The Spanish agent's eyes shone with enthusiasm. "My favourite was *Midnight Dance*," she said. "We got the highest advance in Spain, you know. I don't suppose you could give me just a little more. No?" She looked around the booth. "She is still coming, isn't she?"

Marsha reassured her that Margaret would be there for lunch. The Spanish agent couldn't wait to see her. As good a time as any to ask her for a bit of plot development. Marsha hoped Margaret would not be so distraught at Andrew's demise that she failed to bring the precious ten thousand words. In her mind she kept playing the scene of Andrew's death.

It could not have been a knife. There had been no blood.

She tried to remember all the faces around her. Which one of them was the murderer? Did anyone come close to Andrew while she was there? Who was the woman with the compact? There had been a man behind Andrew's chair, leaning on it. She didn't recall his face.

She had three more agents to see before eleven, and a couple of rights people. She didn't realize how tired she was till one of them asked her if she'd like a cup of coffee and took off towards the nearest coffee stand. Marsha wondered if she had been dozing during the presentation, and returned to it with renewed vigour after a few sips of the thick black brew that Frankfurters call coffee. It tasted like ground burnt toast, but it packed quite a wallop. At eleven-thirty, Bertil came by with a white gift box he must have hastily wrapped himself because the paper was held together with Post-it Notes.

"I did try for flowers," he told her mournfully, "but all I could find this morning were these and a variety of kites. This, I thought, would be sure to remind you of Frankfurt. And me, of course. You can get kites anywhere." He dropped the box into her lap and dashed on to his next meeting. It contained a shiny blue and white butterfly and batteries.

Mechanical butterflies are one of the few attractive features of the Frankfurt Bookfair. Once wound up, they fly around in ever-decreasing circles, making a colourful display and most satisfying whirring sounds. They are sold on the Messe site, along the main thoroughfare between the sturdy, grey box-like buildings. There are six buildings in all, each, unaccountably, called a hall or Halle. Each one turns into a rabbit warren of publishers' booths for the duration of the Fair. The booths are grouped by country. Not surprisingly, the largest group by far is Germany, occupying entire buildings of its own, usually Halle 6 and most of 5. The British are just a part of Halle 9, with the Americans, and across from the French and the Italians who share 9 with other assorted Europeans and the Japanese. German illustrated books, posters, postcards, and maps are usually on the ground floor, and general publishers on the second floor, where they are most easily accessible to the public.

Whatever unkind thoughts you might entertain about Frank-furters, they are a reassuring lot for the publishing industry. They crowd into the German aisles — some five hundred booths on every floor — with the kind of bright-eyed enthusiasm Americans exhibit in lining up for rock concerts. These are not the New York Is Book City frequenters, the annual party-goers who bring their kids for the balloons, the giveaways, the emblazoned t-shirts and canvas shopping bags, the clowns, and the face-painters; these people grab book catalogues, advance copies of as yet unpublished books, they read the handouts on the shelves, and they mob authors for autographs.

This was where Marsha now struggled to reach the Bertelsmann Bookclubs' display area to collect Dr. Gerhardt Gutfreund and take him to the Fünf Hussars. Gerhardt, whom nobody called Gerhardt to his face, was one of the pillars of Bertelsmann's worldwide empire. He had erected bookclubs in Spain, Holland, Norway, France, and all over South America. He spoke eleven languages with precision, had the diplomatic skills of a Weimar politician, the courtly manners of a Habsburg potentate, the ability to stare down opponents, and to fire people with the unflinching preparedness of an executioner. In the Bertelsmann family he was known as the Mechanic, because he could identify the problem in an ailing club, and fix it with a minimum of fuss, without becoming involved in its local peculiarities. He was the best of the numbers-men. He was revered, feared, and suspected of knowing too much of the inside operations of clubs ever to be allowed to leave his employers alive.

When Marsha arrived he was speaking Swedish to someone on the phone. He was leaning over the black Formica desk in the middle of the booth, as if to shield the phone call from any curious Swedes. He wore a charcoal grey tailored suit with thin lapels, a blue tie, and an open vest. He was tall, thin, and angular, too well-dressed to be mistaken for one of the other booklovers hovering nearby. His face was lined, pale, and expressionless despite the animated voice he used on the Swede at the other end of the line. He had a wide, bony forehead, grey hair combed straight back, not a strand out of place. Mousse, Marsha thought, no one can keep hair that rigid unless it's stiff. Though the booth was crowded, a space of some four feet remained around the good doctor, as if even strangers could guess he was not a man to cuddle up to.

The booth was decorated with lit-up posters advertising the clubs' main selections. They had installed plush red carpets to mark the area off from the general path through the hall. Near Gerhardt's head, Marsha was relieved to see a four-foot-high, back-lit colour photograph of Margaret Drury Carter. She was smiling under a broad-brimmed straw hat with pink band and ribbons, and a bouquet of magnolias drooped carelessly over the brim and onto her left shoulder, which was bare. Not at all bad for a woman near seventy, or more, Marsha thought. No one was entirely sure of Margaret's age, and no interviewer had been bold enough to ask her in more than thirty years. Newspapers reported variously between 65 and 80. The *Who's Who* had her at 73, but she had assured Jay Leno that she used to lie about her age when she was young, making herself appear older to gain credibility.

When Gerhardt sighted Marsha, he gave a courtly little bow, stretched his arm to dislodge his gold Cartier watch and strap from the strictures of his lavish white cuff (understated gold cuff links), whispered some parting imprecation into the mouthpiece, and hung up. He prided himself on, amongst other accomplishments, his punctuality.

"It was a tremendous shock, Mr. Myles's death," he said once he had turned his back on his staff (one of whom was trying to show him a piece of paper he had waved away) and was following Marsha through the crowd. "So extremely unexpected. Nothing like this has ever happened at a Bertelsmann party. A few embarrassments, but never a death. It is extremely fortunate our retired chief did not choose to stay very long this time. It would have been for him a tremendous stress."

Andrew was not known to be considerate of other people's occasions, Marsha thought as she struggled against the crowd, many of whom were pushing towards an autographing in the Lubbe booth.

"This is not working," Dr. Gutfreund remarked as he held Marsha's shoulder, propelled her to one side, and took the lead. Given his history of boardroom tactics, it was not altogether surprising that he was an accomplished crowd-parter. He hunched his shoulders forward as if he were running against a storm and slammed through the walls of on-coming duffle-coated browsers without a pause until they reached the exit. Marsha followed closely in his wake.

"It was poison," he told her when they were in the taxi outside the Messe. "The police are not sure what kind, but there is no question it was poison. You were there, weren't you?"

"He was poisoned at the party?" Marsha asked.

"It would seem so," Gerhardt said, nodding rather sadly. "So very embarrassing for the firm. The police will be making enquiries, this whole thing will affect the Fair for everyone."

Inspektor Hübsch was waiting outside the restaurant when they arrived at the Fünf Hussars. He had drawn his collar up against the wind, pulled his felt hat down low on his forehead, and thrust his hands in his pockets as he paced, taking small steps as if he were in a hurry both coming and going.

"Fräulein Hillier," he said when he saw Marsha emerge from the cab. "It is with great regret I had to come to ask you once more about Herr Myles before three, though of course I will be returning at three as you instructed. He was to be here with you now, was he not?"

"If you mean Andrew Myles," Marsha said, "he was certainly to be here, the party is for one of his authors."

"Miss Drury Carter," Hübsch said with a small smile. It was hard to tell whether he was an admirer of Margaret's books or he thought they deserved no more than a smirk. When Hübsch caught sight of Gerhardt, the moment of levity disappeared, he drew back his shoulders, puffed out his chest and all but saluted. "Dr. Gutfreund is also with your group," he remarked with surprise, as if finding someone of Gerhardt's calibre in Marsha's group of motley foreigners was quite unexpected.

Gerhardt said something to him in rapid German, then swept by to open the door of the Fünf Hussars for Marsha.

"Ein Moment, bitte," the policeman insisted, inserting himself between Marsha and the entrance. "Entschuldigung," he said to Gerhardt, "there was just ze question of ze glass." Then, turning back to Marsha he asked, "What did you do wiz Mr. Myles's glass?"

Marsha was baffled for a second, then remembered holding Andrew's glass in her hand when she still imagined that he might want a refill. "I gave it to the waiter. That's what I told you this morning," she said impatiently.

"Ya," Hübsch agreed. "Indeed. Zat's what you told me but I vondered if maybe zere had been some mistake about zat. Perhaps in the confusion, you had slipped it into your handbag." He said this as if slipping wineglasses into your purse was the most natural thing in the world, the kind of activity anyone might indulge in, absent-mindedly, at parties.

"Miss Hillier does not steal glasses," Gerhardt stated, and repeated the same in German, in case Hübsch missed it the first time. "This is most inconvenient, Inspektor," he added. "We are expected inside. You will excuse us." He took Marsha's arm and steered her into the restaurant. "I apologize," he said to her, as if he were responsible for the Frankfurt police. "He is only doing his job."

Marsha shuddered at the possibility that Gerhardt didn't know the historical connotation of that sentence. She was relieved to see her Spanish agent standing at a long table near the window, waving at her; Bertil beside her with a bottle of champagne in his hand; Hideo, slightly flushed, leaning forward to hear whatever Dr. Schneider was saying to him; and Frans van Maeght lurking conspicuously near the head of the table, hoping, no doubt, to be seated near Margaret. Marsha enjoyed the notion that despite his professed loathing for American commercial fiction, Frans would have bought the Dutch rights to Margaret's new manuscripts. Several of her earlier books had been published by Meulenhoff, and after the consistently successful Bertha took over, by Forum. Van Maeght's firm had not been known for commercial fiction. It had a reputation for serious history and large volumes of European memoirs. It seemed that little Frans, despite his protestations, would be on a different path.

Though Marsha was to play host, the lunch had been arranged

by Fay Mercer, A&M's rights director, who had been busily selling pieces of the twenty million dollar pie, though she knew even less about the books than Marsha did. Margaret's track record was all she needed to know for fast Frankfurt sales.

It was easier to sell a twenty million dollar book in Frankfurt than a two thousand dollar one, she had told Marsha before the Fair. A two thousand dollar book had to be read, the twenty million dollar deal was a marketing challenge. Fay enjoyed marketing challenges, and she knew her targets. She had lined them up here for the viewing of the property.

Some of those she had invited today would already have signed agreements in the first two frantic days of the Fair, others would have agreed to the terms, a few would still be waiting to be convinced. One of the most important remained Gerhardt. He commanded bookclubs in six countries. He could make or break a book in Europe. Last time, the clubs had sold a mere 400,000 copies in four languages, and Gerhardt had been disappointed. "This time," he had assured Fay, "they would set their expectations higher, or not engage the book."

Marsha was quick to place him at what would be Margaret's right.

Dr. Schneider, who had already told Fay he would not take Carter's book at the ridiculous price that had been proposed, unless Gerhardt backed it with a bookclub purchase, would sit at the end of the table. Fay settled in between him and the still hesitating French publisher. There were publishers there from Japan, France, Denmark, Norway, and Sweden, the heads of A&M's U.K. and Australian subsidiaries, two Spaniards, a Turk, an Italian, and the two Canadians who had led the invasion of A&M's offices last summer. They had been the advance guard, who appeared as soon as the news was out that a buyer had been found, and they had been the ones who stayed behind once the army of accountants returned to Alberta. What was left of the old staff referred to them as "the cowboys," even though the one called Morris was a recent graduate of a Canadian business school and claimed to have spent time at Harvard.

Morris, as far as one could tell after a few months of casual acquaintance, was not very interested in reading. His specialty was computers and he spent a great deal of his time — when he was not firing people — worrying about inventory. For the Fünf Hussars he had worn a navy blue suit, a blue and white polka-dot tie, and loafers. He had brushed his hair straight back to reveal a widow's peak that made him look somewhat older than his thirty-odd years, and wore black, horn-rimmed spectacles that he must have purchased in Germany, Marsha thought, because they were an exact match for Dr. Schneider's.

Thurgood, the other Canadian, was in his late sixties, and was shorter, stouter, and balder than his countryman. He rarely spoke to anyone at A&M and was generally recognized as the real money-man. He was usually on the phone in his office, talking to Calgary or wherever. He had been the one whose signature appeared on the cheque Marsha had couriered with the signed contract to Andrew Myles's office.

Had he not died the night before, Andrew would have loved this occasion. It had been his idea to celebrate Margaret's new contract in Frankfurt. Though twenty million might not seem like much after Barbara Taylor Bradford's latest deal, it was still a large enough sum to draw mild gasps, and Andrew was not one to hide his accomplishments. For him Frankfurt was just the place for a display.

Fay made her way to Marsha. "I hope you like the centrepiece," she said. "It's not easy to get magnolias in Frankfurt in October. Thought it would be a nice touch for the old lady. A bit of colour to pick her up." Fay was determinedly cheery. Marsha could see that she was not going to let something as inconsiderate as murder encroach on her good humour. She was one of the A&M survivors, loud, assertive, with an implied swagger. Her lipstick was vermilion, her eye shadow a darkish blue, cheeks accented with rust red blush. Even her hair was a statement of battle-readiness. She wore it in a hard lacquered curl, set around her face.

She had arranged the Canadians so they would be facing each other. "Can't do much harm that way."

Marsha asked, "Van Maeght, what did he bid for Carter?"

"He was first off the mark on the two-book deal. Three hundred thousand guilders for book one with an option to acquire the second for ten percent more."

Not bad for a literary snob, Marsha thought. "The Swedes?"

"They haven't made up their minds yet. I think they'll bid after lunch."

She introduced Dr. Gutfreund to the cowboys. Morris smiled vacantly at him while the fat man attempted to engage him in conversation about the Bundesbank and its efforts to bolster the Dutchman. It endured about a minute before they reached Gerhardt's boredom ceiling and he hit out for the tow-headed woman from Denmark. Marsha thought she must have been Helga, who published relatively mindless best-sellers, gaining a reputation for commercial savvy and knowing the value of a good New York scout. Paying the scout a percentage, not just an annual fee, made her more selective.

It had been Fay's idea to invite the *Börsenblatt*. "I've got to take the position that any time Margaret deigns to appear in public, it's a news event," she told Marsha. "She should have been there last night, and you know it. If Atwood could make it to that godawful party, I don't see why you couldn't make *her* come."

"Atwood thinks kindly of her publishers," Marsha said. "That's why she comes to Frankfurt. To support them."

"And Margaret comes because it's in her contract," Fay hissed. "Next time, put the Bertelsmann party into the deal, would you?"

"Next time we can't count on a murder."

"You're right." She smiled wanly at the *Börsenblatt* man who had edged his way to them. "Miss Drury Carter is absolutely heart-broken about poor Andrew Myles," she told him.

"I do hope that doesn't mean she won't be coming today," he said, nodding at Marsha. "Blum," he added grabbing her hand and shaking it. He was chunky, broad-shouldered, and thick-necked. He smoked a half-chewed cigar. His tweed jacket smelled of stale smoke and sweat.

"Hillier," Marsha said. "Miss Carter will certainly come," she reassured him. "She is a professional."

"That's what I heard it was," Blum told them. "A professional murder. Someone was hired to do it. Like the Rushdie killings. A random killer working a common cause with a larger movement. This makes it very hard to catch them."

"I doubt if Andrew had anything to do with Rushdie," Fay said.

"Too cautious for that sort of client, you think?" Connor Sag-field joined in.

"Maybe," Marsha didn't want to be uncharitable to the dead.

"Don't you believe it," Sagfield said. "Last year he offered me a new Rushdie for half a million. Your dollars, not the clean-living Australian kind, at that." Sagfield snorted. He was a big bear of a man with a beer-drinker's belly, and large square hands that flailed about for emphasis. "Luckily I met Rushdie a few days later in Sydney. He was the surprise guest at a PEN benefit. He'd never changed agents, and claimed the last person he'd move to was Myles."

"Andrew up to his old tricks, then," Frans said.

It was close to two o'clock when Margaret appeared.

By then the group was well-lubricated on cheap German cham-pagne. Sagfield had discovered some friends at an adjoining table and started a restrained bread fight; Hideo was discussing in detail his collection of erotic art and literature, which he claimed was the most interesting in Japan — many of the texts he had translated himself — and possibly in Southeast Asia; the Spanish agent was having an animated discussion with Frans about the demise of Spanish literature; and Morris was entertaining Gerhardt with comparisons between the publishing business and the oil exploration business, about which he knew rather more than he did books.

"A best-seller is like a gusher," Morris was saying when Margaret made her grand entrance.

She was dressed in black from head to toe: a black taffeta dress that trailed in a soft bell-curve almost to the floor, black lace ruffles around her throat, matching gloves, soft black suede pumps, a black felt fedora pulled low over her brow, a piece of black gauze veil hanging over her face. Even the silk handkerchief she clutched dramatically close to her ruffled breasts was black. The only touch of colour was her trademark mauve magnolia stuck into the hatband.

"Ah my deahs ..." she sighed softly when all the talk had ceased and she commanded everyone's attention. "Such a tragedy — pooah pooah deah Andrew. How can we eat when we have lost one so deah to all of us?" She held her wrist to her throat in a theatrical gesture that would have done Sarah Bernhardt proud. She turned and wrapped Marsha in her arms and rested her chin on Marsha's shoulder. "Such a pitiful day," she whispered. "It took hours to find the right clothes. What with my concentration all gone ..."

She held the embrace while Fay sorted everyone into designated places around the table. Morris finished the stale bruschetta he had taken before Margaret came and told the waiter he was ready for more beer. His eyes travelled up and down Margaret's heaving back, tilting his head this way and that, wanting to get a better look.

"He died, they told me, in an instant," Margaret went on in Marsha's ear. "No time to say farewell." She was quoting the title of one of her early works. "Perhaps you spoke to him before?" she asked tentatively.

"Not I," Marsha said.

"You were so close to him when he died," Margaret said. "You were the last to talk to him, weren't you? The vewwy last ..." Her voice caught as she exhaled. She made it sound like a very particular privilege to have been there at all. "Such a singulah honour ..." She also chose to ignore Marsha's protest. "What did he say to you?"

Marsha repeated what she had already told Hübsch, but Margaret remained adamant. "Just the two of you," she breathed into Marsha's shoulder, as if she had caught them in the act in some isolated room instead of the crowded Grand Ballroom. "Didn't he have some last wish? Something ..."

"He was already dead," Marsha insisted.

"Ah," Margaret intoned regretfully. "To heah the last words of the dying. The secrets we learn about the world yet to come." She turned towards the big table where everyone waited, still silent. "Sooner or later," she said resting her not inconsiderable weight on the back of Blum's chair.

Everyone nodded encouragingly.

Margaret plopped softly into her chair.

"I hope this will not set you back in your work on the new book," Morris said, leaning forward over the table in an attempt to establish eye contact. The business school manual on behavioural signals was very clear about the necessity for eye contact when making a pitch. It was one of the little tools he used around the A&M offices, in the "one-on-one" meetings he called (Morris loved one-on-one meetings), and even in the group sessions that he favoured for setting out the five-year plan with its shared objectives, common power words, and the new vitality quotient that they all agreed would surely be useful now that about one third of the original staff had been dismissed to make room for "technological efficiencies."

But the black veil covering Margaret's face did not allow for eye contact. One could barely make out where her eyes were, certainly not what she was doing with them.

"She's got till the end of November," the porcine accountant told Morris, *sotto voce*, but not quiet enough for Margaret to miss.

She turned to Marsha. "Who in hell are they?" she inquired, not bothering to lower her voice. When Marsha explained, Margaret said, "Yew gentlemen obviously have a lot to learn. *Ah* always meet my deadlines as deah, deah Andrew might have told you, were he not in heaven right now with the other angels."

Marsha tried to imagine Andrew with wings, perhaps playing a harp, or just hovering overhead, his barrel chest bulging in an oversized nightshirt, and coughed into her napkin. Bertil, as if following her thoughts, gazed at the ceiling, and then informed those within earshot that heaven, if there was such a place, was not cut out for literary agents. "It's not where the action is."

"Please eat," Margaret instructed everybody, but she continued merely to stir her minestrone, not raising the spoon to her lips. Her other hand clasped the high ruffles around her throat, as if the mere act of breathing was causing her pain. "Maybe there is a lesson in that for you," she said to Morris over the babble of voices that greeted Bertil's assessment of heaven.

"Ma'am?" Morris said finding, miraculously, the proper form of address for a Southern lady.

"Being meticulous about time, Mistah Morris. If writers can do it, I see no reason whatsoever why publishers should not." She turned her veil to Bertil and asked, "Do you?"

"None whatsoever, Ms Carter," Bertil said. There was a small but definite grin spreading over his face as he set about enjoying Morris's discomfort. He bit his lip when Marsha gave him a warning look. But the smile lingered.

"Weaall now ..." Margaret fixed Morris once again, stretching her words for maximum effect. "Seeing as how we were discussing punctuality, what pray, Mistah Morris, sir, is your reason for delaying payment of the advance? And while we are discussing that, did you realize that the contract we signed is not worth the paper it's written on until such time as you see fit to send over the cheque?"

"Four weeks ago," Marsha said.

"Cashed within the day," the accountant added. "Mr. Myles's Citibank account in New England."

"Weaall," Margaret said after a moment's hesitation. "Ah'm simply not used to such faahn service, Mr. Thurgood. It's the exception that confirms the rule. Some of y'all do find ways of holding up cheques for the flimsiest of little reasons, don't you, deah? Andrew must've been fairly bowled over by it. Usually it would take a veritable mess of calls just to get your attention to a little thing like money, wouldn't you say? Still an' all, Ah can't worry about such things any longer now, can I? Ah have mah writing to do. Marsha here can tell you I rarely worry about mah own business affairs." She sighed eloquently. "Elinor does it. My niece." Turning to Marsha, she explained, "She's with me, you know."

Marsha had met the niece only once, and it had not been a pleasant encounter. Elinor, who resembled Margaret only in her robust physical appearance, had been going through her aunt's royalty statements, and had taken it into her head that Margaret had been lied to about her sales, or that at the very least, the royalty statements were designed to confuse even the most diligent authors. While Elinor was definitely right about the latter, she was wrong about the former. The statements were accurate, as she herself had to admit after an army of accountants had combed through A&M's files and records to find a discrepancy of less than a hundred dollars, in Margaret's favour. This little exercise in forensic accounting had cost Margaret somewhat in excess of ten thousand dollars.

Myles had been apologetic, as only Myles could be: "The client is always right, my dear Marsha. None of this is my idea. Long as the advances look fine, I know I don't have to worry about the cash flow. I don't actually expect to earn out the advances on Margaret's titles," he confided to Marsha. And he didn't.

"I wish you had told me your niece was here," Marsha lied. "She would have been invited to the lunch."

"You two hit it off so well," Margaret said, before she succumbed to Gerhardt's urging and began to tell the story of *When Morning Comes*, the first to follow *Conspiracy of Roses*. Angelina, the heroine, learns that her father is not the man she has just buried and sets out from Virginia to find her real father, a former river boat gambler, who has fallen on hard times. When visiting her father in jail, she meets Nathaniel, or Nate, as he'd be called outside of the borders of Georgia, a gambler like the man she had loved as a father, and as handsome as he had been ....

The tagliatelle came and went with but one mouthful for Margaret, showing no more than a touch of chin covered in beige foundation and bright pink lips under the veil.

It had all been much too much for her to bear, she told Blum, her voice faltering. She could barely focus on her great undertaking of the three novels. Andrew had been her pillar of strength. She left before coffee, dabbing the silk handkerchief to her ruffled throat, and blaming a headache and lack of sleep.

Bertil held Marsha a little closer than a colleague might, even in Frankfurt, and whispered something in her ear about this evening after the *Reader's Digest* party.

Frans asked her whether the police had visited her as well, and what questions they had for her. He seemed agitated. "They think I had something to do with it," he told Marsha.

"They think everyone had something to do with it, Frans," Marsha tried to reassure him. "It's their way." After some thought, she asked him, "Did you?"

"What do you mean?" Frans demanded. "How would I? Why? This is so stupid, it could be another novel. An American novel. Right? A nonsense novel."

"You were seen very close together, Frans. That's what they call opportunity."

"That's stupid," Frans shouted waving his short arms in the air. "I didn't need opportunity. I had no reason to want to kill the man. That's what I told that Schwein Hübsch. He gets his ... you know ... from harassing the Dutch, like his father did, no doubt, before him. It's a verdammte German pastime. They bring their kids in, you know, to Holland to show them where they marched through during the war and where they slaughtered the Dutch to take over their houses. He is a typical German. No humour. No sense of propriety ..."

Gerhardt did an almost perfect pirouette around Frans, and left muttering something about his father who had been on the Russian front.

"Opportunity isn't enough," Marsha told Frans reassuringly. "You need a motive as well."

"Motive?" Sagfield said, his broad, ruddy face turning even redder, "we all had motive to kill that blighter. Best of times he was a liar and a cheat, gave goddamn agents a bad name, as if the buggers needed one." He offered his best smile to the two Canadians. "Except for you two blighters, and you know tits-all about the business, don't you? But don't let that interfere with your fun." He gave Marsha a big wink and a hug. "Bloody great spread, girl. We'll do one helluva job when Carter comes Down Under. You'll be proud of us yet."

"He doesn't work for us, does he?" Morris asked of Sagfield's receding back.

"It's Australian humour," Marsha said. "He didn't mean anything by it. Joking. They do a lot of that in Australia." She liked Sagfield. He had been in charge of A&M Australia before she had started. Larry Shapiro, her former A&M boss, had usually left him to his own devices in Sydney. "Not a lot to be gained by pushing him around, Marsha," he had told her. "He knows his own market and brings in a fair profit every year. I don't mess with stuff I don't know how to improve."

That sort of thinking was not among the guiding principles espoused by Morris, of course. He stood, feet spread, arms akimbo, staring intently at Sagfield's retreating back, as if he were about to launch a karate attack. "What exactly does he do?" Morris asked. He put the emphasis on the "exactly," a phrase A&M staffers had learnt to recognize as a sure sign of danger, as in, "What exactly does publicity do for this company?" That had been the phrase that presaged Fay's assistant's departure.

"Do you fish?" he had asked Marsha when it was her turn to be called to the sixteenth floor that had until recently been Larry's domain.

"Not for a long time," Marsha had said, thinking that it was probably safer not to draw the general's fishing passion into her first appointment with the guy representing the new owners. "Why?"

"Well," Morris seemed pleased with the answer. He had spread his hands on the smoke-grey glass tabletop he had brought in to replace Larry's imitation Victorian. "Fish you gotta check for size when you bring them in. There's many you throw back in the lake because they're not big enough. There are a few keepers."

"Yes," Marsha had conceded.

"That's the book business, as I see it," Morris had said. "Some have an instinct for the keepers. Some don't. I guess we'll see where you fit."

Once more, Marsha was aware of Morris's appraising glance.

"You don't think there is much humour in Canada, then?" Morris asked with a half-turn, his entire body now directed at Marsha.

"You kidding?" Fay stepped in. "You guys have produced the best humour in America. Bill and Ted, John Candy, Martin Short, Eugene Levy …" She was still the best rights director in New York. Never lost for an answer.

"Rick Moranis," Marsha said lamely. "The thing about Sagfield, though, he is the biggest fish in Australia."

"Small pond, though," Morris whispered to Thurgood, relaxing his battle-ready stance.

Fay laughed a little too enthusiastically.

CHAPTER
FIVE

INSPEKTOR HÜBSCH WAS PACING THE A&M BOOTH when she got there. He still seemed to be in a hurry, though he did stop now and then for a look at the featured books, their covers blown up three feet high, each one mounted on cardboard above a pyramid of tomes of the same title. The A&M people avoided him in wide circling arcs, as if he had a contagious disease. At the makeshift reception desk to the right of the booth, one of the two remaining international rights people looked intently at Marsha, then at Hübsch, tilting his head towards the inspector to indicate that if she wanted to run by it was not too late. He hadn't yet noticed her.

She glanced at her watch. It was 3:15. The only gap in the day. There was no sense in evading him.

"I vill come straight to ze point," Hübsch told her as soon as she came within earshot. "Ve have talked to ze waiter and he has no memory of you giving him a glass. If you gave him a glass." He kept both hands in his pocket, his shoulders hunched forward. "Vill you please try to remember vhat you did wiz his glass."

Marsha sensed he was anxious to be somewhere he could smoke. He had taken his brown felt hat off and was pumping at the rim with thumb and index finger.

She told him about the young waiter's reaction when she had said that Andrew was dead, how he had dropped the tray and probably broken all the glasses on it. "There must have been some shards?"

"Shards?"

"Bits of glass on the floor near Andrew's chair."

Hübsch rested his hat on a display table with a Bill Cosby cardboard cutout and dug his notebook out of his pocket. "You didn't mention the broken glass zis morning." He sounded offended.

"It was too early," Marsha said. "My mind doesn't start turning over till after my morning run. Didn't have time for that today."

"You run?" Hübsch was incredulous. "At the Messe?"

"I don't run at the Bookfair, Inspector, I take some back streets behind the hotel, towards the botanical gardens ..."

"You shouldn't be running around in zat area any more," Hübsch stated. "It's not how it used to be in Frankfurt. It used to be safe before all the newcomers from the East. Not now. Not since the Wall came down. If you must do your exercise, try the hotel."

"Thank you for the advice. Are you finished?"

Hübsch shook his head sadly. "Americans, zey don't listen much, do zey? Zose streets are dangerous. A young woman was killed in ze Palmengarten last summer. Jogging." He said "jogging" with distaste as if it were a four-letter word. He flicked through his notebook, stopping at a thickly scribbled page. "Vat exactly is it zat agents do?" he asked finally. "American literary agents, zat is. What do zey do?"

It had been some years since anyone had asked her that question. She had adjusted her ideas of what agents did dozens of times. Nowadays it was easier to define their jobs by a process of elimination: what they did not do, rather than what they did.

"They are something like a cross between a lawyer and a real estate salesman. They are hired by authors to look after their interests. They find publishers, film studios, magazines to pay for their authors' work."

"Oh," Hübsch rubbed the side of his nose thoughtfully. "Zey get a percentage?" He was swift.

"That's how they make their living."

"In America, is zat a bigger percentage zan in Germany, or?"

"It's not the percentages that vary, it's the demand. The amounts publishers are willing to pay as an advance against an author's earnings from the publishing of a book would tend to be higher in America than anywhere else in the world."

"Advance?"

"We tend to give authors some minimum guarantees against their future income from the sales of their books after they're published. It's become an incentive for them to choose one publisher over another. A higher advance suggests to the author that the publisher putting up the money will do its best to sell a lot of the author's books."

"Why?"

"It's the only way the publisher has of earning back the money it has just given to the author. It's a guarantee. It's not returnable."

"How much vould an advance be?"

"Depends on the author. Or the book. Sometimes both."

"Average?"

"There are no averages."

"What's a large one zen?"

"Barbara Taylor Bradford got thirty million dollars for three novels a while back."

Hübsch whistled appreciatively. "Zat is a lot of money," he said. "What's the agent's portion?"

"At fifteen percent, around $4 million."

"Zere are ozers like her?"

"None quite like Barbara Taylor Bradford; she is a one-woman industry," Marsha said wistfully. She was still smarting from the last time she had lost in the bidding to buy Bradford. She had not been able to convince the upper floor. "But there are few others in her income bracket, if that's what you mean. Frederick Forsyth, Mary Higgins Clark ..."

"And Miss Drury Carter? She is in zat group?" he asked quickly.

"I suppose she is."

"You suppose?" Hübsch lifted his eyebrows. "Vouldn't you *know*?"

Marsha laughed. "You're right, I do know."

"And?" Hübsch seemed genuinely puzzled. "You aren't telling me?"

When she did, Hübsch nodded, as if he'd been expecting it. "Three million for Mr. Myles," he said, shaking a cigarette loose from the package and sticking it between his lips. He didn't light it. "A very nice living. Did he have a number of authors who made zat sort of money?"

"A few."

"Only novel writers?"

"No. He wasn't particular that way. He represented politicians, movie stars, historians ..."

"In wich vay vas he particular?"

"He liked to represent people who were sure to make him money. He never took on beginning writers. He waited for someone else to build a writer's reputation and income, and when he judged the time was right, he would take him or her from other agents. Or he'd go for the public figures who were sure to rake in a handsome advance ..."

"Zat's why nobody liked him?"

Marsha shrugged. "He wasn't in business to be liked. He became an agent strictly to make money, and he was very good at that. If people didn't like him, it's because so many of us are in this business for other reasons."

"More ... how do I say ... noble?" His face remained expressionless.

Marsha was becoming impatient. "I suppose it's mostly that we like words. We actually like books."

"And Mr. Levine, he vas in zis second category. Viz ze people who like words?"

"I believe so."

"He used to represent Miss Drury Carter, isn't zat so?"

"Yes."

"Zo. Ven he lost her to Andrew Myles, he lost three million dollars, is zat not so?"

"Not exactly," Marsha said thoughtfully. "I doubt if Alex Levine would have done a contract like this one for twenty million dollars. But it was certainly the thought of all those dollars that made Margaret Drury Carter leave Alex. Andrew would have told her he could get her twenty million. That was his modus operandi."

Hübsch said, "Hm." He had no problems with the Latin. "But you all did business with him, anyway."

"Yes. And would again."

"An interesting business," Hübsch said. He sounded genuinely impressed. No hint of irony there. "You said Mr. Myles represented politicians. An example?"

"I think he represented Nixon once. Claimed he had Mitterrand's memoirs — the real story. He certainly did have Idi Amin's memoirs, as told to some British hack. And there was something called *History Will Absolve Me,* by Ferdinand Marcos ..."

"All these sold well?" His eyebrows were up again.

"Not particularly, but they all went for remarkably large sums of money. In advances."

"So. Somebody thought they would sell well."

"More than one person," Marsha said remembering the frisson

following the nasty, nauseatingly detailed Amin memoirs as the manuscript travelled through A&M. She explained to Hübsch the typical Myles auction. Andrew had set the date for this one, with first bids in writing by nine o'clock on a Monday morning. Saturday night at a Random House launch for John Irving in the pool room of the Four Seasons, the media were all agog for tidbits of the terrors in Uganda, while Marsha and the other competing houses' senior people were attempting to find out who'd be in and who'd be out. True to form, Andrew opened the bidding by faxing everyone at nine sharp to inform them of a million dollar floor, no topping privileges.

Given that Andrew liked to create his own events, it was anyone's guess whether the floor bid actually existed, or it was part of his marketing plan. "Andrew Myles had a way of bringing large groups of people into his schemes," Marsha told Hübsch. "There were always plenty of bidders for his authors."

"Even for someone like Idi Amin."

Marsha nodded. Afterward, she had been hugely relieved that someone else won that auction. "Even him."

Hübsch thanked her. "You'll be here till the end of the Messe?" he asked as he was finally leaving.

"Sunday," Marsha said. No one of importance stayed beyond Sunday. Monday was for the people who cleared away the debris from the stands. Even a full day on Sunday was risky. Someone might get the idea that she was desperate either to buy or to sell and she'd be viewed with suspicion for some months after. But these were traditions you learnt along the way, not in a few weeks. She had been unable to convince the cowboys of them. Sunday she'd run them around the thoroughly foreign aisles and hoped to leave them in a promisingly dull meeting with the Russians. They were promoting, among other prize offerings, a twelve-volume history of the Red Army.

"I don't think Margaret is going to make it for the press this afternoon," Fay Mercer told her as she was leaving for her scheduled appointments in the British aisles. "She claims she has a terrible headache. She thinks all those deah, deah people will shuahly unnerstand." Fay rolled her eyes and brushed her forehead with the back of her wrist emulating one of Margaret's theatrical gestures. "They are not likely to. A couple have come over from London to see her. Damn woman has been living in a dreamworld. Got about the biggest advance anyone's pulled off this year. Her agent's died in the middle of the Frankfurt Bookfair. That's as close to a media event as I could ever manage. Now she's expecting them to understand she's not going to be part of it. One thing you can be damn sure of, they won't."

"When's the press coming?" Marsha asked.

"Around four. She should be signing some of the German editions of her books."

"I promised Gerhardt ..."

"You talk to her?"

Marsha was already heading for the phone in one of the small cubicles behind the reception desk. It was piled high with boxes of excess books, promotional t-shirts with book titles and blurred faces of leading authors, deflated balloons, cans of soda, a half-empty bottle of wine, and Morris reading the *Wall Street Journal* in the corner. He ignored her entrance.

When she reached Margaret at the Hessischer Hof, she sounded sleepy and very quiet. "Ah'm simply not up to it, mah deah," she told Marsha. "Nobody, shuahly, nobody would expect me to be in public today. It wouldn't be human."

Nevertheless, giving in to her baser instincts, Marsha tried to persuade her. When nothing worked, she referred to the contract, which guaranteed, among other things, that Margaret would make herself available to her publishers during the Frankfurt Bookfair to assist in their efforts to sell her books to a range of other publishers. "The press is very important for us right now, Margaret," she told her. "It's what will drive the foreign publishers who haven't already come up to our expectations."

"Elinor can go and explain to them, if you're not up to it," Margaret challenged.

"Elinor?"

"My niece. It's the best I am going to do for you."

"We could sue," Morris said folding his paper. "A contract is a contract, goddamn it. You tell her ..."

"Is that one of the assholes you report to, mah deah?" Margaret must have overheard Morris's none too restrained tones.

"Yes," Marsha agreed.

"Tell him from me, that I'd surely like to see him try ..." She had half abandoned the phony Southern drawl. "And now, I'm going to rest," she said firmly. "Tomorrow I return to Grand Manan to write." Margaret hung up.

Marsha held the phone to her ear pretending the conversation was progressing well while she considered what to tell Morris. There certainly wouldn't be a reasonable case for a lawsuit, nor any way of making Margaret appear at the appointed hour by delivering a writ, nor any hope of scoring points with the press if it were to leak that they were threatening Margaret Drury Carter with a lawsuit for not coming to a publishing-do the day after her agent was murdered.

"Okay," she told the receiver. "That'll be fine." She smiled at Morris. "All solved."

"Good," Morris said reopening the *Wall Street Journal*.

Marsha went back to Fay who was already setting up the autographing table near the entrance to the booth, positioning Margaret's life-size cardboard cutout figure immediately to the right of it, her name in large mauve fluorescent lettering across her chest.

"I'm sorry," Marsha told Fay. "We'll have to make do with Elinor. She'll tell everyone how very ill her aunt has become since she discovered that Andrew was murdered. And you can tell them everything we know about Andrew's demise. It'll be all right."

"Why?"

"Because at least they won't resent being here if they hear something they can write about."

Fay nodded without much enthusiasm. "And how the hell is that going to help us sell books?"

"You can tell them all the Myles stuff while standing in front of the Margaret cutout. And we'll have Elinor here to do the sad and soft part. You'd want a romantic novelist to be very *feeling*, wouldn't you?" She was making the best of a lousy situation.

Marsha was late for her meeting with the Bonnier trade group. Only two of the junior people had remained — a Frankfurt social reprimand. They couldn't afford a full-fledged snub because their foreign list had been dominated by A&M writers for the past couple of years. Had Albert Bonnier been alive still, they'd have gone the route of complete insult, hang the consequences. Albert would have concluded there were plenty of big-time American story-tellers to choose from and made a big fuss about Simon & Schuster's new publisher to prove to Marsha that no one is irreplaceable.

The young ones treated her to coffee and delight over news of new manuscripts from their favourite authors. Since A&M rarely published foreign authors, they didn't go through the motions of presenting their own. If there was something unusual this year in Sweden, another *Smilla's Sense of Snow*, for example, the scout would make sure she saw a sample in English on her return to New York. Only the Big Books were sold at Frankfurt.

On the way back to Halle 9, she had to pass by Frans van Maeght's booth. The little Dutchman was surrounded by green-uniformed policemen, all slouching over his narrow space, their expressions considerably less animated than his. Two of the five had half-turned away from him, and were gazing at passers-by. When Frans saw her, he waved for her to come over, his arms flailing over his head like propellers. The uniforms made room for her reluctantly.

Frans was damp with excitement. His face was flushed, his hair hung in wet bits down his ears. "You are not going to believe it," he shouted, rubbing his palms together. "I have this threatening letter." He shoved a sheet of paper towards her, but one of the slouching policemen suddenly came to life and snatched it. He said something guttural in German and returned the paper to the round table it had come from.

"We wait for the Inspektor," he said firmly in English.

Exasperated, Frans started reading it out loud for her: "'Death stalks those who defy His will.' All the letters are cut out of the newspaper, just like in the movies," he said triumphantly. "Your stuff about opportunity! Bah!"

"They think it's for real?" Marsha asked.

"Of course it's for real. Why would anyone do something like this as a joke? Why?" He stared at her fixedly. "You tell me!"

Marsha shrugged. "It was just a thought. Frankfurt Bookfair and all, there'd be a lot of people with imagination. Someone might have a little fun at your expense ..."

"Expense? Expense? What do you mean expense?" He was genuinely nonplussed.

Marsha imagined practical jokes were not a Dutch thing, or not Frans's thing, in any event. But the policeman who had snatched the sheet of paper seemed to understand what she meant. He smirked in a rather unprofessional way. "All I meant was that someone might think it a joke ..." when she saw his expression, she added, "not a very good joke, but there's no accounting for tastes ..."

"Someone like Mark?" he asked, outraged.

"I don't think so, but you never know," Marsha told him. "You think it's something to do with Andrew Myles's death?"

"What else can I think?" he was wringing his hands with anxiety.

"You haven't just signed a contract to publish the latest Rushdie novel, have you?"

He shook his head.

"Something else by Rushdie?" All Rushdie's publishers had serious security around Frankfurt, some brought their own bodyguards.

"No," Frans said sadly. "I tried to buy the rights but we were outbid."

The aisle leading up to the A&M booth was already full of people. Some carried cameras, some video equipment, some just giant shopping bags ready for whatever freebies might be given away. Gerhardt was talking animatedly surrounded by a few journalists taking notes. Fay stood in front of Margaret Drury Carter's looming cardboard shape, with her hair in a tight bun on top of her head, her eyes outlined in black, her cheeks rouged. The total effect made her appear taller and somewhat Slavic, a look she cultivated for television. A young man with a microphone was asking her questions while his partner worked a hand-held video camera.

Elinor Drury leaned awkwardly against the table Fay had set up for the autographing. She was a tall, chunky woman of about forty, top heavy, like her aunt. She had cinched in her waist with a wide leather belt, as she had done every day she had appeared at A&M when she was poring over the royalty statements a year or so ago. Marsha had wondered, unkindly, what it would be like never to see your feet.

Above the belt, Elinor wore a cream-coloured tailored shirt with pearls to mark where the collar ended and her neck began. Below she was draped in a soft blue woollen skirt that swished as she walked, its lack of exuberance keeping her look military. Her face was pale, the skin unblemished and still resilient, her eyes wide-set and pale blue. It's how Marsha had imagined Margaret's might have been years ago, before the mauve eye shadow and heavily outlined pink lips had become her trademark. Elinor wore almost no make-up — only a touch of pink lip gloss — leaving exposed long grey eyelashes, small nose, broad forehead, determined chin, and shoulder-length, thick, glossy, dark-brown hair with a hint of grey that, unlike her aunt, she had not bothered to hide. Where Margaret cultivated a rich auburn colour, always fully coiffed, Elinor let her hair hang loosely around her face.

She made no sign of recognition when she saw Marsha.

"Elinor," Marsha said, with as much enthusiasm as she could muster, "very pleased to see you again. Of course, we all wish the circumstances had been different ..." She trailed off, noticing that Elinor did not share in the joy of being seen. She did, however, accept Marsha's proffered hand and shook it, hard. Her palms were dry and silky.

"Oh, yes," she said. "You are the editor, aren't you?" Elinor's blue eyes fixed on Marsha.

Marsha nodded.

"You're still there." Elinor looked at Thurgood, who had materialized at the table. It seemed to Marsha that they had already met. "You've made a few staff changes, haven't you?" she asked him. Marsha wondered how Elinor had managed to keep all inflection out of her voice. There was no way of guessing whether she approved of whatever staff changes she had discovered, or not.

Marsha also wondered how Elinor knew the fat man.

Thurgood shrugged. "It's David Morris. He is running the company now. I have no interest in management."

"Ah," Elinor said without inflection.

"How is Margaret?" Marsha asked. "Perhaps she would like me to go and see her ..."

Elinor shook her head almost imperceptibly. "I think she'll be getting ready to go to the airport. I've changed her reservations. All in all, we think it better she should be home. It's a very emotional time for her, and she's always had trouble controlling her emotions. Unless she is writing — but you'd know that. It's lonely work, but she can channel her feelings through her characters." Elinor gazed sadly at the throng of admirers who were still lining up to meet her aunt. "Today, she would not be happy in a crowd."

Marsha would have argued with her, having seen how jolly Margaret was when surrounded by her fans, not to mention journalists who spoon-fed her questions prescribed by her publicists, but there was no point. Elinor had staked out the territory around her aunt, and judging by Margaret's words at the lunch, it was by mutual agreement.

At first, it was difficult to imagine what the two of them had in common. Margaret was overly soft, with all the exaggerated tones and gestures she must think would appeal to a man. Elinor was quiet, understated, and very private. She was as inviting as a turtle. And about as outwardly emotional. Her aunt, on the other hand, had turned emotion into a fine art. Every gesture was studied emotion. She had become one of the heroines in her own novels, with all the softness and breathlessness that made them so utterly interchangeable, and such favourites with her fans. Yet even more treasured by her fans, they all hid startlingly strong personalities and steely wills that did not yield to the heroes' advances until near the end, and only after a great deal of mutual panting.

Elinor, Marsha imagined, would probably dispense with the flutterings of the first 400 pages and tell the heroes to cut to the chase or cut loose. She was a no-nonsense woman.

Overall, Marsha preferred Margaret.

"I suppose she isn't going to be at the breakfast tomorrow," she asked tentatively.

Elinor was ready to disappoint her. "No," she said. "What breakfast?"

"It's the panel on romantic literature in the twenty-first century," Marsha told her.

Elinor shook her head. "No. I guess not," she said. Elinor clearly thought the panel was a waste of time. "We'll be rather busy over the next year. There are the novels, and the television series."

When Marsha continued to stare, Elinor said, "You do know about the series, don't you?"

Marsha didn't.

"*Magnolias in the Rain*," Elinor explained. "CBS. Six parts, I think. Andrew must have been planning to surprise you."

"That's our book?" Thurgood asked.

"Yes," Marsha admitted.

"How much?" He cut to the quick.

"I think you'll find Andrew controlled all the television rights," Elinor told him. "No money in it for you, but I expect the series will be good for book sales."

Thurgood bristled. "So, how much anyway?"

"Around four million," Elinor said. "Not much, considering she's also consulting on the script. Bradford got more."

"Why in hell wouldn't we have a piece of that?" Thurgood asked Morris, who had drifted close to them.

"Before my time, Arthur," Morris said almost apologetically.

They both looked at Marsha.

"We tried," she said defensively. "Both Larry and I tried but agents keep the television and film rights unless there is some very unusual deal."

"So what does it take to change that little habit?" Morris thundered, his face turning red. He was warming to the topic. Thin veins on his temples grew taut, his nostrils flared. "How many goddamned millions does it take to sup at the table with the movie boys, or do we have to buy the studios as well to cut these geezers down to size? I've never been one to begrudge a guy his slice of the pie, but why in hell would we let an agent walk away with some of ours? Tell me that?"

Elinor shrugged. "You get what you pay for," she said quietly. Her soft upper lip curled in what might have been a smile. Marsha remembered that she had never backed down when the accountants challenged her determination to examine the royalties at

A&M. Some women don't mind confrontation. Most will go out of their way to avoid it. Elinor belonged to the former group.

"And twenty million, you figure that's not enough?" Morris barked.

"Apparently," Elinor said. "You paid only as much as you had to. No more no less. If there hadn't been someone out there willing to pay as much, or nearly as much, and on the same terms, you would have paid less."

"There is no point to all this," Marsha said. "The deal was signed two weeks ago. We agreed to the terms."

"Next time we'll know enough to read the small print," Morris said. "I learn fast, as you'll find out." He stared at Marsha balefully.

It wasn't so much that she worried about getting fired, though she did worry about it some, it was the prospect of being fired over something like a standard agency agreement that bothered Marsha. If she was going to be fired, she'd have preferred it to be over a grand gesture, like breaking Morris's glass-top table with the sharp edge of his framed Harvard degree. So she shrugged and turned her back on him as she said, "I'll be looking forward to that," just loud enough for Thurgood to hear.

She took Elinor's arm and suggested she might like to spend some time with Fay and the press. It wouldn't be the same as if her aunt had bothered to come but better than no one for them to talk to. At least, she told her, Elinor was a relative.

"All that Southern stuff," Elinor said, "grates on my nerves. But it's part of her act. Only don't expect me to give it a try," she allowed herself to be introduced to a stringer from the *Börsenblatt*. Blum would have already done the main story, so this might be for a short sidebar.

Herb Lottmann had come by, much to Marsha's surprise. Margaret was hardly the kind of writer Lottmann would be interested in, but the launch of a twenty million dollar deal was too big an event, even in today's high-flying times, to ignore. He was talking to someone from Frankfurt's W1 station, periodically looking over his shoulder in an effort to catch Dr. Schneider as he passed by. No question, Herbert was working the party.

Fay appeared at Marsha's side. "Lottmann's here," she said as if she was announcing a particular personal triumph. "Please go and talk to him about Margaret."

"What do you want me to tell him?"

"Something brief and quotable. We want to be in the Frankfurt issue of *Publishers Weekly*, don't we?" She made it sound as if any idiot would have guessed as much without prompting. Except that Marsha knew Herbert too well. The press release would have given him all the facts about Margaret's advance. What he'd be looking for was some comic relief from the inescapable reality that a fake, Southern romance-cum-mystery writer had pocketed another record amount for stuff Herbert would never read, nor could he imagine anyone else reading.

Once, they had sat and talked at a Jerusalem Bookfair, an event Herbert attended to show his support, not because the magazine paid his way. Herbert's everyday life was still peopled with writers who could teach you something about the world you lived in, not just offering an escape from it.

Thurgood fought his way through the crowd to reach Marsha just as she drew level with Herbert's gaze. "This, I expect, is for you to read," he said pressing a package into her hand. "Elinor gave it to me before you arrived. She says it's the first part of the new Drury Carter manuscript."

It was thicker than she had expected, comforting to hold it in her hand. What with Andrew's death and Margaret's departure, she had given up hope of receiving even a small piece of the manuscript on time.

"We'll want to know what you think first thing in the morning." Thurgood left Marsha's "Why?" unanswered. It was only when she saw Elinor surrounded by Margaret's fans that she remembered that the next installment was due on acceptance of the first three chapters of the first book. That would mean another two million for Margaret.

"I think I'll want to talk to Margaret first thing tomorrow," Marsha told Elinor.

Elinor had been talking to a tall man with black hair, some flecks of white near the temples. When Marsha approached, he put his arm over Elinor's shoulder, softly, as if he knew she would not resist. Gently, he turned her towards Marsha.

"Mornings aren't her best time," Elinor said. "Why?"

Marsha did not recognize him, though she thought he bore some resemblance to a British publisher she knew.

"We normally meet after I've read her manuscript, she likes to know what I think as quickly as possible," Marsha said. "When do you expect she'll be up?" Marsha did remember that mornings weren't Margaret's best time, but she would be waiting to hear from Marsha about the manuscript. Success hadn't altered her basic anxieties. The first read was still the most important. Margaret had always needed reassurance.

"You could try in a couple of days," Elinor relented. "But I doubt she'll be keen to talk to anyone. Needs some time to herself, gather her thoughts."

Don't we all, Marsha sighed.

"She's on the flight to Halifax this afternoon," Elinor continued. "She'll be spending the night there. Still a long way from there to Grand Manan. If I were you, I'd leave it till Monday."

"There was no problem with the first payment, was there?" she asked Elinor. They had made their way to the taxi stand at the entrance to the Halle. The big-shouldered Englishman stayed with them, though he hadn't uttered a word.

"Why, should there be?" the other woman seemed surprised. "Andrew was most efficient."

"Margaret couldn't remember this morning ..."

"My aunt has memory lapses, that's all," Elinor said, her tone indicating that she, herself, would never indulge in such light-headedness.

A two million dollar memory lapse, Marsha thought. Who could blame her?

He opened the taxi's door for Elinor, waited till she was settled inside, then went around to the other side. He gave Marsha a small parting smile. He had small, crooked teeth, but he was easy on the eyes.

CHAPTER
SIX

JUDITH HAYES HAD SPENT MOST OF THE SUMMER waiting for work. Ever since she had decided to freelance, and that was some years ago, she alternated between feverish work periods and anxious idleness. Sometimes she worked on three or four stories at the same time, afraid to turn down any opportunity offered, in case a magazine never asked her again. She had endured four late June deadlines, each for a different magazine, each requiring its own "voice." Two had been profiles of prominent women, one for *Ms.*, one for *Chatelaine,* but she knew better than to allow a similarity of tone or approach. Though they were both women's magazines, they could not have been less alike. One had maintained its rugged feminism, the other its devotion to recipes and flattering clothes. It was hard to imagine that there were women who read both. Oddly enough, a third story she had been assigned was an examination of the women's vote and its anticipated impact on the next American election. The *Post* still held the fond belief that women voted by gender, and not by political conviction.

The piece was worth three thousand dollars. Judith was certainly not going to talk them out of it.

Through August and most of September she had been waiting for *Saturday Night* magazine to give her the go-ahead on a long story involving an ultra-right-wing organization that had set up its headquarters in Jemseg, New Brunswick, but the new editor was vacillating. He couldn't make up his mind on whether the story had national importance.

She decided she would go to Jemseg with or without his blessing, and try to gather enough information to convince him there was a story worth commissioning. She had been idle for too long, and there was no money coming in. She had tried a variety of other ideas on a full range of her usual suspects but none had taken. This idea, at least, had a chance. Hesitation was not outright rejection. New Brunswick was beautiful. It was also cheaper than Toronto. A tremulous pair of house-hunting newlyweds, whom she'd met through a friend, had offered to rent the nasty semidetached that she and the kids had grown used to calling home since James had left for greener, more romantic pastures in Chicago.

She calculated that the rent coming in would be more than twice what she would pay in New Brunswick for a more spacious house; a handsome profit even before she put pen to paper.

Judith's daughter, Anne, had just left for her first term of university in Montreal. Reluctantly, Jimmy condescended to come East with Judith — in any event there wasn't a place for him to stay. The young couple were not keen to share the house with a surly-looking teenager. Their down payment had taken care of the mortgage.

James had not called. Judith knew the routine. The child-support payment would not arrive for some weeks because James had decided to buy something truly expensive for himself or his relatively new wife. Judith would talk to her friend, the lawyer. He'd send a nasty letter to James. Eventually, James would call, all hurt and surprised that Judith had doubted his sincere desire to live up to the letter of their divorce papers. The cheque, he always surmised, had fallen victim to the post office's legendary inefficiency. He would wait a couple more days to make sure, then cancel it and send a new cheque. By mail.

It was no use her appealing to his concern for their children's well-being. In recent years, James had delegated most of those concerns to a psychiatrist who had promised to put him in touch with his feelings in exchange for tending his aging dachshunds. James had a thriving veterinary practice.

Jimmy had lugged his Christmas Mac — a gift from Marsha — to Jemseg, and had set it up in the old wooden cottage Judith had rented by phone. He figured he could work his way into the main computer in the Pentagon from there.

One thing about Jemseg, there weren't a lot of distractions.

The cottage was spacious, and well-insulated for mild autumn days. There was a fireplace in the living room and a space heater in the upstairs bedroom. The owners were stunned to hear that someone was willing to rent in October. Their ad in the *Toronto Star* was meant to find someone for the next summer season on Grand Lake.

Judith had spent most of the day asking questions about Frank Tranby, the new arrival from Saskatchewan, who had bought a farm to the east of the town and appeared to be running a sort of camp there for men. The *Jemseg Courier* had printed a story about his group's drumming and shouting, but there had been no mention of military exercises.

Sundays, Tranby had a pastor come in from Fredericton and read the men a service. Some out-of-tune singing and a sad guitar that Frank played himself hardly added up to a story for a national magazine. The spread he'd bought was large enough for hunting and the local police delighted in the fact that the men's camp on old Farley's farm set up some target practice. No harm in wearing uniforms, either; the police wore them and it had done them no harm. The butcher thought of them as overgrown boy scouts.

Frank, himself, proved rather elusive.

All in all, Judith was thrilled to get a call from Marsha. When she'd left the new number with Marsha's secretary in New York, she hadn't expected a call until Marsha was home. Now here was just the person to mitigate her sense of isolation and rising concern that she might not be able to meet next month's expenses with no story on the back burner and none coming up.

"What in hell are you doing in Jemseg?" Marsha inquired by way of a greeting.

"That story idea, remember?" Judith told her, "for *Saturday Night*, but so far it's not panning out."

"Is Jemseg some sort of a town in New Brunswick?"

"Not what you'd call a town, but up here in the frozen North it passes for one. The Fair almost over?"

"And none too soon. Not a lot of real work has been done since Andrew Myles was murdered."

"Did you say murdered?" Judith yelled.

"Yes. That's what the police tell me."

"And you were sitting with him when he was murdered?"

"That's what they think, too."

"What? That you were there while someone knocked him off? Sitting next to him? And you didn't even notice?"

"There is a police inspector here who actually thinks I might have done it."

"Given it's Andrew Myles, I guess they won't have to ask why you did it." Judith laughed. "Will they be awarding you a medal?"

Marsha hadn't slept enough to join in the fun. She had gone to the *Reader's Digest* party and had found herself sitting with a bunch of Belgians who preferred speaking Flemish among themselves to making conversation with an American. She had returned to the hotel before the main course to wait for Bertil, who had not shown up at the party after all. He had surfaced long after midnight, well lubricated and somewhat unsteady on his feet. "I love this place," he had informed Marsha. "It's like being stranded on a desert island with a bunch of strangers who suddenly become your best friends, because you are stranded together. No other reason."

He had been with the Bonnier people, and rather enjoyed being courted. Once more, they had decided they wanted his company, and him. The kind of offer a Norwegian loved turning down. Europeans have long memories, and Norwegians, even before the Second World War proved they had been right all along, loved hating the Swedes. "So why did you stay?" she had asked him.

"To make them work for their rejection," he had told her.

Marsha had turned her back and gone back to sleep.

"The bastard spoiled our plans for the Fair," Marsha now told Judith. "Our star author has decided to go home early because Andrew isn't here to hold her hand. We had to cancel all the press. We had been counting on a bunch of hype for her at the Fair."

"Drury Carter?"

"The same."

"The cowboys must be royally pissed off."

"It doesn't take much to piss them off anyway, but this time they have a point. They'd had the notion they would be celebrities in Frankfurt for buying A&M. It's not every day a bunch of rubes buy themselves a hundred-and-fifty-year-old publishing house. And it's not every day they decide to spend another twenty million on one author. They should be courted by everybody. But no one's paying them the slightest bit of attention, now that we've had a murder to take our minds off the real-life business of publishing."

"I do wish they weren't Canadians," Judith said wistfully.

"The cowboys? Everybody does. They spoil your nice, clean-living image."

"That's why you're calling?"

"About your image? No. But it could take some heavy-duty repair work, especially around the 600 block on Fifth Avenue."

"I'll tell the prime minister ..."

"I called because I might have to go to Canada after the Fair. To see Margaret. She's bought a place on Grand Manan island and her niece says she plans to spend the winter there."

Judith whistled appreciatively. "The old duck is tougher than I thought. It'll be bloody cold there through the winter. It's only October and the temperature's expected to drop fifteen degrees by the end of the month. I can imagine what it must be like being surrounded by crashing waves."

"I remember some warm falls in the Vineyard. Grand Manan's in the Bay of Fundy, isn't it? That'd be fairly close to you?"

"Why?"

"I was sitting here looking at my map of Canada, and Grand Manan is part of New Brunswick ..."

"What in hell would you be doing with a map of Canada?"

"You did say you were in New Brunswick, didn't you? Grand Manan's in New Brunswick ..."

"Sure. And Buffalo is in New York State, but you wouldn't want to go there for lunch."

"I might ... if I hadn't seen you since August," Marsha wheedled. "We could check out the whales." When she didn't hear Judith respond, she added: "Maybe there's a story you could do for one of your magazines."

"Not much interest in whales. They've been done. In *Canadian Geographic* and even *Atlantic Monthly*." Judith hesitated. The idea of seeing her old friend was beginning to take root. "On the other hand, someone might like to commission a story about Margaret Drury Carter, mightn't they? There hasn't been much about her lately, and I doubt if there's ever been a Canadian angle. Why in hell would she choose Grand Manan in the winter?"

"It's supposed to be beautiful. She needs a place to write. She has signed a three-book deal with tough deadlines, and she is, despite her phony act of Southern lassitude, a pro. She works hard when she has to. No other way of churning out the steamy volumes she's served up in the past fifteen years. Maybe Grand Manan is just the place to focus the mind."

Marsha had spent the past hour reading Margaret's manuscript and had found it much too pensive and lacking in action. After twenty years in the business, ten of them running a successful publishing division, Marsha knew her romantic historical mysteries and this one was definitely not Drury Carter at her best. That's why it had taken her an hour to read, and then reread, her dismay growing with each page. Normally, reading an entire Drury Carter would take less than two hours. But the new book's opening chapters alone were a hundred pages long, and much too complicated.

The heroine was wasting her time in Louisiana, attempting to run her dead adoptive father's business, ignoring the approaches of all the males within a hundred miles. Though her real father had left her the riverboat to run while he was in jail, she was barely considering that. There had been no abduction, no mysterious stranger, and no one to set her heart a-flutter, as her fans had every right to expect long before the first hundred pages were up. Nate, handsome and brooding though he might be, had yet to make his first appearance. There were long descriptive passages about the dry goods she was to sell, the dogs she lavished her valuable time on, and not nearly enough sense of intrigue. For nine million dollars, the first book's share of the twenty, dark forces should be gathering around the helpless but strong-willed maiden in distress long before the third chapter ended.

"*Home and Garden* might like something on her rural surroundings," Marsha suggested. The thought of crossing swords with Margaret in cold and unfamiliar surroundings seemed more inviting if Judith were there.

Marsha and Judith had been friends since they had both found themselves at boarding school. Neither had had the slightest desire to be where she was, but each had found some instant comfort in the other's company. Marsha's mother had picked Bishop Strachan School because she had grown up on Boston's North Shore with a bred in the bone adulation for everything English. B.S.S. was as close to an English boarding school as she could find this side of the Atlantic. Marsha's father would not hear of letting her go to England. It was too far away, and too disruptive of his plans to train Marsha in the martial arts. He never quite forgave her mother for having a girl instead of a boy, and decided to cope with it, in the beginning, by ignoring the unpleasant fact. He was the only person in Marsha's life who hated little pinafore dresses more than she did.

Judith's mother had assumed that boarding at the big Forest Hill school would lend the family some of the class she had hungered for when she married Judith's father. All that had remained of her family's fortune had been an old house in Rosedale. It had been her inheritance. For the rest, she had counted on Judith's father. There had been some hope that he would meet her expectations while he was working for the bank; none after he had been quietly retired. But Frank Hayes had shown no interest in banking, no devotion to climbing corporate ladders, no ambition beyond the path that took him home to his beloved books early in the evenings, earlier than those who craved the promotions, earlier even than his boss. He had been a painful and enduring disappointment to Judith's mother, and a daily reminder to Judith that a person can survive constant verbal abuse and never bend. Boarding school had provided her with an unwelcome respite. The tuition, her mother had claimed, was painfully scraped together from grocery money. There would be shepherd's pie for dinner filled with leftovers, and the paint would continue to peel off the upstairs walls, but Judith would spend her days and nights among the well-to-do.

Judith thought Debbie Brown might enjoy hearing from her. It had been months since Judith had pestered her with new story ideas. As far as she could remember this would be the first time she'd proposed anything to *Home and Garden* that didn't make her gag. Their favourites were invariably stories of the rich and famous redecorating their homes, redesigning their gardens, entertaining with style, or dressing for special occasions, such as polo with the Royals or skiing in St. Tropez. Regular features included a lavish recipes section in air-brushed full colour, and preparation tips by disdainfully confident chefs. Judith thought Margaret Drury Carter would be an attractive proposition for them. She was rich, famous, appealed to a female audience, and would certainly have a house on the island with some furniture that could be photographed. What appealed to Judith about the grand dame of bodice-rippers was that she had made her fortune from writing. It wasn't Judith's kind of writing but it was encouraging to know that a fortune could be made from any kind of writing.

Home and Garden hadn't done Margaret in over ten years. Judith was becoming certain Debbie would go for the idea.

They agreed to meet on Grand Manan on the tenth. That would give Marsha time to return to her office and try to secure support for her Frankfurt purchases. With Morris in attendance, editorial meetings had become more like gladiatorial contests. If they weren't to the death, at least they could be to expulsion into the job market.

"And it'll give me a reason not to return to Toronto for James's visit. He's been threatening to come for the long weekend, to see 'his son.' 'A boy needs his father,' is what he told me last time. My god ..."

"What?"

"I'd better remind the tenants not to hand out our number here. I doubt if I could stand his lecture on child-rearing and the importance of higher education."

"Could Jimmy?"

"No."

"You're all right then."

"What if ... he tried for custody?" Judith's voice quavered even as she realized how unlikely it was that James would want to be a father again, especially father to a troubled teenager. The idea hadn't occurred to him back when the kids were cuddly and cute, and not in the least judgmental.

"No room for children in his chrome-and-glass condo, remember?" Marsha reassured her. "Besides, they would mess up Muffy's varnished hardwood floors. Can you honestly see her welcoming Jimmy into her palatial home-for-two? With his earring, torn jeans, lumberjack shirt, and tattoo? Can you see them sitting down to candlelit dinners of vichyssoise, prawns-à-la-Marseille and a nice 1967 vintage of Bordeaux?"

Judith couldn't.

"There *is* an urgent call for you, Miss Hillier," the operator cut in, her voice sounding exasperated. She had been flashing the light button trying to get Marsha off the phone for some minutes. "I did not wish to interrupt but zis *is* an emergency."

"I will call you again tomorrow," Marsha said to Judith.

"The Inspector must talk to you *now*," emphasized the operator. "Inspektor Hübsch," she shouted, "Inspektor, sie ist frei jetzt ... Inspektor ..." she was really exasperated now. "Inspektor Hübsch is on his way up. He really couldn't wait," she told Marsha, as if it were all Marsha's fault.

"Naturally," Marsha said to no one in particular as the operator had gone on to another call. "What else would he be doing at seven o'clock in the morning?"

She was still damp from the shower after her morning run. She had been relaxing on the bed with just a towel wrapped around her still-steaming body, another towel around her wet hair. Margaret's manuscript was strewn over the bedspread with little yellow Post-its marking various passages, as she had left them before she went for the run to clear her head.

She drew the curtains on another rainy day. In the steam-clouded mirror above the compact chest of drawers (in a Frankfurt hotel room there isn't room for a full-sized one), she peered at her flushed body. The breasts still seemed firm, but then she had never had big breasts. For many years this had been a major regret, now she was glad there would be no concern for their drooping with age. There wasn't much there to droop. Her stomach was relatively flat, her shoulders could use some work; they were showing signs of stress. When she returned to New York, she would start at the gym again. She had given up going after she finished her tae kwon do course with flying colours. Black.

She wished, as usual, for thinner thighs.

After forty, they were even harder to come by.

Hübsch was knocking on the door.

She ran her fingers through her extra fine blond hair. "Feathery," Judith had called it, like baby hair. When she had decided to cut it, she had not considered how uncontrollable it would become once it was free of the chignon she had worn since her late twenties. In hindsight, she realized that cutting it had been no more than a juvenile impulse to spite her mother. She had not liked her mother's approval of the carefully sculpted hair she had developed for her executive years. It was the compliment her mother had paid her when they lunched at the Russian Tea Room, where Mrs. Hillier could be reasonably sure to be seen. "It suits your style, dear, careful and understated. A trademark of our class." She had then looked around the room with the gaze of someone who invariably belonged. Marsha had wondered whether it was money that had given her mother the airs, or was it some New England presumption that had been with her since she was born. In any event, she had chopped off the chignon on the way back to work that afternoon.

Hübsch was hammering on the door.

She poured a tiny pool of Lancôme cover-up into the palm of her hand, then spread it over her face with two fingers for an all-over ivory effect. The exercise and the shower always made her face splotchy.

She drew on a pair of light wool pants that she enjoyed wearing in Frankfurt because they fitted across her belly, but flared gently from the thighs down, to give her freedom of movement. The material was soft enough to feel snug and luxurious at the same time as it swished around her when she walked.

"Yes," she capitulated to Hübsch's noises at last. It had been pleasant to ignore his persistence. "Soon," she called out somewhat louder.

She put on a blue silk shirt, and her blue leather pumps. She combed her hair and sprayed it back out of her face.

"Miss Hillier," Hübsch shouted.

Marsha opened the door just as he raised his fist to hammer again.

"Hübsch," she said. "What a surprise."

He was not going to indulge in introductory pleasantries. "Zis," he pointed to a black and white photograph he carried in his other hand, "is one of the men who had been with you the night of the party, yes?"

"As I told you before, nobody was *with* me at the party ..." She glanced at the photo Hübsch was holding up to her. It was a most unflattering picture of Jerry Haines, taken close up, but the bright lights blurred Jerry's features. His hair, oiled back the night before, was parted in the middle and flopped carelessly on either side of his feral face. His bow tie had slipped to one side. The sprouting beard cast the lower part of his face in shadow. His eyes were closed, mouth sagged open. Two of his upper teeth showed white out of the shadow. The photographer's flash had caught them. "What's the matter with Jerry?" Marsha asked, her voice unsteady, despite her best efforts.

"Mr. Haines is dead." Hübsch opened the door wider and marched past Marsha into the hotel room. When he reached the windows, he turned to face her. His overcoat was wet, his hat was dripping water onto the carpet, his pants were rumpled, damp and mud-stained at the knees. He looked like he had spent the night in his clothes.

Marsha sat on the bed. She was staring at Hübsch. "I don't understand," she murmured.

"Zat's the problem, Miss Hillier. Neither do I," Hübsch said angrily. He slammed the photograph face up on her dresser. "You, on ze other side, you knew zem both. You must have some idea of what connected zem. I didn't know zem," he was talking much too loudly, and a maid stopped by the door and stared at them. "Weg," Hübsch shouted at her startled face and waved her on, in case she had not understood his shouted instructions.

"Connected them?" Marsha glanced at the photograph again. Jerry's collar was open, the top three buttons of his shirt were missing, a small tuft of hair protruded from the gap just above his breastbone.

"Exactly. What." Hübsch repeated aggressively.

"Whom?" Marsha asked dumbly.

Hübsch was becoming aggressively impatient. "Look," he said, "you haf your Buchmesse. Two nights ago one of your agents is killed in ze middle of one of your parties ..."

"Not one of my parties ..."

"All the same. One of your Messe parties. Now another one of your lot is killed. You haf to excuse me for seeing the obvious. Two people killed in forty-eight hours. Less. Zis one," with his chin he indicated Jerry's photo, "died last night. In his room. To be accurate, he died between two and six this morning. He vas fully dressed. You can see zat. Still has his tie on. Maybe he was going out. You saw him last night?"

"At the *Reader's Digest* party, I think." There had been such a crowd at the Hessischer Hof before the seating for dinner, it was difficult to be sure. She thought she had seen him near the far end of the third room. The reception always started with a cocktail party that attracted most of those invited regularly. Many of them slipped away when the guests paraded inside the dining area. That was when you had to gamble that you'd end up with an interesting table. It was unpredictable.

"When?"

"Sometime between eight and nine, I assume," Marsha said. Dinner always started at nine. "I didn't see him again once we sat down to eat."

"Can you be certain he didn't stay for ze dinner?"

"Not entirely. But it's a buffet and you are bound to bump into people while standing in line."

"What time did you arrive at ze party?"

"Close to eight. There was a long receiving line."

"Ze same people zat vere at ze Bertelsmann party night before last?"

"Not really. For one thing, the *Digest* tends not to have Americans."

Hübsch raised his eyebrows. "You vere zere," he said accusingly. "Bos times."

Marsha shrugged. "I must have slipped through the cracks ..."

"And agents?"

"Some agents."

Hübsch was jotting in his little notebook. "Some agents," he repeated. "French, English, Dutch ... did you see Mr. van Maeght?"

"No."

"Mr. Tanake?"

"I'm not sure. Yes. Perhaps I did."

Hübsch nodded. "Mr. Newnes?"

"I think so. I don't remember. There were so many people ..."

"Not so many as at ze Bertelsmann party, yes?" he flicked open his notebook rather triumphantly.

"No. Not quite as many," Marsha told him. It would have been foolish for the *Digest* to challenge Bertelsmann's prime position on their home ground.

"What happened to Jerry Haines?" she demanded, though from the way Hübsch was going on, there could be little doubt that he, too, had been murdered.

"Ze same," Hübsch confirmed. "Exactly what happened to Andrew Myles. Same method. Zey both smoked, you know?"

Marsha nodded. Jerry had smoked cigars. Often he put one in his mouth and just chewed on the end of it in deference to others. Andrew had shown no such compunction. She remembered him ignoring the no smoking sign in her office and lighting up when he was there to sign the Drury Carter contract. He smoked something extraordinarily offensive. Gitanes, perhaps. At the time, she had assumed that he had bought them specially to be offensive. He had been fond of testing how far he could push people. Once the signatures were done, Marsha told him to stub out the cigarette.

"Why?" she asked now.

"Ze kind of poison zat vas used," Hübsch said. He had removed his hat and was wiping the rim on the sleeve of his overcoat. He stopped to study Marsha's face.

She waited for him to continue. When he didn't, she got up, looked at her watch, and began to rummage in her bag for the day's schedule. Not that she was really interested in the schedule right now, but Hübsch's intense study made her feel both uncomfortable and resentful. She was not going to afford him the satisfaction of noting her resentment. He might have mistaken it for a show of guilt.

"Liquid nicotine," Hübsch said at last. "The laboratory found traces in Myles's blood. At first ve had thought it was his intake of cigarettes, but zen ze, how you call it, ze doctor for ze dead ..."

"Pathologist."

"Yes. He examined the little pieces of ze glass we had found in ze refuse from after ze party. He said zere had been traces of liquid nicotine. Kills very fast. If you are not a smoker, you might detect it in your drink, but if you smoke, you don't. You are used to ze taste of nicotine. Mr. Myles was. Smoked many cigarettes. If he had not been killed, he would have died anyway soon. Had lung cancer. You knew?"

Marsha shook her head.

Hübsch shook a cigarette loose from his mangled package, lit it ceremoniously and inhaled deeply. Again, he didn't bother asking if Marsha minded. "Zis ozer one, Haines, ve looked for zat right away. Zey vere zere. Traces in his blood. Liquid nicotine. Same as ze ozer. Sometimes if you do not know what to look for, it disappears completely before you start to, how you say ... suspicion?"

"It happened at the party?"

"No. I don't believe so."

"Why?"

"Ze poison acts faster zan zat." He shrugged. "It's possible. But even more possible that he met someone closer to his room or even in his room after. Wiz whom was he at ze party?" Hübsch asked with perfect grammar.

Marsha tried to recreate in her mind the picture of Jerry against the windows of the far room where the *Digest* reception was held. The curtains had been drawn. He had a glass in his hand? Yes. Not unusual. Cigar in his hand. Talking? No. Listening to someone on his left. His face had been half turned away towards someone. She thought it was a young woman she had seen before at the Fennell booth but she couldn't be sure. She told Hübsch that.

"Probably Miss Sophie Biddle. She says she stayed at the *Reader's Digest* party after her boss left. Did not know where he was going. She was sure it was business. And she saw him again, but much later."

"They were both killed by the same person?" Marsha asked.

"Is possible," Hübsch said evasively. Then he warmed to the subject again. "Natürlich, zey did business together — Myles and Haines. One is agent, other is publisher. Zey do business, yes?"

"As you say," Marsha agreed. She wondered if, his expression to the contrary, Hübsch was trying some humour. "That's the reason why we are all here." She didn't actually believe that, but there was no sense in giving Hübsch any more publishing lore.

"Some special business. Something ze two of zem were doing zat zey vere killed for. You know what that could be?"

"A manuscript?" Marsha hardly believed it could be a manuscript, but there had been a time not so long ago when she had known several people who had been murdered over a manuscript that barely existed.

"Yes. Maybe. What vas Andrew Myles offering you here?"

"Me? Nothing. I had already bought the package I was going to buy from him before we came to Frankfurt."

"Miss Carter."

"Yes. But he would have had others."

Hübsch looked at her sharply. "What? For example?"

"Nothing I know of," Marsha said, "but you might ask Frans van Maeght what he and Andrew had been discussing so vigorously at the party the night before last ..."

"Ve have already talked to Mr. van Maeght." Hübsch closed his notebook forcefully. "Nothing else you can tell me?"

"You've checked the threatening note he received?" Marsha asked.

Hübsch nodded. "Ze letters zat had been cut from ze paper, zey vere cut out before Mr. Myles's murder. Two days before. Ve do not know who is threatening Mr. van Maeght, but ve believe zey have nosing to do wiz zis." He looked at her over the top of the rimless glasses. "You think otherwise?"

"I don't know," Marsha said irritably. "But, I am not in charge of a police investigation." She wanted him out of her room so she could organize her thoughts.

Hübsch said: "Exactly." He stuffed his leather-bound notebook back into the breast pocket of his raincoat, and put his hat back on his head. From the doorway, he finally apologized for barging in on her two mornings in a row. "You are returning to New York today?" he asked.

"Yes."

"And Mr. Nystrom?" he asked quickly.

"Bertil?" She remembered there was something he had wanted to tell her. He had been late coming to her room after the *Digest* party. So late that she had told him it was too late for stories and sent him back to his own room for what was left of the night.

"As you say, Bertil." Hübsch smirked. "Did he have some business perhaps with Mr. Myles?"

"None that I know."

"Good," Hübsch said. "You vouldn't vant something to happen to Mr. Nystrom, vould you? Your plane's at four. Ve shall see each other at two in ze lobby. Yes?"

"How did you know about my plane?"

"Same way I knew about Mr. Nystrom coming to your room again this morning at one. We do not like to have our visitors killed here in Frankfurt. Ve prefer to send zem home undamaged. At two, zen?" He wet his thumb and forefinger and squeezed the lit end of his cigarette till it stopped smoking, then he flicked it into the waste-paper bucket.

Marsha had no choice but to agree. It was the only way she could be sure he would leave.

Bertil was waiting in the lobby. He stood near the exit where the porters had already piled up the suitcases for the early departures. But for the cowboys, who needed to see every inch of the seven halls, Marsha would have been on a flight to London this morning. She resented another day at the Fair almost as much as the whole nasty business of the murders. In his long brown raincoat, the collar pulled up to his chin, his sandy hair damp and sticking to his forehead, hands deep in his pockets, Bertil looked forlorn. Nevertheless two young things with plastic name tags pirouetted past him, laughing, open-mouthed, shoulder-checking from past the first revolving door to see if they had attracted his attention.

They need not have worried. Marsha could have slipped past him easily as he gazed fondly at their departing rumps. But she waited. Had the morning not been so terrible, she might have walked by and watched from a distance as he became impatient.

Still, it would have been a fascinating manoeuvre for Hübsch's men to observe.

"You've heard," Bertil asked, his arm winding around Marsha's shoulder.

She nodded.

Close up, Bertil looked like he hadn't slept all night. He had a day's growth of light blond stubble, his eyes were red-ringed and blood-shot, deep dark lines had etched themselves from the corners down towards his mouth. There were hollows beneath his cheekbones. Though she had seen him tired and hung over many times, he had not seemed quite as worn out as he did this morning.

Hübsch and a pair of green uniforms came from the direction of the dining room. He glanced at Marsha and Bertil, mumbled "Morgen," as if he hadn't already been with them today, and rushed by them into the rain.

"I saw him last night," Bertil said, "or more accurately early this morning."

"Hübsch?"

"Him, too, but I meant Jerry Haines." When he saw the look in her eyes, he stopped. "You haven't had your coffee," he said sympathetically, and steered her towards the breakfast area.

Marsha allowed herself to be propelled within the embrace of his right arm, as easily as if they were dancing. Incongruously, she imagined how lightly Rita Nystrom would have allowed herself to accept the same comforting direction for some twenty-two years. It would be difficult not to take refuge in Bertil's good-natured protectiveness. Yet, the year Rita had left, she had told him she no longer felt as if she had a life of her own. Later, when Rita returned, she had decided she didn't need one any more.

Bertil had talked about his wife only on those two occasions, when she left him and when she returned. Neither time did he claim to understand why.

Otherwise, his marriage was the only topic he considered off-limits when he was with Marsha. Old world gallantry, or innate cowardice. In any event, it was a greatly refreshing change from Irwin's incontinent burbling about his plans to leave his wife who, he thought, understood him not at all. Marsha had decided she understood him only too well.

Bertil picked one of the tables near the coffee machine and brought Marsha a jug of coffee before she even sat down. He filled all four of the cups on the table and returned for milk.

"Around one in the morning, I think, maybe later. In the Lippizaner, again. He was very much alive. Lively. Drinking Courvoisier, smoking those big Monte Cristos, buying drinks for the dregs at the bar. Not so serious at that hour, whatever it was, maybe seven or eight stalwarts left at the bar, but for Jerry, a vastly unusual outpouring of generosity ..." He fastidiously buttered a tiny Frankfurt croissant, dabbed on some strawberry jam and offered it to Marsha.

She chose to stay with the coffee. "He was celebrating?" she asked.

"Said he had scored his big book of the Fair. He didn't need to go into an auction, no other bidders would be allowed to enter this one — and the price was just right. 'Happenstance,' he said. Being in the right place at the right time." Bertil ate the croissant reluctantly. He had never been much of an eater and Marsha knew how hard he had to push himself to breakfast after a long night. Perhaps that's why he had remained as slender as when she had first met him, despite his bottomless capacity for Scotch.

"He was uncharacteristically shy about the author, the subject, or how much he had agreed to pay, but one thing was for sure ... he kept repeating how surprised you'd be. He couldn't wait for you to find out, just so he could see your face. He said it would make the whole damned Fair worthwhile just to see you squirm. Really. He said that. At that hour in the morning he was obsessed with wanting to hear you admit he had been right about something or other. I wasn't paying him a lot of attention. It was late. You had just kicked me out." Bertil sighed and leaned back in his too-small chair, as his fine features arranged themselves into a perfect frame of anxiety and apprehension. "We were both thinking about you," he said.

Marsha refilled the four cups. "Jerry was wildly insecure," she said.

"For good reason, it seems," Bertil retorted. "He was dead by daybreak."

"What I meant is he was insecure about his abilities. Always trying to impress. Wishing everyone would acknowledge he had made it on his own. Never was able to slide out from under Weidenfeld's shadow. Poor Jerry."

"Such a damnably big shadow," Bertil said. "Don't you think the Fennell group was just right for him? So much business, so little publishing. Perfect choice after his apprenticeship with George. All those glossy books by all those dreadful royals, and monumental biographies of even the most minor of them. No man of title or wealth ever escaped the great one's attentions. The very best training for the conglomerate challenge." Bertil sighed wistfully. "But why anyone would wish to kill him is beyond me."

"Volume analysis. Restructuring. Mission statements," Marsha groaned.

"You suspect one of the Fennell insiders?"

"Except for the fact that Andrew was also murdered, the thought could occur. Are there many of them at the Fair?"

"An immodest booth on 4.2, near Orion. Huge monolithic

display of the unfortunate logo. Fifteen staff, maybe. Aggressive rights people with an inflated notion of the population of Norway. Didn't look like killers ..."

"Wonderful thought, that," Marsha said wistfully. "Murder by memo. Some simple soul who'd had it with synergies. Some brave and furious angel tired of planning meetings, and taking after the philistines. But it's not likely, I'm afraid," she put down a finished cup and started another. "Not if the two murders are connected as Hübsch says they are. Both Jerry and Andrew were killed the same way. Liquid nicotine."

"How would one even get liquid nicotine? Boil cigarettes? Never heard of it as a liquid, have you?"

"No."

"The only reason Hübsch isn't taking me in for some serious questioning right now is that you failed to drag me with you the night before last to meet Andrew Myles."

"He was beyond meeting even you, by then, as I keep telling the dogged inspector. Thank God I wasn't in the Lippizaner last night," Marsha said. "Hübsch suspects us all anyway. He thinks both men were murdered over a book deal. And we're all here making deals."

"Not all of us, I think ..."

The paging system spluttered into life with a guttural sound and something vaguely familiar.

"Who else was in the Lippizaner last night?" Marsha asked.

"I am a little hazy on their names, especially the hookers," Bertil told her. "But I'm sure Frans was there. Couple of guys I knew vaguely. Americans. Someone else. British, maybe. For a while, Alex Levine ... He was with Jerry when I arrived, but he left shortly after. We pissed together in the men's room off the lobby. I do remember that. He thought it rather odd that everyone was searching for kind words to say about Andrew Myles. He had been, arguably, the nastiest bit of work ever to enter publishing.

He had gone after most of Alex's writers, at least all the lucrative ones. No interest in new talent. He'd found it much easier to wait until someone was already established and then go pluck them off the tree. Alex's phrase, I swear," Bertil said defensively.

"Writers aren't peaches," Marsha said. "How about this in defence of Andrew?"

"Oh?"

"They choose to be picked. Unlike peaches."

"Alex did mention greed."

"Andrew's mother is coming to take his body home," Marsha said. "I heard she is planning a memorial service in New York, so all his friends can be there. And I bet the place will be packed."

"Why? Everyone wants to make sure he's really dead?"

"The authors he made rich will come. The publishers will want to see who is there ..."

"Yesterday morning," Bertil interrupted, "there was a note from Andrew Myles. It must have been slipped under my door on Friday evening. In any event, I didn't see it till I got back from here in the early morning. That's what I had wanted to tell you. It said he wanted to meet me in the morning at the agent's booth, he'd be there at ten. That was, of course, the morning after he died."

"Handwritten?"

"Typed. I expect he brought it with him from New York, it even had his letter-head."

"You have it still?"

"I gave it to Hübsch."

"Andrew didn't say why he wanted to see you?"

"No."

"You said you didn't even know each other."

"Only by reputation. We inhabit a small pond. He was a very large fish in it. And I expect I've been doing a fair bit of croaking in my northern reaches of the mudflats." He grinned. Bertil, Marsha knew, rather enjoyed his own immutable renown.

"It's you they're paging, I think," he said. He hesitated for a second as she rose, then reached out to hold her hand. "I'll wait, if you like."

It was the long partings that she hated most about the relationship with Bertil. The long partings at the end of each Bookfair used to reduce her to tears. Bertil had no trouble keeping his lives separate. In one, Marsha was the great love each man is entitled to have, once. In the other, he was married to Rita, was a leading literary light in Norway, and a man used to finding his slippers waiting by the door when he returned home after a gruelling day.

Briefly, the two lives intersected the year Rita had left him. He had been lonely and flirted with the notion that he had failed. A tough act for a man who had had most successes handed to him. The son of a successful architect in Oslo, Bertil was afforded the best education his city could provide, with private tutors for languages, then boarding school in England, and finishing in Oxford near the top of his class in literature and history. He had risen to president of Nillsson within a few years of starting as editor, just as everyone in publishing had predicted he would.

He was not only the best publisher in his country, he was the only Norwegian one the world knew, first on agents' lists for "big books" from England and the United States. When Nillsson was bought by Bertelsmann, Bertil left without rancour. The smallest taste of corporate life had been enough. He had set up Nystrom with all the confidence of a man not used to failure, and he had been right. The agents grabbed Bertelsmann's larger offerings for the predictable best-sellers, but kept Bertil in mind for their more surprising favourites and he prospered.

Perhaps his big, blond blue-eyed looks helped to keep them coming back. At six foot two, with slightly stooped shoulders to take the edge off his height, he still towered over most of the Frankfurt revellers. Male publishers tended to come in short balding shapes, tubby as the years went by. As was his unerring eye for the right books, Bertil's shape was constant.

Though his hair had receded with the years, his forehead became more open, his jaw a little squarer, Marsha knew his body was still covered with silky hair the colour of autumn wheat.

Only once had he asked if she would have left New York for Oslo. The intensity of her response had frightened him. "It's a cold-blooded country, my darling Marsha," he had whispered into her hair. "The long, dark winters are ill suited to big-hearted Americans." And he dropped the idea as if it had never been his.

Rita, Marsha surmised, was perfectly suited to the climate. She wove delicate tapestries and made multi-coloured quilts for charity bazaars. When she had left him, Marsha could no longer imagine taking her place. The thought of hand-made blankets had lost their attraction, though she still loved Bertil, in her own way.

She glanced down at his long-fingered hand, graceful as the rest of his body, and smiled at him in reassurance. Hübsch had been right, she wouldn't want anything to happen to Bertil Nystrom.

She went to pick up the phone in the far corner of the lobby.

CHAPTER
SEVEN

"M<small>ISS HILLIER?</small>"

"Yes," Marsha said.

"Marsha Hillier?" The hesitant voice persisted.

"It's too early for twenty questions," Marsha said.

"It is, Miss Marsha Hillier," the voice said, less hesitant and more irritable.

"Right again. Now, what do you want?"

There was a long, audible sigh at the other end of the line. "I have been calling the room for over an hour. There has been no answering. I worried that you were not all right. It's van Maeght," he said in a rush.

"Frans?"

"Of course. Frans. You have been not answering since six thirty," he said accusingly. "They said you were busy. And I have been pacing up and down here, not knowing what to do. You know about Haines. He has died. Last night."

"Yes. I know ..."

"It's all my doing."

"It's what?"

"My fault. All this. First Andrew Myles. Now this. I do not know where it's going to stop." He was breathing heavily, as if he had been running. "So I am not in my room, I am walking up and down here, not knowing what to do. These things do not happen to people like us, you know. I never thought it was possible. You read about this sort of thing in those trashy novels, but it does not happen in real life to real people. And I never thought it could. Never. And now look. Because I was not thinking." He sighed. "It is all my fault ..."

"Frans," Marsha said when he stopped for air, "I can't imagine what you are burbling on about. We are all upset by Andrew's death and Jerry's. You need a good night's sleep." We all need a good night's sleep, she thought. "Damned Fair is going to be over tomorrow ..."

"No. No. No," he protested. "You do not understand. It's not over. Not for me, it is not over. Maybe not for you, and I do not know how many more. A nightmare it is. You have to come right away. I will wait for you, here," he commanded.

"I don't think so," Marsha said. "I am meeting my bosses over at the booth in an hour and taking them on a tour of Halle 5, Frans."

"How can you talk about Halle 5 at a time like this?" Frans shouted. "Do you hear what I have been telling you?"

"Frans," Marsha said as patiently as her fatigue would allow, "whatever your problem is, I am not the one to solve it. You have to talk to Hübsch, he is the guy to track down the killer ..."

"So you don't give a ... shit ... if you live or do not. That's what you say? You do not care how many others go the way Haines and Myles went. Especially you. I have been here for hours thinking and worrying that you could be the next one. You have been with them both. Both of them. You understand me? You ..." He was hysterical. "I am here at the railway station. Main entrance to the left. There is a big Coca-Cola poster and a bank of phones. I will wait here for ten minutes. You decide what you want to do." He choked on the last word and hung up.

Marsha looked at her watch. It was not yet eight o'clock, though it felt like the day was half over. She had another hour left before she was to meet the cowboys. It was an hour she had hoped to spend with Bertil; they had always found time the morning the Fair ended to say their last goodbyes. She longed to be held and comforted, an antidote for the long journey home, and something to warm her as she prepared for the numbing trek around Halle 5.

Bertil sat with his long arms laid along the sides of the too-small table, his knees knocking the tabletop, his hair falling over his face. He was studying a sheaf of papers, his eyes half-closed. He was trying to concentrate.

There was probably nothing to it, but she would have to find that out for herself. She told Bertil that something had come up, and left him with a puzzled expression on his face, and a promise to make her way over to the Norwegian aisle just as soon as she could. She took the streetcar to the main entrance of the old Hof-bahnhof, because it was by far the fastest route, and she had, for some reason, taken Frans seriously about the ten minutes. Today, of course, there was no shortage of taxis in front of the Marriott. By now, all the important people had left.

She emerged from the underpass just inside the main entrance. There was a stampede of industrious Frankfurters towards the streetcar and the buses on the other side of the gates. She waited for a few seconds before she fought her way through the throng. She saw the Coke sign almost immediately when she made her way into the building. Frans hadn't mentioned that it was over ten feet high and wider across. Coca-Cola must have been getting ready for Christmas already in Germany, because the poster was the heart-warming one with the throng of singing children around the giant tree in Times Square, all of them holding Coke bottles, all singing *Stille Nacht* or some such song.

There was no sign of Frans.

Marsha walked the length of the sign, found the bank of telephones he must have called from, checked around them twice, stood with her back to the Christmas tree around the centre of the sign staring at every passer-by, and still there was no Frans. She checked her watch. It was just nine minutes since she had put the phone back on the hook after his call.

She waited till the full ten minutes was up, added another minute to make sure, then walked around the pillars near the entrance to see if perhaps Coke had gone overboard in Frankfurt and installed two giant posters, but there was only one.

When she was about to give up and walk to the Fair, a woman with too much make-up and straw-like, kinky hair grabbed her by the arm. "Gott sei Dank," she said as she tried to hug Marsha around the waist with her free arm. "You have come."

"I what?" Marsha struggled to free herself from the clinging arm. There was something familiar about the face. The shape of the nose, covered in way too much ivory pancake and beige powder, was certainly like a nose she had seen before. Bulbous. And the grey-blue eyes, intense behind the round glasses ...

"This is excellent," the woman said with a sigh of complete satisfaction. "You do not recognize me." She gave Marsha's waist an extra little squeeze. "We must go into the women's room right now."

"I don't think so ..."

"I will explain instantly ..."

"Frans?" Marsha asked, still disbelieving the evidence of the bulb at the end of the nose and the roundish face she was accustomed to seeing with thin grey hair on top.

"Of course it's Frans," he whispered. "Who else was it arranged to meet you here? The women's room is just around the corner and not at all crowded. We must make plans. I have to explain about what I have been trying to tell you. I doubt we have much time. We don't want to make them suspicious."

"We don't?"

"Come." He steered her towards the big yellow sign with the stick figure of a woman on it.

Frans, even in drag, was hardly a formidable presence but it barely occurred to Marsha to break away. She was addicted to good stories and this one promised to be worth the effort, even without the threatening overtones and Jerry Haines's murder.

Alas, Frans knew less about women's rooms in Germany than Marsha did, so he was surprised to see the robust attendant hovering near the door, her tray of one mark coins on the washstand.

Frans made his way to the mirrors and began to tug at his wig. "I bought this the day after Myles ... Do you suppose she speaks English?"

Marsha turned to the woman who was gazing at Frans with undisguised curiosity. "I wonder if you have some," she opened her purse and dug in among the coins to get her attention, "hand lotions?" she asked.

After a moment's hesitation, the woman pointed to the metal sanitary napkins dispenser on the wall. She smiled showing two front teeth missing and looked down at Marsha's rummaging hand in the purse. "Ja?"

Marsha shook her head. "Nein," and shrugged the international sign of helplessness. "I doubt it," she told Frans, "she is probably Turkish. Trying to feed her family. Now will you get on with it, please."

"Turkish?" Frans asked anxiously.

"Ja," the woman came closer, smiling.

"I didn't expect that ..." Frans said to Marsha, lowering his voice.

"That's funny, everyone else would have."

"Sorry, I forgot. It's Germany." Frans shook his head. "I told you I haven't slept. I have been wanting to keep my head clear but it is not easy. It is, I think, your advice I need. As I said, you are already ... indicated. That is not the word. No matter. You have been with me here ..."

"I haven't been with you ..." Marsha protested, as if by rote. "You mean implicated?"

"It does not matter," Frans said impatiently. "What matters is that if someone did not know you have not been with me, they would certainly think that you have been with me. We have been in the same places. And you were the last to talk to Myles. Someone could jump to the conclusion, nyah?" He dabbed some powder on his nose, quite unnecessarily.

"Nyah," Marsha said, "but have it your way, as long as you get on with it, for Chrissakes."

"It started with my friend from Zagreb," Frans said, glancing over his shoulder at the attendant who had settled into her chair by the door. "We had met some Frankfurts ago. Here."

"In the ladies' room?" Marsha squawked.

"In what was once the Pacific Plaza. The hotel where you are staying. It's where the Motovun group of publishers has been meeting once a year for some fifteen years. For breakfast on the last Sunday morning of the Fair. You know them."

Marsha didn't.

"They do not have many Americans. Maybe two or three. The rest are all Europeans. From all over. Some Croats, and Serbs, yes, I know, and they get along just very well, never any of the war staff, and Montenegrans — what used to be Yugoslavs. Danes. A couple of publishers from Sweden. Three or four from France. Now I think of it, some of those from France aren't going any more. They were ... conglomerated. Yes? Germans. Italians. Czechs. Chinese. We were the first group to welcome the Chinese, back when Mao was still around. William, he is from Oslo, he took me there some years ago, as his guest. They welcome guests to the breakfasts as long as you don't mind being introduced while everyone is eating, and pay your own way. You know. You have the chance to join the group then, if they want you after the breakfast. That's where I started talking with Juris. He is from Sarajevo."

Marsha was becoming impatient.

"He is a Moslem," Frans said in a whisper.

A couple of women had come in to use the toilets. They were now adjusting their make-up on either side of Marsha and Frans. Frans was looking at them balefully. He didn't resume until they were gone.

"At the last Frankfurt, he said he knew some people in Baghdad. There was a manuscript they wanted published. He asked me last year, after the Motovun breakfast if I'd be interested in publishing a book. It's by Saddam Hussein." He returned the lipstick to his pocket and checked to see that Marsha was adequately astounded.

She was. "He's written a book?"

Frans nodded. "The complete thing."

"You have it?"

"Not exactly," Frans said. "But I did tell him I was interested. Anyone would be, wouldn't they?"

A young girl came in dragging a vast knapsack, deposited it in the corner near the attendant, and ran to one of the toilets.

"I never heard another word from Juris till August," Frans said rapidly. "He called me then in Amsterdam and asked if I could come up with three and a half million dollars for the manuscript. I told him my firm does not throw around that kind of money easily. Holland is not America. He said it would have to be cash. One lump payment. The Leader did not trust anybody. None of the 'royalties will come later' stuff. And certainly not from anybody in the West. He said I could meet him in Trieste and he would let me read some of it, and then he'd give me a couple of weeks to raise the cash. He said it could be in Deutschmarks or dollars but they didn't want any guilders."

"World rights?" Marsha asked.

"World rights."

"So why would they have picked you?" Marsha asked with undisguised curiosity.

"Why not me?" Frans raised his eyebrows. "You think I'm not big enough, is that it?"

The thought could have occurred to anyone, Marsha figured, but she said, "If he didn't want guilders, why would he pick a Dutch publisher?" It sounded a little lame, but Frans didn't protest any further.

"The point is, he did pick me," he whispered forcefully. "Maybe specifically because Holland is no longer a big player on the world stage. No more empire. Maybe because we didn't bomb his home town. Maybe because we didn't send in a bunch of guided missiles to annihilate his army. Seemed good enough reasons to me. At the time."

"So, you went to Trieste," Marsha prompted.

"First, I called Andrew Myles to see if he would help me raise the money. It's what he was good at, getting money in advance and doing the big hype. That's why he came to Amsterdam. Maybe he was trying to see if he could cut me out of the deal, if the manuscript was really what I said it was. I never gave him Juris's name."

"And did he raise the money?"

"Yes. It took him less than a week. He was a real operator. But not until I had been to Trieste. I came back with a dozen pages. They were unsigned. Juris even had a contract for us to sign. Also unsigned."

"And you have the manuscript?"

Frans shook his head. "Just the dozen pages from Trieste. Juris didn't let me take any more of it with me. But I did read it all. In English. Maybe four hundred pages. They were not numbered. I was going to get the rest of it in Frankfurt. When the money changed hands. All in one clean transaction, as Juris said. And I have been waiting for Juris to contact me for five days. He has not. We were to meet on Wednesday evening at the Lippizaner, but he didn't show. No messages. Nothing."

"And you have the money?"

"Myles had the money. Of course, he wouldn't turn it over to me without seeing the manuscript for himself. Said he would hand it to Juris, personally, when he had read the entire thing and had satisfied himself it was not a hoax."

"And how does Jerry come into this story?"

The young girl was making very loud noises in the toilet.

"Fennell did the British deal with Myles. I was going to get a ten percent cut and Andrew had carved himself another fifteen off the top. He was going to get fifteen of everything except the Dutch ... This is a very bad smell," Frans said.

Marsha agreed. "We have to get out of here."

"Where else is there to go?"

"The police station is just around the corner."

"They're useless against terrorists."

"So am I," Marsha confessed. "Frans, you have to get some protection, at least."

Sadly dragging his heels, he led the way out the door. Marsha dropped two five-mark pieces onto the tray.

"Protection didn't do much for Nygaard," Frans said, referring to Salman Rushdie's Norwegian publisher who had been shot outside his home in Oslo some three years ago. "And if I go to the police I'll never be able to publish the manuscript. That would be the end of it."

"How do you know it was *his* manuscript?"

They were walking arm in arm towards the main entrance, carried along with a stream of people hurrying to catch the streetcars.

"I told you I read it," Frans said irritably. "That's how I know. It was in English. Not a very literate translation, but good enough to work from once we had it. And with a manuscript like that, it is not the literary quality that makes people want to read on — it's what's in it. And there was plenty in it that would have embarrassed your government. Not so great for the British, but they haven't been big players in the Middle East for some years now, so most of the embarrassment would have followed the dead. But he certainly made your people look like idiots. Lots of details. All the names. He was recording stuff. He has tapes. Akin to your chap Nixon, I think."

"Of course," Marsha bristled. "You don't even know if he wrote it, do you? The only person, so far, who was going to be embarrassed was you. At least Andrew figured the whole thing could have been an elaborate hoax. Still could."

"It's not a hoax," Frans declared as they entered the streetcar platforms.

"How the hell would you know?"

"Because I met him."

"Whom?"

"The author, himself, that's whom." Frans put all the emphasis on the "m." It was an effort, but it served to show he was comfortable with his English grammar. It was amazing, Marsha thought, what people clung to at times of extreme stress.

"You met Saddam Hussein. Sure."

"Shhhhh. What is the matter with you? Two people are dead and you're wandering around saying that name as if it were some ... confection."

They boarded the streetcar towards the Messe. Neither of them had a ticket, but in all the years of coming to Frankfurt, no one had ever asked them for tickets.

"I flew to Baghdad the second of September. I met him." Frans smiled modestly. Or so it seemed. The make-up hid most of his facial expressions.

"And?" Marsha asked impatiently.

"And nothing. We were together for maybe twenty minutes. He had an interpreter, though I'm certain he understood me perfectly. He speaks passable English. He also had some thirty guards around to make sure he was safe. No question, it was his story. He told me so, himself. He was pleased to be able to do something nasty to you and the British."

"And you think he changed his mind?"

"Probably."

"And he had Andrew and Jerry killed?"

"Yes."

"And he had someone cut letters out of newspapers and send you that threatening note?"

"Yes."

"Then why are you still alive?"

"I don't know. Maybe he liked me."

"Sure." Marsha stood up when the streetcar stopped at the second entrance to the Messe. "I'm going to have to take my chances, Frans. I told you the bosses are expecting a guided tour and, as far as I'm concerned, they're just about up there with you-know-who in meanness."

"I tried to warn you," Frans said sadly.

"Thanks."

From the platform she glanced back at Frans in the window. To anyone else he would have looked like a middle-aged woman with just a touch too much make-up and a very cheap hairdresser.

CHAPTER

EIGHT

DEBBIE BROWN WAS NOT WILD ABOUT THE IDEA OF a whole story devoted to Margaret Drury Carter's ruggedly rural surroundings. *Home and Garden*'s regular readers were city folk, more interested in how they could better their own homes (and gardens) than in what obscure vegetation might be coaxed out of the soil on Grand Manan. It was Judith's promise of some unusual decorating touches inside the house that finally gained Debbie's approval. That, and Judith's mention of the new twenty million dollar deal. "Our readers would like to hear about that," Debbie mused.

They both remembered that Drury Carter's last home, in Virginia, had been a designer showcase. The grandam herself had taken *Home and Garden* over every lovingly arranged inch of the premises, all the while telling tales about her various heroines and how she had been inspired to write their stories here. She had written three of her novels in Virginia.

It would be interesting to see, Judith thought, what she finds inspiring on Grand Manan. The folk in Jemseg whistled appreciatively when she mentioned where she was headed. Not a place for the fainthearted, especially in late October. An unusual location for a romance-writer at the best of times.

She had met a couple of women at Basil's variety store who lived with their teenagers and had cast sympathetic glances in Judith's direction while she had collected groceries with the resolutely sullen Jimmy following behind. He had been wearing his customary stained blue jeans, torn so widely at the knees that they appeared to be hanging by mere threads. His bony legs poked out. He had mended the crotch with an old piece of corduroy, itself frayed and sagging. The whole thing slid so low and loose on his hips, it was a wonder they stayed up at all. He wore sandals with thick grey socks, a stained t-shirt dyed splotchy black, his blond hair in matted locks over his shoulders, and the ever-present earring.

She had become so used to Jimmy's appearance she no longer noticed any of this, unless someone else remarked on it.

"I swear it's a uniform they're all wearing," one woman had remarked. "My Pete looks exactly the same." They had had coffee later and Judith could verify that she had not been exaggerating. Both the women were in their forties; housewives, they had said of themselves. "Nothing to be ashamed of, even in these new liberated days. And why the darnation should I get myself some lousy menial job around here if I don't have to, now?" They were both married. The men worked at Irving rigs. Never home except for the holidays.

"There's only two kinds of work in New Brunswick, Irving work or McCain work," so the saying goes. And neither kind pays much, just enough to keep you here. The Irvings owned two thirds of the province, the McCains what was left over, they told Judith. "They even share the government between them. One's oil, the other's potatoes." Amazing how far you can go in one generation.

Judith had once tried to interview an Irving for a business story she was writing on second generation money and how it survived its new owners. They were not interested in talking to her. As far as she could tell, they had little respect for the press. Perhaps, she surmised, that was because they owned all the newspapers in New Brunswick.

Years ago one of the two women had been to Grand Manan. Even in the middle of summer it had been damp and chilly. She could not imagine why anyone would go there if she had the whole world to choose from. Including Virginia. Or was she from Georgia?

Judith didn't want to disillusion them with tales of Margaret's fake Southern airs. They had both loved the novels. They were excited that the change in venue might mean she would set one of her books in New Brunswick. Would there be pirates or rum-runners, or perhaps the headless man who still haunted the shores of the Saint John River near the Reversing Falls, where the Irvings' paper mill had turned the waters to dark brown mulch and stinking suds?

Judith had driven to see the Falls after she landed at the Saint John airport. All she could remember was the stench. Interesting that the tourist booklets still list them as an attraction. But then, the Irvings probably own the booklets, their publisher, the writer, and maybe the local tourist authority.

She had been to visit the *Jemseg Courier* to find out what else they knew about Frank Tranby. The editor was friendly and tried to be helpful, but they didn't have the money or the manpower to do much more on the group than they had already done. He suspected that they were doing more than drumming and shouting, but he wasn't about to lurk in the bushes around the farm to see for himself. He did draw a map of the area for her but he advised her to forget about it. People had talked of hearing gunshots from the farm, but it wasn't illegal to hunt hereabouts, as long as you had a licence.

The Jemseg Constabulary confirmed that Tranby had a licence. They didn't even ask why she had to know. The young policeman said there had been a few complaints of shooting on Sundays. People hereabouts still respected Sunday; alas the law did not. No law against hunting on Sundays. He thought he could cite them for disturbing the peace, but the chief said to leave it alone.

One of the two women, though, had heard that all the men on the farm marched to boisterous German music. There was a large painting of Hitler above the fireplace and in the evening they raised a red flag with a big black swastika on it. She knew someone whose husband had been out there and he came home with all these ideas about the Jews running the world.

"Makes you laugh, imagine poor Mr. Greenfield, the grocer, having a hand in running the world."

Still, one evening, a couple of days after Judith arrived, the grocery store's windows were all broken and someone had tried to set fire to the store.

The police told the editor of the *Courier* they thought it was young kids up to mischief, but it was a fact they had never done anything like that before. "Too many out-of-work young people hereabouts," the editor told Judith and invited her to Dykemans' Pub and Restaurant for a drink, and maybe dinner if she felt like it.

He was bald, bowlegged, fiftyish, eyes close together, shoulders hunched. She didn't feel like dinner. But she did agree to contribute a piece on Tranby's lot for a couple of hundred dollars if she found anything when she went out there.

She chose Monday evening, while Jimmy was hanging out with her new friend's son. She wore black leggings and a sweater, her old black sandals, and a visored cap to hide her auburn hair. She could look like one of those out-of-work youths. If she were caught, she could pretend she had been out for a bracing walk in the fields. Nothing she had read about Tranby suggested he was smart. Only doggedly tenacious. Persistent. One of the Calgary stories hinted at his connections to a mid-Western militia group, but it wasn't connected to the Oklahoma bombing. Just good ol' Rush Limbaugh fans. Gun-lovers. Not killers. He had given a speech in Lethbridge when Rock, the then justice minister, attempted an all-out attack on gun-possession. He talked about "inalienable rights," as if Canadians had some.

She got lost in the dusk and it had become too dark to right herself by reading the *Courier*'s editorial map. The field to the left of Farley's farm had been left too long to lie fallow, there was a hard, scrubby growth of bushes and stunted trees she couldn't see until she was upon them, and though the moon was out, she never did find the hill, or the old barn, or any other signposts that would lead her behind the farmhouse but within earshot of the men inside.

The new occupants had erected a high wire fence around the farm and she did find that. She was close enough that she could smell the smoke from the chimney, and see a patch of light in the distance.

Nobody had mentioned the dogs. They rushed at the fence, hysterical with frustrated anger at not being able to get at her. It was impossible to tell in the dark, but they were black enough and fast enough to be Dobermans. They kept jumping up and down, clawing at the wire. They bit it and shook it and hurled themselves against it, until she heard someone yelling at them to quit. Whoever it was, he was coming closer, carrying a torch, the light streaking the bushes behind the dogs.

By then Judith was thrashing around in the undergrowth beating a hasty retreat to the road. She could still hear the intermittent barking when she got into the car and drove back to the cottage.

She opened a bottle of vodka and shook her hair loose.

Jimmy watched from the corner of the living room where the TV set was just announcing the beginning of a new episode of "ER."

"Why are you wearing my Mets cap?" he asked after a long wait. Generally, Jimmy preferred to let his mother launch into her own stories without help. It allowed him to cultivate his perfected stance of casual indifference. But she hadn't worn a baseball cap since little league when she sat on the sidelines urging on his team. She gave that up after he was old enough to get himself to the games.

"Keeps my hair in place," Judith tried.

"Sure," Jimmy said. He leaned forward to get a better view of Judith's mud-splattered leggings, and the burrs and leaves that had attached themselves to her sweater. She hadn't even noticed that it had torn at the elbow.

"I went for a long walk, and got lost in the dark," she admitted. The vodka tasted delicious as it slid down her throat. She hadn't bothered to put in the mix. A short martini, extra dry.

Jimmy glanced at her again. "Mmmmm ..." he said.

Judith shrugged. "I'm feeling stressed. You know, getting lost in unfamiliar country ..."

"Somewhere near Farley's farm, perhaps?" he asked.

"Since you know already ..." Earlier, she had told him what had led her to New Brunswick. What surprised her was that Jimmy had paid attention. He hadn't been in a listening mood when they left Toronto.

"So you want to know what goes on at the old farm?" Jimmy inquired smugly.

"You know what goes on there?"

"I've been up there," Jimmy said even more smugly.

"You what?" Judith jumped out of the chair she had slumped into.

"Keep your shirt on, will you?"

"Okay, what were you doing with those ..."

"Nazis?"

"Yes, Nazis."

"Checking it out, that's all. Might even tell you about them if you stop the yelling." He sat back comfortably, his eyes fixed on the TV set. Anyone other than his mother might have thought he was following the action on the screen.

Judith took a deep breath. From time to time, Jimmy reminded her uncomfortably of his father. He liked to drive her into a rage, then assume the appearance of sweet reason. She wouldn't play. Instead, she busied herself with energetically pulling stuff off the refrigerator shelves in apparent preparation for making dinner. "Well?" she asked over her shoulder after what she considered an adequate wait.

"One of Tranby's men talked to me and Jed when we sat outside McDonald's yesterday. Said it was a shame there wasn't any work for young able-bodied boys like us. Said it was like that all over the country especially for the young. Like us. Jed's nineteen and no prospects of a job here far as he knew, so he agreed with the guy." Jimmy had wandered into the kitchen. "Too many damned immigrants is the problem, he told us. None of them have any damned skills but they let them in anyway, and then they have to find them jobs, or just stick them on the welfare rolls. Makes no difference either way, we end up paying their way. Jed's not much of a talker but he agreed with the guy, anyway. Sounded reasonable, he thought."

"Who's Jed?"

"What difference does it make? One of the guys I met here. Not too many people my age in Jemseg." Jimmy was exasperated. "Do you want to hear the rest of the story, or play social police?"

"Story," Judith conceded.

"He offered us cigarettes and stood around chatting about lack of jobs and immigrants. I wasn't paying a whole lot of attention till he said he was with Frank Tranby and they had come here from Saskatchewan because the government there had been bought by the immigration lawyers and their henchmen who were selling out the country for some short-term gains for themselves. And the guy's going on about us all being Aryans and having to take a stand before we lose what little we have left of our own country, and Jed's chiming in that we're entitled to have jobs before some foreign bastards grab them. Next thing I know he's inviting us to Farley's farm."

"Did you go?"

"Sure, we went. Bit of a waste of time — there's not much to do down here but waste time." Jimmy smirked at his mother. "Not much there. Grungy old house. The men sleep on bunks that look like they're home-made, gnarled wood. Stinks in there.

The guy gave us some watery stew. Smelled worse. I didn't eat it."

"How many men were there?"

"About twenty guys is all I saw. Old, mostly. They had rifles. Tranby told us they used them for target practice."

"How did you know it was Tranby?"

"You showed me his picture, didn't you?"

"Did he say anything else?"

"Said the government didn't care about the people any more, so one day they would take over the government. They would do a better job. Give jobs to all the young people. He went on and on about how Germany had done it after the First World War. Put everyone back to work. Made the country run. They'd done such a bang-up job they'd almost conquered the world. He had a picture of Hitler over the fireplace. Tranby said Hitler really liked young people because they are the future. Told Jed they were going to have a youth wing and asked if he'd join."

"Did he?"

"Don't be stupid. Crazy old geezer. We laughed all the way home."

CHAPTER
NINE

Most New Yorkers had left at least two days before, but not everyone from New York had been one of the last to see Andrew Myles before the Frankfurt Bookfair pronounced him dead. No amount of argument would convince Inspektor Hübsch that Andrew had been dead when Marsha last talked to him. The pathologist, he had told her, couldn't be sure within the half hour but he had no doubt that whoever murdered Andrew was at the party. Liquid nicotine worked fairly fast. Slower for smokers than non-smokers, but certainly no more than an hour from when he would have ingested it and when he died. The short-term effects include dizziness and double vision. If you're drinking at the time, you might put it down to over-indulgence, and Andrew had been drinking. By the time you realize there is something seriously wrong, paralysis sets in.

Andrew had been at the party for over an hour when Marsha discovered him slumped in his chair. He was probably still alive at the time.

That, Hübsch had hinted to Marsha, left him with some five

hundred suspects. One of them remained Marsha. Most of the others were gone.

As Marsha ushered the dreadful duo around the Fair on Monday morning, she discovered that Hübsch had detained other members of the little group around Andrew. He couldn't do more than request they stay around — he didn't have the authority — but persuasion had worked. They all wanted to come back to the Fair another year. Frankfurt, Hübsch had pointed out, was his jurisdiction.

She had led the cowboys directly to the Russian booth on the second floor of Halle 9. There had been some discussion among the organizers that they should be moved downstairs now that Russia was experimenting with democracy, as a kind of reward for giving up their empire, but Peter Weidhaas, the Bookfair boss, could not convince the French and the Italians that they should give up their perches close to the English-speaking aisles. So, the Russians remained next to the Czechs and Hungarians who were no longer curbing their age-old distaste for their former masters. On the last day of the Fair, however, old battles were forgotten, and even the Finns came by to help the Russians finish off their seemingly inexhaustible supply of Stolichnaya vodka.

Already at ten o'clock, there was a festive air about the booth. The Russians had thrown off their ill-fitting jackets, spread newspapers over the round white tables to soak up the sausage juice (it was only on the last day that they brought out their home-made kielbasa), and offered tumblers of vodka to those who came for their last business meetings. If you wanted bread, which most people did once they tasted the vodka and sausage, you had to bring your own. The Russians weren't about to splurge their last marks on expensive German white bread.

Vladimir, whose prospects under the new regime had not dimmed yet, was lounging before a six-foot poster of the last czar. He had discarded both his jacket and tie, and was directing the much younger staff in their efforts to organize the books into crates. At around age sixty, Vladimir was one of the old Frankfurt hands. He had been with the first delegation after the War. He was one of the few to speak English openly, and was a large, broad-chested man with an infectious smile who managed to look both conspiratorial and irrepressibly cheerful at the same time. Through the years he had lost most of his hair, added a considerable paunch to his barrel chest, but never lost his infectious cheerfulness.

"My dear Marsha," he shouted triumphantly as soon as he spotted her emerging from the Finnish enclave. "I knew you would come back ... but so late." He peered at his watch with a look of disbelief. He pulled the bottle from under the table and filled four tumblers with vodka after Marsha introduced the cowboys.

Morris fixed him with his "I'm here to communicate" glare. Thurgood stood back from the table staring at the vodka.

"Vladimir runs Mezhdunarodnaya Knyiga," Marsha said. "Still the best way to get our books into Russia. The major importer of English language books."

"... And we pay cash, gentlemen. Your cash," Vladimir said, offering the full tumblers to his guests.

Marsha drank hers in one gulp, showing the cowboys how to do it. When neither of them moved, she said, "Russian hospitality has to be accepted if you want to do business."

Thurgood led, as usual, by raising his glass gingerly to his lips and sipping. Morris followed suit reluctantly. They were both coughing uncontrollably when Marsha excused herself. She said she was sure they could handle matters on their own for an hour. She had a few things to do before the return trip.

She looked around Halle 8 for friends or acquaintances. Perhaps there was news about Jerry's death or Myles's.

Mark was lurking around the Fleetwood stand; Brigitte Dombert sat with some agents in the almost-deserted agents' centre; Dr. Gutfreund was also at the agents' centre, in a trance listening to Janet Turnbull Irving describing the newest manuscript of her lead author, and husband, John Irving. Judging by the rapt expression on Gutfreund's face, it would be as complex and engrossing as Irving's previous books. On the other hand, Janet was dressed in a long, clinging, cream-coloured silk dress. It was just possible, Marsha thought, that Gerhardt couldn't hear a word she was saying and was mesmerized, as others had been, by the long, languid features of her exceptionally well-proportioned body.

Hideo had taken the day off to visit some friends in from London, but he had dropped by the agents' centre in case there were messages from Tokyo. There had been some talk, Marsha recalled, that Hideo was in love again and that this time he might even marry.

"You've seen Frans?" he asked Marsha.

"Yes. This morning."

"Did he seem okay to you?" Hideo had a way of raising one eyebrow to indicate puzzlement. It must have taken years to perfect.

Marsha shook her head.

"Not to me either," Hideo stated. "Nothing all right about him when I saw him at the museum. I thought he was wearing lipstick. Hm." Hideo was seeking confirmation.

"Lipstick ..." Marsha said noncommittally.

"Something very pink. It did not suit him, I thought. Still," he shrugged, "a man is entitled to wear whatever makes him happy."

Marsha agreed eagerly. Crazy or not, Frans should be allowed to carry on with his fantasies. "Did he speak to you?"

"No. He avoided me. Odd. He had been very friendly to me ever since I became Andrew's partner in the East." He smiled displaying the gold caps on his front teeth. Hideo spoke almost perfect American English. He had studied literature at Harvard, something else at Columbia. All this less than ten years after the war. Not the best time to be Japanese in America. He had told her this late one evening after a Bertelsmann party when a group had gone on to the Brückenkeller to finish the evening. Hideo had been drinking his whisky neat all evening, and it had taken its toll.

"Did Andrew tell you why he had gone to Amsterdam to meet Frans?" Marsha asked. Not much point in beating about the bush.

Hideo stared at her, expressionless. This was not altogether unusual for Hideo, who tended to excise all expression from his face other than joy at seeing you again. Most people would enter this expressionless void and try to fill it with chatter. Not Marsha. She waited.

"Why do you ask?" He surrendered.

"Frans is worried about a big business deal he and Andrew had cooked up and what might happen to it now that Andrew is dead."

Hideo nodded. "An excellent thing to worry about," he said appreciatively.

It was impossible to tell whether he didn't wish to discuss the subject because he knew all about it and considered it off-limits, or because he knew nothing about it and therefore considered it offensive to discuss something he should have known about but didn't. In any event, he suggested that Frans could take up the matter with Andrew's assistant.

Marsha noticed that even Hideo referred to the assistant by job description rather than name. Andrew had run through a number of assistants, roughly one per year (that Marsha knew of), all starting with gusto and overbearing confidence, revelling in reflected power as they hit their stride, only to disappear as suddenly as they had come on the scene. Andrew, it seemed, had not learnt how to delegate.

"Sam," Marsha said. This one had lasted much longer than was customary for Andrew. He had been at the last Frankfurt Fair, and he was smart enough to conclude the deal with Marsha for the *Vatican Secrets*. Unfortunately, the secrets, once A&M's legal department was finished with them, were thoroughly understated, gentle bedside reading for nuns. "He is still here. Saw him in the morning waddling through the aisles with one of the senior Penguins. He's taken Andrew's demise in stride, hasn't he?" Sam had worn a wide smile, his hands in his pockets, splayed feet, slight swagger.

"For every thing there is a season," Hideo observed obliquely. "In Andrew's absence, this may be his."

Hideo offered to have tea with Marsha later, if she liked, before inspector Hübsch came by for the last time. Hübsch had prevailed upon Hideo to come to the police station for a last chat at five o'clock. He was catching the late plane to Paris, and going on to New York that night. He wanted to be there for Andrew's funeral. Reluctantly, Marsha conceded that she would see him there.

"Ah yes," Hideo said, "Andrew had his critics, but he was the very best literary agent your country produced. He had an eye for the excellent, and if not the top of the literary pinnacle, the most likely to succeed. They will all come to the funeral, just to see who else is there. A strange business we're in." He nodded and pursed his lips to underline his point.

"He certainly changed your business, didn't he," Marsha said, not expecting a confirmation. Perhaps it had been because of his American education, no one knew, but Hideo was struggling even into the nineties, when the Japanese had already discovered Danielle Steel, Drury Carter, John Grisham, Harlequin romances, Larry McMurtry, and a plethora of other American best-selling authors. His contacts in New York were second to none, but he was no match for Tom Mori at home. Until Andrew put him in charge of his list.

"Quite. And perhaps yours?"

"Mine?"

"With Miss Drury Carter, the new novels, you would not have been able to bid for them had she remained with Alex."

Marsha had to admit, no matter what her private feelings towards Andrew Myles, Hideo was right. Alex would have kept

Margaret at Doubleday, the company that had invested the most in developing her talents and fostering her following.

"I suppose the police have asked you about Jerry," Marsha tried again.

Hideo nodded. "I hardly knew him. Couldn't help them."

"They weren't working on something together, were they?"

Hideo shrugged convincingly. "Nothing that would have two men murdered, I think. It's the same question Hübsch has been asking. And I gave him the same answer."

Marsha was not about to mention Saddam Hussein. While she thought Frans's terrorist theory was far-fetched, given that two men had died it was not so far-fetched that she would ignore it. "It's logical to assume that they were connected. Both of them died the same way. Same poison."

"Murder is hardly logical," Hideo pronounced, his eyebrows rising for emphasis. Marsha wondered if he had been reading Sophocles. "But I think Jerry had been to New York in the last few weeks and, yes, possibly, there was something they were both interested in."

"And you?"

"Me? In what context: Me?"

"Were you going to represent a major new title for Andrew?"

Hideo sighed. "Wonderful thing about Andrew, he had so many major titles. Actually, I believe he had only major titles."

It was, as ever, difficult to tell whether Hideo was joking. In any event he was certainly not going to share confidences with Marsha today.

She had hoped to find Bertil at his stand, but the books had already been packed, the posters were down, even the long-playing, incomprehensible video of one of Bertil's Norwegian authors explaining his novel had been shut off, the player left for the Fair staff to take into storage until next year. At the A&M stand, there was a note from him. He would wait for Marsha at the Frankfurter Hof. His plane left at five.

139

In past Frankfurt years they had often made plans to meet on the last morning. It had become something of a ritual. Bertil brought the champagne, Marsha the orange juice and farewell wurst and sauerkraut. It had begun as a joke but, over time, they had grown fond of the strange combination. Nothing about Frankfurt was comfortable, so why should the food taste like home cooking? But today there was not to be a final romp of the Fair. Marsha had to return for the ugly Canadians and assure them that contrary to what her burly Russian friend might have said over the past hour, there wasn't yet a large market for American novels in Russia, certainly not large enough to warrant establishing a joint venture with the wily Vladimir.

On the other hand, she had merely agreed to usher them around the Fair, not to protect them from their own cupidity. Let Joe Kane decide how to handle it when they were back in New York. That is, if Joe still had a job. As comptroller, Joe had survived a range of bosses, but none that claimed to know more about finances than he did. There had been rumours after his last "one-on-one" with Morris. Having spent time in the oil business, Morris had great difficulties understanding the original purpose of a returns policy, in fact, he had trouble with the whole concept of returns. "Why in the world would you send a big bunch of product out," he had asked Marsha," if you stand a predictable chance of getting some thirty or forty percent back?"

"It's the tradition of the business," Marsha had told him. "Booksellers won't take your books if you're not prepared to offer returnable terms. They have the option of not taking your books, and they've been known to cut off publishers who resist. Nothing much we can do about it."

"Has anybody tried?" Morris asked.

"Not for a while."

"We'll see about that," Morris grunted. "A man's gotta have some guts." Marsha assumed Morris didn't think Joe had any. It was incomprehensible to Morris that a financial man should be setting acceptable returns margins and sell-through goals.

They had spent the rest of their "one-on-one" trying to establish what exactly it was that an editor-in-chief did, and why a publishing house needed one if agents found all the manuscripts anyway. "It's just a question of deciding how much you're gonna bid, really, isn't it?" he had asked reasonably.

"We don't always bid," Marsha had told him. Nobody had ever asked her before what it was she did all day. By the time she met people they had usually known. Nor could she have afforded to tell this idiot to piss off, much as she had wanted to, because her job was in the balance.

"Ain't that a relief," Morris shouted exuberantly. He had a habit of slapping his thigh when he thought he had made a particularly strong statement. "You publish too many damned books anyhow. So what you do, is to second-guess the agents, eh? How many times are you wrong?"

The temptation to say never was almost too great to deny, but she was concerned she might not find another job of this calibre for some months. She liked her job. She liked her department, with one notable exception, Aaron Greenspan, the young miracle worker who had never again found a best-seller once he arrived at A&M. This would be her second time being "reorganized," as the industry referred to recent firings. Someone might think she was hard to get along with. Besides, Morris had the endearing habit of calling the victims "redundancies," as if it had taken someone of his superior intellect to discover that whatever job the person had been doing was not necessary in the first place.

"Not very often," she said as ingenuously as she could manage.

"Would you please quantify," Morris had instructed, intent on maintaining eye-contact.

Marsha had wondered whether management school had also taught him the gestures that went with the eye-contact routine. He had steepled his hands and aimed the two touching middle fingers at her. She'd kept her face blank, hoping it would appear attentive and thoughtful. "About a dozen last year that, with the benefit of hindsight, I wish we had left on the table."

"That's all?" Morris raised his ample eyebrows to underline his surprise.

Marsha nodded cautiously.

"Barely accounts for all the unsold inventory, now, does it?"

It didn't. Marsha had gone on to some lengthy explanation about how decisions are made in concert with the marketing and sales departments, and how sometimes one (without being specific about names) became overly enthusiastic about a book and ordered too large an initial print-run which brought them right back to the topic of "returns." By then Marsha was almost relieved to be blaming industry practices older than she was, powerful bookstore chains and demanding wholesalers.

Thurgood seemed reasonably sober, but Morris had acquired the dishevelled look of someone left too long alone with the Russians. There were five shot glasses lined up in front of him, and Vladimir was proposing a toast to "the great state of Alberta." Morris mumbled something about "Eastern bastards," and then downed his vodka in one gulp.

"We must make a study of the documents," Thurgood told Vladimir. He wasn't looking at the papers Vladimir had pressed on him, he was watching Morris, his face as expressionless as if he were gazing out a car window along an expressway. "They do appear to be the basis for a possible agreement. Certainly an excellent investment opportunity. As the markets open up in the wake of reforms in your country, we must be there to take advantage of new market developments. We certainly have the product if you can supply the pipeline." Both Canadians were given to oil analogies.

Thurgood had risen to his feet and was stuffing a sheaf of papers into his shiny mottled brown leather briefcase, a power statement in its own right.

"We have a warehouse full of bloody product," Morris said petulantly.

"As I said, we have the product," Thurgood repeated, cutting Morris off at the pass, and turning to Marsha to announce that they were ready for the next appointment.

Vladimir winked at her once their backs were turned.

CHAPTER
TEN

S HE COULDN'T THINK OF ANOTHER PLACE TO TAKE them in Frankfurt, and she certainly hadn't made them any other appointments. The very idea of carting them along on a serious appointment made her wonder if she had made the right decision not to tell Morris what she thought of his plans for A&M in the first place. She took them through what was left of the Eastern European stands, looking for someone she knew well enough to visit the cowboys on them, or, failing that, someone she didn't need to worry about for future deals, and it didn't matter whether the cowboys bored them to distraction or not.

Help arrived in the form of Dr. Schneider. He emerged from a group of Finns toasting the end of another Frankfurt Bookfair. Alfred Schneider was head of his own family firm, one of the few German publishers who paid considerable attention to each title he published. Rumour had it he was still reading manuscripts, and watched over the cover designs of the firm's books. Their catalogue showed a somewhat eclectic taste in foreign fiction, from Ngaio Marsh to Timothy Findley, Fay Weldon to Alan Paton. He was an exceptionally cautious buyer who rarely made deals in Frankfurt and never improved on his initial offer. Despite this tendency towards firmness he had somehow landed *Conspiracy of Roses* for the German market.

"I think we will be making a deal for the new books after all, Miss Hillier," he told Marsha as he bore down on her and the cowboys. He had combed his sparse blond hair back today — usually, he combed it over his bald spot — giving him a somewhat surprised look. His customary grey suit was wrinkled, the jacket seemed damp, the navy tie askew. "I have now had the indication from Gerhardt that the club will be taking a position on the new books. The results were excellent last time, and we have the confidence now to go ahead ..."

"Which books?" Morris asked wetly.

"Miss Drury Carter, naturally," Schneider said, as if A&M's list consisted of one author. "After all, the terms are acceptable. It is not the way we prefer to do business here in Germany, as you know Miss Hillier, but what is done is done, and we are pleased to keep Miss Drury Carter with Schneider Verlag."

As Fay had said, Dr. Schneider had not wished to confirm the purchase price until he was certain that Gutfreund would cooperate. He was one of the few independent publishers in Germany who managed to hold a middle line between being beholden to the clubs and being angry with them. Whenever a large sum was involved, he would ask for time to consult his friend Dr. Gutfreund and, in the meantime, he would berate the clubs in public for their stranglehold on German literary endeavours. "We have reached a time in German publishing," he had told Herbert Lottmann in a *Publishers Weekly* interview some weeks before, "when no publisher can be the sole arbiter of what he wishes to publish. The clubs have acquired a power beyond any we had ever envisioned. They have become the main conduit to the public. We are merely the second to last stop in the supply chain. Yes, I resent it. We all resent it. Few of us dare to say so."

He was right about that. German publishers did not dare to protest the power of the clubs and none could afford to ignore them. If Bertelsmann did not choose a book you had paid a fortune for, chances were you would not make your money back.

"Two million marks," Thurgood said. His memory for detail was impeccable.

"Three books," Schneider confirmed. "I am expecting the first one to be ready for us in three months. It would be a considerable coup to have the German edition at the same time as the English language, yes?"

"Quite." It had been obvious that Schneider was directing all his words to her and ignoring the Canadians even when he was answering their questions.

"You have the first three chapters, no? At the Fair, Mr. Myles had indicated, yes? I would like to take them with me if that can be arranged."

Marsha thought of the uninspiring pages she had read the night before and declined. "We are under new management now," she told him, pointing to the vacant-eyed Morris with a jab of her head. "We have become very serious about contracts. But I will send you the chapters soon as the contracts are signed."

Schneider shoved his glasses to the bridge of his nose. "As you please," he told her primly. He glanced at Thurgood and Morris for a second and dismissed them with his eyes. Once more he turned his attention to Marsha. "You have, naturally, heard of the death of Mr. Haines?"

"Aha."

"It is a terrible thing to have two deaths at one Bookfair."

Marsha agreed with him. Even Thurgood nodded. Only Morris remained stonily fixated on a Finnish poster. Marsha wondered if he was trying to learn Finnish, or attempting to focus his eyes.

"I didn't very much like Andrew Myles, but the other man,

Haines, he was sympathetic. Yes?" Schneider had ever been a man of few and carefully chosen words, not given to much sentiment, for a German, yet he was now keeping the conversation going, as if he were waiting for Marsha to give him an opportunity for some intimacy, or confidence. He had been out in the rain. His hair was still damp, his face glistening in anticipation of something else to be said.

Marsha nodded encouragement. Though Schneider had failed to appear for their first appointment, he deserved that much.

"Yesterday he talked to me. We had been at the Heine party. Too much noise, as you would expect. A band, they had this year. I think the young people in that company are getting their way too much, no? Noise. No one can listen. It is not the way it had been in the old days when we would go to the parties to talk about books, and make deals. No. Now we go and we have the loud music and you can't hear anybody speak, yes?" He was making listening gestures, cupping his ears towards Marsha, then brushing his hand over his forehead to wipe the dampness.

Morris was becoming restless.

"I don't go to the Heine party any more," Marsha said. "There is too much coke in the washroom."

Thurgood asked, "The women's washroom?"

"The men's also," Schneider said. "And some other things, I don't know what. The cocaine it is easy to recognize because it is always looking the same. But some of the young people they are putting things into their drinks and even sometimes into their noses that you cannot recognize." He rubbed his hands over his neatly combed hair and then over his vest. "That was how the party was last night, yes? And Haines came over to me to talk. He was not completely sober, you understand, but it was a ... bisschen, no, not a little, very strange. I thought in the beginning that he wanted to offer me something, one of those drugs you Americans have brought here in the first place ..."

"He was British," Marsha said.

"Yes. Of course. He was British. Hmmm." For a moment he seemed as if he was about to change his mind and not continue, but then he went on. "That does not matter." He made sweeping gestures with his hand. "What he wanted, it seemed, was for us to have a talk on the terrace. But it was raining so he asked if he could meet me for breakfast today. I had something else arranged, and also, I do not like to make last minute breakfast appointments. But he said he had made the biggest deal of the Fair, and that he thought this would be of some considerable interest to me because he knew I was interested in this author for Schneider Verlag, also. He would be publishing Miss Drury Carter's next two books and he could sell me the German rights for the same price that A&M had set."

"He what?" Marsha squawked.

"He was quite drunk as I had said earlier, yes? But that's what he told me. And he wanted to know if we had already signed the contracts." Schneider shook his head. "It's what I said last night. That we were already dealing with you for the books and we could hardly go behind your back ..." Now he did finally look at both Thurgood and Morris. "Are you sure you have a signed contract for the two books?"

"Damned right we have a contract for the two properties," Thurgood erupted. "What kind of bloody nonsense is this?"

"What's more we paid through the nose for them and no damned way any damned Brit's gonna take them away from us, now are they? Not with our two million gone and more to come ..." Morris thundered at Schneider. "There ain't some stupid publishing rule says they can, is there?" he asked Marsha.

"No." Marsha tried to reassure him. "Jerry must have had too much to drink. We signed weeks ago. All rights," she told Schneider.

"All right," Schneider said defensively. "I was only asking. Better to be safe than surprised, no? Still. It is strange for your friend Myles to sell all rights to one buyer, no? He was himself an agent. He liked to talk up his own game, yes? It was his business."

"He couldn't resist a bargain," Marsha said. "We made the right offer, and he could get on with his other Frankfurt deals." When she saw Schneider's raised eyebrows, she repeated, "He sold us world rights."

"Okay," Schneider shrugged. "We never did have the breakfast, Mr. Haines and I. Sowieso, he was dead by the morning." He shoved his glasses up to the bridge of his nose so he could look at Marsha through the lenses.

Marsha wondered if Schneider thought she had something to do with that fact. He certainly stood waiting for her to say something else.

When she didn't, he shook hands with all three of them, promised to send his contracts in a week, and returned to the Finns. He was shaking his head all the way.

Morris wanted to go back up the escalators to see what the rest of the Americans were doing. When Marsha assured him that no one of importance would be left on Monday, and that they all returned the day before, he refused to believe her. The vodka had made him even more belligerent than usual. Thurgood's first Russian encounter had rendered him more suspicious than usual. "If all the important people are gone, who's to say it is not the best time to find the one deal they all missed?"

The one deal they all missed would be something like *The Mosaic Windows of the Far East*, a splendid photographic number with over two hundred reproductions and costing fifteen dollars a copy. That was the type of book people bought on the last day of the Fair, something showy they didn't need, and would never be able to sell in New York to marketing people who were aware of the Frankfurt craziness.

"Why wouldn't you let him see the manuscript?" Morris asked as they crossed over to Halle 9.

"Something wrong with it? Or didn't the old broad give it

to you?" Thurgood joined in. "All the fuss she made about being punctual."

"I think, perhaps, we could make it better," Marsha said cautiously. Neither Morris nor Thurgood read books, though Morris made vague references to management gurus he admired and was certainly well versed in techniques somebody must have taught him from a book. She couldn't tell whether either had heard of Margaret Drury Carter before she showed them her track record. The sales figures spoke for themselves. The novels were incidental. She was the kind of property Morris wanted to see more of around A&M.

"How?" Thurgood stopped and turned around to face her. Luckily most of the traffic was going the other way.

"Margaret and I could talk over the plot." Marsha didn't like the way the two of them were looking at her. "I think I should go and spend a bit of time with her," she ventured.

"Why?"

"To help her with the beginning. It's always the difficult part."

"For the damned money we're paying, she should do her own work," Morris grumbled. "Besides, it's not what your job is," he said confidently. "You pick 'em. That's what your job is. It's those other people in the production area who worry about the bitty details. Damned if I think we need to treat writers as if they were on some kind of free ride. You pay for the service everywhere else. Should be no different with writers. They want some fixings, they pay for it. Their name goes on the book. They get the advance. They get the money later. Royalties. Like the oil business." He laughed and slapped the rail for good measure.

"You don't think you made a mistake, now, do you?" Thurgood asked. His bald pate gleamed menacingly.

Marsha didn't like the way he said "you." "No," she said with more confidence than she felt. "Margaret's books always sell. She hasn't had a flop in over twenty years. She just needs some encouragement. That's all." Don't we all, she thought.

"Tell her on the phone," Thurgood said gruffly and started his ascent again. "And tell the niece. She is in charge of their business affairs. The contract says the manuscript has to be 'satisfactory.' No more money till she gets it right."

Marsha could barely conceal her joy on seeing an effervescent Fay coming around the corner of the Bantam booths. "Wonderful news," she cried when she sighted them. "The *Börsenblatt* has done a marvellous story about Margaret. They even used an old photograph. Youthful in a bonnet — and in colour yet. She looks so ... here, see for yourselves," she thrust the paper towards them.

Indeed, Blum had done Margaret proud. There she was, taking up most of page one, the picture dominated by her straw hat with pink ribbons, overflowing with magnolias. The headline, as Fay translated for the cowboys, read: "Romancing the Fair." In the bottom right-hand corner there was a tiny photograph of Andrew Myles.

Fay had accomplished the impossible. Margaret Drury Carter's presence had eclipsed her agent's murder.

It was the best opportunity she'd had all day to leave the Fair. She headed straight for the Hessischer Hof. Though it was raining, there was an astonishing array of cabs at the taxi-stand. The Turkish driver experimented with a new route around the Opera, but he got her there faster than ever before. Monday, the Fair traffic had dwindled.

Bertil was not yet finished packing. He had been lying on his bed surrounded by manuscripts and manuscript portions, notes from agents with outlines of manuscripts to come, and catalogue pages he had torn out and kept so as to remind himself of other manuscripts he still wanted to read. This was the part of Frankfurt Bertil enjoyed most. He was wrapped in a towel, his hair still damp from a recent shower, his fair skin lightly tanned (they had been to Majorca this summer), his smile as broad and welcoming as if he hadn't seen her in months.

"I was beginning to worry you couldn't come," he said. She had forgotten how firm his shoulders were, how pale the light hair on his chest, though she remembered the crescent-shaped scar on his thigh and how the muscles bunched up on his arms.

"I am sorry I didn't have time to stop for the kraut and wurst," she told him. But he was not listening. He had slipped her sweater over her head and was licking the space between her breasts.

They made fast and urgent love.

CHAPTER
ELEVEN

"O F COURSE, WE CANNOT KEEP YOU HERE," HÜBSCH confided to Marsha while watching her throw clothes into her oversized suitcase. She had been almost an hour late returning to her hotel, and found him pacing the corridor to her room and back to the elevators. Oddly enough, he seemed less angry at her tardiness than he was relieved to see her. "Perhaps it is better if you all go home, sowieso. Some other people to worry about your safety."

He had brought his own oversized ashtray from the lobby. He carried it with him, as he continued his pacing, and smoked. Marsha noted at least a half-dozen butts in the ashtray when she arrived.

There was a pear-shaped policewoman with him, wearing the regular pea-green German police uniform, most unflattering to a pale complexion. She positioned herself next to the door, which she left half-open after they entered Marsha's room. She didn't remove her cap, and remained almost motionless as she stared out the wide window at the grey sky.

"Ze body of Andrew Myles vill be returning to New York viz

you," Hübsch told her. Marsha could see from the way his lip curled that he thought that was particularly funny. "His mother also. She came zis morning to get him away from us. It is usual to keep ze body when zere is a murder investigation, but it seems Mrs. Myles knew some people viz influence. Zis works all over the world, I think." He stopped to watch her fold her daytime long pants into the case, her black silk dress for the *Reader's Digest* party, her maroon, off-the-shoulder for the Bertelsmann party, the fitted beige suit she had intended for the Japanese party, she wrapped the wet suede high-heeled pumps that went with all the evening-gear in a plastic bag before wedging them into the side. She had another bag for her still-damp jogging clothes.

"You Yankees spend too much time vorrying about your bodies. Fitness." He shook his head in disapproval. "Here, in Chermany, ve don't have time."

Marsha would never have guessed from the formidable effort they had put forth at the last Olympics, but she let it pass. "You have now talked to everybody, and still are no further ahead than you were yesterday morning?" she asked not very tactfully.

"Not much," he conceded. "Zis is not ze best place to eliminate suspects, as your Elizabeth George vould say." He squinted at her through the smoke. "You must read her, I suppose."

"I mustn't read her, but I do," Marsha stuffed in the plastic bag full of catalogues she had promised to study once she was back in her office.

"Ze size of ze Fair is vat is so very difficult," he told her. "Of ze 6,500 people who came zis year, zere vere almost 800 from your country and a hundred more from Britain. As far as I can tell, nobody liked Andrew Myles. None of you had anything kind to say about him, not even Sam Westwood, his assistant. Said he vas a nightmare to vork for. Took credit for everything zat came up trumps — you say zat?"

"Not really."

"And blamed everybody ven things did not." He checked his notes again. "There were four hundred of you at the Bertelsmann party, and zat is not an exact count because, as you know, it is ze party everybody vants to go to — zey crash, is the vord — and zerefore many more go in uninvited. Dr. Gutfreund told me zere are at least fifty more each year, uninvited. They slip through security. Zey borrow invitations, zey lie, zey argue zat zey lost zeirs, zey pretend to be vith the German press ..." He shook his head in amused disapproval. "I do not understand such people."

"It's a game," Marsha said.

"What is?"

"Finding ways to crash parties you weren't asked to. A game."

Hübsch shook his head again. "My neighbour's son does zat, but he is sixteen ... He will grow out of it. Vith your crowd ..." he stopped to let his annoyance hang in the air. "Ve cannot be sure of who vas at ze party. We can only be sure of ze people he came in close contact vith. One of zem is ze Englishman who vas also killed. Similar circumstances. Same poison. No fingerprints on the glasses in Jerry Haines's room, ozer zan his own. Nothing in his room zat vould suggest a killer had been zere. A few odd things in Andrew Myles's room, if you do not know he vas at the Bookfair. Of course, you knew Mr. Myles had a manuscript from Iraq?" he asked suddenly. He had stopped pacing and was looking directly at Marsha.

She continued busily to stuff manuscript outlines, fact sheets, and files into her case. She kept her back turned to him. "Ugh?" she said finally.

"A few pages. In English. I have not had time yet to read it myself, but the man who read it told me it is some sort of autobiography."

"Iraq?" Marsha asked.

"You know something about it?" Hübsch asked instead of answering her question.

Marsha shook her head. Whether Frans had it right or not, whether she believed him or not, she was reluctant to give away his secret.

"I have Mr. Haines' appointment book for ze Fair. Perhaps you would look?" He gave her one of the narrow paperback books the British publishers had. They were hand-outs from a printer. The cover said *Frankfurt International Bookfair.* Inside, there were two pages for every day, Wednesday through Monday. Marsha was surprised Jerry had planned to stay Monday.

"Did you ask him to stay an extra day?"

"Yes. He was one of the people around Andrew Myles."

That explained it. Jerry was too important for Mondays. In any event, the day was left almost blank in his Day-Timer. The single appointment was in pencil with a question mark. It was with Dr. Schneider for 7:30 a.m., the morning after Jerry had been murdered. For Sunday lunch he had pencilled in Knopf supremo Sonny Mehta. Every other day was full. He had appointments every hour, most at his booth. Sunday morning he had a two-hour session with Dr. Gutfreund. Marsha wondered if Fennell was trying to break into the bookclub business in England. Why else would those two need so much time?

His other appointments were the kind one would expect of Jerry Haines at Frankfurt. He saw some foreign agents, Marsha knew them all. He had two meetings with Alex Levine, the first one on Thursday afternoon, the second over lunch Saturday. It was marked down for an hour and a half, and they had been at the Iso-letta. Great Italian food, and longer than your usual Frankfurt lunches. They must have closed a deal, Marsha thought.

His other meals were fast, dinners and breakfasts with Americans. His one Australian appointment was with Sagfield. There was a smattering of Scandinavians, including the Bonnier group and, of course, Bertil.

He had separate times with Andrew Myles and his assistant —

half an hour — and an hour with Sam, the last appointment of the first day. Why? Marsha wondered. What could Sam have been promoting at the Fair that he didn't offer her, and Andrew had not bothered to mention at their last meeting in New York?

Saturday night he had a meeting after the *Reader's Digest* party with Lothar Menne from Heine. Lothar was one of the fixtures of Frankfurt, ebullient, enthusiastic, flushed with wine and good intentions, refreshingly cynical about the innumerable fat, illustrated tomes that floated by all the stands. "I have found it!" he had shouted triumphantly at Marsha across the Hessischer Hof lobby, filled with the older generation of publishers who had been occupying the same rooms for over forty years. Rumour has it that the only way to get into the Hessischer Hof is to be on the spot when one of them dies, but even that isn't a sure bet, because — as in Bertil's case — they frequently leave their rooms to relatives in the trade. He had a grin as wide as his face, his hair was dishevelled from a whole day of being hugged by everyone who hadn't seen him in months, and he was waving a catalogue above his head. "The book of the Fair: *Outhouses of the Mid-West*, in full colour throughout. How can anyone resist?"

Hübsch looked over Marsha's shoulder. "Ve have talked to Mr. Menne. It seems Jerry Haines did not arrive at their rendezvous. Zey vere to meet in ze lobby bar of ze Hessischer Hof at eleven. Mr. Menne vas zere till after midnight. He met some ozer friends while vaiting, and joined zem, instead. Mr. Haines had not arrived ven Mr. Menne left. On his phone zere vas no message. Is zat normal for your Fair?"

"Not when it's Lothar Menne," Marsha said. Despite his casual appearance, Lothar was one of the most powerful editors in Germany. Though he, himself, had a somewhat loose interpretation of appointment times, it would be a rare occasion that Lothar would be kept waiting, let alone stood up.

"Mr. Haines arrived at ze Lippizaner at close to twelve o'clock.

He vas drunk. But he drank three brandies and smoked two long Cuban cigars. He lit a third one, but didn't finish it. Zere vere eleven ozer people in ze bar. Not all at once, zey kept coming and going. You know how it is. People have such memory lapses ven zey drink. Two of zem vere local women who had not yet given up for the evening. Professionals. Most of zem take a vacation when the Bookfair is held. Come back for ze food fair. Your people do not like to pay for zeir sex. Zey like to get it free." Hübsch's upper lip curled. "Publishing ..." he said.

Marsha zipped up her Samsonite suit-bag and hefted it over her shoulder. "I am leaving for the airport now, Inspektor, if you have no objection."

"Perhaps I could drive you?" Hübsch asked. "I did not mean to be offensive."

"Sure," Marsha said. "You didn't mean to be offensive."

"I did not," Hübsch insisted. "It is ze truth. Your crowd has no use for ze ladies of Frankfurt. Ask anyone. Unless zey are in your business. I did not mean to suggest zat only ze outsiders have sex vith each ozer during your Fair. The Germans do it, too. Did Jerry Haines have someone ... how you say ... usual?"

Marsha stared at him. "Usual?"

Hübsch scratched his forehead. He stood at the door decidedly not looking at Marsha. "I do not vish to be offensive. Usual, as with you and Mr. Bertil Nystrom?"

"Not that I know," Marsha resented the invasion of her privacy, the knowingness of Hübsch. The fact that others knew about her relationship with Bertil did not bother her. The others were all in publishing. Some disapproved, some envied her. It didn't matter. So long as her career was on track she had nothing to fear from them. Hübsch was not entitled to the information.

She could have told him that both the dead men had been with Brigitte Dombert. At different times. Brigitte did not seem to have a steady relationship here, or at home. Recently she had been seen with much younger men. One of the French publishers she was hanging around last time Marsha saw her could not have been much over twenty.

Jerry had a reputation for picking up young things from his office. Perhaps Sophie Biddle was one of them.

Marsha allowed the policewoman to take her bag as they proceeded to the elevator. They exchanged smiles. She lifted the bag with the ease of someone used to lifting weights. She made it seem as if carrying suspects' suitcases was part of her job. Hübsch, himself, had not made any move towards the case. The policewoman was taller than Hübsch, and wider. She had still to say a word. Her expression had not changed during the entire interview. It was possible, Marsha thought, that she didn't understand English.

In the car he told her that the others in the bar at midnight included two German booksellers who had come for the end-of-the-Fair bargains, he had talked to both of them. They were from Köln and neither of them had ever met Jerry Haines. They had been surprised that he had offered to buy them drinks. Neither had been invited to the Bertelsmann party.

The American literary agent, Levine, knew both Andrew Myles and Jerry. No love for Andrew, but he had just made a big deal with Haines. Nowhere near Myles when he was killed.

There had been a remainder buyer from the U.K., Levine remembered him, but no one remembered his name. He had paid cash for his drinks. He had been chatting with Jerry when Frans arrived. Jerry had told Frans and Alex Levine that the guy was only interested in bargain books and had been so boring that Jerry had almost gone to bed. It was hard to imagine a remainder buyer would have been invited to the Bertelsmann party, whoever he was. Impossible he would have known an agent like Andrew Myles.

The remainder buyer knew who Jerry was — everyone in the trade in England knew who the managing director of the Fennell group was — but they did not move in the same circles.

There had been a young editor from Fennell named Sophie Biddle.

She had been in the bar a few minutes before her boss. She told Hübsch that Jerry had asked her to come to the bar and meet him there. At midnight. Sophie told Hübsch that she had ordered one drink, a glass of wine; she hadn't even finished it when she left. She said she had gone to bed around one a.m. Alone. She was staying at the Savoy and Jerry had helped her into a taxi. She had claimed she was having a late-night business discussion with him because they had not been able to speak privately all day. She said there had been a major new deal her boss wanted to talk to her about that night. It was new. It had come up late in the evening, and he didn't think it could wait till the next day.

"What was it?" Marsha asked.

Hübsch thought for a few moments while he lit another cigarette. "I'm not at liberty to tell you," he said finally. "I have learnt enough about your business to know zat much."

For a while they travelled in silence.

"You know Miss Biddle?" Hübsch asked.

She didn't. What she did know about Jerry's love life was that many young things from his office went to bed with him in hopes of speedy promotion. To Jerry's credit, he neither promised promotions, nor delivered them to his many lovers.

Hübsch asked Marsha whether Jerry had a reputation for playing the field.

She told him to ask people who had been closer to him.

The others in the bar, Hübsch told her, had confirmed Sophie's story. She hadn't stayed very long and, while their heads had been close together, there had been no touching or kissing.

Sophie thought he was drunk. He had some trouble negotiating his way through the centre of the lobby, avoiding the chairs. But she thought his conversation had made sense.

The barman had told Hübsch that Bertil arrived at a quarter

past one, in time for last drinks. Jerry Haines had bought him a brandy. He had been buying brandies for everyone at the bar.

The British remainder buyer said very little. He left before closing time and seemed unsteady.

Van Maeght had arrived a few minutes after Bertil. He got his brandy right away as the barman was hoping to close. He had sat on the stool vacated by the British remainder buyer. He had been quiet. Jerry Haines was too busy talking with Alex to pay him much heed.

Sam Westwood, Andrew Myles's assistant, had poked his head in once, greeted Levine, Nystrom, and van Maeght, had a few words with Jerry, but refused the proffered brandy. He said he had to go to bed early, he had some big deals cooking.

Alex Levine had almost no recollection of the hour he had spent in the bar. He told Hübsch he thought they had all been talking about Andrew Myles. Jerry Haines had liked Myles about as much as anyone else did. Levine had admitted that he, himself, had hated Myles and took credit for inventing a nickname for him. "The Jackal." But he had no reason to hate Haines. They had concluded a three hundred thousand dollar deal on Saturday, and Levine had thought they were celebrating.

"Something to do wiz ze Harvard Business School," Hübsch said. He was sitting in the back of the car with Marsha. The policewoman drove. "Zat leaves van Maeght." Hübsch lit another cigarette from the butt of the one he had just finished, then threw the butt out the window.

"There was the threatening note," Marsha prompted. She had rolled her window as far down as she could, as had the policewoman. Hübsch seemed unaware or uninterested in the fact that she was choking on the dense smoke.

"Zat," Hübsch said, "does tie him to ze murder. Not ze opposite. Curious, zat. You know ze letters vere cut out of the *Allgemeine Zeitung* two days before Andrew Myles vas killed?"

"You told me."

"You know who cut zem out?" Hübsch appeared to be enjoying himself.

"No."

"Andrew Myles," he said with satisfaction. "Ven ve vent through all ze bits of dirt and little pieces of paper in his room, guess what ve found?" He didn't wait for her to guess. "Ve found some letters cut out of ze same newspaper. Only zey vere not so good. He vas not clever viz ze scissors, Mr. Myles, so he tossed avay ze letters he nipped in ze middle and cut out some new ones to make his little note." Hübsch was watching Marsha for a reaction.

Her mind tried to race over the story Frans had told her. It was hard to concentrate with her stomach heaving, but she did reach the conclusion that Myles could have been motivated by greed. If Frans was scared away from the Hussein memoirs, Andrew could have them to himself. He wouldn't have to share.

"Vat reason, Miss Hillier, vould Andrew Myles have to snip little letters out of ze *Allgemeine* to paste togezer a nasty note to Mr. van Maeght?"

"You should ask Frans that, not me," Marsha said.

"Of course, I asked him zat." Hübsch flicked the ash from the end of his cigarette onto the floor of the car. It was already covered in ash and other debris. "He said it vas a practical joke, zat you do zese jokes in Frankfurt. He said Mr. Myles was a friend of his and zey had made many deals togezer, and Andrew Myles liked ze joking. But ve both know zat Andrew Myles had no friends."

Marsha leaned out the window as far as she could. When the air didn't improve she told Hübsch to stop smoking or she would have to hitch a ride from the side of the road. He seemed surprised, but he did toss the live cigarette out the window.

She wanted to ask him if he believed van Maeght's story, but she had promised him that his secret was safe.

"Haines left ze bar at a little before two. He vas last seen valking towards the elevators. Ze barman said he vas drunk, he had trouble valking. Veaving around ze place. He had been very loud and happy all night, very excited, told everyone it vas ze biggest night of zis Frankfurt business and zat he would go home knowing he had done more here zan any ozer Frankfurt Fairs. Asked ze barman for aspirins before he went to bed, said he had a bad headache. Bertil Nystrom did not seem quite as happy, but you would know more about zat zan I do." Amazingly, Hübsch chuckled. "Haines was found dead at four a.m.," he continued. "His wife had been trying to reach him all night. When she still could not find him at four, she insisted the night manager should go to his room. It is she who found him."

"You think he was killed after he left the bar?"

"No," Hübsch said. "I think he was killed between eleven and two. That's when the poison was administered. Liquid nicotine is not so fast acting when you are a smoker. He vas drinking. He didn't know he vas dying. At first ze poison stimulates ze brain. He would have been very excited. Ze poison can take up to five hours. Not longer. The symptoms vere masked by ze alcohol. In ze end, zere is respiratory failure, paralysis, sometimes convulsions, zen death. But in ze Lippizaner, he vas a happy man. If he felt a bit dizzy, if his heart pounded, he vould have thought it was happiness, and alcohol. He suspected nothing. He vas celebrating. Your friend, Mr. Nystrom, tells me he was not usually a very generous man. Yet he vas buying drinks for everyone, even our ladies. What ve don't know is what made him so happy he forgot to meet a man as important as Lothar Menne. What vas so important he forgot an appointment he had made a couple of weeks earlier by fax."

Marsha had no idea, and the one thought that crossed her mind was too unpleasant and too unlikely to contemplate. He could not have found a way to buy the next lot of Drury Carters. Surely, Margaret would have told Marsha if she was going to deal with Jerry Haines. No matter how close she had once been to Jerry. The contract was signed.

They let her out at the Lufthansa entrance for overseas travellers. "Ve also do not know why he vas talking about you, Miss Hillier." He helped her lift her heavy black attaché case onto an airport cart. "Zat is what I vas hoping you vould tell me. Zat, and where you vere last night between one and three. Did you go out after your friend left you?"

"I have no idea why Jerry was talking about me last night." Marsha wheeled around to leave. "And if you knew Bertil Nystrom visited me around one in the morning, you would also know I never left my room."

"There are stairs," Hübsch said.

"You did not mention I was in the bar."

"No. But a man drinking like Jerry Haines did, he had to take leave of ze bar many times."

"And I was lurking in the men's washroom?"

"Were you?" Hübsch asked as he wheeled around towards Marsha.

"Goodbye Inspektor Hübsch," Marsha called over her shoulder, as she headed for the check-in counters. "Thanks for the ride."

"Goodbye, Miss Hillier," said the uniformed policewoman, and she added in perfect English: "We will hope to see you here again next year."

CHAPTER
TWELVE

MARSHA HAD BEEN WORRIED THAT BY SOME DREAD-ful coincidence Morris and Thurgood might have found their way onto this flight, but they had not. She was able to spend most of the flight sipping wine and reading. She saw no one she knew and a casual stroll up and down the plane did not reveal the identity of Andrew Myles's mother, if indeed his mother was on the plane. As she reflected on Hübsch's various interview and interrogation techniques, it became clear that he had been trying to get something from her she didn't have to give, and telling her that Andrew's mother was going to be on the plane could have been intended to solicit some reaction.

The only woman in business class old enough to have been Andrew's mother bore no resemblance to him. She was taller than Marsha, had a long neck, aquiline features, and a sonorous voice she exercised in cheerful chatter with her seat companion. He was a youngish man with a yellow cravat and bulging eyes that rested uneasily on Marsha whenever she passed. They were much too cheerful to be accompanying a corpse, particularly the corpse of a close relative.

During the last hour Marsha made a few notes on Margaret's manuscript and concluded that her first reading had been almost too kind. The writing was adequate, but the difficulty with the sort of fiction Margaret wrote was that readers came to it with certain, well-grounded expectations, and they had every reason to have them satisfied. This was not writing for its own sake, to please the author's own sense of what fine literature was all about, and it wasn't some form of self-expression that needed an outlet no matter how unappreciated. No, Margaret's brand of fiction had to fit a mould, as surely as a pair of shoes had to fit your feet. You would no more expect your shoes to turn backward, or into snow-shoes than you would expect a historical romantic thriller to decide it wanted introspection.

What frightened her was the possibility that Margaret might be intending her next book to be precisely what Marsha held in her hand. She had seventeen best-sellers to her credit. What if this was the moment she had chosen to explore the realm of serious literature? What if Jerry had been right, and what Margaret was looking for this time was a fitting monument to a lifetime of writing?

It was true Margaret had, herself, insisted on seeing her books in hardcover. She had been happy enough with the gold embossed paperbacks before. But that decision had turned out to be the right one. As if by instinct, she had sensed that her avid readers were ready for the challenge of the hardcover book. *Conspiracy of Roses* went directly to the top of the hardcover best-seller list while *Midnight Dance* was still riding high on the paperback list.

But there had been no change in the formula for success. Only the price changed when they went into hardcovers. Both Margaret's earnings and the publishers' profits followed. That's what had made the twenty million dollar deal so easy to make. The books would be displayed at the front of the stores because book-sellers knew what sold. Borders and Barnes & Noble would lay in huge orders, the computers told them what their Drury Carter sales had been the last time, and, predicting that her fans would not want to delve too deeply into the interior of a bookstore, even if it was a cosy, welcoming superstore, they would instruct their managers to display them in the windows and build islands of them close to the entrance. That kind of display was worth more than television advertising and, except for the chance that more than half the books came back — never a threat with Drury Carter — a great deal cheaper.

What these assumptions did not include was Margaret deciding to write a different kind of book. While her latest heroine was deeply troubled, as she ought to be in a Carter novel, she was not troubled by discovering her own sexuality, nor the over-whelming passion she should have felt for a man she had just met. No. She was troubled by unresolved feelings about her dead adoptive father, for god's sake. She was trying to come to terms with her own identity as the daughter of her real father, the gam-bler, now unhappily in jail. She was examining her soul to deter-mine whether she would follow in his footsteps and take a chance running the riverboat or continue at the dry-goods store her adoptive father had left her. There was every indication she would stick with the flour sacks.

And there was something positively weird about her love of dogs. As far as Marsha could remember, there had never been dogs in Drury Carter books before. It was difficult to imagine what pos-sible role there could have been for dogs either in *Midnight Dance*, or in *Conspiracy of Roses*, and though Marsha had not read all of Margaret's seventeen books, she knew enough about the genre to assume that dogs would not be central to any of them. Sometimes they were decorative, as when the heroine thoughtfully strokes her long-haired dachshund or Pekinese while listening to her family's unreasonable demands concerning a suitable match, or when one of the romantic male leads does a spot of hunting that might involve the baying of hounds, but nowhere was a dog important for the plot.

Why now?

And if the dogs were not going to be pivotal, why did the heroine waste fifteen of the precious one hundred pages agonizing over their fate now that she had to run the dry-goods store her adoptive father had left her when he so thoughtlessly died?

And if she had the choice between the riverboat, ramshackle though it was, and the dry-goods store, why in the name of the nine million dollars for this book alone, did she choose to run the store? The inventory-taking alone occupied the better part of chapter two.

The plane landed a little after six, not too late to call Margaret, she thought. While they waited for the luggage to arrive, she dialled information for New Brunswick, Canada. Numbers for Grand Manan were included in the St. Stephen directory. There was no listing for Drury Carter, or Drury, or Carter alone. When she asked the operator if there was an unlisted number, she got a brief lecture on respecting other people's privacy. If this Carter person wished to be found, she would surely have listed her number, and if she didn't wish to be found, the St. Stephen telephone operator was certainly not going to assist in locating her.

It was too late to call the office. Though she was fairly sure her secretary would still be there, arranging her desk for the morning, the new telephone system the cowboys had installed shut down at five as an austerity measure. In Larry's version of A&M each senior person had his or her own number in addition to the extensions from the main switchboard. Larry thought it prudent to have his people work long hours and remain reachable to the outside world. He knew about auctions, time differences with the West, understood emergencies at home, and had become familiar with a sufficient number of authors over the fifteen years at the helm of A&M to recognize that publishing was not a nine-to-five job. Morris regarded a highly disciplined workforce whose hours only varied by exception as one of the critical success factors that would realize their mission. If your work could not be effectively accomplished within those parameters, there was a problem with your task-orientation, or focus, or both.

She would call Margaret in the morning.

Irwin was waiting behind the customs barrier. At first, Marsha thought she could evade him by attaching herself to a group of Italian tourists, but their guide stopped them five feet short of his stakeout. Even with his glasses off he had no trouble picking her out of a crowd of dark-haired strangers. He was convinced he looked more dashing without his glasses, though he had trouble distinguishing faces at a distance. He had experimented with contact lenses, but they didn't make trifocals, or he didn't know how to use them. It was difficult to understand how a man of Irwin's corporate stature could be so insecure about his appearance, or why he still harboured such a fragile ego. After her days with Bertil, who was at perfect ease with his body and the rest of his relaxed self, Marsha was not looking forward to Irwin's anxieties.

He was a small-boned man, not much taller than Marsha, in his early fifties, he had black, deep-set eyes that darted from side to side as he surveyed the immediate surroundings for signs of people who might recognize him. He had a thin, finely drawn nose, high cheekbones, and a small, somewhat downturned mouth that made him seem more nervous than he actually was. His skin was stretched tightly across his face, the only lines around his eyes and, faintly, from the corners of his mouth. He was an overall beige or oatmeal colour, sometimes tending towards olive after his sessions in the Sixth Avenue body shop where he was massaged once a week under tanning lights.

Marsha had met him two years before at a party the Literary Guild had hosted for Mayor Koch. At that time he still had had some political ambitions, which he had since abandoned in favour of the pleasures of the Dow. Irwin ran an investment firm that commanded the respect of pension-fund managers on both sides of the Atlantic, a fact that gave him the power to influence the stock market. His influence was such that even his competitors listened when he talked.

Unlike his competitors, Irwin was fond of reading. He didn't just follow the financial press from New York to London and Tokyo (he subscribed to the *Times*, the *Wall Street Journal*, *Forbes*, *The Economist*, the *Spectator*, *The Daily Telegraph*, the *Hong Kong News*, the *Financial Post*), he also read *Vanity Fair*, *Esquire*, *The Australian*, *Maclean's*, the *Nation*, the London weekend papers, and two or three books a week. His tastes were eclectic, though he tended towards biography and history on the one hand, and what he called quality fiction on the other. He was fond of William Trevor, T. Coraghessan Boyle, Brian Moore, John Banville, John Irving, and Robertson Davies, among others. When Marsha had pointed out his strong bias in favour of male novelists, he devoured four of Margaret Atwood's recent novels, tried two Ann Beatties, reread Jane Austen and George Eliot, and started on the Brontë sisters.

Finally, he had admitted that she was right; he preferred male writers.

In the beginning, Marsha had found him to be a fascinating companion for the infrequent lunches his secretary arranged. The pretext had been his interest in writing a book about the investment business. It was a subject he knew better than most and he had the personality and the credibility to carry it off. What had puzzled Marsha was why he would bother to write a book. His reputation, where it mattered in his lights, certainly didn't need it. But she enjoyed their conversations, and the elegant milieu he had chosen. His secretary had booked their tables at Le Cirque, La Côte Basque, and Lutèce. Nothing but the best. They are not only elegant places to eat, they are the best places in New York to be seen, and to watch others who like to be seen. Barbara Walters, Marisa Berenson, and Malcolm Forbes are frequent guests. Andrew Myles had favoured Le Cirque. It was a place he took his newest acquisitions, authors who had never dreamt of dining anywhere other than the corner bistro with their publishers. It is here that he had convinced them to leave their current agents, editors, publishers, and to succumb to the taste of real money and what it could bring. It was part of his technique.

Later, Irwin had found the restaurants himself. They were more likely to be on the Lower East side, pleasant and unpretentious, far from both the financial districts and publishers' haunts. He was no longer talking about the possibility of writing a manuscript about the financial business, he was interested in learning more about Marsha. Near the end of their first summer she had abandoned her customary caution and told him about her strange childhood, her more outrageous dreams, and her unfulfilled desires. Somewhere among those was the fact that she was not now and never had been married. Generally, Marsha had taken the position that her lack of permanent relationship had been a mere oversight, that she had no need for a male fixture in her life, that she preferred not to share her apartment, and certainly wouldn't leave it to move in with somebody else.

This, naturally, was a lie.

The facts were that she had endured an identity crisis around the age of twelve, when her mother convinced her that, after all the riding, the military exercises, the judo lessons and shooting practice, she was a girl. Girls, her mother had insisted wore flouncy dresses, pretended they could not climb trees, and went to garden parties with their parents. Her father had fought bravely, but when Marsha began to menstruate, he started losing ground. After a summer of switching from mornings building bivouacs in fatigues to afternoons attending luncheons in pinafores and back again, the old general had given up his daughter, restraining his natural roar of disapproval to mere snorts of derision every time he saw her dressed in her "social clothes."

At first, Marsha had enjoyed her mother's newfound attentions, but found the luncheons dull, the conversations intentionally oblique and, hard as she tried, she could not refrain from offering to beat the boys at whatever battle of strengths they chose. The general had given a rigorous course of training.

The Bishop Strachan School uniform had seemed a relief. Her friendship with Judith had saved her from a deep sense of despair, an indecision of genders, and a conviction that she could never please either parent. She had become frighteningly thin and intro-spective. Judith, though she didn't know it, had saved her life.

Through university and after, she had developed the art of the temporary relationship, fine-tuned it, sometimes enjoyed it, and stayed away from real emotions. Now she was on the prowl for something more traditional. When she met Irwin, she thought she was ready.

Irwin, as it turned out, already had a wife and two attractive children, all living in suitably upscale accommodation in Con-necticut. The 57th Street apartment in New York was there for Irwin's use only, a rooftop extravaganza with Jacuzzi, palm trees and Victorian furniture, to provide him with all the comforts of home when he had to stay in town late. Most weekdays were late. Only the weekends were sure Connecticut days.

It was not until last summer that Marsha had discerned that Irwin was not really planning to leave his wife. Had there not been Marsha's usual command performance in Boston for Christmas, she might have suspected sooner. Christmas would have been the time to put his resolve to the test. But Marsha was at home for two weeks. And, although she had been through this before, the signs were harder to read this time. Perhaps Irwin himself hadn't been sure of his intentions. That's why he kept protesting that it was just a matter of time, of finding the right moment, of setting the announcement in some appropriate context. He had almost convinced Marsha that the relationship with his wife was no more than a formality, a convenience for his business and for her friends. She was, he had insisted, in love with another man, had been for several years ...

Some men remain in marriages because they are convenient.

He wore his black, fur-lined winter coat. It had been a cold, wintry October in New York. He held his gloves in one hand, the other rested on the metal barrier that guided the former passengers into the heart of Kennedy Airport. He had beautiful hands, long thin fingers, a pianist's. His mother, he had confided to Marsha, had had ambitions for him to become a concert pianist.

When he saw her, his face lit up.

He lifted her two cases as easily as if they had been filled with pillows, not paper. Under his slender frame, he was deceptively muscular. "The car is outside," he told her. "I thought you might be early."

She wondered how he had found out what flight she was on. She had given Sheila strict instructions not to tell anyone. Though they had been together for more than three years, her relationship with her secretary had never taken on intimate overtones. Marsha assumed Sheila preferred it that way. At least, she never inquired about any personal matters, and never divulged any of her own. It was unlikely that she would have let Irwin know when Marsha was arriving.

On weekdays he used a corporate Lincoln with a soft, blue leather interior and a smoke-grey glass separating the driver's section from the passengers'. It was soundproof, she had discovered.

"I have booked a table at the Lisanne," he told her, his tone light and cheerful, as if they had made plans in advance. "It has wonderful French cuisine. An antidote to all the weighty German food you've eaten the past week. No sauerkraut allowed by decree of the owners." He took her hand lightly and held it to his face. His skin was hot and dry. "I have missed you," he whispered.

Marsha reached in her handbag for a handkerchief and made some production of vigorously blowing her nose. In the process she was able to extract her hand from his, and demonstrate that she was still suffering from the annual Frankfurt cold that most publishers carried home as a memento of their stay.

"I don't think so," she told him. The last time they had met, she had been fairly honest about her desire to break off the relationship. He had acted as if he had agreed.

"You must be tired," he conceded. "It's a small, unpretentious spot near Brooklyn Heights, more or less on the way, but if you prefer another ..."

"I'm not very hungry." She thought of telling him about the Bookfair murders, but realized he wouldn't be interested. He wanted to talk, himself.

"Of course. As you wish." He pressed a button to open the window to the front and told the driver to go directly to Gramercy Park. He sank back into the seat and observed her as they ground their way through the tunnel. He had the intense, inquiring gaze of someone waiting for an answer, though no question had been asked.

Marsha looked through the window where there was nothing to see but the slowly passing tiles in their yellow glow and her own reflection, pale face and wide-set eyes. She thought she looked sadder than she felt. In September she had been lonely for him still; now, she was impatient with his intensity.

"You can't switch men as you might switch your outfits, a different one for each occasion," he said, finally. "Nor do we change with the fashion. Perhaps less dispensable than you might have thought. Or preferred. When we met you were not interested in more than a romance. You were with a lawyer, I think. Not a keeper, but pleasant for an evening or two. I expect you might have gone to bed with him that night, had I not appeared unexpectedly. It doesn't matter," he said when he saw she started to say something. "Fundamentally I am not jealous. I am not even proprietorial. What I have the right to expect is some respect for my place in this ..." he hesitated before he said it, "affair."

She thought he was going to say "relationship" and she was glad he hadn't. For Marsha, the word had lost much of its currency.

"You were happy to have an affair. Later, you changed the ground rules. Without consulting the other side. Not fair, even in tennis. Certainly not fair to the guy who thought all he had to do was to keep the ball in play."

Irwin, in addition to his gym, also played tennis at two different clubs.

"I have no desire to vanish from your life."

He was right about the ground rules. They had changed when the talk had turned to marriage. It was not a topic Marsha entertained easily. Mostly, she had assumed that marriage was for other people. She had not introduced the subject. But once it had come up, she had grown fond of the idea. It had been disappointing to discover that Irwin had no intention to leave his wife.

"You like to be with me," he stated. "I consider that to be a good start."

Marsha admitted that she did like to be with him. She also liked to be with Bertil. But with Bertil, she had no expectations other than what comfort they exchanged in Frankfurt. "Put it down to exhaustion," she said to Irwin, "but I'm not in the right frame of mind for starting anything. Maybe tomorrow. Maybe you're right about the ground rules. But I don't recall anyone publishing a set of universal rules to have affairs by. I suspect they still come without guarantees. Both sides make up the rules as they go. In September, I decided that it would be better for us not to be together ..."

"There you go again," he interrupted. "Us. Us does not come into it. Us would have to include me, and it doesn't. It is, absolutely, worse for my half of the us. That makes for a fifty-percent vote in favour." He was very handsome when he smiled. His normal expression showed pain. It was the slight downturn at the corners of his mouth.

He handed her bags to the doorman when they arrived at her Gramercy Park building. He gave him a ten-dollar tip to be sure that he took them up to her apartment.

Somehow, she had committed herself to dinner on Thursday night.

As soon as she'd kicked her shoes off and unbuckled her belt, Marsha went to the blinking eye of her telephone to check her messages. The first was from Judith, still in Jemseg, but leaving for Blacks Harbour the next morning.

Marsha called her even before listening to the rest of her messages.

"I have a room at the Compass Rose tomorrow night," Judith told Marsha. "It was hard to convince them that I was going to stay for a week or more, but I've managed to talk them down to twenty-five dollars a night. Jimmy can study in the lounge. Breakfast is included in the price."

"*Home and Garden* must have liked the idea," Marsha surmised.

"Loved it. Once we agreed I would keep the piece nice and cosy, show how a multi-million dollar lady like Drury Carter could tame her rugged surroundings and shape them to suit her innate style, Debbie Brown said she didn't even have to take it to their next ideas meeting, she was commissioning me right away and — get this — six thousand dollars if I take the pictures. She would like a lot of colour. I lied and told her I was a wizard with a camera. If I take Jimmy's point-and-shoot thing and use up four or five rolls of film, I'm sure to get a few right. She wasn't about to question my wizardry — it would cost them a fortune just to send one of their snooty social photographers out here, and he'd charge them extra for every day the light wasn't perfect, and Debbie knows it."

The last time Judith had written a *Home and Garden* story, she had interviewed a Toronto supermarket chief's wife about her successful redecoration of their new house and the design of their patio garden. Judith had spent ten days in the interviews, fit in and around the woman's challenging social schedule, and had had to agree to take time with the landscape architect, the interior designer, the bonsai specialist, and the husband. She was paid three thousand dollars. The photographer came with his own make-up artist and hairdresser, and he was done in a couple of hours. He was paid twice as much.

"Have you talked to Drury Carter yet?"

"No. She arrived back from Europe the day before yesterday, exhausted. Had her groceries delivered up to the house. The proprietor of the Compass Rose tells me she has kept pretty much to herself recently. Working on her book, they say. She and her niece have rented a place about twenty minutes' walk from the village. It's a house Willa Cather had. Did you know Willa Cather had spent time on the island?"

"No. There is a phone in the house?"

"Phone and fax. You hear a short message telling you she is working. Says she'll call you back when she can. I told it I would call again when I'm on Grand Manan. If she spends so much of her time cooped up writing, she'll be glad of some distraction. Everything I've read about her suggests she is a gregarious soul. Likes the media. And she likes *Home and Garden*, in particular — its subscribers are a big chunk of her audience. Debbie was going to fax her a note about my being one of their regulars, wouldn't take much time, wouldn't ask tricky questions, no investigative journalist trying to sniff out her secrets, guarantee of a puff piece, you know."

Marsha wrote down the phone number. "I'll meet you there before the end of the week," she said.

"Something wrong?" Judith asked. Marsha's voice sounded too hollow, too far away.

"Not even sure where to begin. There was another murder in Frankfurt. It happened the night before I talked to you. Remember I had to hang up because the local police wanted to visit? This time it was a publisher. They think the same person killed them both, and nobody knows who or why. A Dutch publisher I hardly know told me a long story about a smuggled manuscript by, of all people, Saddam Hussein. He thought it might be the reason why both Andrew Myles and Jerry Haines had been killed, but it does sound a little fantastic. On the other hand, I would hardly expect to be around two murders at the Frankfurt Bookfair. That's pretty fantastic, too." She took a deep breath. Until she had started talking to Judith, she had not known how edgy and frightened she was. She had wrapped herself in a soft blanket of feathery numbness.

"You knew this Jerry Haines?" Judith asked.

"I knew him as well as we all know one another in this trade. We kiss when we meet. We exchange publishing stories. We show off our wares. He showed off more than most, but he was more successful than most. He ran the Fennell Group. They have swallowed up big chunks of the British book business."

"And this manuscript?'

"I never saw it."

"Great. Keep it that way. The trip to Grand Manan will do you good. Put distance between you and all that. How's Bertil?" she asked, changing the subject.

"Quite happy."

"And cuddly?"

"Very."

"What else?"

"Irwin came to the airport."

"Shit. Why?"

"Long story. He wants to start again." She told Judith of Irwin's point of view and that they would see each other the next night.

Judith knew better than to argue. She had been puzzled by Marsha's unexpected interest in marriage, but hadn't said so. Judith's own experiences in this tricky area were sufficiently depressing, she couldn't lay claim to much authority on the subject.

Sheila had left one of her terse messages listing only those items she considered important to Marsha. The publishing meeting would go on as scheduled the next morning; Aaron had expressed his willingness to run it in Marsha's absence. The fact that she had bothered to tell her this tonight meant that Sheila considered it vital that Marsha be there early the next morning. While never expressing her emotions, Sheila was fiercely loyal to Marsha.

Andrew Myles's funeral was scheduled for eleven o'clock, at St. Patrick's.

Frans van Maeght wanted her to call the moment she arrived. No matter what the hour.

There was an auction for the new Michael Crichton starting at nine. Regis Philbin's agent was offering A&M the floor for his newest. There was a one-page description of the proposed book on her desk. They would wait for her opening bid till ten. They expected to close by four. She didn't need to know what was on the one-page description. After Philbin's first book, *I'm Only One Man* had joined *My Point ... And I Do Have One* at the top of the *New York Times* best-seller list, it was only a question of when he was going to follow with a sequel. Philbin was a hyperactive morning-show host, best-known for his offensive one-liners. His first book would have made little sense to anyone not listening to him regularly, but there were obviously a large number of people who did, and, more surprising still, they bought hardcover books. Her opening bid would have to be at least $500,000, possibly more. She didn't have the authority to go that high without upstairs approval and it would be foolish to expect decisions from accounting with Morris and Thurgood both away.

On the other hand, as long as Philbin kept talking, the book could not fail. She would have to determine what was riskier, to bid without authorization or to let this one pass.

One of her old-time authors had called. He was struggling with the conclusion of his newest novel and needed to talk to Marsha. Clearly, as Sheila had plucked this particular message from a number of author calls, she must have known that Marsha would care about this author personally. It certainly wasn't his sales record that had kept her a fan. He wrote innovative novels that never sold more than a few thousand, though they always earned respectful reviews. They were the kind that Aaron dismissively described as "literary novels." What they needed was a TV production. *Lonesome Dove* had given a permanent boost to Larry McMurtry's sales, though he had continued to write "literary novels."

In the sort of publishing house that Morris wanted, the sort that was as financially rewarding as the other majors were in New York, there was no room for writers like Owen Meen.

Elinor Drury had called to tell Marsha she had decided to come to Myles's funeral. She wished to meet Marsha afterwards. Sheila had set up a tentative time of 12:30 p.m. The Prunelle might be convenient. Miss Drury's flight to Saint John, New Brunswick, was scheduled from La Guardia at three. She did not want to be late and she didn't like to rush, so she'd appreciate Marsha being on time.

Morris was coming back on the Concorde in the morning and wished to meet Marsha for a "one-on-one" at three o'clock. No hint of sarcasm in Sheila's voice when she left that message. Any other A&M staffer would have changed the tone for that bit of news, but not Sheila. She would be in her office before nine to give Marsha the rest of her messages, in descending order of importance.

The apartment was too warm and airless. Marsha opened the big bay windows that looked onto the park. She had loved the view from these windows since the first time she saw it. It was what had drawn her to the old brownstone. The square was small, enclosed, and surrounded by trees. In October they were resplendent in their fall colours. Though it was too dark to see them now, she thought she could smell their moldering leaves. The wind definitely carried a faint scent of earth.

She padded into the kitchen to see how Jezebel, her fiercely independent cat, had fared in her absence. There was a full plate of Kittysnacks in Jezebel's corner of the immaculate kitchen counter. She was probably next door sampling sushi. Marsha's neighbours, a professional couple with no children, treated the cat as one of their own.

Against the building manager's advice, Marsha had a small cat entrance cut into her front door. She wanted Jezebel to have the run of the building and, if she could manage to slink by the doorman, of the park as well. The cat flap was one of her acts of rebellion against the constraints of life in New York. In a city of burglars, it was satisfying to leave an opening in an otherwise triple-chained door.

She turned on the Tiffany lamps in the living room. They had been a gift from an old-world Russian lover. Their shades spoke of hot tea and open fires, and they came in luminous golds and reds.

She walked around the apartment to reclaim her domain. Over the years she had collected some pieces of antique furniture, such as the Louis Quatorze straight-back armchairs and the marble-top table in the living room, the blue and yellow China silk curtains, and the Persian rugs on the hardwood floor. Mrs. Gonsalves kept the floors shiny, the antiques buffed. The only piece she left untouched was the roll-top desk where Marsha kept her manuscripts piled high. Most of these had been read by others already, and there was some debate among the readers whether A&M should offer contracts. Some were first novels a few of the older agents still sent her, remembering her early love of exuberant fiction.

She poured a generous amount of Remy Martin into a snifter and curled up by the artificial fireplace, the phone cradled by her shoulder, Owen Meen's manuscript in her lap.

He answered on the first ring. "I've been waiting for you to call," he told her. "You read it on the plane." What Owen lacked in financial rewards, he made up in confidence.

"A week ago," she told him.

"I haven't been able to write the ending. It's as if the characters won't let go. I simply cannot shut the door on them. They keep on talking. The woman insists she deserves another chance. She makes me feel guilty, as if I let her down ..." He took a deep breath. "What do you think?"

Marsha didn't much like the woman. Yet it was her brittle, funny take on life that kept the novel at such a perfect pitch. "Owen, you have created her the way she is. She cannot change into another person without your sacrificing the whole book and starting again. It's how she behaves, and how she sees things that give everyone else in the novel licence to tread on her in the end. If you were to give her another chance, and change her at the end, you would have to force us to see the others as villainous. There would be no justification for their action."

"I'd have to start again ..." Another deep breath. "A hundred thousand words in third draft."

"Think about it."

"You like the way it ends?"

"Yes, and so will your readers. It's been two and a half years, they deserve a new Meen next Christmas."

He read her the newest version of the final paragraph. It was as brilliant as the previous one, but softer. She laughed at the last line.

It was the confirmation he had wanted.

She dialled Drury Carter's number. The answering machine offered to take messages but gave no hint that anyone would listen to them.

She finished her drink, tossed her clothes into the hamper in the bathroom, and settled into a long scented bath.

CHAPTER
THIRTEEN

Despite the brandy, jet lag woke her at around five. She tried a number of face-down positions on her pillow, lay back to stare at tiny cracks in the ceiling, tried counting the flowers on her wallpaper, revisited warm thoughts of Bertil. Nothing worked.

Marsha had done this too often to fool herself into believing she would toss and turn back to sleep. She wrapped her thick terry-cloth robe around herself and made coffee. Jezebel had returned during the night, eaten her dinner and was still sleeping curled in one of the round shoulders of the white couch.

She drank her coffee and read the *New York Times* propping her back against the couch's other shoulder, making sure she did not disturb the cat. It was a slow news day. There was an interview with Deepak Chopra, the medical doctor who had given himself up to meditation and stardom on PBS. To reach the pinnacle of success, he recommended learning how to get in touch with the innermost essence of your being. When the knowledge offered by Dr. Chopra was incorporated into your consciousness, he promised, "it will give you the ability to create unlimited wealth with effortless ease ..." His newest book, at $24.95, was small price to pay for unlimited wealth, mused Marsha. How many of the three million people who had read the doctor's last book of musings had reached this plateau of success? If they failed, they could try again with this one. Not everyone can delve into their innermost essence the first time.

There was a brief mention of the Frankfurt Bookfair. John Grisham's newest had fetched record sums from all, including the Chinese. His new agent, editor, and friend who had handled the deals for him said it was the first time Chinese publishers had participated in an auction for rights. When they bought rights at all, Marsha recalled, they would decide the winner in advance and bid only once. That was on the few occasions they offered to pay money for a trade book. She wondered what they would make of Grisham's tightly packed American courtroom dramas in a country without juries, without an adversarial justice system, where guilt was not a matter of argument but decree. Perhaps they would prescribe Grisham's novels to school children to show that the democratic way did not work.

Margaret Drury Carter's presence got a brief mention, along with the other major writers who had graced the Fair with their presence.

There was a letter to the editor praising Andrew Myles's abilities as an agent, and protesting the tone of the obituary that must have run while she was away. Judging by the letter, it had included some unflattering quotes from publishers, and fellow travellers. The letter was signed by a Stephen Myles. Marsha hoped that Sheila would have clipped the obituary for her.

Elsewhere in the paper there was an announcement of Andrew's funeral and the wake afterwards at his mother's place in the Trump Tower.

She called Frans van Maeght. It was eleven-thirty in Amsterdam.

"I have been terribly worried for you," he said when he recognized her voice. "I had burdened you with such responsibility. Not at all fair. You did not tell ... anyone?"

"No," Marsha reassured him.

"Juris, my friend, you remember, he did come to my hotel yesterday. As I was checking out. He explained everything. There had been a delay. The ... leader ... you know, he wanted to wait. There were some tricky negotiations with the French, over ... I'm not sure about this phone, but you can guess. He had some other matters on his mind. Not only the manuscript."

"And all that stuff about Andrew Myles and Haines?"

"That stuff? My overactive imagination." He chuckled a little.

"But Myles and Haines are still dead," Marsha remarked.

"Of course they are still dead," Frans was becoming irritable, "but nothing to do with me or this manuscript. I was too quick to jump to the conclusions, that is all. Juris assured me all is as before ..."

"And you believed him."

"Why wouldn't I?" he declaimed. "We are back to where it started: with me. I will try to check if Jerry left instructions about the deal with his staff. I fear it may all have been verbal between him and Andrew. When I asked him about it in Frankfurt, he seemed not to know what I was talking about." Frans sighed loudly. "That was the last evening in the Lippizaner. You know, I had gone there, especially to ask him about it, then. Such a very confusing evening, so noisy in the bar. Jerry was drunk, of course. Later, he died." It seemed Frans was blaming Jerry Haines for his own demise.

"You have the manuscript?" Marsha asked.

"No, of course I don't have the manuscript." Frans sounded impatient. "I explained this part to you before. The manuscript will be exchanged for the guaranteed payment in cash only. With Myles dead, I will have to start again. Simple."

None of this sounded simple, and Marsha was thinking she

didn't really want to read Saddam Hussein's memoirs, after all. "You know who wrote the threatening note to you at the Fair?"

"Note? Which note?"

Was he being deliberately obtuse, or had he really forgotten about his fear of imminent death? "The one that had you dressed like a clown at the railway station."

"That note, I do not know. But it wasn't serious anyway, was it? I am still here. Nothing to do with the manuscript, in my opinion. Probably what I told Inspector Hübsch, it was a hoax. Some fool's idea of a joke. Hübsch had the crazy notion it might have been Andrew himself who sent it to me."

"They found some cut-out letters in his room," Marsha said. To her, it made perfect sense that Andrew would have tried to scare Frans off. That would have given him a clear run at the deal. With Frans out of the way, he wouldn't have shared the commission with anyone else. He would have seen this as his deal the moment Frans brought him into it.

"I know. I know. No matter. Andrew's dead. I will conduct this on my own, now. Question is, do you want to be part of it? Do you want to offer for the U.S. rights? English language, if Fennell doesn't have it on record?"

Marsha thought of the good doctor Chopra's admonition, reached into her spiritual chapbook, and told Frans she would think about it.

He said he would find a way to get it to her while she thought.

She searched in her closet for something suitable for a funeral and came up with a deep burgundy dress, covered it with her black Givenchy coat, pulled on a pair of sturdy white socks over her stockings, stepped into her well-worn running shoes, and hurried down the back stairs to Gramercy Park. In her backpack she carried only those papers she thought were essential for today; she would take the rest of her Frankfurt goodies another time.

It was an hour's walk to the office. She thought the cold morning air would clear her head.

It didn't. She stopped in Mama Jo's for a double espresso and a raspberry Danish. Now she was at least ready for the day.

The doorman at 600 Fifth Avenue didn't recognize her. The cowboys had let the last two men go, rather than agree to shift work. The new guy spent most of his time dozing. Marsha had to produce her new plastic identification card. He barely glanced at her as he shoved it through the automatic style.

The morning sun glinted off the papers in her office. They were settled into tall orderly piles on the left side of her desk, they weighed down the low coffee table, they wedged themselves into one corner of the couch, and they had even mushroomed along the window ledge. Sheila greeted her with a mug of black coffee and a handful of messages. She was wearing her form-fitting black suit, her sensible patent-leather shoes, opaque black panty-hose. She should have been the one going to the funeral.

"Will you be attending the publishing meeting at nine?" she asked, directly to the matter at hand, no time wasted on small-talk.

Marsha said she would.

"I will inform Aaron, then," Sheila said and headed out of the room. It was difficult to tell whether Sheila had some sympathy for Aaron's ambitions. She was resolutely polite to him.

Marsha called Philbin's agent and left a message on the answering machine that A&M bid $650,000 for the floor with ten percent topping privileges. That meant every other publisher would have to start over the six fifty mark, and at the end of the bidding, she would have the right to top the highest offer by ten percent. She had purposely left the questions of royalties and timing of the advance unattended. The agent, being an old hand at these things, would never think of such details this early in the auction and the omission could give her an out, should Morris go crazy about the money.

There was a fax from Rita Fessenbach confirming the contract for the Adenauer manuscript. In the cold light of the New York dawn, Marsha was no longer as pleased with her acquisition as she had been at the Bertelsmann party. Would America still care about Adenauer? Enough to buy a hardcover book? Would the superstores' reading public even know who Adenauer was?

You couldn't publish a book about such a major international figure — albeit a German one — in paperback; that would relegate it to the small press piles, even with the A&M imprint on its spine. She tried to shake off her temporary loss of confidence. A person in her position in New York could not afford to give in to doubt. Altogether a dreadful frame of mind for the coming publishing meeting.

She surveyed the manuscript piles trying to find something promising to take into the meeting. After half an hour all she managed to locate was a collection of some vaguely humorous short stories by another radio talk-show host, all set in Minnesota. Perhaps he had a following in that part of the world. Maybe he could ride on a tiny wave of nostalgia. Minnesota was less a state than a mindset. It was middle America. Coming home for Christmas. Yule log on the fire. Something neighing outside. It would have to do for today. She knew the agent, he would have a number of other encouraging details about the author to think A&M would bid.

A few minutes short of nine o'clock, she called Crichton's agent and registered A&M's interest to be included in the auction. No one had the floor. It was to be open bidding, and the first round would close by ten.

The publishing meeting was a weekly event. It was usually held in the twenty-fourth floor boardroom where there were enough chairs to accommodate the senior members of the editorial department, the production chief, two of the production estimators, the sales director, the heads of marketing and promotion, the field sales manager, and, sometimes, Fay Mercer. She used various excuses not to come: foreign publishers with long names no one had ever heard of before featured prominently among them. Frequently she had to see scouts from obscure Eastern European countries.

She had confessed to Marsha that publishing meetings were her most dreaded times at A&M. Much as she loved selling to outsiders, she lost her confidence when all those little A&M eyes focussed on her around the long boardroom table. It was impossible to predict, even with her years of experience, what the world's reaction might be to a new idea, or an untried author. In the beginning, she had allowed her natural enthusiasm for the manuscripts themselves to show. It had been a mistake, because editors had included her support in their contract requests, and if the books did not fetch big advances from foreign publishers, she got the blame.

It was almost as risky to feign indifference. The editors remembered her lack of support and lambasted her for it when the books, published by their rivals in other houses, earned critical acclaim in *The Bookseller*, or registered in Paul Nathan's *Publishers Weekly* columns as big hits in Hollywood, or auctioned in Frankfurt for record sums.

She often managed to miss the first meeting after Frankfurt as she was the one left behind to close the booths. Today was not one of those days. The first item on the agenda, as demanded by Morris, was her Margaret Drury Carter sales report. When he couldn't be there, Morris read the minutes of these meetings with meticulous care.

Fay had sculpted her auburn hair into a helmet, and she wore her vermilion lipstick, tan cover-up, and navy over the eyelids. She had brought the numbers with her and distributed them, clean sheets of paper, the figures in two columns, before anyone had taken their seats. "I expect a few additional bids to close by the end of the week," she said, all business, "but what you see are the firm offers accepted as of the end of the Fair."

There were some appreciative clucks. "A great job," Marsha told Fay.

"You've recovered a third of the advance," Stan, the production chief, told Fay. "It'll help reduce our risk."

"If there's a no-risk purchase in recent times, this is the one," Marsha said. "There are two Drury Carters on the list, paperback and hardcover. Only Grisham can do that, and we can't get Grisham in the short term."

"Will the manuscript be on time?" Stan asked.

"She is always on time," Marsha said evasively.

"David said you were having a few problems." Aaron smiled at Marsha as he spoke. He was leaning back in his chair. He had the charming habit of tilting the chair back so it balanced on two legs as he swayed gently, one calf resting on the other thigh, just above the knee. He wore expensive J. Crew grey socks, rolled casually. They went well with the J. Crew soft corduroy slacks, pre-rumpled and prefrayed, and the roll-neck sweater, arms casually pushed up to his elbows. Aaron's collegiate look.

No doubt everyone would have noticed that he had referred to Morris by his first name.

"Nothing unusual," Marsha said as gently as she could. "It's first draft material. With Margaret, the first draft is a trial run. She likes to discuss the early chapters to make sure she is on the right track."

"And is she?"

"More or less. The setting is right. The characters are sketched in. The heroine has all the traits Margaret's readers would expect to find." There was no reason for her to feel defensive, Marsha told herself. The Carter bid, though hers, had been supported by everyone, especially the cowboys. Other than not being centre stage himself, Aaron would have been in favour of this one, as well. "The fact is, though, it does need some work and I intend to take the time to get it right."

Jill Maynard, the senior romantic fiction editor, looked up over the tops of her gold-rimmed glasses. "You are going to do that yourself?" she asked. Over the many years of working with romantic novels, Jill had developed the physical characteristics of their heroines. She dressed in soft lilacs and pinks, she wore a gold locket, had dyed her hair blond and wore it in what she clearly hoped would most resemble tresses. She took time to tend her nails and paint them pink or lilac to match her clothes. Her voice undulated.

"Yes," Marsha said.

"I would be very happy to help, you know," Jill suggested. "I would consider it an honour."

"Perhaps when she is further along, when we have a first draft, Jill." Marsha did not feel any personal attachment to Margaret, she wasn't even an admirer of her novels, but she was sure of what they had to offer and she wasn't going to let anyone else in on this disaster. "In another month or so, I think."

"Will you release the cheque?" Aaron asked.

The second two million was due to go to Andrew Myles, according to the contract, when the outline and first chapters had been accepted by the publisher.

"I'll wait for Margaret's instructions on how to handle the rest of her contract," Marsha said. "With Andrew Myles dead, no one knows what will happen to his authors." She called for the next item on the agenda, a package of five Western novels by another of the house's stalwarts.

After some mild debate about the money, they agreed to a modest offer.

Aaron circulated a proposal for a down-home how-to book by a Red Green lookalike who was funding his own shows on PBS. Aaron claimed he had a following of half a million people. They tuned in twice a week, mid-afternoons, to learn how to take grease stains out of shirts, clean shower curtains, soak up red wine from their carpets, and other tidbits of invaluable advice. The man's homespun humour was almost on a par with his advice. Viewers laughed as they learnt. Or so Aaron said.

"There is too much of that stuff on the market," the sales director told them. "Doesn't sound like the guy has a new shtick. I'd pass."

The publicity people looked at the photos and shook their heads.

"We can't sell how-to books in England. They have their own. Europeans don't go for the homespun thing," Fay told them.

"Not for me," Marsha said.

Aaron didn't give up easily. He said he would play the tape for them next Tuesday, same time.

Marsha introduced the new Philbin. Everyone knew his track record. No one even inquired what the new book would be.

"How much do you think it would take?" Stan asked. He was the guy who had to make the costing sheets work. Since Morris's arrival, no one was supposed to make a bid on any new book without an approved costing sheet.

"About a million, maybe a million two."

"No problem on a hard-soft. I'll get the numbers to you this aft." A&M was one of several New York houses that published both hardcover books and softcover mass market paperbacks. The problem was, the mass market people were on a different floor, rarely fraternized with the hardcover people, and preferred to think of themselves as a separate company. They had their own publishing meetings and it was difficult to force an item onto their agenda. They certainly didn't favour former A&M hardcovers in their paperback releases.

"David has set new policy guidelines for hard-soft, Marsha," Aaron said pleasantly.

"Do tell," Marsha murmured.

"You must have missed the memo. It was circulated a couple of weeks ago." Aaron knew damned well that Marsha left management memos in a small mountain on her windowsill. Like most people at A&M, she had developed an allergy to policy guidelines.

"A book must earn the advance in its first format, whether it's paperback or hardcover. No averaging over two editions."

"I'll keep that in mind," Marsha said. She wondered how Aaron would have justified his new spiritual well-being manuscript acquisitions on that basis, but bit her tongue. She'd hold it in reserve for the next battle. It was too soon to determine if the market would accept another series of inner-healing drivel. Aaron had commissioned the series to be related to *The Celestine Prophecy*. He had instructed a visibly shaken Stan to have his people make intentional mistakes in copy-editing to retain the verisimilitude of the original manuscripts. "They have their own integrity," he told Stan without blushing.

Marsha said she would circulate the Minnesota manuscript. There was no rush, so she would put it back on the agenda in a couple of weeks.

Aaron sounded astonishingly keen on the idea. "We have to remember New York is not America," he announced. "Minnesota is. Kansas is. Iowa is. It's our roots as a nation. The heartland. New York floats in its own ether. It is typical of nothing except itself."

Some people nodded. Fay looked at Marsha and rolled her eyes. No opportunity was too arcane for Aaron to toss in Iowa as a reminder of his biggest publishing success to date.

Sheila came in to tell Marsha the Crichton auction was into its second round and the agent wanted to know if she would go beyond two million dollars. Everyone's reaction was a unanimous yes. Marsha ended the meeting and returned to her office for the bidding.

Crichton's agent had asked for the royalties, the splits on the money, and said he would call back when the next round was up. She had topped this one with a none-too-aggressive two hundred thousand. She suspected they might reach three million by mid-afternoon, and she would have to discuss the numbers with Morris. Accounting would not authorize anything over one million, even a sure-fire deal like this one, without Morris's okay.

She called Stan and asked him to prepare an estimate sheet for a book around three hundred pages — average for Crichton — selling 750,000 copies, twenty-percent returns, at a $25 retail price, and try for earn-out of a three million dollar advance. Stan said he didn't think it would work, but Morris might agree to give up some of the publishing profit to get the book. "Crichton's the kind of big fish he likes to catch."

Marsha told him about Adenauer, and set about filling in the requisite forms for approval. At this level of advance, she assumed it would be a formality.

Fay came into her office and sank into the beige corduroy arm-chair, kicked off her spike heels, propped her feet up on the coffee-table, and waited for Marsha to finish writing. "Had a strange call from that little thing at Fennell," she said when Marsha finally looked at her. "Sophie Biddle. You remember, she's the one had been drinking with Jerry before he kicked off?"

Marsha did remember.

"I don't know whose liquor she's drunk on now that Jerry's gone, but she thinks Fennell bought the rights to our three new Drury Carters." Fay dug a long-nailed middle finger into her seemingly impregnable hairdo and scratched languorously. "I think I'm allergic to papaya spray."

"She what?"

"Jerry told her he had bought the lot, all rights, but that he was going to let us publish in the States, anyway. She says he was quite definite about it. Told her to have the contracts drawn up soon as she got home. She was to bundle them up and leave them on his desk for signing. She was going back first thing in the morning. He was planning to stay till the end of the Fair. All this in the Lip-pizaner, the night of the *Digest* party. Is she nuts or what?"

"Jerry told her this?"

"That's her story. She was calling me to gather all the details of our Frankfurt deals so she could include the new advances in her contract memo. She thought Jerry would have wanted to honour whatever commitments we had made. Decent of him, don't you think?" Fay examined her fingernail. "What are the symptoms of psoriasis?"

"Damned if I know what's going on." Marsha told Fay what Schneider had said to her and the cowboys. "Either Jerry was suffering from some kind of delusion or there is something very strange going on with Margaret. Maybe the poison affected his brain. He had this insane idea he had stolen our author from right under our noses. He had been celebrating. He told Bertil he was looking forward to seeing my face when he told me what he had up his sleeve."

"Do you think he talked to Margaret?" Fay asked, worried now. "They used to be mighty close, once." She looked at her nails and blew on them, suggestively.

"You can't mean that," Marsha said.

"Why not? Do you think a little sex would be beyond Jerry's reach? There are those who have done more than that to get ahead in this business."

"I can't see Margaret being interested."

"Hmm. Maybe not, though she is past the time when she could have had the pick of the litter. Any way she could get out of her contract with us?" Fay was leaning forward, her arms interlocked, serious.

"No. We've signed the contracts, paid the money, Margaret's delivered the first bit of stuff." Marsha realized she had been pacing between the desk and the coffee table and stopped. "I can't think what could have given him the idea these books could be his. Did you ask Sophie?"

"He just told her that he had made a last minute deal, and that Margaret decided to come back to Fennell. Makes no bloody sense."

They could both agree on that.

Marsha remembered how coy Hübsch had become when she

asked him what Sophie Biddle and Jerry had discussed. Still, he had said that liquid nicotine had some strange effect on people. Made them light-headed, ebullient. Just before they became catatonic and immobile. She wondered whether both Jerry and Andrew had been aware at the end that they had been poisoned and were dying.

Could Andrew have heard her and wanted to tell her to get help?

"Whom did she say was the contract with?" Marsha asked.

"With Margaret directly. Sophie said that's because Andrew Myles was dead.... You're going to the funeral?"

Marsha said she was.

"Why don't you ask the dear old lady if she talked to Jerry. Maybe they both got skunked in the bar ..."

"She was too peaked to make it to our signing, she certainly wasn't about to go boozing with one of her former publishers. Anyway, she had gone home by then."

"And Elinor?"

"Her too, I phoned the hotel."

"Did you see Elinor out after the botched signing?" Fay asked.

"Yes, I found her a cab."

"Who was the guy with her, do you know?" Fay pursed her lips. "Cute."

"Big, not cute."

"I like 'em big," Fay stage-whispered.

"No idea. Maybe he was also trying to steal our contract. Or she brought him with her. Looked like a Brit." She started to put on her coat. "You coming?"

"You don't mind if I sit this one out?" Fay said. "Never was an enthusiast for funerals." She wriggled back into her high heels. "I'll call the little girl and tell her Jerry was full of shit. In case she hadn't noticed. The fact that he is dead hasn't changed a thing."

Jerry had published more of Margaret's books than anyone else in England. That was before A&M had an active subsidiary trying to gain respect from the British. Fennell had done a fair job for Margaret. Jerry had personally read each of the manuscripts. He had often met with Margaret to discuss editorial matters, just as Marsha was doing now. "I believe he was a real fan," Alex had told Marsha. "Not like you, m'dear. He genuinely likes her kind of book. Looking at Jerry, it'd be difficult to guess that he is the romantic type, but there it is." Jerry might even have agreed to publish Margaret in hardcovers, as she wanted, had Andrew offered him the opportunity to continue as Margaret's publisher in the U.K. Andrew hadn't. He had preferred a simple deal with a twenty million dollar price tag.

As for Margaret, she'd expressed no regrets.

Odd.

Sheila pressed a message into Marsha's hand as she was leaving. Mrs. Gloria Myles and Stephen Myles would be pleased if she could join them at their home from four p.m. This was a personal invitation. The wake was for family and friends only.

CHAPTER
FOURTEEN

JUDITH TOOK THE SCENIC ROUTE FROM FREDER-
icton to Saint John, and along the Bay of Fundy to Blacks Harbour.
She had imagined Jimmy would like the scenery, but he slept
through most of the drive, including the brief stop at the roadside
fish and chips stand. He had been determined to find no aspect of
this trip attractive. Jemseg was as far from Toronto as he had agreed
to go and this new twist hadn't been part of their bargain. He had
been reasonably sure that once his mother dropped the idea for a
story around Tranby and his nutty friends, they would be on their
way home. He had been sure that his trip to the farmhouse would
have been enough encouragement to send her home. If there was
no story around Tranby, there was no story to chase in Jemseg.

She had never mentioned Grand Manan when they struck their
bargain. Not even Jed had ever set foot there.

Jimmy slept vengefully.

Blacks Harbour was the least attractive part of the drive. The
houses were small, flat-topped units made of clap-board, all built
to the same specifications. There were some army barracks,

apparently deserted, and the lone restaurant had Formica tables and a choice of prefrozen specialties. The sardines were canned, even though the town advertised itself on a large stone-pitted sign just off Highway 1 as home of "The World's Largest Sardine Industry." There were no trees to shelter pedestrians from the battering wind. The harbour itself was grim and oily, and a couple of greasy shipping trawlers hugged its concrete walls.

The ferry was almost empty. Only once a day service, this time of year, New Brunswick Tourist Information had told her. It was the end of the tourist season. Another month and they'd be down to every second day. She drove the car over the ramp to the front of the ship and woke Jimmy to the smell of oil and the sound of thumping engines.

Judith bundled up in her oversized hand-knit sweater, yellow slicker, secondhand fleece-lined gloves, toque, scarf, and woollen football socks. She had listened to advice in Jemseg and stocked up at Basil's variety store. She had stuffed her hair into the toque and wrapped the scarf around her neck twice for extra comfort. Jimmy said he was glad, on second thoughts, that there was no one on board he knew.

She led the way up through the smokers' lounge, where Jimmy stopped to read his new Internet guide. He had had to leave the Mac in the trunk of the car. She made for the Upper Deck, where the brochure had promised breathtaking views of the shoreline, harbour seals, a variety of seabirds, porpoises once they set out towards the island. Whales in August and September.

She was leaning over the railing, looking at the debris of past voyages — Coke cans, candy wrappers, plastic cups, mineral water bottles, newspaper, a red toy truck, and a feathery fishing lure. Two men in heavy black coveralls untied the greasy ropes that held the ship to shore and three others winched the ropes up using a clattering motor that all but drowned out the sound of the engines as they geared up for the crossing.

"A grand sight to behold," someone said.

"Ahem," Judith said cautiously. It was a three-hour trip.

"Not as cold as you'd expect, for this time of year." There was no hint of humour in the voice, though Judith could only assume he was commenting on her attire.

She glanced over her shoulder at a blue-clad figure, in jeans and windbreaker, tall, shoulders hunched, black hair, hint of grey, arms crossed, leaning over the railing.

"Too early to set out for Christmas," he continued undaunted by her quiet. "Some people do cross over mid-December, to get a start on the season, but there's plenty of time for that. You have friends on the island?"

Judith shook her head.

He moved closer for a better look at the bundle of clothes. "Are you from hereabouts?" he asked, his tone indicating that he knew the answer.

"No. Visiting," Judith told him.

"Odd time for a visit. Family?" He motioned with his head down towards the gunnel that led to the smokers' lounge. "Taking the lad home to see the relatives?"

She could see him more clearly now. High brow with prominent bones, a flat nose that may have been broken once and had drifted over to one side, square face, blue flat eyes, cleft chin, full mouth. His hands were chapped, nails rough, blackened, and used to some sort of hard labour. "Are you a fisherman?" she blurted out, before she could stop herself. Years of interviewing had never quite dulled her directness.

"Fisherman?" he repeated, laughing. He had a loud hearty laugh that filled the air, and overcame the thudding sounds around them. "Don't you read the papers where you come from? No fish hereabouts, young lady. None since the summer before last. Even if there were some fish we're not the ones can catch them. It's the law. Only the Japanese and the Spanish can fish off the Bay of

Fundy. The locals collect a bit of insurance, and watch television. Not much else to do hereabouts. In November, there aren't even the tourists." He came a little closer and gave her a hard look. "Which end of the island are the relatives?"

"We'll be stopping at North Head Village," she said.

"They'll be glad to see you, I'm sure." He had a lilting voice, a little Irish perhaps. "The Finlays?"

"No," Judith said. "I'm staying in one of the guest houses. Compass Rose." She told him she was a journalist, coming to interview someone on the island.

"Must be the writer," he said. "She'd be the only celebrity staying on over the winter, if she does stay. No one has seen much of her since she landed in August. Keep to themselves, her and the niece. I suppose you should expect that of a writer, though, shouldn't you?"

"Have you met her?" Judith asked.

"No. I met Miss Drury, though. She comes down to the bakery now and then, soon as the bread is out of the oven, and takes up a loaf. The two of them tuck into a loaf a day, if you can believe it. Miss Drury's the niece."

"I heard about her," Judith prompted.

"She walks most days from Whale Cove to the village. Gives her something to do, I suppose."

"Is she friendly?"

"Not particularly," he was laughing again. He had small crooked teeth. "Funny question. She might be friendly to you, I expect. Not much she can gain from being charming to me. You could be another matter. Some people like the press. Gives them status to be in the papers. Who do you work for?"

She told him it was a freelance assignment for *Home and Garden*.

"From Toronto, I suppose?"

"Why?"

"A wild guess," he said.

There had been a time when people from Toronto felt proud of where they'd come from, because it was the biggest and wealthiest city in Canada. But those days were past, and Judith had been feeling defensive about Toronto ever since she'd arrived in the Maritimes. She said, "*Home and Garden* is in New York. I could be from New York."

He looked closely at her clothes again. "I doubt it somehow," he said. "I'm Preston O'Neill, and I used to live in Toronto." He reached for her hand. His was as rough as it had seemed while it was resting on the railing. Her fingers disappeared into his palm.

"Judith Hayes," she said, extracting her squashed fingers. She was glad to have worn the gloves. They had cushioned some of the pressure of his grasp.

"You'll like the Compass Rose. I stayed there when I first came back to the island. June owns that and the Island Arts and Crafts store. She runs summer classes for students from the mainland. They come, they say, to learn how to paint. I had my doubts about that when I saw my first group arrive, but they did try to get the basics over the six weeks they'd paid for. June gives the teachers a bit of cash and room and board at the Rose. The summer ended, the newly hatched *artistes* went home, I stayed."

He was looking intently at the jagged, tall, black shape of the island as it came into view. The wind had picked up as the ship abandoned the shelter of the land and Judith wrapped herself in her big woollen scarf.

"You still paint?" she asked, partly to take her mind off the rocking.

"I stopped couple of years back and started working in stone. When you see Grand Manan you'll see why. Bloody great rocks are irresistible."

It was the rocks she remembered most clearly from her childhood summers in Georgian Bay. They were smooth, grey-white, often scarred with silvery metal. Quartz, her father had told her.

When they were wet they turned pink. The Hayeses had rented the same cottage some five or six years in a row, while her mother had still kept her hopes that her father would amount to something at the bank. There had been a living room with a mess of odds and ends the owners had collected during their travels: spears and ornate shields from Africa, metal sculptures from Haiti, wall hangings from Ecuador, painted boxes and hanging jewellery from Mexico, large, misshapen Inuit carvings, the skin of a llama, whalebones carved in the shapes of whales, and the jaws of a shark ... Her mother had thought them vulgar. When the Hayeses arrived she took all the pieces, and put them into the large trunks the owners used for winter storage. To make sure everything would go back to its rightful place at the end of the summer, she had pinned tiny pieces of paper and a brief description of each piece to the spot it had occupied before. That's how Judith discovered what the various pieces were.

Judith had loved to look at them all. Late at night when her mother had gone to bed, her father would sometimes tell her stories about them. In the dark, the places all came to life in her room, the jungles of Africa, the Amazon river, and the gold of the great Inca kings. It was during the last of those summers that she discovered her father had been writing poetry. He had begun to tell his stories in rhyming couplets, for exercise, he told her. She had promised not to tell her mother.

Later, when Marjorie Hayes discovered for herself that Frank had been writing poetry, she had exploded. There was no future for a banker who wrote poems. She was sure there'd be no room for a poet in the bank, and she had been right.

"There is a bar downstairs, on the port side, if you'd like something to warm you." Preston O'Neill had turned and started without waiting for her answer. "The wind's a bit nippy, I'd say."

Judith hadn't noticed that tears were running down her face, and catching in the rolled neck of her knitted sweater. Some wind.

She didn't take him up on the invitation. She searched for

Jimmy in the two lounges and found him with his nose into the wind on the other side of the ship. He was mildly green, his eyes riveted to the horizon as it rose and fell with the waves. "Just don't say anything," he warned when he saw her.

Judith sat on the damp white bench behind him and watched the shore approach. There was a fine spray of salt water each time the nose of the ship slammed into the next wave. Her hair was wet, but the salt she licked off her lips tasted good. The air smelled of brine and fish, cold and clear as ice. She gulped deep lungs full and felt just fine, while Jimmy retched over the side.

A little closer and she could see the rocks rise tall and black from the sea, waves smashing against them, foaming white. A tiny white lighthouse perched on top of the nearest set of cliffs, its top a pretty red, the light flashing green every few seconds, as it turned.

The gulls were swirling closer to the deck. Their shrieking was now louder than the thudding of the engines. One landed on the railing near Jimmy and watched him, head tilted to one side.

The sea subsided slowly as the ship gained shelter. Jimmy hunkered down next to his mother, close enough that she could feel him shivering. When she put her arm around him he did not protest.

"The first one's always the worst."

This time Judith didn't have to look to know it was Preston; she recognized the slight Irish lilt. He had drawn on a black slicker against the damp. He stood rock still, as if he'd been nailed to the deck, moving with it. "Thing is not to resist the roll," he told Jimmy. "Think of it as music, you sort of go with the rhythm. Might get to like it the second time. I did."

Jimmy grunted miserably.

"Here," he told Judith, and offered her a small plastic cup full of amber liquid. "I thought this might ready you for the island experience."

Judith thanked him and he smiled showing more crooked teeth. "It's rum," he said when he saw her looking suspiciously into the cup. "You drink it like this," and he emptied his cup into his mouth with one gulp, wiped his lips with the back of his hand, and waited for her to follow.

Judith was grateful to all those heavy martinis she had drunk in her life; the rum didn't make her gag, only exhale more forcefully. And it did warm her as at slid down to her stomach.

"That's Swallowtail Light," he told her pointing at the tiny lighthouse at the end of a long thin promontory. "The thing it sits on is called the Swallowtail, looks like a swallow's tail, you'll see when we are closer. There was a lighthouse-keeper there when I arrived. All automated now. If you look closely near the shore, you'll see some harbour seals. Devil of a problem for the weirs but just grand for the tourists."

As the ship veered around the Swallowtail, they could see that the whole piece of jutting land, almost severed from the rest of the island, resembled the open mouth of a fish. Judith couldn't see it, but Jimmy said he thought it looked like a fish head. Preston seemed delighted. "They call it Fish Head," he told Jimmy.

He pointed out the Compass Rose sitting close to the shore on the edge of the harbour. It was a thin blue wooden house with a peaked grey roof that stood out from the brown- and grey-painted houses near the harbour. It appeared to be tilting slightly to the left. A multitude of fishing boats, some no larger than dinghies, were tied up and anchored in the bay.

Jimmy had ventured to the side again when they tied up at the Ferry Wharf. It was still light, but a dull grey colour, as flat and cold as the day had become.

"You'll have a fine view from your window," Preston assured Judith. "Tell June you want the room at the top. May seem like a long climb up each time, but it's the best room she's got. Mornings, you feel the sun rise, and you can hear the men going out to the weirs. Ferry makes a lot of noise, but it only comes once a day now it's October."

He led them off the ferry ramp and up to the door of the Rose. "A few years back they used to hoist the cars from the hold in net slings. Rather tame landings now." He drove a battered blue pick-up truck, paint peeling, licence plate hanging by a screw on one side.

"Charming local character, I suppose," Jimmy said. He had recovered sufficiently to push his baseball cap down on his head, backward. "Part of the scenery. Wouldn't surprise me if he showed up to give us the guided tour."

Judith heaved her suitcase and portable bag from the trunk.

"And it wouldn't surprise me if you liked a bit of local colour. He's your type, I think. Tall, dark, barrel-chested, the strong muscular stuff. Careless about his garb. Twinkle in his eye. Fool you into believing he's got a sense of humour ..."

"Not a bit like your father," Judith retorted.

"No one's at all like my father. He's a case study all to himself. This guy's more like your friend the policeman."

It was the first time Jimmy had mentioned David since he had disappeared from Judith's life. It had been some two years since she had imagined herself being married again. Back then David had been a constant visitor to Judith's semidetached. "He's not barrel-chested," she said.

"Wait till he takes his jacket off. He'll be barrel-chested."

June welcomed them to the guest house. She had been waiting by the door as they pulled up in front to help Judith with the bags. She was a vivacious woman in her forties, strong-boned, ruddy-complexioned. Her arms were tanned light bronze. Her hair was sun-bleached blond. She didn't seem to worry much about the ill effects of the sun. She wore jeans and calf-skin boots and strode up the narrow staircase with the suitcase over her shoulder as if it were as light as a pillow. "I wasn't sure whether you'd want to share, so I made up a couple of the rooms — there are only four — you can have your pick. No other guests now." Her voice was as sturdy as the rest of her.

Judith asked for the room with the view. The bathroom was down the hall, closer to Jimmy's room. They were both beautifully furnished with white wicker pieces, wallpaper that was deep blue with tiny light blue flowers, a tall pine closet, a white wicker washstand and chest of drawers, a blue china pitcher, thin white lace curtains, and watercolour paintings of seascapes with birds and tall-masted ships.

As it was their first night on the island, June had cooked them a dinner of steamed turbot, mashed potatoes, and fiddleheads. Basic fare, but she swore her apple pie was as good as any they'd tasted.

"We had some people here from the States, they asked for my recipe, and they're going to publish the mother of all apple pie cookbooks. It'll have recipes from all over the world," she told them proudly. "Margaret Drury Carter came back for it twice."

"You know her then?" Judith asked eagerly.

June had seated herself on the big fluffy white eiderdown bedcover and waited for Judith to unpack. Dinner was ready downstairs. "We're not exactly chummy in recent times, but she comes in from time to time. They were pretty cosy when they needed my help last summer. Soon after they arrived. She and her niece. They were looking for a place to rent and someone had told them there wasn't much I didn't know about North Head Village. Even from the Deep Cove area, and Castalia, people would post their for-rent signs near my entrance. Everyone comes in here sooner or later. And unlike the mainland agents, I don't take much of a commission."

"Did she say why they'd picked Grand Manan? Had she been here before?"

"Her niece, that Elinor woman, she said she remembered coming here with her family when she was a child. Heck of a long time ago, if you asked me." June laughed.

"Why do you say that?"

"She thought the place had 'charm' — her word. Lunenburg over in Nova Scotia, that has charm. Here we've got wilderness and bloody great tides. 'Charm,' my foot. But you're staying just a few days, aren't you? How long does it take to write a story? You'll be going up there tomorrow?"

"I might be here for a week. Interviews can take a while, especially if she's busy."

"She is working on a new book, I wager." She went to fill the pitcher. "Have you met her already?" she asked from the doorway. "Miss Drury Carter, that is, not the niece?"

Judith said she hadn't but hoped to find her the next day. "Do you know if she's back yet from Europe?"

"Didn't know she'd left, even. Where was she to go?"

Judith told her about the Frankfurt Bookfair and her newest book deal for twenty million dollars.

June whistled appreciatively. "Twenty million dollars. My god you could buy this whole damned island for less." She shook her head. "She sure acts like she is grand, but who'd have thought she is that grand. Twenty million ..." She headed downstairs to the kitchen.

CHAPTER

FIFTEEN

"Did you know he was catholic?" Alex asked in a hushed whisper.

"Sure," Marsha replied. "Anyone might have guessed. It was his profound belief in poverty, humility, and saintliness."

"No. Really. He had even Mother Teresa convinced. He tried to sign her to a slender autobiography, he'd brought a ghost with him to Calcutta. He offered her fifteen million hard cash, no questions asked. All she had to do was to agree that the ghost could interview her as she went about her business, write it all down, and she'd sign over the rights to him."

Marsha had been mildly surprised to find Alex at the funeral. He had not made a secret of his dislike for Andrew Myles. Looking around St. Patrick's, however, it was easy to see that a leading literary agent would not wish to remain invisible. There were too many authors there who might now be keen to replace their dearly departed deal-maker. The scent of money was competing with the incense.

"He actually went to Calcutta?" Paul Nathan asked. He was

sitting in the row immediately ahead of the one Marsha was sharing with Jill Maynard, Connor Sagfield, and Mort Janklow of the famous Janklow agency, one of Myles's most successful rivals. Paul Nathan wrote the rights column for *Publishers Weekly* and it was obvious he was somewhat put out that he hadn't already heard the Mother Teresa story. Not many rights deals went down in New York Paul didn't hear about first.

"Sure, he went to Calcutta. He would have volunteered for a day's work in the house of the dying street women had he thought it would earn him the contract."

"Shhhhhh ..." Connor Sagfield told Alex with exaggerated seriousness. "There is a service going on."

Connor usually stopped in New York on the way from Frankfurt to Australia. He had been hanging around the office all morning trying to interest various editors in worthy Australian authors, with ever-diminishing success. A few years back there had been a brief flurry of Australian chic with Peter Carey leading the trend, but New York had now returned to its ingrained indifference to outside literary endeavour. Marsha speculated that he might have to come to the funeral to pick up a few American authors to add to his list instead. Oddly enough, Australians were less insular than Americans.

Joe Heller was in the row ahead; he appeared to be making notes as the priest spoke. Joe had just signed a deal for a film series with Turner for a history of Africa in the twentieth century. It was reputed to have netted him close to six million, not including the book spin-off Random House was to publish, entitled *The African Century*. In acknowledgment of the obvious fact that Heller was resolutely white, the producers had hired a team of African-Americans to act as consultants, and Andrew had been seeking an audience with Buthelezi to importune him for an introduction. Rumour had it that Andrew had also been to see Abe Moore, the African-American history professor at Yale. Moore had asked: "I suppose you want me to supply the colour commentary?"

"Is that Tom Clancy, next to Heller?" Sagfield asked.

Marsha thought so. She hadn't seen Clancy for some time. He had been busy signing a four-book, eight-figure megadeal for a series of co-authorships with the now famous Desert Storm military leaders. It was going to be called *The Commanders*. Each story gave the behind-the-scenes action as the leaders marshalled their forces over sea, land, air, and the secret incursions of the specialists.

"Do you think they might give me a shot at the Aussie rights?" Sagfield asked. "Down Under, we all watched that bit of action. Good to see you Yanks get it together for once. Heartwarming that it would take all that might — and all those billions of your fancy dollars — to squash a country the size of Florida."

"Aren't you supposed to be on a flight to the Outback about now?" Alex asked. "Damned Australians ..."

"Shhhhh ..." Sonny Mehta said. The Knopf boss sat near Clancy. He appeared to be listening to the priest, but he had a smile on his face too great for the occasion to warrant.

"We brought nothing into this world, and it is certain we carry nothing out. The Lord gave and the Lord hath taken away ..." the priest told everyone. Wisely, he was using a microphone as it would have been difficult to hear him over the loud whispering of the assembled mourners.

From her vantage point near the Fifth Avenue vestibule, Marsha could barely see the top of his head. He was standing in the centre of the elaborate sanctuary, dwarfed by the mammoth bronze canopy over the altar. Marsha assumed the coffin would be at the foot of the steps leading up to the altar. She could not see it from where she sat. It had been rolled in at the beginning of the service, gold-draped, accompanied by four men on either side, two women following behind. She had recognized Sam, the former assistant. She wondered what he would do now. There had been some talk he would try to continue the agency on his own. He'd certainly made no effort to retire from the scene of action once his boss died.

One of the other men seemed vaguely familiar, as did the older of the two women. She had walked with her head bowed, a prayer book clutched to her breast.

"Seriously now ..." Sagfield continued.

"No," Marsha told him a little too loudly, "I can't imagine Putnam giving you the Australian rights. They already have a distributor down there and they tend to honour their contracts. Besides, you just said you didn't think much of our war."

"It's not what I think that matters, m'dear, it's what our market thinks and they watched Operation Desert Storm as if you guys had staged the whole thing for the telly. Made for a good show."

"You might have more luck with Jancie Withers now that Andrew's gone," Jill Maynard said.

"The horror lady?"

"She's at the end of her four-book deal with St. Martin's, and Andrew was going to shop her anyway."

"Did the books work?"

"Not as well as Barker, or Saul, but she is a comer," Alex said. "Only in paperback so far, but she's broken the million copy mark. There should be a movie in there. That's all it takes."

Marsha wondered if Alex was angling to get back Jancie. She'd been another of his discoveries, lost to Andrew's magic. It was probably no accident that he had positioned himself almost directly in front of her. Nor would it be an accident that Avon's new horror and supernatural editor was sitting so close to Jancie. Alex had been glancing back, as if searching for someone, offering both Jancie and the youngish editor his best sympathetic smile.

"Look who's come all the way from Paris," Paul whispered. He was pointing across the aisle under the huge statue of St. Jude, where Brigitte Dombert was sharing a secret with Aaron, the two of them hiding their faces behind their bibles, giggling.

"She must have decided to come at the end of the Fair," Alex mused. "She never mentioned she would be in New York when I saw her."

"She might keep one or two secrets, even from you, Alex," Marsha said.

"Thou hast our misdeeds before Thee and our secret sins in the light of Thy countenance ..." said the minister. "We bring our years to an end, as it were a tale that is told ..." he continued.

"I wouldn't be at all surprised if she's the one that did it," Sagfield said. "Talking about secrets." He leant closer to Marsha, as if he was talking to her alone, but his voice carried across the aisle and into the next one. All the backs straightened in an effort to hear.

"If she killed Andrew Myles?" Marsha asked.

"At least Andrew Myles, but who knows? Maybe Jerry Haines as well."

"Whatever for?" Jill Maynard asked. "Just because they were lovers once? If that were sufficient reason, half the people in this church would be dead."

"Incestuous little shop you fellers run in New York," Sagfield said. "But that's not all. She had a baby last year, don't you know? Andrew's, I heard. Not that he'd made an effort to acknowledge the wee bastard. He told me it could have been anybody's. Why should he belly up to the bar? They had a big fight the day of the Bertelsmann party. She'd tracked him down to our booth around six and insisted he should go with her. He wouldn't, of course, being the shit that he was."

"She gave no sign at the party," Alex said.

"She wouldn't, she's a professional. But she was hanging around close to Andrew, she could have slipped something into his glass, now, couldn't she?"

"She had a baby?" Jill exclaimed. "Brigitte had a baby? I don't believe you."

"Why ever not? Lots of people have babies ..."

"But Brigitte?"

"She's kept it. Has a nanny living with her now. Cute as a button — the nanny that is, I never liked tiny people. They look too fetal for me. Unfinished."

"I heard something about it," Alex said. "She went on a leave of absence last year."

"I heard a voice from Heaven say unto me, Write, from henceforth blessed are the dead which die in the Lord: Even so sayeth the Spirit, for they rest from their labours ..." the minister continued.

"So why is she at the funeral?" Marsha asked no one in particular.

"To gloat, why else?"

"And where does Jerry Haines fit in?"

"Didn't I tell you? They were in the lobby of the Frankfurter Hof together around eleven the night Jerry was murdered. That gave her opportunity," Connor said proudly. "I saw them. They were standing pretty tight, glued together, as it were. And they certainly didn't want to invite me into their conversation."

"I can think of plenty of reasons for that, my dear," Marsha said somewhat unkindly. Various others nodded.

"Point is, that gave her opportunity."

"And the motive?"

"I've got to leave something for the Frankfurt police, don't I? That guy Hübsch was asking some nifty questions about the lovely Brigitte, I wouldn't be surprised if they have something up their sleeve."

They had asked some questions about Sagfield as well, Marsha thought. He had been there both times. Standing around Myles at the party. In the lobby with Jerry on Sunday night. For that matter, Hübsch had furnished Alex Levine with a motive for Andrew's murder, and he had been at the Bertelsmann party and in the bar the night Jerry was poisoned. Van Maeght had been there both times, as had Bertil. And there was still the curious story van Maeght had told her about the Iraqi manuscript, with a whole coterie of possible killers, motive and all. And Hideo had been in the group around Andrew, as well. It was he who had told Marsha that Jerry had been to New York some days before the Fair. What did Hübsch learn from talking to Hideo on Monday? He had been the only one of the group he had persuaded to come to the police station.

But what continued to puzzle Marsha the most was what could have given Jerry the idea that he had acquired Margaret Drury Carter's new manuscripts.

She had seen Elinor come into the church. She wore a black tailored suit, wide-brimmed hat, and short black leather gloves. She had walked in alone, barely glancing around to find an empty pew. She had nodded weakly when Marsha greeted her as she walked by. She appeared to be deep in thought. Perhaps she was one of the few really grieving for Andrew Myles.

The minister said Mrs. Gloria Myles would do the reading for the day. The rustling of paper and whispering stopped as she walked to the front and up the steps to the dais. She was a tall woman with a long, firm stride. She wore a black pillbox hat, far back on her head. Her blond hair was swept back. She had a wide forehead and a pronounced nose. She wore a short black Chanel suit with brass buttons. Her blouse was jarringly purple.

She read one of St. Paul's letters that talked darkly about vengeance and the duplicity of the Philistines. She had a loud booming voice that retreated at the end of each sentence into almost inaudible hush, then rose again to confront the congregation.

On seeing her in isolation Marsha recognized the cheerful woman in first class on the Lufthansa flight. It was difficult to imagine why she would have been so jolly while accompanying Andrew's corpse.

There were no more speeches. Before dismissal, the minister encouraged everyone to hold close to their hearts each memory of

Andrew Myles, as he had given them much in life. Brigitte snickered.

The service was over at noon.

Aaron caught up to Marsha on the Fifth Avenue steps. "There is something you must read before your meeting with David Morris today," he told her.

"I doubt if I'm going to have the time, Aaron. I'm on my way to lunch with Margaret's niece. In fact," she checked her watch, "there's no time to go back to the office before then ..."

"I brought it with me," Aaron told her. "I would have given it to you this morning at the publishing meeting, but we decided it was too hot to pass around. I think you'll agree." He was grinning his boyish lopsided grin. He gave her a yellow manila envelope no more than a few pages thick. "It's from Andrew Myles," he said.

"Huh?"

"True." Aaron was enjoying himself. "Andrew came by with it before you all went off to Frankfurt. He offered us a worldwide exclusive for two million dollars and when you read it you'll see it's a bargain. And David agrees."

"He's read it?" Marsha was incredulous.

"Not much to read. Some stuff is self-evident. Still," Aaron looked at Marsha appraisingly, "he wants to hear what you say." When she started to tear open the envelope he grabbed her hand. "Not here," he said in a loud whisper. "Too many people."

CHAPTER
SIXTEEN

PRUNELLE WAS A&M EDITORIAL'S NEIGHBOURHOOD restaurant. It was close, friendly, and the owner made sure there was always a table for late bookings. The burled maple fixtures lent the room an air of comfortable home ambience, the etched glass partitions provided some privacy, the food was traditional French with no startling surprises, and there were fresh flowers on every table. It was sure to impress out of town authors, and even the most discriminating local agents couldn't find fault with it.

Miss Drury, the maître d' told Marsha, was already there. She had arrived with a gentleman a few minutes before Marsha. They had been seated near the back. Marsha stuffed Aaron's envelope into her canvas bag next to the opening chapters of *When Morning Comes*, and followed the maître d' down the aisle between the tables.

Elinor sat very still, her back against the polished wood, her hands on either side of the silver platter in front of her. The gloves were to the left of the platter, neatly folded. Over the black suit jacket she wore a single strand of cream-coloured pearls. The hat had left her hair flat, but not as flat as the look she gave Marsha when she approached. By contrast, Alex Levine was the picture of good cheer. He jumped to his feet to greet her with an enthusiasm that belied the fact he had seen her at the funeral barely fifteen minutes ago.

"Hello, Marsha," he boomed. "Meet Margaret Drury Carter's new agent." He executed a tiny bow and sat down again next to Elinor. "Margaret has asked me to represent her again and, as you can see, I have accepted. Naturally. I am one of her oldest friends, as you know. I am already familiar with her work, and most of her contracts are still in my care from before ... well, before she left me for Andrew Myles." He smiled as if to indicate there were no hard feelings. "We'll simply take up where we left off, won't we, Elinor?" He was as exuberant as a child with a new toy.

Elinor said yes, frostily. "It's Margaret's decision," she added. Some hint there that Elinor, herself, had had other ideas.

And Andrew Myles is just on his way to be buried, Marsha thought. It was rather uncharacteristic of Alex to have kept his reversal of fortune so quiet during the funeral. Still, she was sure he would be easier to deal with than Andrew Myles had been. He was, at least, a literary agent, in the true, old-fashioned sense of the words. He read what he was selling.

"Congratulations," Marsha told Alex. "Decent of you to jump into the saddle when you're needed." She didn't try to keep the irony from her voice.

"Nothing charitable about it, Marsha. Purely business." Elinor stared hard at Marsha, her eyes round blue buttons, no expression in her face, her voice made it clear she didn't want too much humour at this lunch.

"Alex," Elinor continued, "has agreed to represent Margaret for ten percent. That's less than he usually charges, but this is not a usual situation. Agents do not usually die in the middle of twenty million dollar deals. Margaret expects to have to pay the Myles estate their percentage over the top, even though Andrew

Myles, himself, is in no condition to discharge his duties to my aunt." There was the barest hint of softness in the eyes when she alluded to Myles's demise. The hands remained motionless.

"How is Margaret?" Marsha asked.

"She is better now that she can get back to her writing," Elinor said. "She did not like Frankfurt. She never does. This one was particularly stressful, what with Andrew dying as he did," Elinor sighed and turned to Alex for confirmation, "the pressure of having to appear in public, and the uncertainty about her contract ..." she trailed off.

There were tiny warning bells going off in Marsha's head.

If Elinor was seeking confirmation, Alex was not about to disappoint her. "It would be very difficult for anyone, but particularly so for someone of Margaret's ... gentle disposition." There had never been any suggestion that Margaret was gentle, but Marsha was ready to accept a liberal dose of gratuitous flattery as the price Alex was going to pay for his newfound fortune. "I am sure we can sort out the problems with the contracts easily enough ..."

The warning bells grew louder. "What is wrong with the contracts?" Marsha asked. "Bearing in mind, that is, that they were signed several weeks ago by all the then extant parties ...?" She emphasized "all." Andrew might have died, but his signature would have survived him.

Elinor glanced at Alex. He answered, "The fact is, my dear, that through some sort of misunderstanding, the author never received her share of the money."

"The two million dollars?" Marsha asked, her voice rising with each word.

"Seems Andrew didn't have a chance to send Margaret her share," Alex said matter-of-factly.

Marsha stared at Elinor who remained quite still, her back pressed tightly against the banquette, her shoulders squared, her formidable breasts jutting out like the prow of a ship. Even in the sedate wide-cut black suit, they made a considerable statement. Marsha suspected Elinor was aware of that, because she had kept the jacket buttoned all the way to the top, even though it was warm in the restaurant. There was the merest hint of a grey shirt collar above the buttons. Her face was paler than usual, the skin taut over her high cheekbones, dark around her eyes. She had not bothered to hide the beginnings of loose skin on her neck. Unlike her aunt, Elinor would be comfortable with aging.

Margaret had taken to wearing high fluffy collars to hide the wattles in recent years, and had instructed photographers to shoot her picture with a low, diffuse light, the camera angled down to make the most of her rouged cheekbones and the least of her chin.

"I believe I asked you that question in Frankfurt, Elinor," Marsha said very precisely. "You were sure the money had been paid. So was Margaret. She assured us you had taken care of the business matters. And Andrew cashed our cheque weeks ago." She knew they had discussed the money with Elinor, and she remembered now that there had been some strange exchange between Elinor and Thurgood that made her wonder if they knew each other. "Arthur Thurgood was there, don't you remember?" she asked.

"I certainly recall seeing Arthur Thurgood," Elinor said evenly. "I had occasion to talk to him before our meeting at your booth. Perhaps he mentioned it to you?"

He hadn't.

"I called him around the time the contract was signed and suggested we could avoid the customary delays if he divided up the advance before it was paid. Seemed perfectly logical to me. Send Andrew his share, and send Margaret her share. That would save time and paperwork. For some reason, he refused. Now Margaret hasn't got her share of the money." Once again, she glanced at Alex. "The point is, and Alex will bear me out on this, the contract is not valid if the terms haven't been met, and they haven't been met, as far as my aunt is concerned."

"Surely, that's between you and Myles's estate," Marsha protested. "I assume Alex can get the money for you. Have you spoken to Andrew's assistant?"

"Not yet," Alex said. "First we wanted to talk to you. It might take some months before the financial stuff around Myles's death is sorted out. You know how these things are. It could take months."

"Elinor, I asked you if the money was in order, and you told me it was," Marsha repeated.

Elinor folded her hands in her lap. "Margaret assured me that there was no problem. She had been told by Andrew that the money had been deposited in her New York account. She always believed him. She thought it would be only a matter of days before the cheque cleared. It hasn't."

"In the meantime," Alex said, "you could validate the agreement and, in a spirit of goodwill, make the second payment immediately and directly to Margaret." Alex had lapsed into a legal tone unusual for him. Marsha assumed he was feeling uncomfortable with his new role.

"The next payment," Marsha protested, "isn't due till Margaret has provided an acceptable outline and three chapters. I have neither. That's why I wanted to meet with her in Frankfurt, Elinor. She needs some direction. In fact, I have decided to go to Grand Manan at the end of the week to see — "

"Why?" Elinor asked. She leant forward over the table so her face came close to Marsha's. Marsha held her intense blue gaze. "Why would you want to do that?" she asked again, her voice barely over a whisper.

"I am going to Grand Manan to see Margaret," Marsha said. "We need to discuss the manuscript."

"I'm afraid that won't be possible," Elinor stated, as she relaxed against the back of the banquette.

"Why ever not?" Alex asked.

"I thought we had covered this already, Alex," Elinor said. She was looking at Marsha, not Alex. "My aunt has not been well. She has still not recovered from her travels. She has had a nasty shock with Andrew's death. She is still weak."

"She did not seem particularly weak to me in Frankfurt," Marsha mused.

"That's ridiculous, and you know it," Elinor said.

"Actually, she seemed rather ... theatrical," Marsha continued, unperturbed.

"She is always theatrical. It's her act, she does it by rote, you both know that. She is an old trouper; she'll rise to the occasion every time. Wouldn't let her audience down." Elinor smiled indulgently. "But she has not been well, and I am not going to subject her to your badgering about the manuscript. Why don't you tell me what the problem is. Now. Or you can put it in writing."

"I really don't see why this is such a big deal, my dear," Alex intervened. "Personally, I think it very admirable of Marsha to offer to go to ..."

"Don't patronize me," Elinor turned to Alex. Her voice was as flat as a pancake. "I'm not your dear. And I do know what is best for my aunt. I have been with her for over fifteen years. It seems to me that her health is what you should worry about, not whether Marsha is ... admirable."

Alex was pleating his napkin.

"Unfortunately, the manuscript," Marsha said, keeping her voice level, and as pleasant as she could, "is not acceptable. The contract stipulates that an 'acceptable' three chapters be completed before the second payment. I have worked with Margaret before, and I am quite confident that we can fix what needs to be fixed in a couple of days. That's why I am going to Grand Manan." She could match Elinor's stubbornness, if that's what it took.

"As I said, we can review your problems now, or you can send Margaret your comments in writing," Elinor repeated. She straightened her back even more.

"Marsha, I do understand that you want to make these chapters ... perfect," Alex said. He had, obviously, decided to ignore Elinor's rudeness. "But we both know you are dealing with a professional. This will be Margaret's eighteenth book. She has always delivered on time and all her work has been consistent."

There had been a few exceptions along the way, but Marsha had to agree that Drury Carter was nothing if not predictable. The exceptions had been so few that her fans were willing to overlook them.

"We are talking about an author with two best-sellers on the list," Alex continued, "at the same time. Last I looked *Conspiracy of Roses* was still in the number one spot. After six months. That isn't your average author."

"Nor is twenty million dollars your average advance," Marsha said.

There was a brief truce while they ordered. Elinor had the salmon mousse and the boeuf Tolstoy. While Alex reminisced about Margaret's past triumphs, Marsha observed the niece. She ate with considerable gusto, quite unlike her aunt's somewhat delicate approach to food. Where Margaret preferred the graces of Southern belles, or what she thought were appropriate graces for Southern belles, Elinor was direct, and whatever grace she might possess, she kept hidden from view. Where Margaret was circumspect, Elinor was dauntless. In a room like this, Margaret would be aware of everyone around her, checking for celebrities, fans, journalists. Elinor appeared to focus on her food. Margaret had a friendly disposition. Around A&M she had talked to the receptionist, the secretaries, even the copy editors — at least before Andrew began to represent her — as if they were people. Elinor kept to herself. While she was conducting the audit at A&M she never once engaged another person in conversation beyond questions pertinent to her inquiries about past royalties.

It was difficult to imagine what they had in common.

While they ate, Alex managed to carry on a friendly mono-logue about his experiences with a range of authors, all of whom had been wonderful people, and no doubt had also delivered per-fect manuscripts on time. Neither woman helped him work for his lunch.

When the last of the boeuf Tolstoy disappeared, Elinor asked Marsha to tell her what she thought was wrong with the manu-script. She sounded friendlier than before, showing that she was interested in being as helpful as possible. Nevertheless, her tone made it clear she expected Marsha to be nitpicking, concentrating on the details, ignoring the big picture.

Had she been talking to Margaret, herself, Marsha would have sugar-coated her critique. As it was, she saw no reason to be gentle. She was certain Elinor would not respond well to gentle. She would interpret it as weakness.

Elinor listened without interruption. When Marsha reached the part about the dry-goods store, and the needless lists of its con-tents, she took out her airline ticket and checked the departure time. She asked the waiter to order a cab to take her to the airport.

"There's more," Marsha said, annoyed at what she took to be Elinor's lack of concern. "I wondered why Margaret has suddenly acquired a personal interest in dogs."

"Dogs?" Elinor asked.

"The two dogs in this manuscript have a greater role than any of the humans. They are labradors, I think. Has she got a dog?"

"Two," Elinor said. She pinned the hat on her head using two small pearl-studded clips. She was preparing to leave. "The writing itself," she asked Marsha, "is it much as it has always been?"

"You mean her style?"

"Yes, I do mean her style. Is it not up to the standard of her other books?"

Marsha had to think for a moment. Margaret was not the kind of writer one talked about in terms of style. "I suppose it's about the same," she agreed grudgingly. "But that is hardly the point. The story isn't there. If she continues in this vein, we're not going to be able to sell the book. That is the point. When you explain that to her, I think you'll find she will want to see me. No matter how lousy she might feel, she knows it's the only way we can fix this thing. Margaret is, as Alex said, a professional."

"Well then," Elinor announced. "There doesn't seem to be a problem. She'll fix what needs to be fixed. I will discuss it with her when I get back. You can send your comments by fax if you like. I've installed a machine in the cottage. Alex has the number." She had risen to her feet and was collecting her oversized purse. The gloves were already on her hands when she offered to shake Marsha's. "As for the contract, Alex has power of attorney to deal with both you and the estate. If I were you, though, I would listen to his advice about goodwill. Margaret wants to buy the place on Grand Manan and, frankly, she needs some of the advance for the down payment. So far she's had none."

Alex seemed visibly relieved when she left. He slouched back in his seat, crossed his knees, and heaved a loud sigh. "Not everyone's cuppa, that one, is she?" he asked rhetorically. "But she does have a point about the advance. You can't seriously doubt that Margaret will get it right for the eighteenth time, now, can you? She hasn't missed in ... how many? Twenty-five years." He smiled expansively. "Damned shame, though, Myles didn't get the cheque over to her, but that's not her fault. Some agents like to keep the money for the extra few weeks, collect interest, you know. ... No doubt he was one of those ..."

"Dammit, Alex, I didn't pick the bastard, she did. I'm not going to tell the Canadians the manuscript is all right when it isn't. A few days with Margaret, a few hours, if she's up to it, and we can fix this thing. What in hell is her hurry, anyway?" Marsha was not about to be appeased by Alex's warm and cuddly routine, she'd seen it before. "Besides, what can a house cost on that island for

Chrissakes? Three or four hundred thousand dollars? She doesn't need the two million and you know it. She collected a pile of royalties this year, she's got the television deal, didn't I hear four million dollars?"

"You know how those things work, Marsha, a few thousand for the options, a whole bunch when they sign, no more till they start rolling the cameras. Besides, it seems she's made some rather bad investments," Alex said. "Worse, she's got a hare-brained daughter in California with three kids and no husband, she's been supplying her with money for years. Have you ever met Charlotte?"

Marsha had seen photographs. Margaret was proud of Charlotte. She was not at all like Margaret. Slender, tall, almost willowy, she was beautiful in a way Margaret could never have been beautiful, even if it weren't for her strong chin and short neck. Margaret had the square shape and big frame of an ocean freighter. Her daughter was a sleek sailboat.

"Charlotte hasn't had a job since she gave up modelling because she was pregnant. Married twice, unsuccessfully, both men took what they could of her money and each one left her with a kid. Margaret supports the lot of them. Big house on the coast south of Los Angeles, a nanny for the grandchildren. Nothing's too much for little Charlotte. Margaret told me once that she still feels guilty about her lack of mothering skills. Thought she neglected Charlotte as a child and has been trying to atone for it ever since." Alex ordered coffee and an Amaretto for himself. He had loosened his tie and seemed ready to relax into a long afternoon of conversation.

Marsha recognized Alex's easy negotiating manner, his sharing of concerns, his eliciting sympathy for the author, building an atmosphere of mutual trust, his trademark light-handed approach to publishers. Had it not been for the size of the advance, she might have given in.

"Have to hand it to her, though, Charlotte has charm," Alex

continued. "It's Elinor who was short-changed in that department. It's hard to believe but she actually had a brief career on the stage. Didn't work out, though. And her mother didn't stay around long enough to screw up her childhood. Died when Elinor was only ten, or so ..."

"I'd love to hear the rest of that, Alex, but Morris wanted a meeting at three, and I've got a couple of auctions running, so why don't I work things out with Margaret, and I'll get back to you." She had twenty minutes to make it back to 600, and being late for a Morris one-on-one was living dangerously. He had announced in true Morris style that time was money and that his time was more money than anyone else's because he was paid more than anyone else. He had fired the comptroller for being half an hour late for a meeting.

"You're going to Grand Manan?" Alex asked.

"Do I have a choice?"

Alex shook his head. He had listened carefully to what Marsha told Elinor about the manuscript and, unlike Elinor, he understood the problems were more than cosmetic. "I'm sorry I couldn't help you with that today, but I have just received the material. Haven't had a chance to read it yet. I'll call you when I have. Tonight okay?" Alex was one of the few agents who had Marsha's home telephone number. She knew from past experience that he used it only in emergencies.

"There is one more thing," Marsha said. She had decided to leave it till last. She had also decided, once she knew Alex was Margaret's new agent, not to raise the matter with Elinor. "Jerry Haines seemed to be under the impression that he had somehow acquired Margaret's manuscripts, the three-book deal that we signed with Andrew."

Alex stared at her. "Jerry Haines?" he asked. "But he is dead, isn't he?"

"He is dead now, but he thought he was going to publish the

Drury Carters before he died. He told Dr. Schneider that he would be negotiating the German rights. He told Sophie Biddle they had the deal ..."

"Who?"

"Sophie Biddle, a junior editor at Fennell." She couldn't really believe it of him but she had to ask, "You didn't talk to Jerry about this at Frankfurt did you?"

"About what?" He had gone rigid.

"You didn't offer Drury Carter to him, did you? In the bar while he was buying drinks for everyone? That wasn't what you were celebrating?"

There was a moment's silence while Alex examined his Amaretto. Marsha thought he might cry. "Marsha, you know me better than that," he said, finally, his voice husky with emotion. "Have you ever known me to go back on a deal? Ever?"

She hadn't. But if Alex was telling the truth, he hadn't started to represent Margaret until after the Fair. Jerry's story about having bought the Drury Carters was going around earlier.

"All that talk about a contract not being valid until the money had changed hands?"

"Talk. Agent talk. You *should* know better."

"Someone must have put Jerry up to it. I don't think it was Margaret, do you? She might have had a few drinks to drown her sorrows over Andrew's demise, and they had been friends. She was closer to Jerry than she's ever been to me."

Alex shook his head. "Margaret's delighted with you. She said last night that she hoped you would continue to handle her manuscripts personally, not pass her on to that ditsy Maynard woman. She didn't want to feel like just another item on A&M's romance production line."

"That leaves Elinor."

"Selling the manuscripts for a second time?" He seemed genuinely nonplussed. "It's against the law. And why would she? Why would anyone? It's a great deal. Twenty million dollars even for someone of Margaret Drury Carter's mettle is serious money."

"Sophie Biddle thinks Jerry was serious enough, she was preparing the contracts for our books. She was calling this morning ..."

Alex sighed. "I think these damned Canadians have you spooked. Normally you'd laugh at that sort of rumour. Jerry, God rest his sinful soul, was a fun-loving troublemaker. He'd been trying to take you on over the Drury Carters ever since you snatched her from his clutches. Don't you remember?" He was still looking hurt, but he took another sip from his glass and twirled the amber liquid around, sniffing the fumes with obvious enjoyment. "In the Lippizaner right after Andrew's murder, he was going on at you about publishing Margaret in hardcovers, and how much money you were going to lose."

"It's odd, all the same. He told Bertil Nystrom he couldn't wait to see my face next day when he told me of his surprise."

"No doubt. Jerry in his cups as ever. You couldn't possibly think it true, could you?" Alex had resumed his avuncular self.

On the way out Marsha agreed that she would release the money as soon as she was satisfied that Margaret would do the work. "Have you seen Margaret's contract with Andrew?" she asked.

"Not yet. She couldn't find it, she told me. But Elinor will send it to me as soon as she has a chance to look around."

Hurrying along Fifth Avenue she opened Aaron's yellow envelope. There were a dozen pages and a covering letter on Andrew Myles's letterhead. It was marked "Personal and Confidential," and at the bottom of the letter: "Hand delivered." It read:

> *Aaron,*
> *I enclose the material we discussed. You will*
> *understand its highly explosive nature instantly and*

I trust you will treat it with the care it deserves. The complete manuscript is available after we have signed an agreement. Total advance to be only one and a half million. Payable in full on receipt. The royalties will be fifteen percent. There will be no announcements until March, unless you decide to rush into print earlier than that. There will be some additional stipulations.

My client will not wish to deal with any editorial questions. Direct them to me. He will not, as you may have guessed, participate in publicity, though he had told me that he might be willing to stage some kind of attention-grabbing local event.

I am staying at the Hessischer Hof. Call me by Friday morning 9 a.m. After that, I will sell to another bidder.

Andrew

The date was the Tuesday before the Bookfair.

The thickly typed sheets of paper were old-fashioned typing paper, the letters sunk into the sheets where the typewriter keys had hit. The first line read: "My name is Saddam Hussein. I am the ruler of Iraq. This is my story." The manuscript went on to tell of the Iraqi leader's unsavory childhood, including a couple of examples of his early initiation into torture and killing his father's opponents. There was brief mention of his brothers, one of whom had to be assassinated earlier in the year. He praised Israeli intelligence for their help and suggested that there would be more details in the manuscript. He set the scene for the Iran-Iraq war and mentioned the documents that would be included to show the U.S. and British arms and technology that were supplied for the build-up. There were a few names of State Department officials, arms dealers, and CIA bosses of the time. He referred to direct conversations he'd had with the President, and said there was a transcript with the manuscript.

He outlined his reasons for the planned invasion of Saudi Arabia, claiming to have the encouragement of both his former allies. There was to be a common trade pact that included exclusive access to Saudi oil.

There was some longish stuff about oil pricing, Shell, and Exxon, and lists of senior executives of both companies that had been paying him for his role in the eventual invasion. He would supply a full transcript of his conversations with the American ambassador who claimed to be acting on the President's orders.

The double-cross by the U.S. was sketched in a few lines, mentioning the American ambassador by name, referring to taped conversations and coded messages, from the White House no less, leading up to his invasion of Kuwait, the ill-fated attempt to regain land that was always part of Iraq. There were to be true stories of the victims of Star Wars. There were some unkind words about the Saudi royal family and its unbridled greed at the expense of the Arab world being overwhelmed by the West.

The recent defection of part of his own family was kept till the end. Naturally, the CIA had full responsibility for that fiasco. More names. Then the promise that all his enemies would suffer early death.

The six pages ended on that high note, followed by a short disclaimer which said that the supreme commander had dictated this outline, and had not read it.

Marsha slipped the foolscap sheets back into the envelope. She was already in the A&M building, digging for her plastic identity card to satisfy the elderly doorman. She stopped to look behind her. There were a few stragglers coming back from lunch, none seemed focussed on her. Some were familiar. She remembered Frans's warnings in the railway station. It was possible, she thought, that various people would be loath to see this thing published. And there had been two deaths.

Was Andrew Myles selling the book for Frans, as they had agreed? Frans couldn't have known that the thing had been given to Aaron. He would have told her, had he known. It was more likely, as she had suspected, that Andrew had gone into business for himself. It was also becoming more and more likely that his murder and Jerry's had both had something to do with the thin paper package she carried under her arm.

She stood near the last set of elevators, pretended indifference as a couple of elevator doors opened and people filed in. Finally, when there was no one else waiting for the upper floors, she jumped into an elevator just as the doors were closing. She was alone all the way to the 56th floor.

New blue carpets had been installed on this floor since the Canadians moved in. The walls had been stripped of framed design awards and best-selling book jackets and painted a reserved pale blue. Glass had been installed between the receptionist and the elevators. You had to announce who you were by picking up the white phone attached to the partition. You had to be expected by someone on this floor to gain admission.

Though the receptionist had seen Marsha some dozen times in the past month alone, she showed no sign of recognition. She never did.

When Marsha told her she was going to a meeting with David Morris, she checked her Day-Timer before buzzing Marsha in. Morris's office was in the corner at the end of the corridor, with windows looking onto both Fifth Avenue and 52nd Street. There was only one point of entry and that was guarded by his personal secretary. She had been described as "personal" in the five job descriptions he had posted on the inter-company notice board and in *Publishers Weekly*. "It means she has to pick up his laundry," Fay had suggested. The fact that the job had to be filled five times merely confirmed everyone's views of Morris. Being his personal secretary probably meant being his slave.

The most recent secretarial acquisition had held the position for less than a month. She still smiled when someone arrived to see her boss. "Mr. Morris will be right with you," she said and she returned to her typing.

Since Morris's arrival, a couple of chairs had been added to this small space. They were lined up, side by side, near the entrance, facing Morris's door, sideways to the secretary's desk. The idea was, Marsha figured, that you would feel like a kid outside the principal's door, waiting for some reprimand. The narrow, straight-backed chairs closely resembled chairs a school would have. They were built to keep you alert, not comfortable.

The only attempt at decoration was a framed photograph of a yellow and ochre wheatfield with a red silo, both dwarfed by an aggressively blue sky. Marsha chose to examine the not very inter-esting picture instead of taking one of the chairs. Close up it was even less interesting than it had been from a distance. It was the only picture on the wall, the only attempt at a personal touch — if you could call a photograph of the prairie personal — that Morris had allowed.

The door opened and Connor Sagfield marched out. He saluted when he saw Marsha. "Your turn, chief," he said. He had a broad smile on his face, not the face of a man about to look for another job, Marsha thought. In response to her raised eyebrows he gave a thumbs-up signal and swaggered down the corridor.

The newish secretary scrabbled around her desk and leapt ahead of Marsha just as she reached the door. "Miss Hillier is here for her three o'clock appointment," she announced breathlessly.

Morris sat behind his smoke-grey glass-top table. It was bare except for a thin sheaf of foolscap centred exactly in front of him. Aaron occupied the low-slung leather-backed designer chair to the side. He was slouched down in it, his ankle resting on his knee, his left hand fingering the brownish sock that exuded from the cuff of his corduroy pants. In his right hand he held a manila envelope that looked exactly like the one he had handed Marsha on the steps of St. Patrick's Cathedral. He did not look up when Marsha entered. He continued to examine his nails. There was something about both his posture, the way he had so casually folded himself into the low chair, and the studied casualness of looking at his nails, that was intended to suggest to Marsha that he was comfortable with Morris.

"You must be very busy catching up after Frankfurt, Marsha," Morris said, gazing over the tops of his horn-rimmed glasses. "I won't keep you long. I asked Aaron here, to join us because it's his project, perhaps you'd like to sit there?" He indicated the other leather-backed chair.

Marsha hated the chairs because they were so low that her knees jutted up when she sat upright, which was particularly awkward in a fitted skirt. The burgundy dress had a short skirt that ended a couple of inches above the knees. Morris would be looking straight down her thighs. "I'd rather stand, if you don't mind," she said lightly. "Big lunch today. Too much sitting down."

"As you like," Morris said. "I assume you read the proposal?" She said she had.

"And?"

"It's an interesting proposal," she lied, "but very difficult to know what the manuscript might be like until we can read it."

"Not much chance of that, I'm afraid," said Aaron, as if he were stating the obvious. "It's the kind of thing you either believe in or you don't. Personally, I think it's a no-brainer. Can't miss. Once in a lifetime opportunity to publish a document everyone will want to read, comment on. Think of the news coverage, the serial rights in England alone would go for hundreds of thousands — covers of *Time*, *Newsweek*, debates on the morning shows about whether he was telling the truth or not. Maybe the Pentagon would try to stop us publishing it. More stories. Some carefully planned leaks before publication. *People* magazine, you know the stuff." He was getting so excited he had lost his composed stance.

Playing to Morris, Marsha thought. "One and a half million, Andrew's letter said?"

"Not much for such a property, wouldn't you say, David?"

Morris steepled his fingers over the glass and peered at Marsha over their tips. "Question is, what you think, Marsha? That's what I would like to know. Organizationally, your view is in the matrix. You're the editor-in-chief. What do you think?"

Marsha was relieved to note she was still in the matrix, whatever that meant to Morris. She pretended to be deeply in thought. She rubbed her chin, she hoped, pensively. She glanced out the window. She took the pages out of the envelope and frowned at Andrew Myles's letter. "It's difficult to imagine that seventy-five thousand Americans would fork out twenty dollars each, just to find out how Saddam Hussein grew up and what his version is of the events leading up to the war, or even of the war itself. They were fairly pleased with their version of the war. Far as I'm concerned it's what we needed to pull us out of the Vietnam doldrums."

"Seventy-five thousand?" Aaron asked.

"She's working out the royalties to earn back the advance," Morris told him. "One of the critical success factors. That's all?" he asked Marsha.

"No. There is also the fact that Andrew Myles has been murdered."

"The deal doesn't need an agent," Aaron said, trying to regain lost ground. "I can work on it directly. Andrew told me the manuscript was completed and Saddam Hussein is waiting for the advance in cash before he hands it over."

"You are actually planning to send him the money?" Marsha's voice rose part of an octave despite her best efforts.

"Of course not," Aaron said dismissively. "I will go to Baghdad and read the manuscript myself. Then, I will give him the money."

"Personally," Marsha assumed. The ghastly photograph of Jerry Haines, dead, flitted into her mind.

Aaron didn't bother to respond.

"Thank you both," Morris said. To Aaron, he added, "I will think about it and let you know." He turned to Marsha. "A moment, if you don't mind," he said. "We have another matter to discuss. One-on-one."

Aaron seemed crestfallen as he went out the door.

There was not a single private object in this office. No pictures of the wife — did Morris have a wife? Nobody knew. Or children — did he? Not even a desk lamp, no memorabilia, no comforts whatsoever, nothing except the framed Harvard Business School degree. Had he read somewhere that this was the way to run an efficient office or did he not have a life?

"Margaret Drury Carter has hired a new agent," he told Marsha. "I assume you know him."

Marsha said she did know Alex Levine.

"I assume, then, you know that she has not yet received the payment on signing. Though the cheque was cashed by Andrew Myles's Citibank account the day we had it run over to him, he did not send her share on to her. He had two weeks in which to do it, and he didn't. Is that very peculiar, you think?"

Marsha shrugged. "Not really. Agents have been known to keep authors' money for several weeks. Months even."

"For the interest." Morris understood right away. "Miss Drury Carter thinks it might take weeks before the dead man's affairs are settled and she gets her money. Fair enough. I want you to follow your plan and go to whatever island you said it was and settle her down some." He was maintaining eye contact in vintage Morris fashion.

"Grand Manan," she said.

"Wherever," he pondered. Obviously, people from Alberta didn't spend much time in New Brunswick, Marsha thought. "If you feel you must take a few days with her mucking around with the manuscript, go ahead and do it."

That certainly described the editorial process accurately. "Thank you," Marsha told him. "Have you read my note about Regis Philbin?"

"Not beyond a million," he told her.

"Can I have some leeway on that?"

"Two hundred, if you must."

"Crichton?"

"Stan's numbers don't add up. If you can't get it for three million, leave it." He had walked around his desk and was standing nose to nose with Marsha. "You don't think this Hussein thing will fly. Do you?"

Marsha composed her face into noncommittal. "I think it's a gamble," she said.

"I will let him go to Baghdad," Morris added.

"I see," said Marsha. A man of vision, after all. She didn't think Aaron was going to like it there, but why interfere?

CHAPTER
SEVENTEEN

OVERNIGHT THE FOG HAD ROLLED INTO FLAGG Cove and overtaken the harbour, the road, and even Swallowtail Light. All you could see from the scenic window of Judith's room was a blanket of white. There was a great stillness that came with the thick fog, a sense of being closed in, coddled in soft, cotton wool. Except for the regular, distant, haunting boom of the foghorns, there was not a sound. The thin, white light diffused through the fog, suggested daylight. Judith had been waiting for the fog to clear since ten o'clock. It hadn't budged.

She had breakfast alone. June had set out canned orange juice, dry toast, jam, butter, fresh muffins still warm from her oven, and percolated coffee. She, herself, was nowhere to be seen. Jimmy had wrapped himself in the eiderdown cover and slept. Judith walked about his room for a while, hoping he'd wake up. When he didn't, she left him sleeping.

There was an old black phone hanging on the wall of the narrow entranceway of the Compass Rose. After a couple of attempts to call Marsha, Judith concluded the phone was wired so as not to accept long distance calls. She had a lively discussion with the local operator who finally accepted her credit card number and then put her on hold for a person-to-person call to Debbie Brown in New York. "Have you heard from Margaret Drury Carter yet?" she asked Debbie.

"No, but I'm not worried. She's sure to want to talk to you," Debbie assured her. "Her publisher sent out a press release today about all her international sales at the Bookfair."

She called Marsha. Sheila told her Marsha was busy all day, best to try her at home in the evening. Sheila divided Marsha's calls into professional and personal. She knew Judith was a friend. She did not like to interrupt Marsha's business meetings for mere friends.

She tried Margaret again.

The phone rang seven or eight times before it clicked as if it had been picked up but it was only the answering machine. "Hello," it said in Margaret Drury Carter's unmistakable fake Southern drawl. "Ah'm not fah from the phone but much too deep in my fictional world to talk to you now. Do leave a message and Ah'll be shuah to call yew just as soon as Ah come back to the real world."

At least she was on the island. Sometime she would decide she needed a rest from her writing, and Judith would get her interview. Meanwhile, she would work on the local colour, to get a sense of the place. *Home and Garden*'s devoted readers would want to know why a great Southern writer — they had no idea she was a fake one — would come up here for the autumn. She found the fat ring-bound stenopad she had purchased for the trip and stuffed it into her extra-large purse — really, more of an ungainly carry-all — with the handy map of the island that the tourist office had supplied.

A perfect day for her hand-knit sweater, scarf, socks, and toque. While June kept the inside of the small house warm with space heaters and the soot-blackened log-fireplace in the dining room, outside the temperature had dropped at least ten degrees. No longer was there the feeling of gentle cotton-wool about the fog. On close encounter it was chafing cold, tiny particles of icy dampness grating against her skin. In a few seconds she felt wet through to her underwear. Time to return for a quick change and — to hell with Preston O'Neill, and whether she would look like a Toronto tourist — the rain-proof canary-yellow slicker.

From the evening before she remembered something resembling a sidewalk on the far side of the road, but she couldn't see across, so she stayed on the side of the Compass Rose and attempted to make her way towards where the harbour had been. The ground was packed gravel with potholes. She had to be careful where she stepped. Past the guest house there was a sharp-edged picket fence, maybe a house behind it, and two more houses closer in, shadows in the fog. Far off, the foghorns bellowed their eerie warnings. It was hard to imagine there would be boats about on a day like this. Nearby she could hear water slapping against wood and stones shifting in the waves. She came to a storefront with cans of paint, a chainsaw, and shovels in the window. She tried the door. It was unlocked.

Inside, it smelled dusty, dank, and mildewy. There was a single lightbulb hanging from a wire in the ceiling. A man in brown, shiny overalls, check sleeves rolled up to his shoulders, was sanding the counter. He glanced up when he heard the door slam shut. Then he started to work again. "It's the dampness, you see," he told her between lunges at the counter. "It eats away at everything. We're not really open today. Too much fog to be out shopping. But then, I guess you're not shopping are you?"

Judith looked around the store. There were shelves with cardboard boxes full of nails and screws; hammers, wrenches, chisels, and screwdrivers of different sizes hung on the walls; on the floor, metal wheelbarrows were piled on top of one another; assortments of garden rakes, shovels for all occasions, and a full range of mysterious tools she was sure someone, not herself, would find very useful. She smiled at him and said, "You've guessed right."

"You're a new arrival, then?" he asked. He was a big man, muscles bulging on his arms as he kept working, face ruddy, nose flat and bulbous, hair sparse and plastered down with sweat.

"Last night," she told him, "on the ferry."

"Visiting someone?"

"Miss Drury Carter," Judith said.

"The writer woman up in the old Whale Cove Cottage?" He stopped sanding for a moment and looked at Judith.

"Yes, have you met her?" she asked, friendly, and casual.

"Uhuh, couple times."

"I suppose she's been in here to buy things for the cottage," Judith said, still very casual, though she was already thinking of an angle for a lead into the story.

"Not exactly," the man said. He went on with his sanding, while Judith wandered over to a shelf with lightbulbs and fixtures. "Old place like that needs more than a few lightbulbs, I daresay," he continued, angling towards her as he spoke. Though he hadn't looked up, he seemed perfectly aware of where in the store Judith was.

"Especially if you intend to stay over the winter," Judith hazarded.

It had been a good guess. "Never been used in the winter, that house," he told her, becoming a tad more animated. "Needed the walls insulated, a basement dug, heaters put in. All they'd had in there was one of them log-jobs, more for show than heat, if you ask me. Something nice to look at on a summer's night, but not much good to you when the chill sets in."

Judith was scrambling around in her grab bag of memories for something that would keep him talking about Margaret's place. A flash of her father attempting to winterize the cottage he'd built in the woods near Georgian Bay. "The cheap end of the lake," her mother had commented. For years, she had grumbled that they could only afford to rent other people's cottages for the summer months, but she was not going to praise him for trying, at last, to have a cabin of their own.

"Can't keep the heat in without a basement," she said at last, echoing what her mother had told her father at the time. Her mother had gone on to ridicule any thought that he might have succeeded.

He hadn't even tried to drill through the rock. He had contented himself with laying wooden sheeting along the windward side and putting in a second layer of glass. Years later Judith realized he had not intended the cottage to be so warm that Marjorie might have been tempted to use it in the cold weather, as well. That would have defeated its purpose.

"Right you are," he said, and he went on to tell her what her mother had said at the time. "Tough to cut a basement here."

"Too much rock," Judith said, still echoing her mother.

"Up on the bluff where the house is, there is a bit of earth, not much. You can tell from the trees. Even spruce needs some soil. It took us three weeks to dig down. Left it rough, too, they don't need to use it, not for just the two of them. There are two big bedrooms, and the study." He stopped as suddenly as he had begun. "You're staying there, aren't you?" he asked suspiciously.

"No," Judith admitted. "I'm at the Compass Rose."

"Hm. I wondered how you'd gotten yourself down here in this pea-souper. Isn't there enough room up there for you?" he asked.

"Margaret's finishing a novel," she said, telling the truth, but still pretending she was a friend of Drury Carter's. "She doesn't like to have houseguests while she works. I'll be heading up there just as soon as the fog clears."

"Be a while, then," he said.

"You did all the work on the old house, then?" Judith asked, drawing him back to talk about the house.

"Me and a couple of men," he told her with some pride. "I do all the building contracts up the North end."

"How was she to work for?" Judith asked, smiling as if to indicate that she expected Margaret to have been a tough client.

"She is just fine. She likes islands. Told me this place was just darling." He chuckled. "She's okay, though. She loves the house, she loves the idea that another writer had lived there way back. Woman called Willa Cather, do you know of her? People around here still talk about her and that friend of hers she always had with her. Name of Edith. Something funny about those two, if you ask me."

"Who?" Judith asked. She had been examining a box full of Christmas decorations and wondering where she was going to spend Chrismas this year. "Margaret and Elinor?"

"Of course not. Elinor's a bit particular, but they're fine. Willa and Edith." He had returned to his sanding and spoke in brief takes following the rhythm of his movements. "All before my time, but you still hear the stories. They had rented the same place in the twenties. Came every summer for over a decade, they did. Willa Cather wore a tie and jacket, if you know what I mean." He winked conspiratorially. "My grandmother knew them. I told Miss Drury Carter that Willa Cather had used the large attic as her study. There is enough room there for a table and chair, even one of those recliners if she gets tired, and on a good day she can look across the cliffs to the sea." He rubbed the counter clean with a soft cloth and admired his work. "That's where Miss Drury Carter told me she was going to do her writing. 'Good enough for Willa, good enough for me,' she said." He looked up at Judith. "Have you read her stuff?"

"Willa Cather's?"

"Margaret Drury Carter's."

"I read *Conspiracy of Roses* and *Magnolias in the Rain*," Judith said. After she had been given the assignment, she had borrowed *Midnight Dance* from one of her newfound friends in Jemseg. But she hadn't finished it. "Have you?"

"The wife likes that stuff," he said, dismissively, as if they'd been discussing doilies, or cosmetics, or some other strictly female thing. "I never even heard of her till she came here," he added proudly. "You a relative or something?"

Judith said she wasn't. Then, because she was sure June was going to tell everyone anyway, she told him that she was working for *Home and Garden* and she was here to interview Margaret about what it was like to live and write on Grand Manan. That, as she had assumed, was the end of their conversation. Clearly, he wasn't a man who liked to think of himself blabbing to journalists.

He didn't say another word, except to direct her to June's store. He told her she'd have no trouble finding it even in this weather. There wouldn't be any cars on the road, so she should walk to the end of where the rails and chain barrier ended and turn sharp right. She'd know she had reached the other side of the road when she stumbled into the sidewalk. Island Arts and Crafts would be immediately in front of her.

He surprised her as she opened the door to leave. "I shingled the roof for her," he said. "Hand-cut shingles, all from the island." He didn't want to be quoted in her article, but he sure did want that roof to be mentioned.

She had no trouble following his directions. When she reached the end of the chain-link fence, the wind obliged by whipping the fog around and clearing the way for a brief, hazy view of the arts and crafts store. It was a blue two-storey building, tiny windows with white trim, peaked roof. Halfway across the road it had all but disappeared again.

A tiny bell signalled Judith's entrance.

June was writing in a big leather-bound book, perched on a tall stool near the window. "Can't think how you found your way down here," she said. "Great start for a foreigner — that's what we call mainlanders here, don't you know."

"Even Torontonians?"

"Especially Torontonians." June laughed. "Suddenly we've

become popular in Upper Canada. Last summer we had over three thousand visitors. Couldn't go anywhere without some guy with a backpack wanting to know where the trail started. No complaints here, mind, they love all my stuff. Even if the weather turns nasty and they can't take pictures, there's plenty in my store to remind a tourist when he gets home that he's been here." She brandished her pen in the direction of the interior. "I'm just doing my year-end accounts. Sales are up again. I'm closing in another week." She was balancing the big book on her knees by propping her feet up on a black-faced wooden sheep, complete with white fleece coat and button eyes. "Got this idea from a gallery in France, if you must know," June said when she noticed Judith examining the sheep. "Americans just love them."

"Why sheep?" Judith asked.

"Why not sheep? This island used to be full of the little wool-bearing critters. All the trails in the *Heritage Trails Guide* — you got to get a copy — used to be sheep trails. They're marked in red now for the tourists. The sheep knew where to go without the signs or the guidebook." Without abandoning her perch, she leaned forward and picked up a paper-thin booklet from the window. "Your Margaret Drury Carter got one of these first day she arrived. She and her niece came in here. They were planning to walk all over the island. Elinor said they would be hiking, but her aunt corrected her. Said she was too old for hiking; she'd walk. I said, far as I was concerned, hiking is just walking with an attitude. Go look around, yourself, maybe you'll find something you can't be without."

Judith walked about the soft-lit store admiring the polished wooden carvings of whales. All species of whale could be had in the store, June assured her. She had run out of humpbacks now, it being the end of the season, but there were two craftsmen on the island who could deliver an order in a month. They used only local wood. There were oven mitts with different patterns of waves and fish, big hand-knitted sweaters, not unlike Judith's own, but with the colours still intact. There was a table with Grand Manan mugs, the island the shape of an upside-down footprint with a dominant big toe. There were miniature Swallowtail lighthouses, hand-painted cards, bookmarks, and earmuffs; a whole set of shelves with fishtail-handled tableware, embroidered napkins, tablecloths, whalebone-handled knives; there were quilts of every size from baby's bed to king's.

"Did she buy one of these, as well?" Judith asked, admiring a quilt hanging on the wall, blue on darker blue patches that were made to look like rolling waves.

"She certainly did," June said proudly. "She bought two of them. One for herself and another to send to her daughter in California. She picked the ones with pink and mauve. Told me those were her colours. 'Ma deah,' she'd said," June was trying for a Southern accent and doing about as good a job as Margaret herself, "'We all have our trademark colours, and those are mah own.' She came in here done up like she was off to a reception with the queen, in all those fancy flouncy clothes, her white gloves, and her big straw hat with ribbons hanging off it in the back. She wore a white blouse had more handwork on it than most stuff I sell, lace here," she ran her hand up her neck, "and lace here" indicating her wrists, "lace just about everywhere. And her mauve skirt all gathered at her waist, she was the best-dressed tourist this island has ever seen."

"When did she first arrive on the island?"

"Late June, it was, the flowers were blooming, and she loved that: columbine and garden lupine, pink, white and violet; she picked them, she told me, to decorate the house. You know she is in Willa Cather's old place?"

"The man in the hardware store told me about that," Judith said.

"Fred?"

"He didn't exactly introduce himself. Preston O'Neill mentioned her as well. Willa Cather must have been quite the celebrity around here." In any event, Judith thought, Willa Cather would make one hell of an opening to her story for *Home and Garden*, one writer succeeding another in the same house, contrasting tastes, comparing styles.

"Only one we had living on the island, till Drury Carter came."

"I think Fred might have been suggesting Willa Cather was gay. She and Edith must have raised some eyebrows here in the twenties."

June shrugged. "On Grand Manan that would still be a bit of an eyebrow-raiser. Did you say you met Preston O'Neill?"

Judith told June about her encounter on the ferry.

"The paintings on the far wall are all his. Did he tell you he used to teach painting in my little summer school? Damned fine water colours he used to do." Though she was still sounding gruff, Judith thought some tiny whiff of gentleness had crept into June's voice.

They were indeed beautiful; very soft lights, big skies, rolling clouds, green and purple pastures. There was one big painting of a giant rock rising out of the water, black, menacing, white foam gathering in its crevices, water breaking on its sharp edges. The sky was as dark as the water, both shimmering green. June, who had joined her in admiring the painting, had turned a light on to let her see it more clearly. "It's scary," Judith said, "and beautiful." On the edge of the painting there were white gulls circling, their wings shining in the sun that must have been coming through the clouds somewhere though its rays hadn't yet reached the rock.

"You might have asked him about the famous writer," June said. "Preston's babysitting the dogs for Elinor Drury while she's away on the mainland."

"He didn't tell me that."

"He wouldn't," June announced. "Doesn't like to tell you more than he figures you need to know. It took me over a year to find out he'd been married once and has a couple of kids. Wife stayed behind in Toronto. I was surprised he'd struck up a friend-ship with those two women, they wouldn't have much in common, I'd have thought."

"Why do you say that?" Judith asked.

"They've got too much pretension and way too much money; he has neither. And I used to think he didn't care. When he first came he'd take any job he could get. Helped Fred out with his building business, did odd jobs for the women in the summer when the men were off fishing, fixing this and that, you know. Everyone liked him. I met him through Fred in the hardware store, and that's when he told me that he had studied drawing at the Ontario College of Art. He'd gone into an architect's firm in the seventies, but the work dried up when the building industry collapsed in Toronto — but you'd know all about that, wouldn't you." June looked at Judith suspiciously. "You didn't know him back home, did you?"

"No."

"Well, I took him on as an instructor. I suppose he told you that he used to work for me?" June's tone changed again, as if she was annoyed about something. She turned off the light over the paintings.

Judith said he had.

"And I suppose he told you he's stopped painting, then." June said peevishly. She fussed with her hair, sweeping the sides back and trying to capture a short ponytail with a ceramic hair clip she had picked up from one of her display boxes.

Men, Judith thought sympathetically. "Something about working in stone," she mumbled, picking her way through the minefield. "I had no idea Margaret Drury Carter had dogs," she added brightly. "What kind?"

"A golden retriever and a Newfoundland." June seemed happy to change the subject. "They make a heck of a noise when they start up barking. Set up a proper chorus with the seals down in the cove, you could hear them a mile away. Elinor must have had a word with them about that because they stopped after they all moved into the house. At first it was just for the summer, but they decided they liked it so much they'd stay for the year. Wouldn't surprise me if Margaret bought the place."

Near the window there was a wire rack for paperback books. Almost all the ones displayed were Margaret Drury Carter's. They all had garish mauve, pink, and gold-lettered covers, and not one of them was thinner than a brick. Judith picked up a copy of *Midnight Dance*. At five hundred pages, it was one of her flimsiest tomes. She toyed with the idea of buying it, but at nine dollars it was no bargain. Nine dollars would probably buy her and Jimmy lunch. James had managed to make his infrequent alimony cheques seem like acts of charity, rather than part of the divorce settlement their lawyers had negotiated so many years ago.

Of course, James had hired one of the best divorce lawyers he could find, and Judith had had to settle for what she could afford: a friend who specialized in libel work and knew about as much about divorce law as Judith did herself. In the end they both got what they had paid for. James left for Chicago with the pretty young girl who had brought in her collie pup for his shots. In the beginning, the girl never ceased to be amazed by James's gentle ways with animals, and had found him irresistible though he was at least fifteen years her senior. "That'll be why," Marsha had told Judith, "she'll outgrow him," she'd predicted, and she had been prophetic. Five years later, James signed on for yoga and self-realization lessons, went to an analyst, and told Judith he was searching for his true self. No doubt, it had been the other self that was left behind by the now not-so-adoring young thing, who was newly in love with another man.

For a while James had even entertained the notion of coming back to Toronto, at least until Judith shattered his illusions about the home fires still burning for him in what he liked now to think of again as his home. Left to his own devices, James met another woman who found him charming.

Luckily, his third marriage was still ticking.

In the end, Judith bought a copy of *Death Comes for the Archbishop*, one of two slender Willa Cathers on the rack. It was only $4.95.

The fog had lightened to a filmy grey veil that allowed a glimpse of the harbour across from the Compass Rose. She could see the faint outlines of boats both large and small, all tilting this way and that, as if they had been tossed there by a drunk. They barely moved as the wind whipped them.

"It must be low tide," June said, following Judith's gaze.

Judith asked for directions to the bakery. She would pick up a few things for Jimmy and herself for lunch.

"There's some butter in the fridge, if you need it. Coffee's on. There's a couple of beers if you prefer. You can replace them when you can drive up to the liquor store. This'll clear in the afternoon." She was preparing to return to her accounts. "I suppose you'll be heading up to Whale Cove soon as the weather lets up?" she asked.

Judith said she would.

The wind had gathered momentum, whipping up the gravel on the road, and Judith thought it must have been driving the rain along the top of the sea because it tasted both icy and salty. When she crossed to the harbour side she saw that all the boats were out of the water, lying this way and that, a few up to their gunnels in mud. There were seagulls stamping around in the mud and circling in shrieking flocks overhead. In the distance the foghorns kept up their wailing. She could hear the seals bark close to shore.

She wished she had brought her rubber boots so she could go down to the water. In spite of the cold, swirling fog patches, or perhaps because of them, the harbour was beautiful.

The Island Bakery, June had told her, was a dozen houses south of the Compass Rose. Judith had no trouble recognizing it from June's description. It was the only place she had seen along the road that anyone might suggest was picturesque. All the other houses were low-slung, brown brick buildings with small square windows. The bakery was in a white wood-shingled building with gables and a latticework-covered porch, white-painted wooden pillars and tall windows that had been outlined in blue. Each window had its own separate gable. There was white ironwork furniture on the porch, including a canopy-covered swing set. There were two hand-lettered signs with cute blue arrows. One pointed towards Reception, the other towards the Island Bakery.

The door to the bakery was locked but it opened a moment after she pressed the button designated as "Press to Enter."

There was a wonderful smell of fresh baking bread inside. The small room was painted white, like the outside of the building, and there were two sets of wooden chairs and small round tables near the window. A long counter at the back displayed various sizes of breads and a couple of pies. Behind, there was a big oven as tall as the very pregnant young woman standing in front of it. She wore a crisp white apron that tied over her shoulders, a blue dress with rounded white collar and matching cuffs. She was writing on a notepad she had rested on her bounteous tummy, the phone cradled between her shoulder and her ear.

"Not until three," she was saying into the telephone, "and I could set it outside for you just before I leave ... No, not today, the weather is terrible for driving ... No, I haven't seen anyone ..." She motioned with her chin for Judith to come right in. She was blond with a pink complexion, dark-blue eyes, hair pulled back off her face into a squiggy. She had pinned stray bits into place. She had a wide forehead and flared nose not unlike June's. Beads of perspiration gathered over her brow. The oven was warm enough for Judith to feel it near the door.

"He hasn't been here yet, but I am expecting him around eleven ... yes, he did call ... No ... Okay ... Thank you. Hope you do, too. Goodbye." The young woman hung up the phone and wiped her hands on the apron before turning her attention to Judith. "You've chosen a heck of a time to visit," she said. "Can't see much past your feet out there. Staying at the Compass Rose?" she asked without missing a beat.

Judith introduced herself, though she was fairly sure there was no need to.

"I'm Nan Cheney," the young woman told her. "And this is Ross." There was a tiny boy hiding behind the counter. He was chewing on a toy car and, at the same time, picking his nose. He was not particularly interested in Judith.

"Smells like you've been baking today," Judith said with a warm smile she hoped was disarming.

"I bake every day except Sundays and Mondays," Nan said. "Supply everyone this end of the island. Even your friends the Drury Carters." She returned Judith's smile.

"I guess you must have talked to June?"

"You guessed right. Have you been up to see them yet?" She was peering through the glass door of the oven.

"Not yet," Judith said. "I phoned this morning but Margaret is working on her book this morning."

"Not now, she's not. You call her from here, if you like. She just phoned in her order of bread and pies, extra muffins, too. Be a sure thing she's down in her kitchen planning the meal. Her niece is coming back on the ferry tomorrow morning, she said she needed more than yesterday, when Elinor was in New York." She started to pack a dozen blueberry muffins into a brown paper bag. "Can't get fresh blueberries this time of year, of course, not in this part of the world in any event," she said when she saw Judith looking at one of them. "Next best thing, though. Mrs. White, down in Grand Harbour picks them fresh when they're in season, and bottles them herself. You ought to try one, and take another for the lad, won't you?"

Judith was already digging in her purse for the money. The pungent scent of still-warm muffins was too hard to resist. "I heard Ms. Drury Carter loves your baking," she said. "Quite a compliment from a woman who's had the best of everything, at least since she's become such a great success." Over the many years she had spent interviewing for her freelance assignments, she had learnt that one of the easiest ways to a story was to compliment the storyteller.

Nan did not disappoint her. "They both love 'em," she said, "specially the blueberries. And in the summer I made some strawberry muffins just for Miss Drury Carter. She said she could remember having strawberry muffins when she was a child. Her mother used to make them for her and her brother when they were kids. Devil of a job, though, the strawberries are too juicy. They make the dough run."

Ross began to cry. Nan Cheney picked him up and sat him on her hip, his feet scrabbling for purchase around her big belly. When he didn't succeed, he cried harder. His mother came out from behind the counter and sat on one of the little chairs near the front, laid him against her bosom and stroked his head. "Won't be long now before he has a playmate," she mused.

Judith remembered the feverish anticipation of Jimmy's arrival; how Anne, only three at the time, had been certain the whole thing had been arranged for her benefit, to provide her with a new toy, something like the furry creatures she had grown used to around their house. James used to bring home animals their owners had abandoned, puppies no one wanted, and a few of the pedigree dogs he had operated on and thought they might get lonely in the animal clinic during the night.

James had been wonderful with animals.

In hindsight, it seemed to Judith that she had fallen in love when she saw him giving mouth to mouth resuscitation to a kitten. There had been something about the gentle, careful way he had held the cat's dainty face in his hand, breathing into its tiny pink nose. Another woman might have thought it was revolting, but Judith found it knee-buckling.

"I bet he thinks you're having the baby just for him," Judith said. "My daughter, Anne, was the same. She was so disappointed when we wouldn't let Jimmy sleep with her. Ross is around three, isn't he?"

"Weren't you scared she might do him harm?" asked Nan, sharing a common fear.

"Sure I was, but I got over it. You watch them for the first few months, then they settle down. Besides, babies are not as fragile as they seem." Judith slid easily into the woman-to-woman banter. She had done all this before.

"Pour yourself a cup of coffee," Nan said. "Phone's on the counter."

"How did she seem? Friendly?"

"She was in a great mood just now." She was rocking the boy on her bosom. He had quietened. "Don't mean that the way it came out. She's usually in a fine mood. That's how she was when they got here, cheerful all the time. Sure, she wore all those flouncy dresses, and carried a parasol with tassels for the sun, but she did like it here as much as Miss Drury liked it. I suppose you've heard that Elinor Drury remembers coming here as a child?"

"June told me. Do people remember her folks? Did Margaret come with her then?"

"They had a cottage near Castalia. Close to the harbour. There had been a little colony of summer cottagers around there, in the fifties and sixties. Nothing fashionable, but nice. My mom remembers them. The kids travelled in packs, looking for trouble, like kids do, you know."

Judith nodded, yes.

"Except there wasn't much trouble you could get into in those days, not on this island in any event. It sure is a beautiful place when the sun shines. You'll see. Supposed to brighten tomorrow."

"Did Drury Carter come with them?"

"Not that anyone remembers. A few remember the O'Neills, though. Couple of boys were real roughhousers."

"O'Neills, as in Preston O'Neill?"

"The same. He's another one that came back."

Judith dialled Margaret's number. After a few rings, she got the same message as before. Judith figured she must have gone back up to her study. She left another message that she was still staying at the Compass Rose and hoped to visit as soon as Margaret thought was convenient. How about early the next day? "Would you let me know what time suits you? I am completely flexible," she added. To Nan, she said, "I hear she walks down to the village every day. What time is she likely to come?"

"I don't expect to see her today. She's been too busy. Ever since she started on the new book. Takes her daily walks along the paths near the Light. Says it's all the exercise she needs. Elinor's been running most of her errands for her. Treats her like a queen, she does. Nothing but the best for her aunt. I figure those two have been together so long, she can guess what her aunt wants even before she says it." Nan got a faraway look on her face. "I wish I'd been that close to my mother. And it's too late, now that she's gone. Ah well," she smiled. "We all have our problems." She was stroking the boy's head with one hand, absently, as he snuggled against her.

It would be so comforting to hold a child again, Judith thought, watching. There had been a time when Jimmy loved being hugged. He had been clingy as a child, James had thought too much so. "You're making a Momma's boy of him," he had told her. But Judith hadn't cared, she'd felt that the children were entirely hers, not James's as well. They were what she had created to keep loneliness at bay. As luck would have it, mothering was one thing she was exceptionally good at. It was as if she had found her true calling in life. James had his work, this was to be hers, alone.

As it turned out, he didn't have much to worry about. When Jimmy hit his tenth year, he was not interested in cuddles any more. But James was already in Chicago and no longer cared.

"What does she buy from you?" Judith asked.

"Is this for *Home and Garden*?" Nan had been well-briefed by June.

"Yes. They like to have recipes, food photos, and table settings — you know. You've seen the magazine?"

Nan shook her head. "We don't have too many magazines on the island. Something like *Chatelaine*?"

"I suppose so. Lots of colour photographs, they'll want to see what the island looks like, as well. A feeling for the place, and her house, of course, the furniture, the garden, the view, her kitchen, how she lives, what she eats. They'll be more interested in that stuff than what she actually says in the interview." Judith knew Debbie Brown's audience as well as anyone on her staff. You couldn't sell story ideas to a magazine unless you knew all about it. She had even observed the subtle changes that Debbie was allowing into her feature pages. Of late, she had developed a taste for strong, independent women. It's not that she had abandoned the socialites, or the wives of the rich and famous in their fabulous settings, she still starred plenty of those, but she had taken more of an interest in ambitious career women. They had even made it into her column, "Women Who Make a Difference."

"They had the house done up for winter. All-new basement, Fred down the road did the insulation, space heaters they brought in from the mainland. All the rooms repainted. I haven't been up there but I heard it's done up like a designer had planned it for them. But Fred said it was all Elinor's doing. She's got all the ideas for colours and she's the one who had the furniture made. Pine, mostly, from Quebec. Only piece Miss Drury Carter ordered for herself was the desk she uses in the study. And the few trinkets she bought down at June's. You know that study used to be an attic before the house was bought by Willa Cather and that Edith woman she travelled with."

"They bought a whole lot here, too, June told me," Judith prompted.

"On the island? Sure. Quite a few of June's things. Some wicker chairs in Castalia."

"Where do they buy their groceries?" Judith was thinking about a sidebar on local produce. It might provide her with a paragraph before the obligatory plates and food display shots.

"There's a market at the crossroads at Cedar Street. Elinor does most of that, too. Looks after her aunt as if she were a housekeeper proper. They hired Mrs. Dollins when they first came but Elinor decided they don't need her any more. Not even for the cleaning. Margaret complained she was making too much noise with the vacuuming. She asked her a couple of times if she could keep it down, but no way you can keep a vacuum quiet. Now, I hear Elinor just sweeps the place when Margaret's working at her writing and does the noisy stuff while her aunt's on her walks. Only thing Elinor doesn't do is the baking."

"And they like all your fare."

"I told you about the muffins already. And she likes corn bread, too. Takes at least a couple of pies a week. I make different ones every day, you know," Nan said with pride. "Today's specials are still in the oven. Ten minutes to go. She ordered the steak and kidney. Said it was Elinor's favourite. Good to know she's thinking of her niece's homecoming."

"When is she coming to pick them up?"

"She's not. Said she'd love a walk, but the weather's crummy and she's got her deadline for that book. Twenty million dollars, you told June?"

"That's for three books," Judith explained.

"Oh well," Nan giggled. "My eyes glaze over when you get past a hundred thousand." She hoisted the child higher on her hip and went to check the pies in the oven. "You can take a picture of the pies if you like," she said coyly.

"I'll go back for my camera," Judith said. "Can I come with you when you deliver her order? I could maybe set up a time with her then, wander about, get a feel for the place."

"Did I say I was doing the deliveries?" Nan was indignant. "Don't I have quite enough to do here with all the baking, tending the store, watching over the guest house? Even if we don't have any guests right now, there's plenty to get on with. No, sir. Preston O'Neill does that little bit of the work for me. Used to be Harry's job, but he's gone off to Fredericton to work in a gas station. Closest he could get a job." She was panting as she removed the pies, one by one, each glossy beige to light brown, fork marks in perfect circles on the crust. "You better get your camera while they're still steaming."

Ross began to wail again.

Judith bought a couple of blueberry muffins to brighten Jimmy's morning, and left to pick up her camera at the Compass Rose.

CHAPTER

EIGHTEEN

J UNE HAD BEEN RIGHT IN PREDICTING A CHANGE
in the weather. "This time of year, nothing lasts more than a
couple of hours. The midday plane should be able to land now."
The sun was shining when Judith returned to the Compass
Rose. The wind had picked up and driven the waves up against
the pilings, a fine spray of salt water drifting in gusts over the
path to the door.

Jimmy was working at his computer. He claimed he had
plugged into a flat-earth group in Poland and had joined, briefly,
the debate over physics. He showed her some game he had
invented using a program-destroying virus; a clever gamesman
could catch it before it devoured everything he had worked on. It
was a race between the computer and its master.

Judith didn't even pretend to understand. All she asked was,
"Isn't that a bit risky?"

"Not a game for the faint-hearted," Jimmy told her. He gave
her the lopsided grin he had developed for just such occasions. It
made him feel great to have staked out a territory his mother had

no chance of invading, and certainly no hope of showing she knew it better than he did.

She gave him the blueberry muffins for his breakfast, and asked to borrow his camera to take pictures of the steaming fresh pies from Nan's oven.

"Your friend was here," Jimmy told her. "He brought me this," he pointed at the *Grand Manan Heritage Trails Guide*, "and asked if I'd like to go on a tour of the island tomorrow."

"What friend?" Judith asked blandly.

Jimmy laughed. "I suspect he thinks you'll want to join us," he told her.

"I'll have to work tomorrow. The lady author would be ready to see me by then, for sure. She didn't phone, did she?" Judith felt somewhat disappointed she would not be able to go on the tour, and that surprised her.

"There was a call from a woman with an odd accent, could barely make out what she was saying, didn't leave a message. All she said was that she'd call back when she could. She was very busy."

"Did she sound Southern?"

"No idea what that sounds like. She lisped, I'm pretty sure of that."

"Probably Margaret," Judith said.

"She said she was 'vewwy, vewwy busy,'" Jimmy mimicked. "Sounded like a drip." Judith had told him a bit about Margaret Drury Carter. She could tell this was not going to be one of her projects he'd find interesting, though he had admitted it would be a change from chasing white supremacists in Jemseg, and a lot less dangerous.

Judith returned to the bakery, took her photographs and waited for Preston O'Neill to come by.

Instead, he phoned Nan to tell her he had been called away on an urgent errand and wouldn't be able to help her out today.

"Men," Nan told Judith, "they're so bloody unreliable. Not

as if I hadn't been paying for his services. I was ready to take him on soon as he arrived. Couldn't make a living out of the pittance June pays her teachers. 'Tutors,' more like. 'An honorarium,' she calls what they get, makes it seem like it's something they should be honoured to get. Not a living, not if you want to pay your rent. Then, it took Fred and the others an age to decide it was all right to hire a foreigner. Not me. I thought any guy would choose this place, though he's not born here, he's all right by me." She went on grumbling about Preston and what could have come up that would make it so hard for him to take just the hour for the deliveries, then the diatribe subsided and she began to make plans to do it herself.

"I'd be glad to do it for you," Judith offered eagerly. "It'd give me a chance to see the cottage, maybe take some shots of the outside ..."

Nan hesitated. "You wouldn't find your way around," she said finally. "Besides, she's not my only delivery. I've got a bunch of others to make."

Judith suggested she could accompany Nan, hold the baby while she drove the car, but Nan would have none of it. "If there's one thing Margaret does not like, it's surprise visitors," she said.

When Margaret Drury Carter first moved to Grand Manan, tourists were so desperate to catch sight of the famous writer, that they would sneak up to the guest house the two women rented and knock on the door to try and get her autograph. They bought copies of her books in the Island Arts and Crafts store and hiked up the Whistle Road, their books held proudly aloft. Some just came to ogle through the windows. Elinor used to chase them away. By September they'd become so tired of the unwanted attention, she had put white blinds on the lower windows. The upper floor was well protected by tall spruces in the back and the cliffs overlooking the sea on the other side discouraged all but the most athletic gawkers. Now that they were planning to buy the house,

Margaret was thinking about having Fred put up a fence to block the view of the house from the trail.

"I think," Nan said rather primly, when Judith continued to press, "you should wait until you're invited." She went to strap Ross into his car seat first, then she returned for the bags and cartons of her baking to put into the trunk of her car.

Judith and Jimmy ate a lunch of steak and kidney pie on the porch of the Compass Rose, overlooking the harbour, watching a couple of fishing boats lurch in the wind, a lone sailboat flap at its moorings, while, towards the entrance to the harbour a couple of seals barked. They both thought they could get to like this place. It no longer seemed so crazy to Judith that Margaret and Elinor should have chosen to buy a house here. It would, she thought, be great to come back next summer and rent a cottage herself. A perfect place to try her hand at writing something other than commissioned pieces for magazines.

She would have told Jimmy what she was thinking, but she was sure he would just bring up Preston O'Neill.

She tried Margaret again. This time the answering machine was rather more personal. Margaret's voice had a special message for Judith Hayes. "Ah'm so vewwy sowwy to be difficult," she whispered, throatily. "I did tell Debbie Brown this was not a good time for me. She knows Ah do try to cooperate with the press whenevah Ah can, but there is a deadline.... Would you consider coming back in a couple of months?" Long deep sigh. "Ah'd have finished the first of the three books by then."

If the Jemseg story had shown any sign of coming to life, or if her debts had diminished, or the mortgage wasn't waiting, Judith would have considered that option. As it was, she thought she would wait for Marsha to arrive and open the door to Margaret's cottage.

Meanwhile, she bushed around for more local colour. She could give Debbie sidebars and little boxed highlights, the sort of stuff *Home and Garden* often had to pay another writer to supply. That's where the bakery would fit, the sidebar about the village, June's gift store, and the artsy life of the island in the summers. She jotted down some more questions for June on her courses, looked over her notes from the day, and decided to visit the grocery store on Cedar Street before nightfall.

It had begun to rain.

She dodged small puddles over to the street beyond the Island Bakery. The lights were on in the corner store though it was past six o'clock.

The woman behind the counter looked up as soon as the door opened, and gave Judith a small welcoming smile. "Not a lot I can tell you about Miss Drury Carter," she said pushing her glasses to the top of her head. "She doesn't come in here much. No need to. Has someone else pick up her groceries. Or did you come to shop?"

Judith introduced herself, though there seemed to be no need. Mildred already knew who she was and why she had come.

"You heard from Nan Cheney, I suppose?"

"Everybody knows you're here," Mildred said. "But I'm the only one who reads *Home and Garden* regularly. When I can get it, that is. We don't have any subscribers on the island, but I bring back copies whenever I go to the mainland. It's a nice magazine. Gives you ideas for decorating and has some very fine recipes. My Arthur doesn't like too much fancy food, but he enjoys me trying my hand at a few new dishes now and again. Haven't seen you in it, though." She talked very fast, clipping the ends of her words off and carrying on from one word into the next so quickly Judith had trouble piecing them into intelligible sentences.

"I write for a bunch of different magazines," Judith explained. "I'm a freelancer. Haven't written for this one in a while. Last time was a story about Lucy Maud Montgomery."

"Ah, her." Mildred was very pleased. "A wonderful story, *Anne of Green Gables*. We saw the whole thing on television. I bought the series on video so we could watch it again." She had come around from behind the counter and walked with Judith as she approached the fruit display. "Arthur and I went to P.E.I. once to see it in the theatre." She seemed somewhat crestfallen that she had to tell Judith she hadn't actually read her Lucy Maud piece. "Margaret Drury Carter never much cared for our fruit," she confided. "Prefers to bring in her own from the mainland."

"Why is that?" Judith asked, picking up an apple and rubbing it on her sleeve.

"She thinks she can get better stuff there, but we buy our fruit from the same people she goes to. We have twice a week delivery, and it's no more expensive than what you'd pay in St. Andrews." She watched Judith polish the apple. "Granny Smith," she said. "Fresh."

Judith put it into a paper bag she found next to the apple bin and went up the aisle to see if there was anything else she might find for their supper tonight. "I guess if she can afford to fly over for fruit, that's fine for her, though it does seem like a dreadful waste." She was using jaded old interviewing techniques, covering the subject with a comfortable blanket of sympathy, hoping Mildred would give her something she could use.

"All right for some," Mildred said. "She uses the rent-a-plane whenever she has a mind to. Less trouble than waiting for the daily service, and a lot quicker than the old ferry. Would you like to try the corn?" she was pointing at a desultory stack of yellowing corn husks in a cardboard box. "We do grow our own corn and some years we get two growths. This is the last of this year's." As if that needed explaining.

Judith stuffed a couple into her bag. Only thirty cents each. No big deal if she had to throw them out later.

"Make sure you wash them, though." Mildred tossed an extra one into the bag. "On the house," she said.

"Why?" Judith asked. "Don't usually wash corn."

"It's the bug killer we use on the island. Old-fashioned stuff, home brewed and works like a charm. But it's not so good for people. Even watered down, it can give you an upset stomach."

CHAPTER
NINETEEN

As soon as Marsha reached her office, she called Grand Manan again. She wanted to talk to Margaret before Elinor did. But the answering machine told her that Margaret was working, she could not come to the phone, and she promised to call back if Marsha left a message.

Regis Philbin's agent said he had closed with a million dollar bid by Bantam. There had been fourteen bidders, he told her, preening. It had gone six rounds. Marsha told him she would top by the ten percent. She was glad she had asked Morris for the extra room to negotiate. "I'll fax you over a deal memo," she told the agent.

"Regis will be so pleased," gushed the agent. "He has such respect for your editorial judgement."

That, and a million ten, Marsha thought, will get you a long long way to being viewed as a publishing whiz.

The Crichton auction had gone into its fourth round, and was well past the three million dollar limit Morris had set. "You'll regret this one," the agent told her.

"I know," Marsha said. She already regretted it.

She stuffed Saddam Hussein into the only drawer in her desk that had a lock, and wondered why anyone would kill over that anemic outline. Yet Frans had been right when he told her it was the only obvious connection between the two murdered men. Andrew Myles had made a deal with Jerry. He had been well on the way to another deal with Aaron. Or, as only Andrew would devise, he had been on the verge of selling the same manuscript twice. He'd pretend to accept the Fennell offer, then shop it around for a better one. If Aaron came through, he'd use some small undiscussed clause to tell Jerry they didn't have a deal after all. If Aaron didn't come through with fifty percent more than Jerry, what the hell, he still had Jerry on the line.

That was the kind of double-deal that had helped make Andrew so popular among publishers. It was the way he had bagged Jancie Withers. At the time, she had been represented by Alex Levine. Some unsuspecting soul had told Andrew how much Alex had been offered for Withers' fourth spinetingler. Andrew decided he could do better. He surveyed the scene for paperback houses whose horror lines had gone into decline, picked one, told the editor in confidence that he was empowered to offer a six-figure deal for two new Jancie Withers. Within the hour of receiving the offer in writing, he took it to another editor foundering in Stephen King's giant wake. Withers, as everyone knew, had some of the same magic as King, if not the name. The new mark upped the first offer — one that Andrew had been able to display with confidence — by some thirty percent. It was only then that Andrew had gone to see Jancie herself. He was offering a package worth more than twice what Alex had given her, and she bit.

Being an old-fashioned agent, still hanging on to honour and the value of mutual trust, Alex didn't have contracts with his authors. He didn't want to represent someone who wished to leave him, he had often said. And Jancie had left without regrets.

It was around that time that Alex had started calling Andrew

"The Jackal." "It's a wild, gregarious creature," he had explained. "Much like Andrew Myles. And it feasts on the remains of animals killed by others, claiming part of the spoil without facing the danger of obtaining it."

Jancie had been a young aspiring writer with little prospect of success and a collection of fifty or more rejection slips, when Alex decided to take a chance on her. He had reworked the first manuscript, himself, turned it into a generational horror story from the small-town saga she had originally written. She had made a decent living from writing the next three, and had been ready for the breakthrough. Only the breakthrough had been engineered by Andrew, not Alex.

She looked up to see Sheila standing in the doorway. "You're expected at the wake," she told Marsha. "Trump Tower. Twenty-third floor. Your name's been given to the security guard. You will be late," she added firmly when she saw Marsha fingering her telephone messages. She could tell that Marsha had no desire to go and she was doing her best to convince her that it was important. "Mr. Thurgood has left already." Sheila had a well-developed sense of propriety; not showing up for events you had committed to was on her list of unacceptables.

"Thurgood is going to the wake?" Marsha asked. "Why?"

Sheila shrugged.

It must be the Drury Carter contract, Marsha thought. Margaret's got him spooked about the money. It was Thurgood who had decided to follow the rules of the standard author-agent contract and send the whole advance to Andrew. Now maybe he was going to try to recover Margaret's share at the wake. It would show the Canadians' wonderful sense of occasion.

The rain had turned into a steady drizzle on Fifth Avenue and the homeward bound crowd was rushing more than usual. Nor were they displaying their customary good cheer at the prospect of getting home. They were wet and grumpy. They jostled for position at the curb, stepped in the line of cars as they ran to beat the changing lights, swore, grunted, and shoved. They made the five blocks to Trump Tower heavy going. In rush-hour New York you have no chance to worry about personal space; all you can do is establish distance by not looking directly at anyone else. Despite that, Marsha had the uncomfortable feeling that someone was following too close behind her, yet when she glanced back, she recognized no one and no one was looking directly at her.

It was almost five o'clock when she made her way through the too-pink marble atrium, past the waterfall, to the elevators serving the condominiums. The security guard checked her name on the list and waved her on. The elevator was all gilt and mirrors, the carpets two inches of soft shock absorbers. She slipped out of her wet coat, wiped the shoes on the carpet and finger-combed her hair. She hated wakes. She particularly hated going to one for Andrew Myles.

The doors swished open to reveal both Hideo and Joe Heller.

"We've paid our respects," Joe said seriously. The doleful look he had been practising at the funeral was becoming a habit. "It'll be hard to imagine New York without him. For me, Andrew *was* New York."

Hideo wore an all-black suit and black shirt, somewhat like a bad-guy extra from a Van Damme movie. He looked haggard, the exhausted mien of a recent Frankfurt survivor. "It's all very confusing," he said. "I expect to go back to Tokyo tomorrow and no one can tell me what will happen to the authors I have been representing for Andrew. His mother doesn't have any interest in the business. I'm not even sure she's his mother." He was talking to Marsha, but it was Heller who answered.

"She's not," he said. "Stepmother."

"Doesn't much matter," Hideo said sadly. "I suppose you're going straight home after?" he asked Marsha.

He had guessed right.

"No time for a drink, then?"

She told him she'd been up since before dawn, struggling with jet lag, and wanted to get to sleep early. Her mind was beginning to play tricks on her. She thought there had been a man following her from the 500 block, someone too close, as she had struggled through the swirling crowd.

"Perhaps you'd like some company on the way home then," Hideo suggested sympathetically. "I'll wait for you in the shrubbery." He was referring to the array of the lush green plants in the Tower's atrium. "I assume you won't be long."

He had guessed right again. Marsha was not going to spend more time than absolutely necessary, and she was pleased by Hideo's offer.

The apartment was much too bright for a wake. The white marble floors reflected whatever light came through the sheet-glass wall looking onto Fifth Avenue, and sparkled in the lights of the silver-footed standing lamps that dominated the sparsely furnished living room. It was a vast open space with an astonishingly high ceiling that was painted white, as the walls were. Adding to the gallery effect were six-by-seven-foot black and white paintings on the walls, each lit by its own set of lights. A couple of Rothkos, maybe a Jackson Pollock. Three Franz Klines.

The people were all gathered in the middle where there was an arrangement of low white couches, armchairs, and lamps. Two men in tuxedos stood discreetly between the group and the mirrored bar that jutted out of the wall near the entrance. One of them approached Marsha and offered her a glass of white or red wine from a silver platter. He wore white gloves.

Had Andrew planned his own wake, Marsha thought, there would have been over two hundred people, or however many it took to fill this room to back-to-back capacity, but he could not have wished for more pretension. He had loved big parties because they gave him a chance to shine. Only a year ago he had hosted the mother of all publishing parties at the Museum of Modern Art.

Over a thousand people, liberally dotted with celebrities — Anjelica Huston, Carl Bernstein, Barry Diller, Peter Jennings, Tom Brokaw, even Elizabeth Taylor had come for a brief appearance. The flavour of the evening had been champagne and peach juice in honour of Margaret Drury Carter.

"Perhaps you would care to join us." It was more of a command than an invitation. Marsha instantly recognized the ringing voice of Andrew Myles's mother or stepmother. Even if she were stepmother, it was difficult to imagine why she would have been so jolly on the plane with Myles's body in the deep-freeze. There was a touch of New England about the voice, a tone that reminded Marsha, none too pleasantly, of her own mother.

Gloria Myles sat on the sofa with its back to the window. She was very tall and very erect, and her regal appearance was enhanced by her long neck, flowing black silk dress, and heavy costume jewellery that hung in layers of gold from her neck. It was all a little too much, a little too baroque. Andrew, Marsha thought, would certainly have approved of that.

The circle included Arthur Thurgood, Jancie Withers, Connor Sagfield, Brigitte Dombert, and Andrew's longest-lasting assistant, Sam Westwood, who had sold Marsha the wildly disappointing *Vatican Secrets*. The young man sitting on Gloria's right was her yellow-cravatted companion from the Lufthansa flight. He, too, had walked by the coffin. His bulging eyes followed Marsha into the room with the same close attention he had paid her on the plane.

Marsha introduced herself to Gloria and shook the proffered soft white hand as she murmured something about deep regrets, profound sympathy, and how proud Gloria must feel of her Andrew's accomplishments.

Gloria picked up on the last piece of Marsha's condolences. "Andrew was very much his own man," she said, too loudly for it to be intended for Marsha alone. "He could have chosen any field at all, he was so full of talent. I think he chose yours because it was the one most needful."

Marsha refrained from asking in what way.

Gloria explained anyway. "It's such an old-fashioned, moribund business," she said.

Sagfield coughed into his white paper napkin and stood up to turn to the waiter for help. He downed his wine in almost a single gulp.

"Andrew was so much like his father," Gloria continued. "I lost my husband two years back," she sighed. "He, too, was an innovator. Very much his own man. He brought his own ways to whatever he touched."

"He threw open the windows and let in the fresh air," Sam added with the tiniest of smiles.

The man with the bulging eyes, on Gloria's right, introduced himself as Stephen Myles, Andrew's brother. He seemed a great deal younger than Andrew. Maybe in his late twenties. There was certainly no resemblance between the brothers. "I admired him greatly," he said. "Andrew," he added, as if he'd needed to explain. "But we didn't know much about his business, did we?" He included Gloria in this rhetorical question.

Marsha perched on the arm of the chair occupied by Sagfield and thought, briefly, of the last time she had sat down like this: at the Bertelsmann party, when Andrew Myles was already dying, or dead, in the chair. Sagfield, apart from the thin line of perspiration on his forehead, seemed quite vigorous.

"As I was telling your Mr. Thurgood ..."

"Arthur," the fat man said modestly.

"... Andrew kept his own counsel. He did not confide in us." It was Gloria's turn to include the young man on her right, "Nor did he inform us of his business dealings. Sam has agreed to meet with all the authors, the publishers, whomever," she made a sweeping gesture towards the room and perhaps all of New York, "and answer your questions. I have none of the answers."

Sam was wedged into the sofa next to Brigitte. He was looking at the space between his black brogues.

"Sam?" Thurgood demanded, "What's your last name, son?"

"Westwood."

"You heard the question," Thurgood boomed, "there is the matter of the advance owing to Margaret Drury Carter, you do know who I mean, don't you?"

"Of course I know miz Drury Carter," Sam protested. Having been Andrew's assistant, he would be used to being bullied but, unlike A&M's staff, he was not afraid of Thurgood. "I worked for Andrew for well over a year."

Marsha thought he sounded appropriately proud of that fact.

"Well then?" Thurgood persisted.

"I will look into the matter in the morning, as I told Alex Levine already."

"Vous êtes Canadien?" Brigitte whispered loudly to Thurgood. She had piled her hair up into a carefully dishevelled knot and added long tear-shaped silver earrings just perfect for a wake. Marsha wondered whether Gloria Myles knew about the child.

Thurgood gave her one of his intense stares.

"On ne parle pas des choses d'affaires à une occasion privée comme ça. Ça ne va pas, monsieur. Vraiment." She gave Gloria a warm smile first, then returned Thurgood's intense stare.

There was a pause, while everyone waited for Thurgood to respond. Meanwhile, his gaze changed to puzzled, then offended.

Slowly, it dawned on everybody that whatever it was that Albertans did, it certainly did not include learning French. Thurgood had no idea what Brigitte Dombert had said. To make matters worse, he wasn't sure whether he should be insulted or flattered that she thought he might. In the event, all he could utter was a long vowel that could have been either "weeeell" or "heeeell," and then subside into the general silence.

"Elinor Drury came to the funeral," Stephen said helpfully. "It was good of her to come all the way from New Brunswick, don't you think? A pity Margaret could not make it. But she sent a lovely note, didn't she?"

"Lovely," his mother confirmed. "And flowers."

"They were very close," Jancie added, "Andrew and Margaret. She owed him a lot." She sighed prettily. "We all owed him. I don't know where I'd be had it not been for Andrew. He made it possible for me to be a full-time writer. It's all I ever wanted." She had tears in her eyes. A drop of black make-up ran down her cheek.

Since Andrew took over Jancie she had taken to wearing clinging black dresses, dyed her mousy brown hair black, changed her make-up to almost white and used heavy black mascara to accentuate her eyes. It was, clearly, Andrew's idea of what a horror writer should look like — sort of early Addams family — if she was going to take on Stephen King. King's uniform was resolutely ordinary. Jancie's would be the opposite. The media loved it.

"It's one of the biggest advances our company had ever paid out." Thurgood had rallied from the linguistic fiasco. "And Miss Drury Carter hasn't had her share," he said decisively. "And you, young fellow, had better send her cheque on first thing tomorrow. By courier. Then, his business accomplished, he stood up, nodded to the group, warned Sam he would be in his office by seven in the morning, waiting for his call. Unusually early for a believer in regular hours, Marsha thought. He took Gloria Myles's reluctant hand and gave it a squeeze. "My sympathies," he announced, and he left.

"Well," Jancie said.

"One of a kind," Sagfield added after a careful look over his shoulder to make sure Thurgood had gone. "They sure don't make them like that in Australia. You ever been there, Miss Withers?" It may have seemed a bit of a non sequitur to anyone else, but Marsha realized that Connor was about to make his opening pitch for Jancie's next book. Indeed when she shook her head, he told her quietly that he was amazed her publishers didn't think it worth their while to fly her down there. No substitute for direct promotion and publicity. They would turn out in droves to see her, he promised. When he saw that he had her attention, he went on with a jumble of numbers various Australian talk shows could bring.

"What did your brother do before he became an agent?" Marsha asked Stephen Myles. She had heard enough about the wonders of the Aussie book world.

"Didn't he tell you?" Stephen asked. "He was a trader. One of the best. A tough act to follow."

His mother cast him an encouraging glance. "They have such different styles," she said. "Stephen is more circumspect, less of a gambler. He has staying power, though. Andrew didn't. Our Andrew was always after the big one, you know, Drexel Burnham, the shooters, people who changed Wall Street forever."

"Andrew used to work at Drexel Burnham?"

"Of course," Gloria said.

Connor Sagfield was still talking about how things worked in Australia, but he had lowered his voice and was focussing his attention only on Jancie.

"Isn't that where Michael Milken was?" Marsha inquired, though she knew the answer to her own question.

"Andrew left before all that trouble. Had nothing whatever to do with it," Gloria said, waving her arm as if to fend off a fly. "Months before. He wasn't even part of the investigation."

"They did ask him some questions, mother," Stephen said, adjusting his cravat. He had small, almost infantile hands, the nails were shiny and clipped to perfect rounds. "He was one of their mergers and acquisitions specialists. Among the youngest to work on his own." He smiled. "I'm in commodities."

Marsha thought Stephen Myles hadn't much liked his brother. It was not only the way he spoke about him just then, and the way he looked at his mother when he suggested that Andrew might have been somehow involved in the Drexel fiasco, Marsha also remembered mother and son enjoying themselves on the flight back from Frankfurt knowing that Andrew's body was encased in ice somewhere in the hold. Despite the general picture of grieving projected by the wake, she found it hard to believe that either of them cared much for Andrew.

"He liked all the good things in life," Brigitte said breathlessly. When she spoke English her voice took on a sensual, vapid quality, in contrast to her rather commanding French. "In Paris, he always preferred the Ritz. In London, he stayed at the Grosvenor. He had such a grand style." She said "grand" the French way meaning "large." "His clothes were all specially made. He found a tailor in Paris who could do the cut exactly as he liked it. Very chic. His boots, they were handmade for him. Did you know?"

Stephen looked like it didn't surprise him. "I buy mine off the rack," he said.

"He had such expensive tastes," Brigitte continued.

"His father was like that," Gloria said with some pride. Marsha wondered if she included herself in her husband's expensive tastes. This vast, airy room with its uninterrupted view of the New York skyline, its marble, and overwhelming paintings spoke of taste and ostentation, and of someone who could afford both.

Jancie was beginning to take Sagfield seriously. There was a whispered exchange about dinner.

"Did he have a will?" Brigitte asked out of the blue.

"A will?" Gloria seemed surprised by the directness of the question. "Why do you ask?" Obviously, she did not know about the child.

"I just wondered. Did he?"

"Yes, I think he did. Didn't he, Stephen?"

"We haven't looked for it yet, Miss Dombert," Stephen said. "But I believe he did have one done a couple of years back. He mentioned he would. Why do you ask?"

There was an awkward silence. Sagfield downed his third glass of wine. Jancie took a black compact from her purse and began to repair the damage to her make-up. She powdered over the tear stains and dabbed around her eyes with a smudged tissue. Brigitte lifted her glass for the waiter to refill. "Perhaps you will find my name in his will," she said finally.

The way mother and son looked at each other, there was no doubt almost everyone else in the room knew more about Andrew's private life than they did. "Your name?" Stephen asked.

"That's what I said," she simpered. "My name. And maybe someone else's, as well. Someone called Elise." Brigitte stopped for effect. She was enjoying the raised eyebrows and nonplussed expressions on the Myles's faces. "I will be staying at the Plaza for the next two days," she added. I gave my card to the butler, you'll have no trouble finding me after the will is read." She gave everyone a warm smile and took her leave.

Sam was still engaged in a study of the floor between his shoes.

"I think I must go now," Marsha said. "So nice to have met you," she lied. "Very sorry about Andrew. We shall all miss him," and for a moment she actually thought that they would miss him. Though he had not been likable, he had been exciting to watch in action.

Stephen rose to see her to the door. "Perhaps I could call you sometime?" he asked when she put on her coat.

"Why?" was Marsha's stunned response.

"The usual reason," Stephen said, grinning.

"I don't think so."

He took a business card out of a gold card holder and slipped it into her hand. "You call me, then," he suggested still grinning. She was grateful that the elevator doors opened immediately when she pushed the down-button.

Hideo was perched on a bench near the waterfall, reading *Vanity Fair*. "I'm tired of reading about Sonny Mehta," he told Marsha.

"This is the fifth profile I've seen this year. As far as I can tell nothing has changed since the last one." Sonny, the brilliant Indian-born editor whom Random House had imported from London, had not yet ceased to fascinate New York. "Do you suppose," Hideo asked, "there would be all this attention if he were Irish from Chicago?"

Marsha didn't think so.

"Hm." He led the way out of the atrium. The place was full of tourists in furs and Armanis milling about, ogling the rich merchandise in the shop windows. Outside, a blind man in a weathered blue raincoat was playing a polka on his accordion. He smiled and bobbed his head when he heard a coin drop.

The rain had stopped but there were no cabs in sight. Marsha suggested they walk across to Lexington; cabs on Fifth Avenue prefer to go uptown at this time of the day. It was close to six o'clock and the streets were still choking with end-of-the-day commuters. "Sometimes I grow nostalgic for this place," Hideo said. "Not for the people I met when I lived here, but the feel of the place itself. It's strange how unlike Tokyo it is. Two big cities, about the same population, but that's the beginning and end of the similarities." He stopped to admire the crystal figurines in the Steuben Glass Company's windows. "Jim Houston used to work here," he told Marsha. "I sold one of his books in Japan years ago. Something about Eskimos before the white man came. It was made into a movie."

Marsha couldn't remember the film, but she had met Houston once at a Houghton Mifflin party in the Plaza.

"Andrew had thought Houston was worth trying to get away from his agent. He had even invested in a collection of Steuben sculptures to discuss with Houston, but it didn't take. Houston had been with the same agent for twenty years and he was only marginally interested in money." He took a deep breath. "I think that was all that interested Andrew. He believed that enlightened greed had driven the world along the path of evolution and that anyone who denied another's right to increase his own wealth deserved to be pushed out of the way."

"I thought you liked him," Marsha said.

"I admired him. It's not the same thing."

"Did Hübsch think you, too, had something to do with his death?" Marsha asked suddenly. "Why did he want to see you last Monday? You were the only one of us he asked to come down to the police station. Why?"

"That's not quite true. They asked young Sam to go down as well. They thought we could explain some of the things they had found in his room. The cut-up newspaper, for example. Hübsch couldn't understand why Andrew had gone to such lengths to scare Frans van Maeght. You know he was the one who sent Frans the threatening note?"

Marsha said she did. "You do know why he did it, don't you, Hideo?"

"Money, I expect," Hideo said with a shrug. "With Andrew everything led to the same obsession. By the way, he did have the Mitterrand memoirs once, despite what Brigitte said. They were worth two million dollars after only five phone calls, easiest money he'd ever made."

"What happened?"

"Mitterrand changed his mind. A statesman's prerogative."

This time she would not allow him to be evasive. "Do you suppose that's what happened with the Iraqi manuscript? That Saddam Hussein changed his mind?" she demanded, facing him as they swung around the corner of 56th and Lexington.

Hideo stopped. He had been walking with his hands in the pockets of his black Burberry coat, and now he took one out and slipped his arm through Marsha's as he ushered her down Lexington. "Not you, too?" he asked. "He didn't sell you that piece of garbage as well, did he?"

"No. He picked Aaron at A&M."

Hideo laughed showing a row of gold-capped teeth. Marsha wondered whether they were a status symbol, or had he lost his front teeth in a fight. It was difficult to imagine Hideo in a fight. He was smaller boned than Marsha, and about the same height. But she remembered the stories about the beatings he had taken when he was a teenager in New York. Back home, in Japan, he had endured only ostracism. Though he didn't stand out as a foreigner, he was no longer seen to be Japanese. He had been away from his own people for too long.

"He picked the right guy for the job," Hideo said.

"Why did he send the note to Frans?"

"I can only guess. He tried to scare Frans away from the deal. As simple as that," Hideo said. "Somehow he had found his way to Saddam Hussein, directly, and he decided there wasn't enough cash all around for him to share the deal with Frans. With Andrew it would be nothing personal. As I said, it would be only about the money." Hideo stopped and looked back in the direction they had come from. There were crowds of people going in all directions, but no one seemed to be keeping step with them. "You haven't read the manuscript, have you?" he asked.

"Only the outline."

"Andrew had the whole thing. He picked it up in Baghdad before he came to Frankfurt, in early October. He delivered the money and they gave him the script. Frans didn't know. Jerry might have known. They had agreed to terms before Andrew went to Baghdad. Andrew told me that he put the manuscript into safe-keeping for the duration of the Fair. For some reason, he decided not to show it right away."

"Did you read it?" Marsha asked.

"No." Marsha thought he didn't sound convincing.

"Do you think that's what all this is about?" Marsha demanded. "Is it the memoirs that got him and Jerry killed?"

"Perhaps," Hideo said. "In any event, I'd stay away from the damned thing." He stopped at a vendor on the corner of 49th and bought a hot dog with sauerkraut, chili, and Keen's mustard. "I've had no lunch, and it doesn't look like I'm going to have dinner, does it?" He peeled back the foil wrapper fastidiously to reveal one bite-sized piece at a time. "For sheer taste, it sure beats sushi," he said.

"Do you suppose he gave them the million bucks?" Marsha asked.

"Hm," Hideo said raising his eyebrows. He had his mouth full.

"Not like Andrew to go the whole way without insurance. Unless Jerry gave him all the money and a bunch more for his trouble. But if that's what happened why was he trying to sell it to us as well?"

Hideo shook his head.

"And if the Iraqis gave it to him to have it published, they would hardly be knocking off their agent, and Saddam's publisher to seal the deal, would they?" Marsha asked. "And if not them, then who? Who would stand to gain by all the fuss around the murder of two men who were going to get the stuff between covers and out on the market?"

Between bites, Hideo said he had no idea, and was going to make a point of not trying to find out.

At the corner of 42nd Street Marsha decided she was too tired to walk the rest of the way to Gramercy Park. It had been a long day and she desperately needed to rest. Hideo insisted he would see her home, an act of unusual chivalry for a man who was doubtless as tired as Marsha was herself. While they argued the point, Marsha started to wave at passing cabs.

She stepped off the curb as one began to pull up.

Hideo was still turned towards her, his back to the approaching taxi, remonstrating that it made no difference whether he went back to the Algonquin via Gramercy Park or direct from here — the cab would take him on a scenic tour anyway.

Marsha moved forward to make sure the driver could see her. It was then that it happened.

In a sudden burst of speed a car careened left from the line of cars next to the cab, its engine racing, tires squealing as it rushed towards her. There was a split second of disbelief, hesitation, then she leapt backward, bumping into Hideo, who had turned at the sound of the gears shifting and the tires hitting the sidewalk. He reached out in time to catch her.

They both fell backward onto the pavement and lay in a jumble of arms, legs, and coats, most of Marsha on top as Hideo grunted something unintelligible, probably in Japanese. She jumped to her feet, adrenalin racing, to see the car take the next corner onto 41st and disappear, its back lights fishtailing as it sped away. Through the grimy window it was impossible see more than the driver's shape.

"Shit," Marsha shouted, at last giving vent to her anger. The car's back plate was missing. "Have a nice day!" she yelled at the corner where she'd last seen the car that had tried to run her down. "Fucking idiot."

Hideo stood up rubbing his hands and elbows. "Who says it's not safe to walk in New York City?" he asked brushing the dirt off his coat. "A lot safer than trying to take a cab, for example, wouldn't you say?" he was talking to the backs of two passing women in running shoes.

No one had stopped to see what the commotion was about.

CHAPTER
TWENTY

As IT TURNED OUT, JUDITH DIDN'T HAVE TO WAIT until the morning to see him again. After an uneventful afternoon reading Willa Cather's *Death Comes to the Archbishop*, Judith would have been glad to see almost anybody coming through the guest-house door, but she was particularly pleased to see Preston O'Neill.

"Another month, and you could have fresh Grand Manan lobster, but the best I could do until the season starts is North Head tuna, caught today," he told her as he peeled off his wet black sou'wester and soggy socks. He had left his rubber boots outside.

"I thought you said there was no fishing around here," Judith said.

"No real fishing, not the kind that would allow a guy to make a decent living. But the government does allow us a couple of fish a day, just to keep us in hope." He shook some water off his hair. "Bit of a drizzle over top of the island. Fog should be coming back overnight, I wouldn't be surprised. Any luck with your story?" he asked absently as he surveyed the living room. "June?" he called.

"She isn't back yet," Judith said. "She is working on her year-end accounts."

"And how is your story going?" he repeated, maybe attempting to show more interest.

"Not much to do until the great lady deigns to see me."

"Bit of local colour in the bakery, I hear. Nan expects to see her pies on the cover of your magazine." He had proceeded into the kitchen with the easy familiarity of someone who had spent a lot of time at the Compass Rose, opened a drawer, pulled out a towel and began to dry his hair with it. "Between her and June, you'll soon be an expert on the island."

Jimmy had been right when he predicted that Preston would be barrel chested. He was. And he had wide shoulders, and thick forearms with a sparse growth of black hair. The hair on his head had begun to grey. Jimmy, it seemed, knew his mother's "type."

While Judith wasn't sure if she would like Preston when she got to know him better, she was sure she wanted to knew him better. She certainly did like the way he looked and sounded.

"I saw your paintings at the store," she told him.

"June try to sell you one?" he chuckled. "Trouble is she's put the price up so much no one can afford them any more. Margaret Drury Carter bought the last one June's been able to unload at an exorbitant seven hundred dollars. Not that it's any business of mine any longer. She's paid me for them in full over a year ago. A hundred each. Helped to keep the wolf from the door." He opened the fridge and flicked the cap off one of June's rare Labatt's Blues. He drank it straight from the bottle. "I expect she told you to replace whatever you take. Liquor store's open tomorrow. I'll get her a case of beer. Always do. You can stop looking so worried. She'll know I'm the one drank her beer."

"I thought the paintings were very beautiful," Judith told him. Jimmy rolled his eyes.

"Really. Especially the one with the giant black cliff."

"Ashburton Head," Preston said. "I painted it from a boat seine-fishing just off the main ferry line. Not the whole thing, just the bare outlines. Can't hold a brush still when the sea swells. It's where the Lord Ashburton was wrecked. All but seven men on board were killed. It's what gives the rocks that ghostly aspect."

"When was that?" Jimmy asked.

"Over a hundred years ago, but time passes exceedingly slow on this island. People still talk about how the seven men were rescued by a Boston whaler, or some such boat. The man who interests me the most, though, is the one who climbed all the way to the top of the cliff without benefit of rope or pulley, and made it alive."

"What happened to him?" Jimmy wanted to know.

Preston shrugged. "He had to give up his sailing career. Lost both his feet to frostbite. Nan will tell you he stayed on the island and became a herring smoker down in Woodwards Cove." He pulled off his drenched socks and wrung them out in the sink. "I think I know how he felt. Damned cold out there." He looked around for some firewood and kindling. When he found none near the fireplace, he padded down to the basement and emerged with an armful of logs.

"Are you in charge of the fireplace?" Judith asked.

"You could say that." He set the logs up in a peak, leaving space for the kindling and paper in the centre. It was what Judith's father had called a "teepee formation" — his favoured method of starting a fire. "I try to help her out with odd jobs."

June had not seemed like the kind of woman who needed much help with odd jobs, or much of anything. Judith thought of how she had hefted her suitcase over her shoulder as she bounced up the stairs. Perhaps she paid Preston for some maintenance work. Still. More likely, there had been something between them, or still was, judging from June's strange reaction to Judith's questions about Preston.

"I hear you do quite a few odd jobs around the island," Judith said. "Fred told me you helped him with the work on the old Willa Cather house."

He gave her a quizzical look but didn't say anything.

"And you're taking care of Margaret's dogs," Judith went on.

"Only while Elinor's away," Preston said. "She wants to make sure Margaret has as few interruptions as possible. Dogs take up a lot of time. And these two are barkers. Need heaps of attention, and they're used to it. They're fine dogs, the pair of them, but one of those women has spoiled them rotten." He grinned at her disarmingly. "Me, I'd put my money on Margaret."

"Yesterday," Judith said, opting for the direct approach, "you never mentioned that you knew them. Let alone walk their dogs. Why didn't you?"

"Why," he repeated, turning his back to the now lively fire. "Hm," he mused. He had put his hands on his hips and stared at Judith with flat blue eyes, as if he was seeing her for the first time. "Back then," he continued at last, "we were barely acquainted. Island people, you'll find, don't like to bare their souls the very first time they meet you. We're an odd lot. Insular. Keep to ourselves. But now," he grinned his crooked grin, "now that we are practically old friends, I don't mind revealing to you that sometimes I walk Margaret Drury Carter's dogs. And that they've been staying with me while Elinor Drury is away on business. You've already discovered that I deliver the bread and pies and such when Elinor can't make the trip herself. Sometimes I pick up their groceries and liquor. I've been doing Nan's deliveries for a couple of months. And yes, I do help Fred with one or two jobs, pretty much whenever he asks, which is not quite as often as I would like, but more often than he would. He prefers the real local folk, boys he's known all his life. Is there anything else you would like to know?"

Judith scrabbled around in her bag for the notebook. She made quite a show of flicking it open and searching for the questions she wanted to ask. She heard Jimmy snorting with amusement as he watched. She knew he'd be noticing her embarrassment and concluding that whatever would begin between her and Preston had already started.

There had been a time when Jimmy was wildly jealous of any relationship his mother might contemplate with men, when he needed to occupy a large chunk of the space left empty by his father, but that time had passed. He no longer coveted her total attention. In fact, he had been glad when Judith fell in love with the Toronto police inspector. David Parr had been the right tonic to lift her out of a depression. He had been considerate, easy-going, reliable — and barrel-chested. In the year or so since that ended, Judith had shown no inclination to become involved with anyone else.

"Well," Judith prodded. "How did Margaret or Elinor happen to ask you to do all this for them?"

"I'm glad you asked," he declared, his hands patting his chest. "It's because I am trustworthy, punctual, and don't interfere in their lives. I don't ask them a bunch of questions, for example." His voice lightened. "There is another reason. I'm broke. Or didn't June say? I'm the odd-jobs man in this neck of the woods. No task too lowly, no pay too small. I like it on this island and will do most anything to stay. That includes dog-sitting. It does not include cooking, but that's precisely what I plan to do this evening: show you two a bit of island hospitality. A formal invitation to O'Neill's for grilled tuna steaks with dill sauce, mashed spuds, braised fiddlehead, Nan's famous blueberry pie and mainland ice cream. What do you say to that?"

"Sounds perfect," Jimmy said, "especially the last part."

Judith agreed.

Preston told them the chariot would be outside in fifteen minutes. He had to go home and leave behind the motorbike he'd been using.

They were ready when he returned with the battered blue pick-up truck. In Jimmy's case ready meant he had put on his Adidas;

in Judith's, that she had changed her bulky hand knit for a store-bought green sweater that she hoped would bring out the green in her eyes.

The rain was so heavy by then that they could only see a few yards in front of them. Preston drove as if by rote. He hardly slowed for the bends in the road. They passed by a couple of white-painted churches, small, with squat steeples, no doubt so as to stay aloft in the winds. As they turned inland there were fewer houses and less fog. They pulled up in front of a squat, one-storey house, with brown brick walls and dark brown shingles, and windows with white trim.

"A heritage home," Preston told them. "Built in the early eighteen hundreds. The present owners come for a few weeks in the summer, and then scurry back to Maine at the first sign of the cold. I look after the upkeep — and a fine job I make of it, too." He showed them into a narrow, low-ceilinged room with a black pot-bellied stove. The walls were painted a pale yellow, the floor carpeted in thick white shag. "Hard to keep clean," Preston said, "but I need something to do during the long winter months. Come, sit by the fire."

Two big dogs emerged from the back room, barking, and bounded at Preston, jumping up until he patted them. The black Newfoundland came to investigate Judith and Jimmy, and then returned to jumping around Preston.

"They're harmless," he told Jimmy who had made a hasty retreat behind the floral sofa. "Girls," he shouted at them. "Enough." He gave each of them something he took from his pocket, and they lay down near the sofa, chewing loudly.

The stove was belching heat. A couple of wrought-iron standing lamps cast an orange light over the soft watercolours on the walls. They were all island scenes: high cliffs, boats with nets, fields strewn with juniper and columbine, and tiny houses — like this one — clinging to scrubby ground with wind-bent spruces leaning over them. Judith didn't have to ask if they were painted by Preston. She knew.

"It's a pity you stopped painting," she told him.

"Perhaps," he said thoughtfully. "I think I was beginning to repeat myself. You know, when you can tell in advance exactly how a painting will turn out, because you've seen it somewhere before. These ones, they're stuff I did when I first arrived here. I was discovering everything. They hold that sense of discovery, still." He pointed to the one with the high black cliff. "That's the first time I saw Ashburton Head. It was like a revelation. I could see that poor bugger scrambling up those icy rocks, the air full of shrieking gulls, the waves crashing around him. There's no turning back and nowhere to go. Every breath he takes he's dying. And he knows he's dying. But he keeps climbing anyway. I tried to capture all that when I painted." The picture showed the same high rock, and exuded the same sense of menace Judith had felt when she saw the scene painted the first time. "The one in June's shop is about the fourth or fifth Ashburton Head. June liked it. She asked me to make more for the tourists." Preston turned his back on the painting and went into the kitchen. He had to duck his head under the doorframe as he passed.

"There have been artists who paint the same things year in and year out," Jimmy said. "Never tire of it. Monet, for example. Did those water lilies like he'd never seen the damned things before, though he'd just done them, looking much the same — except to Monet. And Cézanne and that damned mountain. Must have done a hundred of those, and he thought they were all different."

Judith couldn't believe it. "What do you mean, Monet?" she asked. "How do you know about Monet and Cézanne?"

"Still waters," Jimmy said.

"What do you mean still waters?"

"Not just the pretty face you know and love," Jimmy winked at her. "Or didn't I tell you I took part of a course in art history last year. One of my friends was in the class and on his off days I sat in for him. Fran. Enjoyed that course.

"Where's the stuff you do now?" he shouted at the kitchen door.

"You go out through the back, they're not hard to find," Preston said.

The next room was no bigger than the living room, but a great deal colder. There was no fireplace here to take the edge off the dampness. There were brown bean-cushions scattered on the white shag-carpeted floor. A three-foot-wide television set occupied pride of place in the centre. Sturdy shelves displayed the spines of colourful children's books and toys. In the corner, a spindly loom with a straw basket of yarn. The two dogs followed them as if to police their progress, walking with their heads down, ears back, keeping their distance.

A narrow passageway with closed doors on either side led to the back door. The retriever stood guard outside one of the doors as Judith and Jimmy passed by.

The rain had steadied to a drizzle. In the darkness, outside, they could discern some large, looming, white shapes that caught a touch of the light through the door. At first they seemed like tall megalithic stones, something out of Stonehenge, in a random arrangement that stretched back away from the house and disappeared into the darker shadows of the trees. But when Judith approached the closest one, a few feet from the house, it developed massive, rounded shoulders and an enormous head. It towered over Judith, who was five foot seven. Jimmy tried to wrap his arms around it. His hands didn't quite meet.

"A monster," Jimmy said. "Frankenstein's monster." He put his shoulder against its chest and shoved to see how stable it was. It didn't budge. Looking up where the face might have been, all Judith could see was a glowering brow, wide and angled towards her. The back door light that glinted off its long arms hanging straight down from the hulking shoulders made the figure seem to be bound so that it could not move, though its knees were bent as if it wanted to jump forward. The whole shape was smooth to the touch, chiselled, rounded. "Cool," Jimmy announced.

Judith found the figure fierce and threatening.

The rest of the stone figures stood around it, as if they were waiting for something to happen. They made her think of the huge stone markers in the Arctic that the Inuit had made from giant boulders, to ward off evil spirits and sometimes to show the way to lost travellers. They called them "inukshuks" and the local people treated them with reverence. No one over the centuries had dared change the shape of one of these giants, though all it would have taken was one push. She had been in the Arctic only once, on commission from *Ms.* magazine to find a woman hunter north of Frobisher Bay. It was a summer of blackflies and mosquitos; the hunters, if they were ever there, had followed the caribou northward, so Judith made do with a story about the inukshuks, which she eventually sold to *Canadian Geographic*.

Preston shouted that dinner was ready.

He had set out plates and cutlery on the kitchen table. It was a small pine tabletop with red woven mats under the plates. One tall red candle glowed in the centre, next to a bottle of red wine. The air was steamy, and smelled of rosemary and dill. "An island recipe," he told her with a wink. "For very special occasions only. We pay riveting attention to presentation. I hope you brought your camera."

"I wish I had," Judith said. "I'd like to take a picture of your stone sculptures."

"You like them?" he asked hesitantly.

"They're too huge and imposing to be simply liked," she said. "I like the scent of rosemary. Those things out there, at least the ones I could see, they're overwhelming. They're also frightening. Where did you find the stones?"

"That's one thing we don't lack around here, young lady," he said, his blue eyes twinkling in the candlelight, "stones. We have all kinds. Volcanic, Paleozoic, Precambrian — some of the rocks on the east coast are two billion years old. On the west coast, they rise three hundred feet high out of the sea. There are rocks here that take on shapes before your eyes. If you have time, I'll show you around Southwest Head Light, where some of these stones were born."

"How the hell did you bring them here?" Jimmy asked.

"I'm not the only one broke," Preston said simply. "Paid a few of the guys to haul them up with their tractors."

The plates were white gloss china. The tuna was grilled in brown stripes, accompanied by white sauce, lemon wedges, mounds of mashed potatoes, and green islands of limp fiddleheads.

"The green things look vicious," Jimmy said. "But the rest's okay. Didn't believe you could actually cook. None of her other guy friends could. I doubt if David ever boiled an egg. And my dad doesn't. Thinks it's woman's stuff."

Judith aimed a powerful kick at his knee, and buried her foot in fur. There was a high pitched yelp followed by a growl. The two dogs took up most of the room under the table. She had to make do with a nasty look.

"What are their names?" Jimmy asked to change the subject.

"The golden retriever's Edith, the Newf's called Willa. Really. Can you imagine standing in some public place and calling them? Can you?" He was laughing. "Two big dogs with sissy names."

Judith said, "They must be named after Willa Cather and her friend, I suppose. Did Margaret buy them after they came to Grand Manan?"

"They're at least two years old," Preston said.

"Hm," Judith said. "I guess she must have liked Willa Cather before they moved here. Maybe she read her back when she and Elinor used to come here first."

Preston continued to eat.

"Back when you first met them, I suppose?" Judith went on. "Your folks used to rent near Castalia. As did some of the Drurys, right?"

"You've been busier than most today," Preston said.

"A strange coincidence you'd all end up here again, isn't it?" Judith asked.

"You think so?" Preston responded with a question. "Haven't you wanted to go back to the places you liked when you were a child?" He was about to go on, but caught himself and quickly veered off the subject to tell Jimmy he didn't have to eat the fiddleheads if he didn't like them.

"Not many places I liked as a child, at least not as much as you and *they* seem to have ..." she paused to give him a chance to speak, "... liked it here. Your parents must have been nice people."

Preston nodded. "I liked them."

"And Margaret? What was she like back then?"

"Margaret?" Preston laughed. "I didn't know Margaret. It was her sister who used to come in the summer."

"Elinor's mother?"

"Hm."

"You were close to them, then?" Judith chimed in fast before the moment passed. Maybe she could pick up a few more morsels of information about Margaret tonight.

"Was I?" he responded, digging into the mashed potatoes.

"Were you close to the Drurys when you were here twenty-five years ago?"

He shook his head but said nothing.

"And you met Margaret through Elinor?" Judith pressed on.

He didn't answer the question directly. "You and June had a good old yarn, did you?" he asked at last.

"Is that why they came here, because they knew you were on Grand Manan?" Judith was not about to give up. "You've known them all that time?"

"Hardly. We don't move in the same circles," he said gruffly.

"But you did meet Margaret a long time ago?"

"I hadn't clapped eyes on her till last summer, and that's a fact." He offered Judith more wine and poured some into Jimmy's glass. "Here's welcome to you both," he said, raising his glass for the toast.

There was no chance she could reopen that subject for a while.

CHAPTER
TWENTY-ONE

MARSHA DIDN'T BELIEVE IN COINCIDENCES. IF A car tried to run her down, there was reason to think that it had intended to do just that. The picture of the car and driver, hunched over the steering wheel, waiting by the curb, then lunging as she stepped off the sidewalk was clear in her mind, as was the sound of the engine revving. The only question was — why?

Hideo suggested that the driver was having a bad day, and that Marsha had stepped into the line of his rage. "New York drivers are famous for their bad tempers," he said. Only the day before, on the way from the airport, he had been in a cab that tried to hit a bicycle courier. The driver told him later, in shattered English, that he was only going to hit the courier "a little bit." He hated the way bikes weaved in and out of traffic while cars had to wait their turn.

Hideo was working on his second Scotch, and becoming more animated with every sip. After the encounter with the cab, Marsha thought a very dry martini would help focus her mind, and she was not in the mood to tackle a martini alone. So she had invited him up to the apartment.

"It's the Saddam Hussein manuscript, I'm convinced of it," she told Hideo. "Logically, it's Aaron they should be after, but they don't know it."

"Maybe an ad in the Baghdad *Daily Jihad*?" Hideo ventured. He had settled into the couch after a brief survey of Marsha's bookcases. "Generally speaking, what a person reads will tell you more about them than hours of intimate conversation," he had told her. "But it doesn't work around publishers. They display stuff they've worked on even if they don't much like it, books they would never buy for their own pleasure. I suppose we'll have to settle for intimate conversation."

"Maybe it's the Brits," Marsha went on, ignoring Hideo's effort to make light of the attempt on her life. "There was all the fuss about their selling arms to Iraq while they were grandstanding at the United Nations and offering to back us in Star Wars. Maybe there were some prominent Brits not named by the Scott report. Maybe the government itself would wish to see this whole thing go away. It's embarrassing for them."

Hideo disagreed. If the British wanted to have Marsha killed, they would come up with a more sophisticated method than a car on Lexington Avenue. They still had MI5, for example. "And what's a Scott report?"

Marsha had a hazy recollection of reading about Sir Richard Scott's inquiry into the British government after it relaxed its policy on selling arms to Iraq, which was getting ready to invade its neighbours. No one had bothered to tell Parliament. Parliament had also been kept blissfully unaware of Iraq's Project Babylon — the technology of the supergun, and Saddam Hussein's venture into the production of nuclear weapons. It would be reasonable to assume that the expensive imports from America's major ally included the material to build nuclear weapons.

"Andrew had said there was information in the manuscript that would cause a furor in Britain," Hideo said. "But he didn't tell me what. And," he said, taking a long sip of his drink, "under the circumstances, it hardly matters. If someone wants to stop this thing from seeing the light of day, they're going about it the wrong way. And they're going after the wrong guys." He poured himself another drink and made a brave effort to change the subject by telling Marsha about his new friend, an exquisite woman who shared his interest in erotic art. He had met her, as it happened, at an exclusive art and rare manuscripts auction in Paris. It had been a small event, by invitation only. He found they were often bidding on the same prints, and antique books. He had heard of her before, as a collector, but had no idea she would be so beautiful. It had been love at first sight of the collection itself. It was more than love, it was a union of kindred spirits — "Andrew would have thought of it as a merger," he chortled.

Judith called at ten o'clock. Her big news was that she had met a wildly attractive local character called Preston — "can you believe that name?" — O'Neill, who made gigantic stone sculptures that looked like a cross between primitive Inuit markers and Rodin's French peasants. "He has hands like hammers and he cooks better than I do. He arranges food on the plates. He has a slight Irish lilt ..."

"Broad shoulders?" Marsha asked. But she had already guessed the answer.

Unlike Marsha, who took casual affairs in her stride, Judith fell rarely, and always hard. She got involved with her men. Given the amount of time and effort she expended on them, it was no surprise that she had only had three relationships since James left her over ten years ago. Marsha knew James had been Judith's first. Years later, Marsha had even listened to the wincingly horrid details of their unconsummated honeymoon. It was amazing that they succeeded in making two very normal children after that fiasco.

Watching Judith's marriage unfold had been quite sufficient reason for Marsha to shun the institution. It had also quite soured her on veterinary surgeons, though she rather liked the guy who took care of Jezebel's annual shots.

"Need you ask?" Judith laughed.

"Can you keep yourself at bay till I get there?" Marsha asked. "You should check out the ... pool before you dive in, don't you think?"

"Why?" Judith asked. "Your success rate with relationships is hardly a measure to judge by."

"I don't have relationships," Marsha stated, which was not altogether true, but she certainly didn't have the kind of all-consuming relationships Judith had. She had always endeavoured to keep it that way. Once, only once, had she been in danger of being captured by what Judith would call a relationship, but that was a few years ago. It was a testimonial to her willingness to overlook personal pain, that she still loved Bertil — each successive Frankfurt, if not in-between.

"You been drinking, or do you have somebody with you?" Judith knew Marsha too well.

"Now, there's quite a claim," Hideo said, nodding thoughtfully. He had been listening to Marsha, one eyebrow raised in puzzlement. "Is it an accident, or determination?"

"Both," Marsha said. "I am having a drink with Hideo, Andrew Myles's former Tokyo agent," she told Judith. "But he is leaving soon," she added pointedly. She already had her ticket to Saint John, she told Judith, and if the ferry left on time, she'd be on Grand Manan by late afternoon. The murderous driver had convinced her, if she had still needed convincing, of her need to be on Grand Manan. "Any luck with Margaret?"

"Not yet. She claims she is busy meeting her deadlines on your extravagant contract. Wants to postpone the interview until she's finished the book. Can't say I'm sympathetic. Even small fry like me like to meet deadlines."

"Comforting that she is working," Marsha mused.

"Not for me. I need the money for this story. If Debbie postpones it now, she won't pay me a thing. She never pays unless I deliver."

"How is our hotel?"

"The Compass Rose is beautiful," Judith said. "It's a short walk from the docks, and I'll be waiting to show you the way."

Hideo, displaying no inclination to depart, launched into a long peroration on the nature of human relationships and what was common to all species, even people as remote as the French and the Japanese. It was no accident, he mused, that translators found it easier to translate Japanese fiction into French, than into any other European language. Japanese films, even obscure art films, found enthusiastic audiences in France. Americans, in contrast, were most interested in old martial arts, which are as remote from modern Japanese experience as wagon trails from today's Americans.

Alex called next. He had read Margaret's manuscript. He was trying to do his best for his new client, but he had to agree that the chapters were not up to Margaret's standard. "Maybe it's best that she should be on that island. Gives her the uninterrupted time to get it right."

"What did you think of the dogs?" Marsha asked.

"Unnecessary," Alex admitted.

"And the heroine?"

"It's just a first draft," Alex said, dodging the issue. "I suppose you're determined to go to Grand Manan."

"I have no choice."

"And the money?"

"I'll take your advice. Reluctantly. It's not so much Margaret, it's Elinor I don't trust. Somebody gave Jerry Haines the idea that he could still get this contract away from A&M. And it wasn't you."

"Perhaps you're right, but it's Margaret that chose Andrew Myles, and like attracts like, ancient Chinese proverb."

Marsha laughed. "Inca, I think," she said.

It was almost midnight when Margaret called.

"Mar-cia," she whispered into the telephone, "Ah'm so glad yew are theah." The voice was faint and far away but there was no mistaking Margaret Drury Carter's forced Southern tones.

"So am I," Marsha agreed ardently. "I've been trying to reach you ever since I read the first three chapters of the new novel. All I'm getting is your answering machine."

"So tewwibly sorry," Margaret whispered. "I did so want to finish the writing, I quite forgot there are people out theah, whom I do wish to talk to. You, mah deah, are at the vewwy top of that short list. Each day mah list abates, as mah friends pass away."

"So sorry, Margaret," Marsha said.

"Ah was shuah yew would understand." She put all the emphasis on the "yew." "When Ah am in the middle of writing a book, Ah must cre-ate a space for mah characters, another world for them to live in — if Ah can't have that time alone, Ah can't breathe life into them. That's how Ah work, yew know, mah deah." Marsha could hear the soft intake of breath between each phrase, though the line was crackling and fading.

"You do like to hear from me after I've read the first chapters," Marsha said somewhat defensively.

"Quite, quite," Margaret said, flattening the word into something resembling "quaint." "But this time, Ah needed to be alone. It's Andrew, yew understand. Ah tried to explain to yew in Frankfurt. Ah simply haven't the stamina I once had. So difficult, with dahling Andrew dying like that. And then Jerry had to go and die, as well. We'd been so vewy close, don't you know? I loved that man. Such talent. So young." The voice trailed off into a sob.

"Yes, of course, I understand," Marsha said, though the Jerry who sprang to her mind had been neither.

Jezebel chose that moment to crash through the cat flap. Hideo jumped to his feet, and the two of them stared at each other in utter amazement. Jezebel recovered first. She rounded her back, bared her teeth, and hissed at Hideo. He swayed gently. "Racist pig," he told the cat, finally, and returned to his seat.

"Ah just had to get away from all those howwible events." Marsha could hear faint choking sounds above the buzzing of the phone line. "Without deah Andrew to guide me ..."

"But you have a new agent now," Marsha interrupted, a trifle unkindly. She had recovered from the first attack of sympathy. With twenty million dollars at stake, she could ill afford to feel so sorry for Margaret that she would let her off the hook.

"Ah yes," long sigh, "Alex has stepped into the breach. He is such a deah, deah boy," swallow. "He talked to you about the advance?" A small hint of greed, Marsha noted. She must be feeling better.

Marsha told her she had seen Alex and Elinor at lunch. "They told me you never received the initial payment from Andrew?"

"Perhaps theah wasn't time," Margaret sighed again. "So sudden it was, so unexpected. Alex will handle that for us now. He told yew about the house I want to buy heah?" A little heavy-handed, but there was no doubt now that the push for the money was not just Elinor's idea.

"Maybe you'll be able to show it to me tomorrow," Marsha came directly to the point.

There was a long pause with static.

Jezebel padded around the apartment making sure nothing else was amiss. When she completed her tour, she jumped up on the windowsill and glared balefully at Marsha. Evidently, the neighbour hadn't fed her enough.

When Margaret's voice came back, it was a little weaker than before. "Ah don't see that that's a vewy good ideah, mah deah. Not so soon. Ah'm doing so well now, Ah expect to have the whole manuscript to you even before the contract says. Absolutely shouldn't interrupt me with minor editorial things we can discuss when it's all done. Better that way, don't yew agree?"

Marsha said she didn't, and told Margaret there were too many problems with the manuscript to leave it till the end. In fact, she was so worried about the direction the novel was taking, she thought it best that Margaret should not continue till they had talked.

Another long pause greeted that news.

"Drury Carter?" Hideo inquired from the kitchen, where he was helping himself to the last of the Scotch.

"Perhaps you could explain," Margaret said, forgetting for a moment her Southern drawl.

"It's too long and too complicated," Marsha insisted stubbornly. "I think we have to meet. I'm booked on an early flight from New York."

"Theah are no direct flights to Grand Manan," Margaret stated.

There was a flight from Saint John, but Marsha told her she would take the ferry from Blacks Harbour. She was looking forward to being aboard the ship. The sea air would be lovely after the fumes of Frankfurt. She'd take a couple of manuscripts to read. Blissful. Uninterrupted by telephone calls and by Japanese agents who, seemingly, had nowhere to go in the middle of the night.

"Elinor says yew will not even release the cheque. Ah simply do not understand. She says yew will not even indulge me to that tiny extent." She exhaled heavily. "Ah don't know any more if Ah want to write this for yew-all. Yew-all have no faith in me. Seventeen books and where am Ah? Where Ah began ..." she trailed off into an audible wheeze. "And myself ill, running a high fever. Ah've been awaiting deah Elinor's return, she'll go get me some medication. Ah have no thermometer here on the island, never needed one before, but Ah just know it's vewwy high. Hardly slept all night, Ah've been so worried about the money, and poor Andrew's death. I thought at first it was the grief, but no, Ah'm as ill as Ah've ever been."

Marsha relented. "I'm going to try to get your share of the advance to Alex tomorrow. I'm sure we can sort it all out with Andrew's estate."

Hideo had come back into the room. He was walking somewhat unsteadily, but there was no uncertainty about the emphatic way he was shaking his head. "No way, you'll sort this one out in a hurry," he said. "Mmm, mmm ... no chance. Not if she doesn't have it now." He sank back into the sofa.

"Mar-cia," Margaret gushed, "Why don't you call me heah tomorrow, dahling, Ah'll be by the phone. If yew can fix the money for me, Ah'll even come to Saint John for the day to save yew the trip on that awful ferry. Couple of weeks, another three chapters. Storms tonight. Fog. It's been raining all evening. Ah'll bring yew the new chapters, if yew like."

Marsha said she would let her know in the morning.

"Elinor will be back then," Margaret said. "She has been such a saint, yew don't know how much she's done for me."

"What did you mean by that?" Marsha asked Hideo after she hung up.

"By what?" Hideo was all golden smiles of exaggerated innocence.

"You know. About Margaret's money," she urged him on.

"Ah, that," Hideo waved aside the matter, as if it was of no consequence. "Didn't you know? Andrew was playing the futures market. He didn't have any money. He was broke. Kept betting the wrong way every time. It's what drove him off Wall Street in the first place, didn't his brother tell you?" When he saw Marsha's wide-eyed look, he went on. "I guess he didn't. Andrew played the market the way other people play the horses. He loved it. He used to know a lot about the stocks and took reasonable gambles. Often won. But he lost a bundle in the crash of '87. That's when he got off the mouse wheel, and decided to try his hand at agenting. And man, was he good at it." Hideo chortled with happy memories of Andrew's successes.

"You lost me back there. Whatever happened to the money he's made since?"

"The same, Marsha, the same. He never left the market. Gave it a rest for a year and went back to show he could win, after all. Not a good loser, our Andrew. Didn't know how to give up."

"He used his authors' advances to buy futures contracts?" It was hard for Marsha to believe that, even of Andrew Myles.

"Yup," Hideo confirmed with a hiccup. "That's the way your Drury Carter money must have gone. He kept it churning. A new advance would come in to cover the one he'd just sent off to cover old futures contracts whose dates had come up — you can go through a lot of money that way." Hideo whistled. "Oh yes. A lot of money. Remember that young whiz kid who put Barings out of business? Nick Leeson? Speculated in Japanese real estate. Thought it was the safest bet he could place. The yen was strong and stable, real estate in Japan had only gone up since the war ended. It was the earthquake that wiped him out. Never imagined there'd be an earthquake. Lost billions for Barings. Lost the whole bundle — bank and all."

"What's that got to do with Andrew?"

"He was a comer, like Leeson. Didn't know how to give up, kept betting other people's money. Only he didn't have as much to start with. Lost mere millions, not billions. Anything that wasn't cashed in by his authors before he died, you can pretty much forget about. That's the thing with futures: you borrow against the future. He owed too much. Can't replenish the well now that he's dead, can he?"

"I don't understand," Marsha mumbled, though she was beginning to.

"Few people do. That's the problem. Way it works is you speculate that the price of a currency or commodity will rise, or fall, by a certain date. If you bet the wrong way, you have to pay the difference between the price of the stock on that date, and what you bet it would be when you signed your futures contract. As simple as I can make it. Never played the market myself. Too busy with books."

"And our two million dollars?"

Jezebel ate noisily, pushing the newly opened tin of cat food around the countertop, indicating to Marsha that she could be ready for seconds.

"On signing the Drury Carter contract?" he chuckled appreciatively. "Went the way my modest commission money's gone." His hands flew up, fingers waving to simulate the flight of a bird.

It was almost one in the morning when she finally hoisted him, singing "On the Road Again," into a cab. The driver was Russian, and when Hideo asked him about his sympathies for the great *jihad*, he said he hated everyone from the Middle East, especially Iraq. Unfortunately, he had but the vaguest notion concerning the whereabouts of the Algonquin Hotel.

CHAPTER
TWENTY-TWO

IT WAS STILL DARK WHEN MARSHA WOKE UP. DURING the night she had made a few decisions, and she wanted to have time to act on them before the day dragged into everybody else's morning. To counteract her sense of soporific fatigue, she did a hundred sit-ups, ate two oranges, downed a handful of vitamin pills with coffee, and took a long shower. In the end she felt almost like her normal self. She packed an overnight carry-on bag with warm clothes and bare necessities.

Dawn came at six. She called van Maeght in Amsterdam, and left him a message that if he had not already sent the manuscript they had been discussing, he should not bother. Aaron already had it from Andrew.

The park was empty when she left her apartment. The only sign of life along the street was a man sweeping the pavement in front of the National Arts Club. He paid no attention when Marsha hurried by. She could ignore the park side of the street because the fence kept the park isolated. It would not be easy for someone to leap over it, and it would be even harder to run across the road unnoticed. The iron gate, to which only dues-paying neighbourhood residents held keys, was padlocked.

She walked up Park Avenue to 42nd, keeping an eye on the few people who came level with her, waiting at each crossing till there were no cars in the vicinity. From 42nd she took Fifth Avenue. She was not followed, and no cars threatened to leap out at her as she passed.

At a quarter to seven she was in front of the A&M building waiting for Thurgood to arrive. She stood on the corner at 52nd, where she could survey both entrances. Thurgood climbed from the back seat of a standard black Cadillac limousine a few minutes before seven. He wore a rumpled light grey suit and a striped blue scarf that looked like an old college scarf. He dragged his coat and legal-size briefcase from the seat beside him, and then he leant in to talk to the driver. The wings of his jacket parted as he bent over, exposing his rotund behind. The pants had been worn thin and shiny where they stretched. Thurgood, unlike Morris, had no fashion sense.

If he was surprised to see Marsha, he didn't show it. He dug in his pockets for the keys to the A&M offices. Before the Canadians, each senior person had been endowed with a set of keys that allowed them to come in late at night, and start early if they wished. Now only Morris and Thurgood had keys. The elevators simply didn't open on the A&M floors after 6 p.m. and before 8 a.m. Morris had explained that the policy was part of his plan for steady working hours and full accountability. After the keys were confiscated, he had the locks changed.

"We are going to have a problem with the Margaret Drury Carter contract," Marsha told him as she followed him into the building.

"We already have a problem," Thurgood said.

"Andrew Myles used Drury Carter's money to buy futures contracts, or pay up on maturing futures contracts, or whatever one does with those things," Marsha tried to explain in the elevator to the top floor. "In any event, it's all gone."

"Commodities," Thurgood mumbled. "Son of a bitch could have lost the lot. Goddamn mug's game."

"I think he might have," Marsha said, "lost the lot." She repeated what Hideo had told her.

Thurgood was silent all the way up to the executive floor. He watched the lights go up behind each number as the elevator went up.

She had never been in his office before. She had been there many times while it was Birnbaum's office, but never since. Birnbaum had been chairman of the board during Larry's tenure as president. He rarely came to the office, but when he did, he liked to ask people to have tea with him. He would ask them leading questions about the business for the sole purpose of appearing more knowledgeable at directors' meetings than any of the other people there. In his spare time he had set up a small putting green with indoor-outdoor carpet and a sandbox in the boardroom. He practised his strokes there.

If Thurgood had any hobbies, he kept them hidden.

No one knew precisely how often he came to the office, or what he did when he was here. He rarely talked to anyone except Morris. He spent time with stacks of computer printouts and he had an IBM with all the software.

His office, Marsha noted with some astonishment, had been painted a powerful yellow. He had a Chinese lacquer credenza against one wall, and a bookcase with an assortment of A&M titles on the other. A big walnut desk and a blue leather swivel chair faced the window. There were two other chairs — metal-backed, with blue cloth seat cushions — but their backs were to the window. On the windowsill, blocking part of the view of Fifth Avenue, there was a big metal sculpture of a cowboy riding a bucking bronco. The cowboy's hat was pushed to the back of his head, and there were drops of metal perspiration on his face. It might have been a real Remington.

Thurgood threw his coat over one of the chairs facing his desk, and waved Marsha towards the other. "I'm going to sue the bastards," he informed Marsha. With the morning light on his face, he was even uglier than usual. His skin was soft and deeply pockmarked around the nose and chin. He had tiny black button eyes embedded in puffy layers of skin. His skull showed through the thin hair on his head. He, too, was perspiring.

She imagined that would be quite a trick as the real bastard of this fiasco was dead, but she didn't say so. What she said instead was that she doubted whether suing was going to solve the more immediate problem with Margaret Drury Carter. Her new agent was taking the position that the contract was not valid because she had not had her signing payment.

"She's the one who hired the son of a bitch to be her agent in the first place," Thurgood shouted. "It certainly wasn't our goddamned idea. What in hell are we supposed to do about it now?" His soft upper lip puckered as he extended the "now." "Our position is that we paid the money to her designated representative, and it's up to her to fucking collect it."

"Alex Levine, her new agent, says they had asked you to split the payment between her and Andrew, but you refused," Marsha said quietly.

"Of course, I damn well refused," Thurgood thundered. "The contract was care of the little son of a bitch, and when I checked whether we could split the money and send him only his fifteen percent, he went ape. He said a contract is a contract even if I'm a goddamned Canadian. If it says send all of it to him, that's what they do down here in America."

Marsha concentrated on picking lint off the sleeve of her coat. She thought she might start laughing if she looked at him.

The phone rang.

"Thurgood," Thurgood yelled into the receiver. He listened for a while, his eyes wandering over Marsha's shoulder. "Will you just explain that to me, son," he went on with an effort to sound patient.

Marsha was sure he was listening to Sam. If Hideo had told the truth, this could be a long conversation.

"No. I do wish to see it." Long pause. "I know it's confidential between the author and the agent, any fool knows that, but that hardly matters now that he's dead, does it?" Sam nattered on in response for what seemed like five minutes. Marsha was bored with studying Arthur Thurgood's pockmarked face.

She wondered if he'd had teenage acne and had been persecuted at school. That would account for his nasty attitude, as well as his preference for staying away from people.

There had been a couple of people at Bishop Strachan whose faces had erupted. That was in the days before Oxy. They had been desperate, smearing on lemon juice, scrubbing with facial soap, squishing and pummelling their faces till they were raw. Judith had missed most of the socials in her senior year when she came down with the dreaded zits. She would stand glowering at her reflection in the mirror, her face a pulpy mess, willing the zits to vanish. She tried to imagine Thurgood as an insecure teen. Did they have school dances in Alberta? Would he have been able to dance?

"That's Stephen Myles, right? Which firm?" He scribbled on a card he had pulled from his pocket. His desk was as bare as Morris's. "I know it's the Citibank, but if the account is empty, as you say, there is no sense in writing any more cheques on it. No." He listened some more while Sam talked. He was chewing the inside of his cheek.

Neither of the Canadians had ever mentioned a family. Was it possible that there was a Mrs. Thurgood somewhere who doted on this ugly mug? She cast her eye around the office looking for photographs. On the bookcase, there was a gap between a couple of hardcover Margaret Drury Carters, where a small rectangular frame faced the desk. A black and white photograph. Too far away to make out the features.

"Our lawyers will contact you in the morning." He slammed the phone down, crossed his arms, and rested his elbows on the desk, his small eyes fixed on Marsha. "There is no money. The account is overdrawn. There is an overdraft. He says Andrew Myles conducted his businesses — both of them — out of a limited company. All the contracts are with the company. The Drury Carter contract, the same as all the others, is with the company. The one that has no money." He let his eyes rest on the buildings across the street. "And there is no money to cover her share of the advance." The thick folds of his skin almost touched as he narrowed his eyes.

No eyelashes, Marsha observed. She waited for him to make the next move. Instead, he continued his hostile contemplation of her face. Then he asked, "What do you propose to do?" as if the problem had been one of her making.

Marsha had the answer ready, having spent some of the night thinking about it. "We should pay her the author's share of the next million, hold the agency's hundred thousand dollars against what we have already paid out, and let the lawyers battle over how Margaret gets her money from the first installment that we paid Andrew Myles."

"Why?" Thurgood demanded.

"Because it will keep her happy and working on the manuscript, and because Alex Levine will agree that we are acting in good faith and not try to get out of the contract for non-payment of the advance."

"Our lawyers can stop him in his tracks. It's Myles's fucking company that owes the money, not us." He was shouting again. Beads of perspiration had gathered around his neck and were starting to stain his clean white shirt.

"Yes," Marsha said. "But that will take months, maybe years, and meanwhile we have an unhappy author."

CHAPTER TWENTY-TWO

"You told us in Frankfurt that the chapters were not acceptable."

"Right. They're not. But I propose to go to see her in New Brunswick and we will make them acceptable."

"When?"

"Today."

Thurgood lumbered to his feet. "I will tell Morris to have the cheque drawn up. But you better be right about this. I don't intend to lose three million dollars on this blasted deal."

Marsha checked the photograph as she went by on her way out. It was a picture of a woman, young, with short kinky hair, smiling. She had flowers in her hair.

"One more thing," Thurgood bellowed when she was halfway to the elevators.

Marsha turned to see him standing in his doorway. He took up all of the space. "Did you know Myles's commission was fifty percent, not fifteen?"

"Fifty percent?" She thought she hadn't heard it right.

"Half," Thurgood yelled.

Marsha said she'd had no idea. No matter how much an agent was doing for an author, half didn't seem possible. Not even if, as Jancie had said, Margaret owed him a lot. "Will he let us see the agreement?" she asked.

"Said he would fax it over. You better take a copy with you and ask your author about that." There was something ominous about the way her referred to Margaret as Marsha's author.

She called Irwin when she was in her office. He started at seven most days to keep in tune with the London and Tokyo markets while they were still active.

He was not altogether surprised that she would not be able to have dinner with him that night, though he had not been prepared for a reason as imaginative as the one she offered. He had never heard of Grand Manan. When she asked him about Andrew Myles, though, he became quite voluble. "There have been a few rumours about his trading recently," he said. "Myles used to deal in stocks, himself, while he was at Drexel. Known as a shooter. An instinct for the jugular. Got into arbitrage and made a mint agreeing to sell back to the original shareholders after some of his efforts became public. Crashed in '87, along with a lot of other people."

"That's when he joined the book trade," Marsha said.

Irwin didn't catch the note of irony. "You didn't actually invest with him, did you?"

"Indirectly, it seems. With one of my authors. It seems he was using our money and hers." She had picked up on Thurgood's suggestion that Margaret was her very own author. "I hear he lost a lot of money."

"Playing on the Chicago Exchange. Futures. He's been shorting oil, of all things. Dumb enough to follow the economists who have been predicting a glut in oil and a price slump for years. Never happened. Worse, he hinted he had some private source of information. There've been rumours that Iraq would be allowed to start selling oil again. That might, actually, have brought the price down. None of it happened." Irwin was chortling.

"Can you explain how it would have worked?" Marsha asked.

Irwin sighed. "It's too complicated."

"Try me."

"You think the price of oil will drop. You sell a bunch of oil contracts at, say, twenty dollars a barrel. One contract is a thousand barrels. If you sell two hundred contracts, that's two hundred thousand barrels, two thousand contracts is two million barrels. What's so tempting about it is that it's highly leveraged."

"It's what?"

"You don't have to put up more than about three hundred thousand dollars for the two thousand contracts, if the broker knows you well and Andrew Myles was certainly well known. He used to cover his debts. You want me to go on, or is that enough?"

"On."

"If the price of oil goes down to twenty dollars or less a barrel, he makes money. If it goes up, as it has been, despite the rumours, you lose your deposit and about another eight million dollars. That's what seems to have happened to Myles. I don't know the amounts, but that's how it's played out. Of course, you knew he died?"

Marsha told him she had been there in Frankfurt when it happened.

"He was a little prick," Irwin opined. "Gave the Exchange a bad name. You can read all about him in tomorrow's *Times*. There's a reporter been following the story for a week, ever since the obit appeared. He is racing the *Wall Street Journal*'s guy who has been collecting rumours as well. Were you at the funeral?"

"Yes. And the wake."

"Met the brother, then?"

"Stephen?"

"A piece of work, that one, too. Used to be at Solomon. The two of them competed right down the line. Hated each other. If Stephen had been in Frankfurt during your Fair, the police wouldn't have to look much farther to find the killer."

"They were blood brothers?"

"Half. Their father married four or five times. All the wives had children, except Gloria. She still a beauty?" It was Irwin's working voice. Loud, brittle, bombastic. Marsha recognized it as the voice that helped convince clients that he was one of the boys, confident, unruffled, and on the track towards making more money for them. She hated this voice.

"I still don't understand how you can sell a whole bunch of barrels of oil you don't actually own," Marsha ventured for the last time.

Irwin laughed or guffawed, making a noise like a dog's sharp bark. "Welcome to the market," he barked into the receiver.

Despite the way she felt, she agreed to call him from the island.

She phoned Margaret and told the answering machine that she would be arriving in the evening with a piece of the second advance.

She hoped this would put her in a more cheerful frame of mind for their meeting. Tomorrow morning, around ten, she suggested.

She spent an hour returning her own messages, including one Alex Levine had left. He was delighted with the news of the money and agreed to wait for his cut until after Margaret's situation with Andrew had been settled.

True to his word, Sam faxed Margaret's agency agreement to A&M. It was a simple four-pager, containing all the usual items, including his right to collect all sums due to her, as her agent. The only bizarre bit was the split of income from all sources: fifty percent to each. It was signed by Margaret and Andrew. No one had witnessed the signatures. The contract was dated September twelfth, only days before he sold Marsha the three-book deal.

The preamble said this agreement replaced all previous contracts and was the sole contract between the two parties. That meant Margaret's previous contracts, including the ones for the two books now on the best-seller lists, and even the film deal for *Magnolias in the Rain*, would now be superseded by this one. All her income would be shared fifty-fifty with Andrew.

Why would she have agreed to that?

A modest parcel of manuscript proportions had arrived by courier. It bore Frans van Maeght's company's name. Marsha redirected it to Aaron.

Sheila called for A&M's usual driver to take her to the airport.

CHAPTER
TWENTY-THREE

JUDITH AWOKE TO THE AGGRESSIVE CAWING OF crows. The sun shone through the lace curtains and settled on the blue flowers of the wallpaper. The sharp golden rays changed the flowers to almost green. When she opened the window the cawing grew louder, mixed now with the shrieking of seagulls, the churning of motors, and chains screeching as the small boats moored in Flagg Cove started to go out with the tide. The water reached all the way to the seawall now, splashing against the wood logs along the harbour. The air was crisp and salty.

A platoon of crows had settled on the wind-stunted spruce that spread towards the back of the inn. Their black beaks pointed sea-ward as they jockeyed for position on the higher branches. A man in thigh-high rubber boots pushed his wooden dinghy along the path under the tree and launched it by plopping it into the water under the window. He threw in a bucket and a pair of oars, jumped in himself, and began to row facing the sea. Judith had never seen anyone row that way before. She continued to watch him till he boarded a somewhat bigger boat near the mouth of the harbour.

The foghorns were less persistent than yesterday, or they echoed less when the fog was out. She could hear sounds from the kitchen below. She pulled on a pair of jeans and her woolly sweater, and padded down to the kitchen in her stockinged feet. The night before it had been so cold, she had gone to sleep with her socks on.

"You're up early," June remarked, her back towards the door that led into the dining room. She was frying bacon in a deep iron pan. The coffee was already bubbling in the percolator on the counter next to the range.

"I know," Judith said. It was seven in the morning and, except for the crows, she would have been asleep still.

"You must have had a really good time last night," June said, her back still turned. The slight tension in the air had nothing to do with her being up early, disturbing June in her breakfast preparations; Judith knew that, even though she had been up for only ten minutes. It had to do with why she had come in so late the night before.

"Ahem," Judith rejoined, waiting for the rest of it.

"He is an excellent cook, don't you think? Or didn't he make you his famous grilled fish and fiddleheads? It's not his, how do you say, his pièce de résistance, but I must concede he does it well." She was turning the bacon slices, squishing them against the hot metal, the fat sizzling and popping over the edge of the pan.

"Yes, fish and fiddleheads," Judith said. "And ice cream."

"Showed you the carving he's been doing?" June asked, her voice low.

"As much as you could see in the dark."

"Coffee?"

"Please." Judith filled the mug halfway with warm milk from the top of the range, and June added the coffee.

"I suppose you asked him about his friends, the Drury Carters?" June was busying herself around the kitchen, getting eggs out of the fridge, testing the heat in the oven, cleaning the sink with a wet check dishcloth. What she was not doing was meeting Judith's eyes, or even looking at her.

Judith wanted to say something reassuring but she didn't know the other woman well enough to do so without risk of invading her privacy. Besides, she had gone to sleep thinking warm thoughts of Preston O'Neill. There was no denying he had made her shiver when he kissed her good-night, though it had been no more than a friendly gesture. Jimmy had snorted derisively when the truck's door slammed shut and they were, once more, alone. "Didn't kiss me good-night," he'd said.

There was no denying the familiar way Preston had with the Compass Rose, the way he knew where everything was, nor the way June was holding herself too stiff and upright in her own kitchen. The best Judith could come up with under the circumstances was, "I will be gone in a few days, when the interview is over."

June glanced at her over the lip of her own coffee mug. They had understood each other without either one of them coming directly to the point.

Then Judith answered the other question. "I didn't find out very much," she said. "He says he does odd jobs for them for money. Helps take care of the dogs, takes up their groceries. He'd met them when he was a kid, didn't he? Known both of them a long time. Is that why they are all here now?"

June shrugged. "Ask him, not me. Scrambled, fried, over-easy, or poached? How do you want your eggs?"

Judith said poached, and she offered to wake Jimmy later and make breakfast for him herself.

June poured some vinegar into a pan of boiling water, popped in four eggs, covered the pan, and turned to face Judith. "For the record," she told her, "whatever there might have been between that man and me never happened. I'm not saying there wasn't a moment when there might have been ... something. But there wasn't. Not entirely his fault, this sort of thing is never only one person's fault. He is too damaged. A messy divorce. Seems to have agreed to an uxorious settlement. Had to give up the kids. Only allowed to see them once a year. You know the kind of thing."

Judith knew quite a lot about nasty divorces.

"Can't give more than the fish and the fiddleheads, or stuffed lobster when the season's right," June continued. "He's tied up in his private hell. Like one of his new stone sculptures, he's strong, weather-beaten, and immovable. Keeps shovelling the money home to Toronto. A boy and a girl, I think. Told me once he'd kidnap them if he could get away with it. Change identities. Go to South America. They're the only necessities in his life. Everything else is dispensable." She looked sad, her hair in dishevelled bits around her face, the skin freshly scrubbed, a few deep lines where the pillow had creased her cheek. "It's a pity. He could have been a good man. Maybe was, once."

Judith mumbled that she would barely have time to get to the heart of the matter. She hoped to have her first interview today, now that her friend Marsha, Margaret Drury Carter's editor, was arriving on the ferry. They'd all be gone by the beginning of the next week.

June slid the eggs onto two of her canary-yellow plates, took the warm bread out of the oven, the coffee percolator from the stove, and carried the lot on a tray into the dining room. The tray, like the yellow plates, was from her crafts store. It was painted in blue wave patterns. "Let's have some civilization around here," she told Judith with the smallest of smiles. "Even when there's only one guest, I prefer to serve breakfast out here."

Judith mumbled a grateful thank you, though she would have been perfectly happy to eat standing up in the kitchen. It would have reminded her of her not-too-civilized breakfasts at home. When she had breakfast at all, she ate it while cleaning the dinner dishes. Frequently she promised herself a dishwasher from the next freelance cheque, but there was rarely enough left over after the mortgage, tuition for Anne and clothes for Jimmy, and the groceries to indulge in a movie. When, after months of nagging and sending threatening letters from her lawyer — the same libel expert who had handled her divorce — a cheque arrived from James, every dime was already spoken for by impatient plumbers, roofers, and other handymen. The semidetached had low rates but high maintenance.

"You had a call from Drury Carter while you were out last night," June said when she sat down facing Judith.

"Oh?" Judith brightened.

"She sounded really sick. Told me to tell you she would be spending the day in bed with the flu. She is running a fever, her voice is almost gone, coughing up a storm she was. Elinor had gone down to Dollins to get her some medication." June piled her egg onto a thick piece of white bread, and bit into it. "In other words," she said, her mouth full, "I doubt if she'll want to see you today."

"Did she say that?"

"She didn't have to." The egg was dribbling down her chin. "It's a nice day, you could get around the island. Try a couple of the trails. The boy looks like he could use a bit of fresh air, and so could you. Make the most of it while you can. More weather coming our way tonight. Hey, you could even look at the old Willa Cather place, long as you stay far enough away that the dogs can't sniff you."

"I could take a bath, to be on the safe side," Judith suggested.

"You're not that bad," June said laughing. "Long as you stay downwind. What I meant is they're a noisy pair when they don't know you, especially the Newfoundland. Elinor's got them trained so that they keep intruders out."

"They might remember me from last night."

"Don't count on it."

"If the Drury Carters put a fence up, how could I see the house, anyway?"

"You take the trail from Eel Brook Beach along Seven Days

Work, and you'll be coming to the cottage from the seaside, the cove, not the Whale Cove Cottages side. They have no fence up towards the sea. It would wreck the view."

"Preston offered to show us around the island," Judith confessed. "Maybe he'll take us along that path."

June picked up the dishes noisily and packed them back onto the tray. "And maybe he won't. There are plenty of other sights. He and Elinor are thick as thieves. He wouldn't do anything to piss her off, no sir." On the way to the kitchen, she turned. "Odd that he'd be so friendly to you. Never known him to chum up to anyone else, though he's had plenty of opportunity. Those lonely ladies in my art classes thought he was the cat's meow but he left them all alone. Except for me, of course, the one lonely lady I thought he fancied for a while."

Jimmy appeared just as the front door flew open to admit Preston O'Neill.

Jimmy stopped and stared at him, made a great show of checking his watch, then he said, "It figures. Never too early to make our day. Hello Preston." He shuffled into the dining room, wiping the hair from his eyes, dragging the blanket he wore down to breakfast behind him.

"Too cold for you?" Preston asked.

"Don't tell me," Jimmy replied, "us too-too-spoiled Torontonians can't bear your ordinary, down-home October weather, we're too soft, been living in luxury, and so on. Spare me." He surveyed the cereals June had set out on the sideboard and picked a package of Special K.

"Eggs?" Judith asked.

"Yech."

Preston chuckled. "Thought I'd show you where dulse is made," he said. "Nothing spectacular, but you'll never see it in the big city." He took a bag of salt candy from his pocket and offered it to Jimmy.

"What's dulse?" Jimmy asked, looking in the bag but not taking it from Preston's hand.

Preston said he would wait for them to get dressed and show them what it was and how it was made. "Grand Manan, they say, is the dulse capital of the world." He was much too cheerful for this time of day. Too aggressively hospitable, Judith thought, but she didn't want to look for reasons, she was happy enough with the obvious.

June announced that she was sure they'd find dulse fascinating. She had not come in from the kitchen since Preston arrived.

Judith thought he was looking particularly handsome and barrel-chested this morning in a sleeveless blue t-shirt and jeans that rode low on his hips. His arms were suntanned, their muscles like cords. His hair was still wet from the bath or shower. He carried a case of beer into the kitchen and packed it noisily into the fridge. "Would you like to come along?" he asked June after a long silence with both of them rummaging around in the kitchen.

"I think I've seen dulse," June said without inflection.

Affording them some privacy, Judith called Margaret in case June had exaggerated her condition.

She answered the phone herself. "Yes," she croaked.

"It's Judith Hayes," Judith said brightly. "I was hoping I could come and talk to you today, Miss Drury Carter. It's been a long way for me to come, and I was so hoping that you would spare me just an hour maybe. I wouldn't take much of your time. Really. Then we can do a follow-up piece, if you like, when the book is finished. Debbie Brown will have told you all about the kind of piece I'm writing for *Home and Garden*. When would it be convenient?" The whole pitch came in a flood, she was so pleased to get Margaret on the phone at last.

"Oh deah," Margaret sighed. "Didn't you get mah message?"

"Well, yes. And I'm sorry you aren't feeling well, but ..."

"Beyond not feeling well, mah deah, beyond all those words

so cavalierly used. Ah feel to the fah side of dweadful. Ah have no choice but to spend the day in mah bed. Just when the novel is reaching a climax. A tewwible thing. With mah editor coming from New York." She coughed. Her voice had been coming and going, ranging from a whisper to a growl. "Ah'm most sowwy, Ah simply can't see yew-all today. Perhaps we could talk on the telephone ..." she choked on a series of coughs.

"We could certainly do that, but I must get a few shots of the house, perhaps the garden ..."

"We don't have a gaaden."

"Maybe you'll feel better tomorrow," Judith suggested. She didn't mention she knew Marsha. She'd keep that trump card until the end.

"Oh Ah hope so, Ah do indeed hope so," Margaret breathed.

"I will call you later," Judith wheedled.

"If you must, mah deah, if you must." Margaret said, not very graciously, and hung up.

"You don't give up easy," Preston said with a smile.

Judith wondered whether he'd meant that as a compliment, or as criticism. She asked him whether he thought they could visit Eel Brook Beach, but he insisted that, as they had most of the day at their disposal, they should start at Dark Harbour, and get on the Island Coast Boat Tour at noon. He said he had talked to the Russells and there was still a chance of seeing whales in the Bay, though Dana Russell wouldn't guarantee more than two different kinds, as he did for most of August and September.

The way to Dark Harbour was a deeply rutted dirt and gravel road bordered on either side by a scrubby forest of beech, spruce, larch, and a few white-trunked birch. The harbour itself was in a deep inlet between towering cliffs that Preston said were over a hundred and twenty feet high. It was as dark as its name implied it would be: the cliffs blocked the morning sun. The road itself dove into the outlet suddenly. The engine screeched as Preston put it in low gear for the descent. On the beach there were tar-paper topped huts on wooden stilts, which, he said, were summer places for residents in the dulse business.

There were nets laid in line along the rocky shore, with pinkish leaf-like seaweed draped over them. Preston said the seaweed takes a day or so to dry, depending on the weather. You pick it in the briefly shallow water when the sea recedes during low tide. Whole families come here during the summer to collect and package the stuff. The government tried to make an industry of it but none of the big firms thought it would make money. They took the government's exploration funds, gazed helplessly at Dark Harbour, and went home pocketing the dough.

For a dollar, he bought them each their own package of dulse. "It's very good for you," he told Jimmy, who was not even going to look at the foul-smelling stuff. "Full of minerals and vitamins. Makes you strong."

Judith thought it tasted salty and chewy, though Preston insisted it was crisp. "Dulse takes only a day to dry when the sun is high, but there wasn't much sun yesterday," he explained without an apology.

After an hour of clattering over the stones, and watching the tide turn, Jimmy was so bored he accepted Preston's suggestion of the boat trip with the Russells. Judith asked him if he thought she could look at Drury Carter's cottage from the outside, even if Margaret was too ill to be interviewed today.

"I'll call Elinor if you like, and ask," Preston said. He called from the Island Bakery while he picked up the day's provisions.

Predictably, Elinor declined.

"It isn't as if *Home and Garden* expected an in-depth interview," Judith said on the way back to Flagg Cove. "Hardly the height of investigative journalism. A few glossy pictures of the cottage, some shots down towards the sea, a few gentle questions about her new novel, all self-promotion."

Preston said he thought some writers were just too private, at least when they were in the midst of a novel.

"Not this one," Judith assured him. "She loves to ham it up for the cameras." She told him about the *Vanity Fair* piece, when Margaret dressed up for the photo shoot in one of her heroine's Southern period costumes. For the *People* profile, last year, she had ordered in ten dozen magnolias so she could be photographed among her favourite flowers, though the picture was not even a feature in the magazine.

"Perhaps she's been burned by bad press, lately," Preston said.

"Hardly. They're all fawning over her because she got the biggest advance of her career. Twenty million dollars. Bunch of people in the media love that sort of thing. She's hot now, and I expect she knows it. Maybe that's why she's holding out. I wouldn't put it past her to be a prima donna."

"And she is really ill," Preston said. "She sounds like hell, and she's taken to her bed. She doesn't strike me as a woman who would invent an illness just to keep you at bay."

"How well do you know her?" Judith asked quickly.

Preston stared straight ahead. "You never give up, do you?" he said.

They had come to the Russells' boat, a small wooden thing with a tarp cover, and Preston could ignore her question by giving Dana Russell a playful punch on the bicep, and shaking hands with his wife. "Only one for you today," he said. "But you had better find a finback. These two are plenty critical." He introduced Jimmy and Judith to the Russells.

Judith had already decided she would not take the boat trip. She would get herself up to Whale Cove and find a way to ingratiate herself with Margaret. She'd done enough interviews with reluctant subjects to know that she had the knack for pulling their guard down once she gained admittance. She was ready to convince herself that Margaret might even like a break in the middle of her day if she was feeling lousy. In fact, if she was too ill to work on her manuscript, this could be the best time to visit.

She thanked Preston for arranging the boat trip and told him she was looking forward to it. She didn't even feel badly about lying. He'd made it obvious he was not going to help her gain admittance to the Drury Carter cottage.

Preston waited till she had paid for the passage before he said goodbye. "If you're still here tomorrow morning, we can go down the other end of the island," he told her before climbing back into his truck. He had his deliveries to make. When the truck disappeared from sight, Judith told Jimmy he'd be on his own for this trip, she had to get back to work if they were to make any money in October. They agreed to meet back at the Compass Rose in time for Marsha's arrival. She told the Russells she would be back another day to use her ticket, and clambered back to the shore.

She watched while they helped the last two tourists into the boat and cast off. Jimmy was being unusually reasonable. She had expected him to put up more of a struggle when she left. Then it occurred to her that they had been in each other's company for two weeks straight now, longer than any time since he was a baby. He might enjoy a few hours by himself.

She lingered at the dock for a while, watching a man rig his sailboat. The sail flapped wildly in the wind.

"An Albacore," a familiar voice said just over her shoulder. "Not too well suited for the sea, but he is a determined bugger, saw him take it out day before yesterday."

"Oh," Judith said, not turning around to look at Preston.

"Talking about determined, seems like you changed your mind," he said putting his arm around her shoulder. "A pity. It's a once-in-a-lifetime opportunity. Nowhere else can you see whales like these."

She thought of the six thousand dollars she would get for the piece from Debbie Brown and the mortgage that was due the end of the month. "I think I have to try to see Margaret," she told him.

"You're sure, now?" he almost pleaded. "You'll find her more elusive than the whales."

Judith decided not to mention her mortgage.

"At least I could see their cottage," she told Preston. "Take a couple of shots of the place, maybe catch sight of her ..."

He nodded. "June told you how to get there."

"It's not far," she said. "I have the trail guide."

They watched in silence as the Russells' boat left the mouth of the harbour, Jimmy sitting between two other winter-garbed tourists. He waved at his mother only once, and then turned away to show that he was independent.

"She used to be a scallop dragger," Preston said as the boat disappeared around Swallowtail point. "Now even scallops are scarce." Then he rested his hand on her shoulder and pointed her towards a large blue rowboat tied up near the Compass Rose. "Well, if you really must see the place, I could take you over to Whale Cove, the ocean route, by boat. You'd see some of the island on the way. What do you say?"

She could feel his hand through her sweater. It was heavy and warm, and she remembered its rough calloused fingers, the tall rugged stone sculptures, the intense blue of the paintings, and melted into agreement. The sun was still high and going out into the gently splashing waves suddenly seemed like a wonderful idea.

The boat's only power was an outboard motor wedged onto the stern. As soon as he untied it from its moorings, it began to rush out to sea. He hadn't even started the motor. They were swept past the ferry wharf and towards the rocks near what Preston said was Net Point.

"Tide's going out," he told her when the tiny engine kicked in as they rounded the point. "Doesn't need much to get you out. Trick is to come in while it's still out, or just as it's beginning to come in. Bay of Fundy has the highest tides in the world, did you know?"

She did.

"About a hundred billion tonnes of sea roll in every twelve hours or so. Then they roll out again."

Four bottle-nosed dolphins jumped out of the water and flopped back in alongside the boat, raced to the prow, and swam effortlessly matching the speed of the boat, while they looked up at Judith, who was shouting with delight.

"Local fishermen know the tide without even having to check the tide tables for timing, but the bozos who come down here for sports fishing get stranded on the beaches or they're swept out to sea." Preston talked as if the dolphins weren't swimming sideways and spying up at him. He was leaning forward, his hand on the throttle, his face set in a grimace of concentration. The sun cast a shadow over his prominent brow, while his eyes scanned the horizon. The effect was not unlike the face of his stone monster.

"Pettes Cove," he gestured at the wide inlet to their right. "Pirates used to get stranded here. They'd come in on the tide, hoping to raid the farmers on the island, but they were stranded when the tide went out, and the farmers shot them for target practice."

Judith thought Preston disquietingly nervous. He talked rapidly, as if he had learnt the words and was reciting them by rote. She thought maybe he was annoyed at her persistence in wanting to get to Margaret, even though she had no invitation. He'd made it clear the night before he didn't want to help her as long as she went uninvited.

The dolphins smiled and whooshed their deep intake of breath each time they surfaced.

There was a brush weir across the other side of the cove, two men on a rusty boat pulling in a net. "Only two left, now the fishing is down to what we can eat," Preston said, barely looking at them. "There used to be over a hundred around the island. You know about weirs?" An army of seagulls milled around the weir, shrieking in excitement, and a small fish jumped as the net tightened and pulled the fish onto the boat.

Judith said she had once done a story in Newfoundland, where they use weirs like these in the coves.

"Must be nice to be a writer," Preston remarked over the splashing of the waves, as they changed direction and headed out to sea again. Swallowtail Light rose to the left, above a long green meadow overlooking a rubble of giant rocks.

"It's close to a living," Judith said, forgetting that she had decided not to talk about her own poverty-line existence once she had learnt from June about his.

Several large seals lazed about on the rocks under the lighthouse and more circled the weir, swimming near the nets, waiting for a fish to fly their way. A big bull seal came close to their boat, lifted his head to check if they were fishing, noted they were not and dived under again. His breath was a vast sigh that smelled of dead herring and salt water.

They puttered around the rocks below Swallowtail, the small boat struggling against the waves that rushed from the shore and battered its side. For a few minutes they bobbed in the swell, the boat unable to right itself, and then they began to scoot along the jagged coastline towards the next promontory. A couple of seals swam alongside the boat replacing the dolphins that had peeled off towards the open sea.

"A society columnist like you should be able to pick and choose what she wants to write about," Preston said. "You must have a bunch of assignments waiting if this one doesn't pan out."

Judith thought he sounded angry, at least when he shouted the bit about a society columnist. Again, she resisted the temptation to whine and just sighed along with the seals.

"Fish Head on your left," Preston said as the boat rocked near a cliff that didn't, from their vantage point at least, look like the fish head he had pointed out on the ferry. It was grass-covered flat land, over scraggy rocks, and deeply furrowed mudflats where the ocean had retreated. All along the shore there were logs and massive tree trunks with roots that clawed the air as if they had been only recently wrenched from the earth. "Reminders of the winter storms," Preston explained when Judith asked about the trees. "Whatever logging there used to be on the island is all but over. All we have left is the Bradford forest and now that the tourists are coming we'll likely keep it for its scenic value."

From Fish Head, they headed inland again, the wind to their backs, and the motor struggling with every wave. A great black arch rose from the water near the shore and it seemed to shudder with the receding sea. Its legs were like a spider's, the ridged head and shoulders hulking over some imaginary prey.

"Hole-in-the-Wall," Preston pointed to the great spider. "Northern Head up there where the lighthouse marks the northernmost point of the island. That's Long Eddy Light, some people still call it the Whistle, the tallest marker to lead you into harbour on a night crossing from Passamaquoddy Bay. It's the only light along the west cliffs, nothing to show you the way between here and Southwest Head. And there, can you see Ashburton Head?"

Judith recognized the massive cliffs rising straight up from the sea. They were as forbidding as the painting, and looking up at them, even more intimidating. On the shore and scattered all the way to Ashburton Head there were black rocks, each eroded around the middle, their tops diving sharp-nosed towards the sea.

"They look like your stone sculptures," Judith yelled over the sounds of the waves, "this must be where you found the rocks."

"They're all over the island," Preston shouted, "sturdy ... denying the battering of the sea. ... There are dozens near Ashburton Head. Brave, they are, like the flat-earth society, not giving in, no matter how overwhelming the evidence. They're bloody stubborn, like the people around here."

"It's why you like it," Judith said, fully aware that the sea would drown her words.

"And that's Whale Cove in there." He pointed to a wide inlet with one old wooden shack near the water. Up on the headland a few more cottages sat close together, clusters of birches stood close to the water, tall spruces and poplars stretched along the top near the cottages. Their leaves had started to change to gold, and red.

"Which one is Drury Carter's?" Judith asked as they neared the pebbled beach, navigating among big flat boulders and an old abandoned weir.

Preston pointed to a house they could barely see through the dense foliage. It was painted white, with blue shingles. Visible from below was the blue-trimmed top window, just beneath the pointed roof. Judith assumed that it was the attic where Margaret did her writing. As the dinghy rolled onto the beach, she lost sight of the house, it was so well hidden behind the trees.

He pulled the motor up and stepped from the boat, telling Judith to follow his example. They pulled it farther up the beach over rough stones and driftwood, till he could tether it to a bent metal structure that must once have been the footing for a dock. Between the stones it was muddy, and the stones themselves sank down as Judith slithered over them, her shoes also sinking into the mire.

"We don't have long," Preston told her. "Tide's going to fall, which gives you about fifteen minutes for your snooping, that's it." He said "snooping" with all the emphasis on the word's oozing sound. "I'll start back with or without you." He was fiddling with the rope, his back turned to Judith.

She wondered why he had offered to bring her at all. But with only fifteen minutes there wasn't time to explore that thought. She headed up the path from the beach. It was a rutted track, slippery and muddy, and there were tall apple trees on either side, an incongruous sight in this wild place. There were still a few apples on one of the trees. Farther up there was an old cherry tree, its leaves the colour of ochre.

When she stopped to take a picture of the trees, Preston came up behind her. He stood so close she could feel his breath on her neck. His face brushed against her skin. It was coarse and stubbly. He smelled of balsam, she thought. When his arms circled her she stood still, feeling the muscles she had watched flex around her waist and move slowly up over her breasts. The sun played tricks over the leaves of the cherry tree turning them blood red, as her heart pounded in her ears. Then he turned her and kissed her softly on the lips. It was as she had imagined; his tongue was salty and rough like a cat's. The stones at her feet suddenly felt soft and inviting but when she opened her eyes she saw that his eyes — black-fringed, alert — were watching her.

"Oh," she said, that being the most brilliant observation she could make at the moment. Her knees slowly unbuckled as she felt her feet touch the ground again. "Well." Close by a seagull shrieked. Somewhere in the trees, there was a late songbird that should have known better and left for Florida weeks ago.

"It's not far to my house," he said, rather awkwardly, but that predatory look was still there in his blue eyes. "Be better than hanging around where you're not wanted."

Much better, Judith thought, at that moment wanting nothing as much as seeing what the bed was like in the room off the corridor that led to the back garden with the stone figures. That room might reveal something personal about the man that his sculptures were too stoic to reveal.

She was afraid she might fall when he let go of her.

There was no reason for James to barge into her mind at that moment, but he did anyway. She remembered with a great surge of sadness how much in love she had been, and how utterly dreadful their honeymoon was, when they had both learnt by trial and error what sex was, and how it differed from their inept fumblings in the back of James's father's car.

In hindsight, the fumblings had been infinitely preferable. It had been years before Judith recovered from her honeymoon.

"I don't think so," she said firmly. "At least not now." She grabbed Jimmy's camera for comfort, and pointed it at the nearest apple tree. She didn't want to risk the cherry, in case it turned red again. "What," she asked quite unnecessarily, "are all these trees doing here?"

"This used to be an orchard," he said gruffly. "When Willa Cather rented the cottage, it was called Orchardside. You really should not go closer than the top of the path. You can take a couple of pictures from there."

Judith followed a badly marked trail to the right of the inlet, through a thick growth of ferns and creeping plants that gathered in notches along the rising cliffs, obliterating the borders of the path on either side. They had been climbing long enough that she had to catch her breath when the house emerged from the fruit trees and tall fronds of fern. There was no path from the house down to where Judith was standing near the edge of the cliff, periodically shuffling forward to get a better shot of the gabled windows and covered porch.

"That's far enough," Preston said at her elbow.

"It won't be nearly enough for the assignment," Judith said. "They're expecting some shots of the garden."

"There is no garden."

"And they'll want to see how she's redesigned the house." She was edging closer for a better look.

"No."

The dogs began to bark inside the closed porch and Preston turned away from her, back towards the path to the beach. As she approached she saw a figure through the wire-mesh screen. It was a broad-beamed shape in something dark brown, with just the barest hint of dark hair and a blotch of pale face. It stood very still, as the barking of the dogs reached a hysterical pitch. Then it opened the screen door.

Judith was on her haunches taking photographs with her usual attitude of the more the better, the camera between her and the house. The two dogs shot out at a full run, baying at the camera, and lunged towards her in a blur of flying fur and bared teeth. She stood up quickly and started backing up, thinking only that these were the same dogs that had lain at her feet only the evening before, when her foot slipped over the edge of the path and she felt herself falling down the steep slope, her hands grabbing at brambles and fern, and her mind turning, incongruously to the camera and how lucky it was that she had looped its string around her wrist so she wouldn't lose it.

"Stupid," was the next thought in her mind as she hung over the splintered, sharp-edged rocks, her hands around a thick dry root, one foot caught on a gash in the rock-face, the other dangling over some thirty feet of rock wall angling straight down into the sea.

There was silence all around. Two friendly dog faces peered over the edge where she had fallen. It seemed to Judith that they were smiling.

There was no sign of Preston O'Neill.

CHAPTER
TWENTY-FOUR

A SOFT FOG HAD STARTED TO SNAKE AROUND THE island as the ferry approached Grand Manan. One moment, Marsha could see the black cliffs rising from the water. It was a craggy, barren, windswept place, and the lights at the two points that faced the ocean turned on and off, the sun still shining on the waves. The next moment a silky blanket of fog had rolled over the ship, enveloped the island, and the two lights became green ghostly apparitions with no connection to land. The foghorns seemed to herald the fog, loud, then remote, then close again.

She had been standing in the prow of the ferry, hoping to see Judith on the wharf, but by the time the ship came to a shuddering stop along the moorings, it had become difficult even to make out the shore. She was one of the first people off the ferry.

The passageway led to a parking lot, only a few cars with their engines idling, the air full of the smell of heavy exhaust and salt-fish. When she didn't see Judith, Marsha was sorry she hadn't bothered to get to get to know anyone else on board. She had spent most of the journey trying to make sense of what had happened to Andrew

Myles and Jerry Haines, and whether the intensely boring Iraqi manuscript could possibly be the key to their fate. Only half an hour before she left New York, she had a call from Inspektor Hübsch — a man she had thought never to hear from again.

"You know about ze Saddam Hussein manuscript?"

She did.

"Process of elimination has now finished viz it. Some here vere convinced. Not I. Ze ting was announced in the papers here yesterday zat it is about to be published by your friend in Holland and no one has even attempted to kill him. I did not go viz zat one anyvay, not I. No trouble at Westermann, and zey haf signed for ze German rights. Mr. Tanake has told us about Andrew Myles's continued need for money. He tried to grab the Saddam Hussein autobiography all to himself. Wanted to cut out ze Dutchman. Zat's why ze threatening note."

She told him about the car that had tried to run her over the night before.

"Have you gone to your police?"

"No." The idea had not crossed her mind.

"Why?"

"They have more serious things to worry about than cars trying to run down people. They wouldn't even investigate unless I were dead. And if I were dead who would tell them about it? Hideo Tanake was with me. He thought it could have been the Iraqis."

"It's not likely," Hübsch had said.

One of the four cars in the parking lot directed her to the Compass Rose.

"You must be Marsha Hillier," said the blond woman in the entranceway, her hand already reaching for Marsha's. "I've been expecting you for dinner. Judith said you'd be sure to come on the ferry today. Don't, as a rule, have dinner for guests in October. Too late in the season, but I thought what the hell. Judith will have trouble getting you fed tonight, so I threw a few things in a pot ... she with you?"

June had grabbed Marsha's bag and started up the stairs, just as Marsha said, "No, she wasn't. I don't suppose you'd have a drink in the house." She had progressed into the living room, its large fireplace lit and inviting, a couple of obscure bottles on the coffee table near the worn sofa.

"Single malt? Or mixed?" June asked, as she dropped the bag halfway up the stairs.

"Single. What do you have?" Marsha was already at the coffee table, lifting the bottles, looking at the labels. One was an almost full Ballantine's, the other a half full Glenfiddich. "Yes sir, that will do very nicely," she said holding the Glenfiddich aloft. She waited for June to pour her a shot glass full of the amber liquid, and drank it in one gulp. "Very, very nice," she said, "the perfect drink for a foggy crossing," she gave June a big grin, "wouldn't you say?"

"Your friend was going to be at the dock," June said, filling her own glass with the Ballantine's. "Doesn't seem like the kind of gal who would forget. The boy's up in the bathroom having himself a warm up after being out on the sea, says his mother's disappeared with one of our local characters and hasn't shown up since she put him on the whale-watching cruise."

"Preston," Marsha muttered, but June must have heard her because she snorted with derision and downed her whisky. "Best thing for me is to follow Jimmy into the bath. Judith didn't tell me to bring my winter underwear."

"I doubt if you're going to have time for a bath now," June told her. "Elinor Drury called to say she'd be down here by six. She thought she was giving you plenty of time to warm up, but the ferry was about ten minutes off today. I suppose they must have been expecting you. Only had one other visitor since they came to the island. As I told your friend they've been keeping pretty much to themselves."

She showed Marsha to the room below Judith's. It had pink and blue flowered wallpaper and gauze-thin curtains over a tall picture window that overlooked the harbour. Through the swirling fog she could see a couple of fishing boats bobbing in the water below. The bed was covered by a pretty quilt of fish and boat squares, each one a different blue against the white background. It would be perfect on a summer day.

"Has Judith been up to see them?" Marsha asked.

"No. The old lady has the flu. Didn't want to do the interview. Might be different for you, though. No reception committee when she came," June turned on the bedside lamp with a blue shade with pink flowers. It lit up the small painting that hung over the bed. Birch trees overlooking a bay, Marsha thought. "Though, I suppose, you could call Preston O'Neill a reception committee. He's certainly been keen to show your friend around the island. Last thing we heard, the two were tootling over towards Swallowtail in his putt-putt of a boat. Was still sunny, then."

"Maybe they got lost?"

"Nah. Preston knows his way around these waters. He'd find the harbour if it was dark."

She struggled to pull out a couple of the drawers of the pine tallboy in the corner. "Damned weather makes everything stick," she complained between vigorous tugs at the recalcitrant drawer. "There. You can put some of your things in now. I'll get a few sandwiches going and some tea. I think that's what Elinor drinks. Earl Grey. If I have time, I'll go next door and pick up a few date squares. They're the surprise of the day at the bakery."

"It's not like Judith to miss my coming in," Marsha said. "She simply wouldn't, not without a damned good reason."

"Preston's not a bad reason," June ventured.

"Oh give me a break," Jimmy yelled from the bathroom. "That you, Marsha?"

Marsha ran up the stairs to where his voice was coming from.

"Come on out and give me a hug, will you?" she said to the bathroom door. "She wouldn't, even if there was the best-looking man on the island. Even if he's an Adonis. Not like Judith at all," she told June. "Where do you think they went?" she asked Jimmy through the door.

"Mom was determined to get to Whale Cove," Jimmy said. "That's where the Drury Carter woman is. She's having trouble getting her to talk, and you know what she's like around deadlines."

"You said they had another visitor," Marsha asked June. "Do you know who it was?"

"He didn't stay here," June said. "Picked one of the Whale Cove Cottages, to be close to the two of them, no doubt. Orchardside's just down the path from the Cottages. Vera manages it for the owners while they wait for an offer to sell. The Drury Carters used to take their tea in the dining room at the Cottages, before they had their kitchen redone. Didn't need to bother going up to the dining room any more."

Jimmy came out of the bathroom, all pink and steamy, his thin shoulders and legs sticking out of the towel he had wrapped himself in. He looked so much like the little boy Marsha had loved from the first moment she had seen him that she forgot he was a teenager with status and attitude, and wrapped her arms around him, squeezed, and lifted him up in the air. "It's great to see you," she enthused into his damp hair.

"Dammit woman," Jimmy growled in his newly acquired baritone. "You're about to expose me to the elements. Put me down," he ordered with all the authority he could muster.

Marsha was not so easily put off. She carried him into his room, and dumped him squealing onto his bed. It was only when she saw how anxious he was to keep the towel covering up his private places, that she said she'd leave him alone to dress and rejoined the still surprised June on the landing.

"You know him pretty well, then," June said.

"Jimmy?" Marsha asked. She was slightly winded from the exercise. For all his skin and bones, Jimmy weighed about the same as her hundred and thirty pounds. "Judith's my best friend. That's how I know what lengths she'd go for a man, no matter how wonderful. And that's how I know that little fellow up there," motioning towards Jimmy's closed door, "better than I know any other fellow in the world. And, believe me, he's not easy to know." She went into her room to get a sweater. She'd brought a couple of her Versace stringknits, which, she realized, were wholly inappropriate for Grand Manan, now that she saw it.

"If Elinor's on her way here," she told June, "what I need is one more shot of your Glenfiddich, to hell with the tea."

June was already pouring when Marsha got downstairs. It was promising to be an interesting day, after all.

"The man you said came to visit, what was his name?"

"Vera said he'd signed the guest book 'Myles,' but we all thought that was odd because it was a first name, not a last. That's the only name he gave her, and he wasn't particularly friendly. Stayed overnight. Spent all the time at Drury Carter's place. Never even looked around the island. And when he left, he didn't even pick up his own bill, she did." June gave Marsha a steady gaze to see if this was much too much gossip for a woman from New York. Marsha was halfway through her shot glass. She had tossed her shoes into a corner upstairs and was now curled up in one of the wicker chairs, ready to listen.

"Andrew Myles?" she repeated. "Dammit, Andrew Myles would not come to a place like this island unless he had no choice in the matter. He was a pretty rarified New York literary agent, most comfortable around large dollops of money, and in rooms filled with cigarette smoke. What did this Myles look like?"

"Short. Stocky. Red-faced. Wore fancy cowboy boots, Vera thought, because they had heels. Barely talked to her. Not very polite."

"Definitely Andrew Myles." She was thinking about what Hübsch had said and what she knew about the contract Margaret had signed with Andrew. Maybe he came here to talk her into something as nefarious as a fifty-fifty arrangement. But why would she agree to it? Even if he promised her more money than she'd ever seen, even then, why would Margaret agree to give him half the pie? And why would the otherwise savvy Elinor Drury go along with it?

"When was he here?"

"September, I think. Whales were still running. Tail end of the season."

There was only one explanation, Marsha thought, that Myles had something on Margaret, something that would make her sign a deal not even a novice writer would agree to sign. But what?

If he had something on her, and he needed money, he'd use it. Andrew Myles was best at looking out for his own interests. But then, would she kill him? For the fifty percent? She shook her head and took another sip of the Scotch. Very unlikely. Very unlike everything she knew about Margaret Drury Carter.

Jimmy came down, fully dressed in his torn jeans and baggy sweater. "So. How you doing?" he asked Marsha. He was attempting to look casual.

"Fine. Better to see you again. How's the Internet?"

"I've been working on a new program for idiot-proof maths and algebra. The one I got is too confusing and you gotta know a lot about computers to figure it out. I think if you already know a lot about computers, you can probably figure out the answers to your algebra questions. It's all logic." He was standing at the bottom of the stairs, one foot balanced on top of the other, still very much the child, but he was talking like a grownup. It's that awkward age, Judith once said, neither one thing nor the other yet.

He was beginning to look, disconcertingly, like his father.

"I brought you a couple of fancy new programs from Apple," Marsha said.

"Can I see?" he asked, already at her side, looking into her over-sized handbag that he knew carried everything important. When he took out the package, he was all concentration and delight. "I read about these," he said. "Got to install them now. Can I?"

"Sure."

Jimmy ran up the stairs again to his room. On the way he almost bumped into Elinor.

"Hello," Elinor said to Marsha as she progressed into the living room. She acknowledged June with a half-smile and a friendly nod. "I had hoped you wouldn't bother to come just now. Margaret called you last night, didn't she?"

"Hello, Elinor," Marsha said.

"She's ill. Didn't she tell you? She has the flu. Can barely talk." Elinor looked better in her country garb than in the funeral special she'd worn when Marsha saw her last. She wore grey flannel pants, cinched in at the waist with a wide leather belt, a blue and red check shirt, and brown lace-up workmen's boots with reinforced toes. She'd worn a plastic hat over her head. It was an odd-looking wide-brimmed thing in navy blue with a ribbon to hold it in place.

"Sounded all right when she talked to me," Marsha lied.

"Would you like to come in, Miss Drury?" June asked rather formally. "I have some Earl Grey brewing for you. Got it out soon as I heard you were coming."

Marsha thought June was overdoing her selling mode; she had become almost obsequious all of a sudden, but perhaps she did roaring business serving up dinners and lunches to Margaret and Elinor.

Elinor took off her plastic hat and hung it on one of the nails by the front door. She shook her hair loose. "She should have told you she's ill. She didn't want to worry you, I suppose. Still, she could have saved you a trip out here."

"I was determined to come, anyway," Marsha said. "I know we can fix this thing if we work on it together, and I'm sure she'll be glad to see me when she knows I'm here."

Elinor shrugged. "Maybe it doesn't need fixing any more."

June had brought in a pretty china teapot and two matching cups and saucers. "Would you like a couple of date squares?" she asked Elinor.

"Don't trouble with it, I won't be staying long."

"No trouble," June was already heading out the door.

"I came down to give you a new batch of manuscript. She's been working on it right up to the time she got sick. She is sorry she couldn't come, herself," Elinor said. "She asked me to apologize. But she is not well, no matter what she may tell you. She's been driving herself too hard. She needs rest and medication. Though she might not admit it, she is an old woman." There was a hint of cruelty in the way Elinor said it. Marsha thought it was particularly unkind, given the fact that Margaret went to such enormous lengths to disguise her age.

By contrast, Elinor barely made an effort. Her determined lack of make-up, her long brown hair, now greying, her casual clothes, all revealed a woman who did not care about appearances. There was only the wide leather belt she seemed to like wearing. Marsha wondered if it was a reminder of some former, happier time.

"I can wait till tomorrow," Marsha said. If Elinor thought she had come all this way to be put off by a truculent niece, she had not yet seen her mettle.

"I do not think she's likely to be much better tomorrow," Elinor said with a tone of sad finality. "It might be weeks. I'm going to take the doctor up tomorrow, as soon as he can make it. The way she's wheezing, it wouldn't surprise me if she had bronchitis. Her fever was almost a hundred and one."

"Look, Elinor," Marsha said, trying not to show her disappointment. "I have come a fairly long way to see her, and see her I will. Unless she, herself, tells me otherwise. You may be her niece and her business manager, but you are not her representative when it comes to her writing. It's her work."

Elinor's unyielding blue eyes fixed on Marsha with a look of pure hostility. But she didn't say anything. She poured herself a cup of tea and set about drinking it. She held her pinky aloft as she clasped the dainty handle.

Marsha thought of what her mother said about women who did that. "Déclassé, my dear Marsha, totally déclassé. Never, never, do that, or people will think you haven't had an upbringing." Marsha shuddered at the memory.

"I thought, perhaps, we could have a reasonable discussion," Elinor said sadly over her teacup.

"We can," Marsha said. "After I talk to Margaret."

"Here is the manuscript." Elinor rummaged through her green knapsack and drew out a plastic bag. "She has been working very hard, as I told you. It's why she's ill, no doubt. I think she is almost halfway. Ahead of your schedule. And I think it's very much better than the first draft. You'll agree, I'm certain of it." She thrust the plastic bag at Marsha. "There are over two hundred typed pages there. I know, I did the typing. Been doing it for her for years."

Marsha thought she had heard that from Margaret. She was so old-fashioned she still wrote longhand. She took the sheaves of paper from the bag. "Great work," she said, trying for a friendlier tone to match Elinor's attempt.

Jimmy poked his head in through the door. "Thanks, Marsha," he said. "Nifty stuff. But I better go and look for Mom. It's been hours, and she hasn't even called."

"This is Jimmy Hayes, Miss Drury," Marsha did the introductions. "I think his mother, Judith Hayes, has been trying to get an interview with Margaret. They've been here for a couple of days."

Elinor was staring at Jimmy as he grinned at her and left. She was still staring when the front door banged shut.

"What did you decide you'd do about the money?" Elinor asked Marsha, her eyes still fixed on the doorway where Jimmy had appeared moments before.

"I've released the first million of the next two due on the first chapters. This morning. Left it for Alex and Arthur Thurgood to deal with the details. Thurgood is our details man." Even as she was saying this Marsha registered a small voice of protest in her mind. There was something definitely not right about this, not right about the fact that either Margaret or Elinor had encouraged Jerry Haines to think that he was the proud possessor of the three-book contract that Marsha had signed with Andrew. And it wasn't right that Elinor had threatened to nix the contract, though she had known, she must have known, that it was Andrew who had been dealing in bad faith, not A&M.

And Jerry Haines had been murdered by the same person who had murdered Andrew Myles.

"That's very wise," Elinor said, with an undisguised note of satisfaction in her voice. She liked to win, Marsha thought. Maybe she liked to win enough to let her guard down for a moment.

"I was thinking about Jerry Haines, Elinor."

Elinor almost smiled, a tiny grimace played around her pale lips. "Ah yes, poor Jerry."

"Did he offer you more than our contract?" Marsha asked quickly.

"Not much more," Elinor said. "But the terms were rather tempting." Her face returned to its usual impassivity almost as soon as the words were out, but she had not bothered to hide her enjoyment of the moment.

Back then, Marsha thought, she would not have known yet that Andrew hadn't paid. Or had she?

"If you're so clever, Elinor," she asked, keeping her voice conversational, and the other woman still off her guard (was Elinor ever really off her guard?), "why did you let Margaret sign a fifty-fifty deal with Andrew Myles?"

She didn't answer immediately. She still hadn't answered when June came back with a plate full of date squares and a big smile on her face.

Elinor turned to her and asked, "Where did that boy go?"

"I think he went up to Whale Cove, looking for his mother."

Elinor stood up quickly and headed for the door.

It was only when she was already there that she seemed to remember Marsha. She half-turned her usually expressionless face, and Marsha was surprised to see something that resembled shock or fear.

"I will call in the morning," she said.

"And Margaret?" Marsha asked.

But Elinor was already out the door. She had left behind her blue hat and the knapsack.

CHAPTER
TWENTY-FIVE

JUDITH HAD NO IDEA HOW LONG SHE HAD BEEN THERE. At first there was shock, then disbelief. Then she saw the dogs grinning down at her, and realized she must have fallen some twenty feet down towards the rocks. Then she waited and hoped that someone — honestly, Preston — would appear where the dogs' muzzles had been until they had lost interest in her. Damn that songbird. It had no business carrying on in late October.

She had slowly, very slowly, edged her foot farther into the crevice that seemed to have stopped her fall, and then she had gripped the root that her right hand held with both hands. When she aimed for another root, it broke. She held on to the root with one hand, barely daring to breathe. Farther over to the left, she saw a long thick-leafed creeper dangling down the rock face. She inched towards that.

The rock was overgrown by scrub bushes near the top, and all the way up there were patches of earth that must have washed down and adhered to the rock. Small plants cringed in the crevices. Brownish, slippery moss clung to the rock. She was aiming at a series of sharp edges that angled upward, thinking they might provide enough purchase to drag herself up to solid ground again. With both hands holding on to roots and creepers, she could move her feet an inch at a time.

It was difficult to abandon the relative security of the deep crevice that held her foot, but once she had made that decision, there was no turning back.

Someone overhead whistled for the dogs. A door slammed.

"Help." The sound came very tentatively at first: "help" was not a word Judith was used to shouting. When there was no response, she tried it out again, louder this time. Her throat was dry. "Anybody there?" Her breath came in short gasps, not enough for big sound.

No response.

She was barely aware that one of her elbows was bruised and bleeding. Her knees felt raw. She had done a mental inventory, feeling each part of her body in turn, and had concluded that nothing was broken. At least not yet.

The waves had become louder under her, and when she looked down, she saw that the tide had started to come in again. It was hitting the rocks, creeping up over the seaweed-covered stones, then sucking back over the mudflat. It was reaching higher with each onslaught. A small group of crows had settled on an overhanging branch and were eying her curiously.

The first sign of fog had been the loud booming sound of the Whistle, followed by the farther away keening coming from Swallowtail. Soon, the offshore foghorns joined in. The sun turned grey, then disappeared.

Judith remained very still. Waiting for Preston, she thought. She wasn't afraid, only surprised that she had fallen, and that he wasn't there to pull her up right away. He must have known that she had fallen. Where had he gone? One minute he was there with her, the next, he had disappeared. Why? Had he gone back to make sure the boat was secured? Turned and not seen her slip?

Her fingers became numb.

If Margaret and her niece were inside the cottage and had seen her fall, they would have come to help. It was one thing to scare off gawkers, quite another to let them hang on to life by a thin thread while you enjoyed some tea and Island Bakery treats, she thought.

Intermittently, she shouted. "Anybody there?" was too long and cumbersome. She no longer found "help" embarrassing. Later, she tried "hey" because it was shorter and she was tired. Only the crows paid attention. Two of them flapped their wings, shook themselves, made their neck feathers bristle and fan out, and then pulled their heads in again. There was something both comical and intimidating about the way they were looking at her. One of them, it occurred to her, had almost perfected the disapproving glance that Marjorie Hayes was wont to cast towards her daughter.

She would never forgive her for dying here, on some inane mission typical of her unstable employment. Her mother had always taken the position that Judith's work was not real work. "Scribbling," she had called it. She considered her daughter's various magazine assignments to be mere excuses for vacations from her day job of childcare. In her view, had Judith hung on to James, she would have been well looked after. She had made it sound as if losing a husband were akin to losing one's car in a crowded parking lot. Inexcusable carelessness. When they first married, Marjorie boasted to her acquaintances — Marjorie didn't seem to have friends, as no one measured up to her standards — that James was a doctor. "It's the same thing," she had told Judith, "he doctors animals."

Judith's clothes were wet now and she imagined her fingers were blue where they had attached themselves to the rock. She would have to try moving. She thought when she reached the top she'd probably remember to be cold. Somewhere down below a seal blew air bubbles, and another started to bark.

There might be some handholds farther up the rock face. Another jutting bush that could hold her feet. She edged up and across, taking shallow breaths, stopping to take stock, and then starting again.

What was the name of the man who climbed all the way up Ashburton Head? They should have named the cliff after him and not after the stupid ship, *Lord Ashburton*, which had sailed off course.

She was only inches from the step-like rocks she had been moving towards, and her hands and feet felt numb. Her elbows were bruised, and ached with every move. She saw the blood coursing down her arms and settling into her stretched armpits where the sweater had pulled in tight. The sweater must be torn at the elbows. The knees of her jeans must also have been shredded; she knew her knees had been scratched bloody by the rocks because the jeans were sticking to her below the knees. Clutches of earth gave way as she tried to rest her weight on them. She had to rely on her hands, holding onto roots and leafy plants, to pull herself back up to another perch. Amazing how strong the plants were. She was definitely not going to cry. And she was not going to slip and fall.

The ocean was rising under her, and the rocks shook as it heaved itself against them.

She thought of Anne and Jimmy, and what they would do if she died.

She tried to imagine them in Chicago with James. The immaculate white condo in the neat glass tower. James's spanking new wife, with her designer wardrobe, yoga classes, aerobic workouts, and steady flirtation with self-discovery. She had met James during one of his group sessions with the newest psychiatrist, who had promised to put him in touch with his feelings. "God help us all." There was an echo from the rocks around her. She had said that out loud, because she was quite certain that it would not do. It would not do to have her children hanging around a spotless condo while their father was worrying about getting in touch with his feelings — no telling where he had left them — and not theirs. She was not going to let go, no matter how hurt and numb she felt.

She was more angry now than hurt. It was anger that propelled her towards the "stepping rock" she had been aiming at for so long. When she reached it, she was sure she'd be able to step up onto the bluff again. It was becoming dark. Night was falling — or was it the fog?

The dogs set to barking again, and in the distance she heard a very familiar voice yelling "Mom." She was so happy she almost let go.

Her voice had gone completely hoarse, but she gave it all she had and croaked "Jimmy." The barking had become so loud she didn't think she could be heard. She heard him calling them, "Willa, come here, stop that, come on Edith, don't be an idiot. Come on, now." The barking subsided. "There. Hey, isn't that better? Willa, what do you say?" Luckily she didn't say anything. The lull gave Judith the pause she needed to gather all her strength and shriek "Jimmy!" Just hearing his voice had launched her up another rung of the "steps," but the new roots were slippery, and the next lot were too high up to reach unless she took a chance and leapt. Ever since the thought of the spotless Chicago condo, she had decided she was not going to take any chances. She had to make it all the way up.

"Mom?" Jimmy's voice was closer now.

"Hey."

"What the hell are you doing down there?" Jimmy's face came over the edge, and he peered at his mother.

"What does it look like? I'm making sandwiches for my picnic, of course."

"Fine time for jokes," Jimmy said, taking off his shirt and jacket and tying the arms together to see if the two combined would be long enough to reach his mother. It wasn't. "One of the ladies must be inside," Jimmy said. "I'll see if I can get a rope."

"Jimmy?"

"Yes."

"Don't be long."

He was gone. Judith heard some half-hearted barking by the dogs, more soothing words from Jimmy, and then yelling for Miss Drury Carter.

There was no response from the house.

"Somebody?" he yelled again. "Anybody at all?"

Where had Preston gone?

It seemed like an eternity of silence, then Jimmy was back again shoving a long orange cord down towards Judith. "It's an extension cord. Best I could do on short notice. I've tied the other end to a tree, so you can put your weight on it," he told her. It amazed her how calm he seemed.

She grabbed the cord with one hand first, just testing. No. Her hand slipped. The cord had a rough, serrated surface like the extension cord she used for the outside Christmas lights. It had endured, she thought fondly, some fifteen years. Each year they strung it along the prickly branches of the young Scotch pine she had planted the year they had moved into the house. Thinking about the Christmas lights made her stronger. Or she maybe just forgot the pain. She wrapped her fingers around the rough surface, edged her shoulder up against the rock and when she had steadied herself she grabbed the cord with her other hand. She took a deep breath, tested the cord's give, and then she began to walk up "her steps." They were waiting for her, exactly as she had imagined.

When she was close enough, Jimmy reached down, gripped her wrists, and pulled her up in one fluid motion. Amazing how strong he was, Judith thought. She was going to cry.

"Jesus, you're heavy," Jimmy said spoiling the moment.

A wonderful boy, Judith thought.

At the top she stood shaking for a while, her heart pounding.

She looked back down the rock face to where the sea had been smashing against it, coming harder now than before, the fog drifting gently over the waves. She would not have survived a fall. With a hundred billion tonnes of water moving in and out, who knows where they would have found her body, if at all.

"What happened?" asked Jimmy. Judith told him.

"All you need is some water to clean you off and you'll be as good as new," Jimmy said. "Come on, no one's in the house, and I'm sure they won't mind."

"The dogs?"

"They're my buddies," Jimmy said keeping his arm, protectively, around his mother. "Aren't you, Edith?" he asked the retriever soothingly.

There was a well-tended gravel path with sharp edges leading to the cottage. More stunted cherry trees, an old gnarled apple tree with a few wizened apples, a row of uniformly clipped rose bushes near the porch, a few still in flower, lilac bushes, and rows and rows of wilted peonies. On either side of the entrance, there was a tall stone figure, arms held down close to its sides, its chest expanded as if with a sharp intake of breath, each with a thick-necked, rough-hewn face that craned towards the cliffs. Two sentinels. Their jaws were set, mouths thin lines, foreheads low and heavy; they were glowering at any intruder that might come this way.

"Aren't they some of Preston's guys?" Jimmy asked.

"Who else would make stuff like this?" When she could think straight, she would figure out where Preston had gone and why. Right now, it wasn't convenient to think about that.

"Looked better at night," Jimmy said, pushing towards the porch. The screen door swung open and they were inside with white wicker armchairs, a round white table with a cup and saucer, and azaleas spilling from white wicker baskets hanging from ceiling hooks.

"Miss Drury Carter," Judith called hoarsely.

"You think she's here?" Jimmy asked. "No one answered when I was yelling for help."

"Did you see her leave?"

"No, but the place feels empty. The other one's down at the inn with Marsha. You know she arrived?"

Judith groaned.

"I wouldn't worry," Jimmy said. "You have the best excuse ever. Gives new meaning to being hung up. This way," he directed her to the stairs. "The bathroom must be upstairs. I didn't see one down here."

Judith tried calling for Margaret again.

The house was strangely quiet. Judith could smell something she couldn't identify, but it was very unpleasant. Sweet, sickly, and rotting.

The stairs were uncarpeted polished wood. Pine? Judith wondered. Too dark for pine. The banister was so shiny that it reflected the pale blue light filtering through an upstairs window. Three paintings hung on the wall, each one the same size, perfectly placed, the upper left corner of the first one touching the lower right corner of the next one up the stairs. Two of them were long views of the sea in a calm mood, sunny days. The one in the middle was Ashburton Head with the waves crashing into it.

"They need to open a few windows in here," Jimmy said. They were in a small bathroom, towels tidily hanging from freshly painted bars, the floor gleaming new tile, a small gilt-edged mirror hanging over the old lion-footed sink. Too clean to wash her dirty hands without permission of the owner. But Jimmy was already turning on the tap and opening the medicine cabinet. "They've got to have some iodine," he said. "Everybody has iodine."

There was a bedroom to the right of the bathroom, a big double bed with one of June's blue eiderdown covers. The steps continued, steeper, to what Judith knew to be the attic where Willa

Cather had worked, and where now Margaret did her writing.

She asked Jimmy to wait and she headed up the stairs, her feet making hollow sounds on the wooden steps.

"She may not want to see you," Jimmy suggested. "Not the way you look."

There was a tiny landing, dark, covered with a patch of pink carpet.

When Judith opened the door to the attic, the smell became overpowering. Light streamed through the open window. The air was damp and stale, though she could feel the wind from the sea. A big oak table faced the window, papers strewn over it, weighted down by a china mug full of pencils and pens. The papers were curled at the edges with dampness.

Margaret Drury Carter was reclining in a blue floral chaise longue. Judith first saw her mauve stockinged feet, her hands in white gloves. She was wearing one of her trademark mauve dresses with lace around her neck and wrists. Her feet were half-covered by an Island Arts and Crafts shop pink and mauve quilt. Her chin was resting on her ample bosom, as if she were asleep.

Even from the short distance between them, Judith knew she was dead.

She took a couple of steps towards the inert figure. It was amazing how well-cared-for she looked. Her hair was coiffed into a bouffant auburn halo around her head, there was a thick layer of make-up on her forehead, though the skin had begun to shrivel and the lips were just thin bits of brownish flesh. There were still vestiges of pink lipstick clinging to them. She had no eyelids.

"Mom," Jimmy called up, exasperated. "You're snooping. You're supposed to get cleaned up. Come on now."

Judith backed out of the attic room, slowly. She shut the door on Margaret Drury Carter and breathed in some cleaner air as she ran down to Jimmy, who was standing at the sink in the bathroom, and grabbed him by the hand. "We are getting out of here," she whispered.

"What the hell?"

"Now."

Jimmy reached for the tap but Judith didn't even wait for him to turn the water off. She was pulling him along, down the stairs, past the living room door where she now saw, for the first time, not one but two of the black-faced fleecy sheep.

"You're nuts," Jimmy observed, but he knew there was something wrong and followed along as if by instinct.

There was a tall woman standing just inside the porch. Her dark hair was wet, strands clung to her forehead, and her jacket was dripping water onto the blue outdoor carpet. Her arms were crossed over her chest as if for protection. She had a pale face and broad forehead, her very blue eyes stared at Judith, then Jimmy, then Judith again. She was panting.

For a while nobody said anything.

Finally, Jimmy did the introductions, "This is Miz Drury, Mom — met her down with Marsha."

"Oh," Judith said.

"You're the journalist," Elinor said. An expression of despair flitted across her pale face. She did not bother to disguise it. "What are you doing in our house?" she demanded.

Judith was going to mention Margaret Drury Carter, but thought better of it. She pointed mutely at her knees and hands where the blood had begun to cake.

"You've been up to the bathroom," Elinor stated.

There was no point arguing with her; the tap was still running, and they could all hear it. Elinor's eyes followed the muddy footprints up the stairs.

"My mother hurt herself," Jimmy explained. "She fell from the rocks where your path ends. Probably trying to take some photos of the house. She's hopeless with a camera." Jimmy stopped and looked at his mother. "Where is my camera, anyway?"

When she didn't answer, he said, "Okay, don't tell me. Fish food? Right?"

Judith whispered, "I'm sorry."

"You have been up to see her, then?" Elinor asked lightly, as if Margaret Drury Carter was still alive and perhaps even receiving unwelcome guests.

"Who?" Jimmy asked.

"Yes," Judith said. To hell with *Home and Garden*, this was going to be for *Vanity Fair*, or whoever paid the most, she thought. The *National Enquirer* had been known to spring for twenty thousand for one story, if it was weird enough and involved famous people. This one had everything except Anthony Perkins. She could have an auction, and sell to the highest bidder. Make it an exclusive. There'd be headlines, newspaper pickups. "Mummified Author Signs Multi-Million-Dollar Deal." She could see it now. TV news. All carrying Judith's byline.

She made a serious attempt to look friendly.

"Perhaps you should come back in," Elinor said stiffly. "Finish washing up." She pointed rather unnecessarily towards the bathroom, whence they'd just descended. "I have some disinfectant in the medicine cabinet."

"Stuff in the plastic bottle?" Jimmy asked.

Judith would like to have told him to go back to the Compass Rose but Elinor was blocking the entrance to the porch.

"No. Come, I'll show you." She ushered Judith and Jimmy upstairs but followed close behind. In the bathroom she handed Jimmy a black jar from the medicine cabinet. "You'll have to spread it around a little, don't think it'll hurt much." She appeared almost sympathetic for a moment.

"What's the smell up here?" Jimmy asked quietly, but not quietly enough, because Elinor froze for a moment.

"Old houses," she said finally. "Would you like some tea," she asked Judith pleasantly. "Better still, I have some brandy left over from our celebrations last summer. Margaret pretended to like those nasty concoctions with fruit and paper umbrellas she thought a Southern lady should like, but she really preferred brandy."

Judith said she'd prefer brandy, too, and thanked her.

Jimmy asked for a damp cloth.

"Take the one in the bathroom," Elinor told. "Don't worry about getting it dirty."

"You'll hardly feel a thing," Jimmy assured his mother as she let him wash her elbows and wrists with warm water. She had taken off her blood-caked sweater and dropped it on the pristine tiles. It was a small bathroom with no windows. It might be too much of a drop down from here, anyway, she reasoned. The thing was to get Jimmy safely back to the guest house and away from the dead woman in the attic and the friendly demented one downstairs.

Jimmy had been right, she didn't feel the sting when he poured the brown liquid disinfectant over her elbows and wrists.

"Smells like fish," he said. "Not like the house. There's something really foul in here."

"Maybe," she whispered to him, "you could go back to the Compass Rose. Tell Marsha I'm all right, she'll be worried. Maybe she'll come here."

"You're going to need a shoulder to lean on when we're done. I'll wait."

No sense in alarming him. "I might want to stay for a while. Why don't you go ahead?" She was washing the gashes on her knees. There were barely a few strands of jeans left there. There were grains of dirt and bits of leaves adhering to the dried blood that made them hard to clean.

"No. We'll both stay then," Jimmy said. He started to dab disinfectant over the knees and down at her ankles. "If you want to talk to her alone, I'll play with the dogs."

"Go outside."

"Okay, no problem."

"Maybe Marsha will come and pick us up," Judith told him in an emphatic whisper.

"Make sure you cover your bruises, as well," Elinor said. "It may not smell great, but it'll do the job." Elinor followed them down the stairs. She took two snifters from the hall corner cabinet, and half filled them from the crystal bottle that had been sitting next to them. She gave one to Judith. "You'll need this, after your fall," she said. "Amazing you made it."

"Jimmy is going to see the dogs," Judith said anxiously. She wanted him out of that house.

Elinor stared.

"We're buddies," Jimmy said. "Preston introduced us last night. Okay?"

Judith gave him a small shove.

"I've made some cordial for you," Elinor said, reaching for the tumbler on the hall table. "Raspberry. Would you like that?"

Jimmy accepted reluctantly. If there was one thing Jimmy hated, Judith thought, it was raspberry cordial. But just to make sure, she said, "You're allergic to raspberries."

"Yup," Jimmy said.

Elinor didn't try to stop him when he went out the swinging door.

"I usually keep the place locked up," Elinor said. "Lately, I've become careless. Heard the ferry come in, and I was keen to give the manuscript to Marsha Hillier. She is Margaret's editor. Here from New York. But you already know that. You two know each other. That had somehow not occurred to me before." She wiped drops of water or perspiration from her forehead. She smoothed her thick hair back and wrung it with one hand before letting it drop over her shoulders. "I thought I'd be gone for such a short time. I never imagined ..."

She never imagined that I was still alive, Judith supposed.

"She's been dead since late August," Elinor said, conversationally. She took a sip of her brandy and showed Judith into the living room.

It was an odd mixture of antiques and hand-carved wooden furniture. Judith recognized evidence of June everywhere: quilted wall hangings, carved whales, a patchwork tablecloth. An old washstand, dark wood, and blue tiles. In the corner a pine credenza. Preston O'Neill on the walls.

"She had a massive stroke," Elinor resumed quietly.

Judith's experience as an interviewer told her that if someone wanted to talk, it was best to let them. Interrupting with stupid questions could put them off stride. She nodded.

"She used to do her writing up in that study. We had tried to make it into her special place. Exactly as she had imagined it when I first showed her. The place needed so much work to make it right for her. We had it done exactly as she wanted it, every last detail." There were tears coursing down her cheeks, but she didn't stop talking. "It's where she died."

They were both quiet for a while, then Elinor resumed. "She'd developed her own work habits over the years, I think most writers must do that, or they'd never get anything done. Quite disciplined, she was, though you wouldn't have thought so when you met her. She had such an act." Elinor smiled. She was pacing around, adjusting things as she talked. She straightened a couple of silver boxes on the credenza, pulled at the tablecloth to align its edges more precisely with the table's. She turned a flowerpot of pink azaleas towards the window. "We had breakfast around eight, and then she went to her room. When I took her tea up at ten she was dead. We'd barely moved in, then. My god, did she love that attic. Loved it. You know, she'd actually read Willa Cather when she was a girl. It's the main reason she agreed to come to Grand Manan. She thought *My Mortal Enemy* was the best book she'd ever read. You know it," Elinor stated.

Judith wished she'd opted for that, instead of *Death Comes to the Archbishop*. She attempted a noncommittal incline of her neck.

Luckily, Elinor had no questions about *My Mortal Enemy*. "Myra Driscoll is like one of Margaret's heroines: headstrong, romantic, beautiful, imperious, and clever. She married for love. You know what she says at the end?" Again, she didn't wait for an answer. "She says 'people can be lovers and enemies at the same time.'"

Judith thought, again, of Preston O'Neill.

"A scene right out of a Drury Carter novel." Elinor stopped in front of the window and gazed out over the darkening garden. "I brought her here because I thought she would be better off away from all the distractions in Virginia. Too much social whirl. She hadn't been well for some time. You know she lied about her age?"

"Doesn't everybody?"

"I don't," Elinor announced.

Judith lowered herself into the chair nearest the door. She rested her cool glass on her burning sore knee.

"You don't like the brandy?" Elinor asked, standing over Judith, her clear, unyielding eyes fixed on Judith's glass.

Judith pretended to take a gulp and tried smiling encouragingly. Strange — although she hadn't tasted the brandy, she felt drunk. *Psycho*, the movie, she said to herself, that's what she'd been trying to remember. There is the scene when the mother turns around and it's only a skull. She'd been dead for years. Would she have changed things around for the movie version? Judith giggled. Then hiccoughed.

"She'd had a couple of small strokes," Elinor continued. "Her doctor warned her to take it easy, to rest, you know. She ignored him. That's why I had to get her here, where she could really rest. Sometimes she became distracted. Nobody else cared. Certainly not her daughter who's been bleeding her dry for years. Never amounted to much, little Charlotte. Mummy's golden-haired girl." Elinor's lip curled. It was an old resentment. "I was worried people might notice she wasn't right. She'd wander a bit. All around the house, as if she'd lost her sense of purpose. Nothing serious at first, but I thought it might get worse." She sighed. "Knew about this place from my childhood. We came here one summer and rented a cottage in the middle of the island. Castalia. It's such a wonderful name, don't you think? So romantic." She sighed. "You've been there?"

"Not yet."

Another sigh, longer this time. "My mother died the year before and my stepfather — he was stuck with me because my father had scarpered — thought it would do us both good to get out of the city for the summer. He didn't have much, ran a grocery store on the Lower East Side. We lived simply. It was the happiest time of my life." She took off her jacket and dropped it on the floor. Then she looked at it and picked it up again. She suspended it from one of the arms of a very tall, wooden hat-rack by the door. "I was sure she would be all right here, it's so peaceful. And people on Grand Manan don't crowd you."

Judith's arms and legs were starting to itch. The disinfectant was making up for not stinging before. She rubbed her hands over the itching. Her flesh felt hot and still sticky with blood. Her headache was getting worse.

"You'll be stiff tomorrow," Elinor said with a smile, as if her aunt's body hadn't been decomposing in the attic. "Would you like some more brandy?"

Judith said she couldn't. In fact she thought she might throw up if she had any brandy at all. Her heart was racing.

"At least she was happy here," Elinor said. She was crying again. "We went for long walks, ate in the guest houses in the village. She liked the food here. It's simple. Lots of greens and starches. Home cooking. I introduced her to Preston. She liked him, too. You see, I knew Preston back when I was here that summer. We were both young, then. He was going to be an architect, did he tell you?"

"I don't feel very well," Judith said. The nausea was worsening, and her heart was pounding.

"You've had quite a fall," Elinor said, smiling sympathetically. "And you've had a shock. Where was I? Yes, he was going to be an architect. I was going to be an actress. We both made it for a while. I was an actress, and a fine one at that, you know. Margaret sent me to acting classes. She was my mother's sister. She wanted to do something for me. I suppose she wanted to do something for her sister. My mother died young. Odd, to think she was younger than I am now. She thought — that's Margaret — she thought I had talent. And she was right. I did well for a while. Small parts. I could have been one of the best. You know why it didn't work out?"

Judith was feeling dizzy.

"Look at me," Elinor came closer and stood in front of Judith, her legs apart, her arms akimbo, a big woman with a pale face, soft brown hair, too thin lips, and eyelashes so pale they vanished. "That's right," Elinor said triumphantly. "I'm not the leading woman type. No simpering little thing, as they liked them even then. But I was good enough to fool everybody after she died. All those people who thought they knew her, they didn't know her at all. I could have pulled it off except for that grasping little agent my aunt liked so much. He had to get his share. But his share wasn't enough any more. Greedy bastard. He pretended to go along with it at first, he said he'd sell the three-book deal and maybe I could try my hand at finishing the bit she had been working on when she died."

Elinor's voice seemed to be edging away from Judith and her solid shape was losing definition. "I think I am going to throw up," Judith formed the words very slowly but wasn't sure she had uttered them, they hung in her mind. She tried to stand.

"You'll feel much better soon, I promise," Elinor said firmly and gently pressed her back into the seat. "She wrote longhand, never learnt how to type. Last ten years I've been doing all her typing, correcting her mistakes, cleaning up her grammar. She wouldn't have been able to do it without me, you know. And don't misunderstand her, she was grateful. She was not a bad woman." There was that grin again, parting the lips, showing teeth.

Andrew Myles. She must have killed Andrew Myles. Judith didn't think she had said the words out loud, but maybe she had, because Elinor picked them up and tossed them around.

"Andrew Myles was a greedy little pig. That's what Andrew Myles was and no one is going to miss him. He wouldn't leave it alone, he had to get more and more and more and why the hell would I want to give that little shit everything I was working for. Tell me, why?" She seemed to be pacing again. She stopped for a moment and looked out the window.

"What about Preston?" asked Judith. She really did want to know about Preston, even if she was having trouble catching her breath.

Elinor turned. "Ah yes, Preston. I told you, we are friends. And he needs money. He has a bitch of a wife and two lovely kids he's never going to see again unless he keeps paying and paying his dues every month. Maybe now he'll have a bit of luck. He deserves it. Why do you ask about him?" She had come closer and was examining Judith's face, as if the answer was to be found in her expression.

Such blue eyes, Judith thought. "I was waiting for him to come back," she mumbled.

"Oh that," Elinor smiled. "Don't hold your breath."

"He brought me here," Judith said, her voice sounded petulant, even to her own ears.

"Specially, no doubt," Elinor said. "Preston doesn't necessarily stick around to find out how his problems resolve themselves, or haven't you figured that out yet? His heart is in the right place, but he lacks follow-through. Margaret told me that. She said men like that are dangerous. Their minds don't extend to the conclusions of their actions. In the end, their courage may fail them. 'They scarper,' she said."

Judith thought she was gulping air, trying to defeat the nausea. "Maybe I could get that wet towel again," she said.

"She owed me." Elinor continued, ignoring Judith's request. "She never paid for my work. Just room and board. In all that time. You'd think I'd resent that. I could have hated her and that useless bit of fluff, Charlotte. She never did anything. Married an idiot. Couldn't support herself in all her life. Margaret," Elinor sighed forcefully, exuding patience, "she sent her money. Any time she called, there it was. More. Oddly," Elinor turned and gave Judith a look of forbearance, "I didn't resent it. I thought Margaret was a fool. But I loved her. I really did. Nobody else ever loved her. She had fans, and admirers, some men she called her "beaux," mostly users, people waiting for her to provide. Not me. I took care of her." Elinor glanced up the stairway expectantly, as if Margaret was about to join them. "She couldn't have done it without me."

Judith imagined, vaguely, that she was about to rise from her chair and go to the bathroom. She thought of where the bathroom was and saw her feet turn in that direction. Then she knew she didn't want to go there any more, that she had to get out of this house, away from Elinor's droning words. She had lost interest in the story. The words hung between nausea and the dreadful pain that had been growing inside her stomach. But it was the itching heat that finally propelled her out of her chair. She stood, weaving. Or the room weaved. It contracted and expanded. The light was so much brighter, though somewhere she knew it was dark.

Her heart was pounding harder.

Suddenly, Elinor was standing in front of her, close enough for Judith to see the dark lines under her nude eyes. Her hands reached out, ready to steady Judith, or to catch her as she fell.

"I think, maybe," Judith mumbled. She wasn't sure if she had continued. She had meant to say that maybe she should go home. But the words would not form.

The room spun. All the colours of the quilts were running together.

There was a sound of pounding and shouts. She thought she saw Marsha. She wanted to say how sorry she was for not being down on the ferry dock waiting for her, but saying that now seemed rather illogical. There was shouting and she felt herself being carried. Somebody was panting in her ear. Big swatches of blue and white swished by, and Marsha was yelling at her to stay alive. Damn it, Marsha, why wouldn't I, she was going to say as soon as she could speak.

The white tiles were cool under her knees as she hugged the toilet seat and vomited into Elinor Drury's pristine toilet bowl.

The next moment she was looking up at Marsha's face swimming in the white light. Warm water closed over her face and the rest of her body floated away.

CHAPTER
TWENTY-SIX

"IT'S INSPEKTOR HÜBSCH TO ZE RESCUE, IN ABSENTIA, as it were. And you've never even met the guy," Marsha said. "Not sure you'd like him if you met him. He's the one who told me what the symptoms were."

"Soon as I saw you I knew what it was," June was saying. "You're not the first person on the island to have nicotine poisoning." The two of them were sitting on the rim of the bathtub, taking turns holding up Judith's head. Judith was barely conscious of their presence at first, as she passed into a dream world and back again. She was soaking in a tub of chalk-white hot water, her arms and legs huge, numb swollen logs.

"The tea's what we give them for it. Whether they like it or not. It's a diuretic. Cleans the system. Most pretend it was an accident. Funny thing, usually happens in the dead of winter. Not when the stuff is used in the gardens. Old Mrs. Dollins says we should keep it away from people in the winter, seeing as no one needs to keep the bugs off their plants in January." June kept up a patter, as friendly and normal as if they'd been sitting in the parlour of her bed-and-breakfast. "Some take it by accident, of course, though I've never been able to figure how you can mistake liquid nicotine for anything else. They boil the tobacco here, you know, that's how it's made. Cheapest and best bug-killer there is. Not many would put it on an open wound, though."

"Good thing about the island," June said, "we know home-made first-aid. Can't get a doctor every time you think you need one, here." She had given her Valium to try to control the convulsions that started when the poison began to leave her system.

Jimmy sat on the floor outside the bathroom, waiting.

It was some time before Judith realized that her skinny son who couldn't finish high school had saved her life twice in the same day. He had received her signals, listened to the conversation while he watched through the window.

He had run all the way to the Compass Rose to bring help. Jimmy had been fairly sure his mother was frightened of Elinor Drury. If she was frightened, she had reason to be, he concluded.

Marsha had scrubbed her with soap till the blood from her wounds had coloured the water dark red. June had brought a poultice for her body. Then they had soaked her in hot water and baking soda.

All the time, Elinor waited in her own living room. She had made no attempt to escape. She was very calm now. She had stopped crying. When June went to see her, she said she didn't need anything. She refused even the tea.

When the island's lone policeman arrived, Elinor led the way up the stairs to Margaret Drury Carter's study. She watched as the doctor came and examined the body. And after he left, she returned to the armchair and waited till the policeman was ready to ask his questions.

Then she told him what she had told Judith. Her aunt had died of natural causes. Elinor's only crime was she hadn't given her a proper burial. Not yet.

She claimed not to know how the liquid nicotine got into Judith's system. "Maybe the boy used the wrong bottle in the bathroom," she said. "Happens."

It was no use Jimmy's protesting — his word against hers, a long-haired teenager's against that of a middle-aged woman.

Around midnight, Judith began to feel alive again. They were sitting around the fire at the Compass Rose.

"She used the same stuff in Frankfurt," Marsha told June. "Andrew smoked Gitanes, Jerry cigars. She must have put it into their drinks, and this stuff acts much slower if you are a smoker. Jerry must have taken the longest. She poisoned him between ten and eleven. He thought he could get Margaret to sign with him again if he saw her, personally, but he found Elinor instead. He didn't die till after 2 a.m. Didn't even know he was dying, poor sap. Went happy, though. I think Andrew might have known. Hübsch said the victims become paralyzed before they die."

"Charming," Jimmy said.

"None of that for you, Jude, if the stuff's rubbed on your skin you don't have a lot of time to contemplate your life as it passed. Itching and burning, nausea, headache, rapid heartbeat, coma. Fifteen minutes, if you're lucky. You were lucky. If Jimmy hadn't come down ..."

"I'm the one who almost killed her," Jimmy said, "I thought it was iodine. Smelled funny, but the whole place smelled horrid."

Judith drew the blanket closer around her shoulders. She looked over at him, crouching by the fire, his pale bony knees poking out of his jeans. "My hero."

"They can't charge Elinor; she didn't attempt to kill you. It's Jimmy who put the stuff on. It could have been an honest mistake. It's what Elinor told our policeman. And they can't get her on her aunt's death, if the old lady did die of her own accord," June said. "Most excitement we've had here in years."

"What about Andrew Myles?" Judith asked.

"Maybe she was at the party and no one recognized her. She was a good actress. I didn't recognize her the next day. Everyone thought it was Margaret. She got the accent down right, every nuance. She killed Andrew Myles because he got so greedy. If he'd been happy with his usual commission, he'd still be alive. But when he found out Margaret was dead, he decided to cash in on Elinor's ability to write much like her aunt had written. It's strange, the first three chapters Elinor had delivered to me in Frankfurt really had been written by Margaret. Jerry was right, she wanted to make a literary contribution. She thought she was, finally, doing one for posterity."

"Elinor wrote the new material?" Judith asked.

"She did. And it's vintage Drury Carter. I've no idea when she found time to work on it, but she did have me fooled. If we'd all stayed away, she might have been able to write the books her aunt would have written. She could have had it all."

"Do you suppose Preston knew I had fallen down that cliff?" Judith asked after a while.

"Did he know Elinor had killed those people?" Marsha answered.

"Does it matter?" June asked.

It was a couple of days before everyone realized that Preston O'Neill had fled the island in one of the fishing boats. Elinor Drury said she didn't know where he had gone. Elinor was able to prove beyond a reasonable doubt that she could not have killed either Andrew Myles or Jerry Haines. Both times, she had perfect alibis. Both times, she had been in the company of other people at Bookfair parties.

It was weeks before the New Brunswick Provincial Police were able to produce a photograph of Preston and show it to Marsha. She knew at once that he was the man she had seen with Elinor.

CHAPTER TWENTY-SIX

Inspektor Hübsch began his rounds with the picture some weeks after that.

In mid-November, *Maclean's* magazine ran an exposé on Preston. They printed his photograph, not a recent one, but still recognizably Preston, pictures of his old home in Toronto, his ex-wife shielding her face from the camera, and one of his children through the window of the family station wagon. The boy, the story went, had heard from his father. He'd phoned from the Halifax airport. Preston said he would come for them both when he had enough money. Meanwhile, they had all his love. The police, the *Maclean's* story said, were looking for him. They wanted to question him about two unsolved murders in Frankfurt.

No charges were ever laid against Elinor Drury. She moved to New York and completed work on the three Margaret Drury Carter novels. Although Margaret's faithful fans must have noticed the sad stories of her death, they chose to ignore her demise and pretend she was still writing the books herself. In the great tradition of V.C. Andrews, Marsha thought.

And Judith Hayes finally got her breakthrough story.

Saddam Hussein's memoirs were published to lukewarm reviews and deeply disappointing sales six months later. Aaron, according to *Publishers Weekly*, was pursuing a full range of interests. Rumour had it that he was going to start a literary agency.